Susan Cliff wri⟶ ...
for Mills & Boon⟶ ...
given a starred ⟶ ...
lives in the San D⟶ ...
daughters. She draws inspiration from the diverse
neighbourhoods and spectacular scenery of Southern
California. You can find her on Twitter much too often.
Her other hobbies include reading, hiking, and going to
the beach.

USA TODAY bestselling author **Barb Han** lives in
Texas with her adventurous family and beloved dogs.
Reviewers have called her books 'heartfelt' and
'exciting.' When not writing or reading, she can be
found exploring Manhattan, on a mountain, or
swimming in her backyard.

Carla Cassidy is a *New York Times* bestselling author
who has written more than 125 novels for Mills &
Boon. She is listed on the Romance Writer's of America
Honour Roll and has won numerous awards. Carla
believes the only thing better than curling up with a
good book to read is sitting down at the computer with
a good story to write.

Heroes in Hot Pursuit

Heroes in Hot Pursuit:
Romance on the Run

SUSAN CLIFF

BARB HAN

CARLA CASSIDY

MILLS & BOON

First Published in Great Britain 2021
By Mills & Boon, an imprint of HarperCollins*Publishers,* Ltd
1 London Bridge Street, London, SE1 9GF

www.harpercollins.co.uk

HarperCollins*Publishers*
1st Floor, Watermarque Building,
Ringsend Road, Dublin 4, Ireland

HEROES IN HOT PURSUIT: ROMANCE ON THE RUN
© 2021 Harlequin Books S.A.

Witness on the Run © 2018 Susan Cliff
Sudden Setup © 2018 Barb Han
Scene of the Crime: Means and Motive © 2016 Carla Bracale

ISBN: 978-0-263-30269-1

MIX
Paper from
responsible sources
FSC™ C007454

This book is produced from independently certified FSC™ paper
to ensure responsible forest management.

For more information visit: www.harpercollins.co.uk/green

Printed and bound in Spain
by CPI, Barcelona

WITNESS ON THE RUN

SUSAN CLIFF

Chapter 1

December 11
62N
14 degrees

Tala Walker was a woman on the run.

She'd fled Canada six months ago and never looked back. Now she was living under an alias in Willow, Alaska. She'd rented a room at a quiet boarding house. Every day she got up early and walked to the diner where she worked.

It wasn't much, but she felt safe here.

This morning, the diner was in disarray. There were beer cans all over the countertops and broken glass on the floor. It reeked of booze and cigarettes. She sighed, shaking her head. Walt must have really tied one on last night.

A quick detour to the office down the hall revealed the man responsible for the mess. He was dead to the world, snoring away on a dilapidated love seat. His barreled chest rose and fell with every breath.

Tala didn't bother to wake him up. Walt was her boss, the designated cook and the owner of the diner. If he wanted to sleep on the job, that was his prerogative. She'd opened on her own before. She could handle the early-morning customers herself. They were heading into the dark days of winter, and business was sparse.

She cleared away the trash and cleaned the floor. She thought of Duane, the husband she'd run away from, who'd also indulged in drunken antics. Only his hadn't been as harmless as Walt's. She pushed aside those memories and focused on her morning tasks. Alaskan truckers liked their coffee. She prided herself on brewing a good cup.

At 6:00 a.m. she turned on all the lights, flipped the Closed sign to Open and unlocked the front door. Soon after, a black-and-white squad car pulled into the parking lot. An officer in a navy blue uniform emerged from the vehicle. The sight reminded her of Duane also, and she had other reasons to be nervous about lawmen, but she knew he wasn't here for her. Cops liked coffee, too. They drank it at Walt's for free.

"Morning," he said, hunkering down on a bar stool.

She put a mug in front of him and filled it up. The cream and sugar was within reach. "Can I get you anything else?"

"Just this."

Tala nodded and inched away. She felt the familiar urge to flee, so she grabbed a clean rag and started wiping down the counter. She didn't strike up a conversation with him. She didn't strike up conversations with anyone. She wasn't the friendliest waitress. Walt always told her she'd get better tips if she smiled once in a while.

A few minutes later, three roughnecks strolled in. Truckers were their regular clientele, but the diner took all kinds. These men had the weathered look of loggers or oil riggers. Tough guys weren't unusual in these parts, or where she was from. She'd been born on a land reserve in the Northwest Territories. She was no stranger to hardworking men.

She brought them three mugs and three menus, glad for the distraction. As she poured their coffee, she noticed one of the men exchanging a glance with the police officer. She got the odd feeling they knew each other.

"You need another minute to decide?" she asked.

The man closest to her had dirty blond hair and bloodshot eyes. His friends were dark-haired. One had a long, skinny face and a goatee. The other was stocky, with boyish freckles. "Three breakfast specials."

She collected the menus. "Coming right up."

The police officer watched her walk away from their table.

"Ready for a refill?" she asked him.

He checked his mug. "I'm good."

She retreated to the kitchen and turned on the griddle. She considered waking up Walt. Something felt wrong to her, like a bad spirit. Men made her nervous, especially when she was working alone. She told herself it was just her imagination. Not her past, catching up to her.

Not Duane, coming to get her.

She took a deep breath and scrambled eggs. By the time she was finished with the sausages and toast, she'd regained her composure. She brought them their plates.

They acted like normal men. The blond one looked her up and down as he bit into his toast. She'd been leered at before, so it didn't faze her.

"More coffee?"

The boyish one nodded, shoveling food into his mouth. She refilled his mug, noting that he had a better appetite than his companions. He also seemed more relaxed.

"Anything else?" she asked.

The blond one smirked, as if he'd thought of a funny joke. She waited a beat before she walked away, aware of his gaze on her backside. Her waitress uniform was a basic blue dress with white tights and a white apron. She wore sensible shoes and scraped her hair into a bun at the nape of her neck. Some customers were disrespectful, but lewd behavior was rare. Most of the truckers who frequented the diner were old married men, not young bucks on the prowl. They didn't bother her.

There was only one customer so far who'd caught *her* eye. He was quiet. Strong, but not a roughneck. He was young and fit, for a trucker. He tipped well and didn't leer. He smiled even less than she did.

Tala got busy rearranging some pies in the refrigerated case. The police officer left, tossing a few coins by his empty mug. The three men finished their breakfasts soon after. They paid in cash and walked out. She frowned as she cleared their table. Only one of the plates was clean, which was odd. Roughnecks usually ate every bite. Shrugging, she dumped the contents in the trash. It was full, thanks to Walt's late-night party.

She put on her jacket and picked up the trash, grabbing the keys on the way out. The dumpster was in the back corner of the parking lot. It had to be kept behind a wooden fence, because of bears. She hurried forward and unlocked the gate. Male voices carried on the wind, which whipped around her stocking-covered legs. It was still pitch-black outside, and the air smelled like snow. She hefted the trash into the receptacle. Then she heard a loud pop.

Gunfire.

Close-range, small-arms gunfire. She knew guns. Her dad had taught her how to shoot. Duane had been an enthusiast himself. The sound was unmistakable, and chilling. Hunching down, she peered around the fence to locate the source.

Light from the diner windows illuminated three figures in the parking lot, less than twenty feet away. The blond man who'd leered at her was holding a pistol. One of his breakfast companions was slumped on the ground. The policeman stood right next to the killer. His badge glinted like an evening star.

She ducked lower, smothering a sound of panic. She wanted to run, but she was afraid she'd be spotted.

Two men loaded the body into a car while the officer stood guard. He was watching the street with his back to her. He clearly had no idea she was there. She clapped a hand over her mouth, horrified. Someone slammed the trunk, and the officer turned around to speak. His face was angry.

"Take care of this mess," he said, pointing at the diner. "All of it."

The blond man's reply was lost on the wind.

Tala stayed hidden, trembling with terror. The officer strode to his squad car and got in. After a short hesitation, the two men headed toward the diner's front entrance. She glanced at the back door, which was still ajar. They'd come out and find her any moment.

She couldn't breathe properly. She couldn't blink. She felt like her eyeballs might freeze inside the sockets. The mental picture of her frozen corpse got her moving. The instinct to flee was impossible to ignore. She had to run, now. She leapt out from her hiding place and bolted across the parking lot. She tripped over the first cement parking block she encountered and went down hard. Gravel bit into her hands and knees. It hurt like hell, but she didn't dwell on the pain. She got up and kept moving.

There was a truck stop on the other side of a wide-open space. She ran toward it, because there was no-where else to go. Dogs barked in the distance. She couldn't hear anyone following her, but she couldn't hear anything except her pounding heart.

She enjoyed running, under normal circumstances. She'd been on the cross-country team in high school and college. She could run for miles without tiring.

She reached a group of big rigs—huge trucks with trailers. There were four or five in a row, sitting idle while the truckers rested inside the sleeper cab or some-where else. She didn't know what truckers did when they weren't driving. Maybe they didn't sleep. They were magical, mythical creatures.

She hid behind one of the trailers and tried to catch her breath. Her blood was half adrenaline. Her veins might burst from the overload. She was having trouble with her eyes again. Everything in her peripheral vision was fuzzy. It was as if fate had decided she only needed to see what was directly in front of her.

Ice Storm.

Chapter 2

Cameron Hughes deliberated for at least ten minutes before he started the engine.

He hadn't planned on going to Walt's Diner. He'd been avoiding Walt's Diner. To be specific, he'd been avoiding one particular waitress at Walt's Diner. Which was ridiculous, because she'd never acted interested in him. She poured his coffee and took his order with brisk efficiency. She didn't flirt. She didn't even smile at him. There was no reason for him to keep his distance from her.

Although she'd done nothing to encourage him, he felt uncomfortable in her presence. Her cool manner and pretty face unsettled him. The last time he'd visited the diner, he'd found himself staring at her. He'd realized, with a surge of guilt, that he was attracted to her. And he'd decided not to go to Walt's again.

This morning, he'd glanced across the parking lot and studied the neon sign in the diner's front window. He'd imagined strolling in for breakfast. He knew what would happen. He'd avert his eyes when she approached, and let them linger as she retreated. He'd think of her at night, instead of Jenny. Cam studied the picture of his wife that was affixed to the dashboard. Jenny smiled back at him, not judging.

Shaking his head, he fired up the engine and prepared to leave. Maybe Jenny wanted him to move on, but he wasn't ready.

He left the truck stop and headed north on the highway. He had a radio app with more music than he could ever listen to and several audiobooks on queue. He enjoyed mysteries and true crime. He liked stories about bad guys getting caught, and hard evidence that led to convictions. If only real life mimicked fiction.

He'd forgotten to select listening material for this leg of the trip, so he drove in silence. Some days he surfed through the CB channels to hear the latest trucker chatter. This morning he didn't bother. There was light traffic and good weather. He concentrated on the lonely lanes before him, feeling restless. He needed a workout. He'd stop at the twenty-four-hour gym in Fairbanks. Hit the weights, jog a few miles.

Stretching his neck, he continued down the road. He'd gone about thirty miles when he heard a strange thump. He checked his mirrors and didn't see anything. Maybe one of his tires had kicked up a chunk of asphalt. His gauges looked fine. He kept going. A few minutes later he heard another thump, along with a rattle.

What the hell?

It sounded like something was banging against the

metal plate behind the cab. His mirrors didn't give him a full view of the space. A loose piece of wiring wouldn't make that noise. The rattling started again, and then stopped. When he reached a long straightaway, he pulled over, shifted into Neutral and engaged the brake. It was still dark, so he grabbed his flashlight before he climbed out.

First he checked the back of the trailer, which looked secure. It was locked up tight. He dropped down to his belly to shine his beam underneath the rig. The wheels were intact. He didn't see anything amiss.

He got up and inspected the space behind the cab. To his surprise, he caught a glimpse of gray fur.

Wolf?

He blinked and his eyes adjusted, making sense of the shape.

Not a wolf. A woman.

Holy hell. There was a woman in his hitch space. A stowaway. He'd never had a stowaway before, and he'd never expected to see one here. Any hobo with a lick of sense would climb into the cab or the trailer. He kept his trailer locked, of course, and there was no way to get inside his cab unnoticed.

"Come out of there," he said. "It's not safe."

The woman didn't move. She was crouched down like a cornered animal, shivering violently.

He attempted a softer tone. "Come on out. I won't hurt you."

She didn't respond. Maybe she didn't speak English. It was difficult to judge her ethnicity because most of her face was hidden behind a fur-lined hood. She appeared to have dark eyes.

Cam turned off the flashlight and pocketed it. She'd

been here since he left the truck stop, or earlier. She might be hypothermic, unable to move. He reached into the space with both hands. She leaned sideways in a feeble attempt to escape his touch. He captured her arm and pulled her toward him. She didn't fight, but she didn't cooperate, either. He had to drag her out of the narrow space. As soon as she was free, she crumpled to the ground. Her legs were ghost-white. Other than the gray parka, she wasn't dressed for the weather.

With a muttered curse, he scooped her into his arms. She was tall and slender, but heavy. He carried her toward his open door and climbed the kick-step, grunting from exertion. He skirted around the driver's chair and deposited her in the passenger seat.

Now what?

He grabbed a wool blanket from his supplies to cover her trembling body. She had on white stockings, ripped at both knees. The sight triggered his memory. He knew those legs. Startled, he lifted his gaze to her face.

It was *her*. The waitress from Walt's Diner. The one he had a crush on, and had vowed to steer clear of.

He spread the blanket over her legs and retreated, rubbing his jaw. In any other circumstances, he'd call the police and let them handle the matter. He was reluctant to take that step with this woman. She wasn't a stranger. He knew her. She clutched the edges of the blanket in a tight grip, still shivering. His first instinct was to help her, not report her.

He closed his door and cranked up the heat. Then he removed his jacket, placing it over her lap to add another layer of warmth. He didn't think her condition was life-threatening, but it concerned him. "Do you need to go to a hospital?"

She shook her head, vehement.

After a short hesitation, he put the truck in gear and pulled forward. He couldn't leave her on the side of the road, so he might as well drive. He monitored her progress as he continued north. She shivered less and less. Some of the color returned to her cheeks. Her grip on the blanket relaxed and her expression softened. No smile, but that wasn't unusual or unexpected, given the circumstances. The only drink he had was lukewarm tea. When he offered it to her, she accepted the cup and took an experimental sip.

"You work at Walt's."

She seemed surprised that he recognized her. But every trucker who'd been to Walt's would have recognized her. There was chatter about her on the radio. Pretty young things were rare in the frigid interior.

"Why did you stow away in my truck?"

"I needed a ride," she said, passing back his mug. She inspected the palms of her hands, which were scraped raw.

"You're hurt."

She hid her hands under the blanket. "I'm fine. I just tripped and fell."

Cam knew she wasn't telling him the whole story. She wouldn't climb aboard his rig and risk serious injury for no reason. She was either lying, or crazy, or scared to death. He guessed it was the latter, and his protective instincts went into overdrive. "Are you running from someone?"

She glanced into the side mirror, as if searching for a bogeyman.

He checked the highway. It was dark and deserted. "Maybe I should call the police."

"No," she said in a choked voice. "Please."

"Why not?"

"If you don't want to give me a ride, let me out. I'll walk."

He gave her an incredulous look. She'd rather freeze than contact the authorities? "The nearest town is thirty miles away."

"I can hitchhike."

"Are you in trouble?"

She stared out the window again. Her eyes welled up with tears, but she blinked them away quickly. She had a stubborn chin, bold brows and a soft mouth that reminded him of tulips. Her upper lip had a distinctive bow formation, like two little triangles.

With a frown, he returned his attention to the road. He needed to concentrate on driving, not her mouth. He didn't care if she'd robbed a bank, or vandalized Walt's Diner. He wasn't going to leave her out in the cold.

"Are you a cop?" she asked finally.

He drummed his fingertips against the wheel. "Do I look like a cop?"

"You don't look like a truck driver."

"I'm not a cop," he said, raking a hand through his hair. Not anymore. He'd abandoned his career in law enforcement a few months after Jenny died. He'd stopped believing in justice. He'd lost faith in himself.

An uncomfortable silence stretched between them. Her defensiveness could be an indication of guilt, or another manifestation of fear. He didn't ask any more questions. He knew from experience that aggressive interrogations made victims clam up. But it didn't matter, because he wasn't getting involved. Her problems were none of his business.

"I've seen you at the diner," she said.

He cleared his throat. "Yeah?"

"You order the veggie omelet and wheat toast. Black coffee."

He was surprised she remembered him. He'd only been in the diner a handful of times. The idea that he'd made an impression on her appealed to him. She tugged off her parka, revealing some other things that appealed to him.

Cam pulled his gaze away from her. She was an enticing package, with her slender figure and lovely face. Her presence in his cab felt like an electric charge. He couldn't prevent the rush of warmth that suffused him every time their eyes met.

He'd been alone on the road too long.

"Where are you headed?" she asked.

"North," he said shortly.

"Fairbanks?"

"For starters."

"Can I come with you?"

The temperature inside the cab had gone from toasty to sweltering. Cam turned down the heat, contemplative. He'd never picked up a hitchhiker before. He'd seen his share of "lot lizards" in the lower 48. They were hard-looking women, desperate for hard-up men. Nothing like this fresh beauty beside him.

She waited for his answer in silence.

"I'll take you to Fairbanks," he said, against his better judgment. He knew it was the wrong choice. She needed help, beyond a simple ride north, and he couldn't give it to her. He had nothing left to give. "From there you're on your own."

"Thank you," she said stiffly. "I appreciate it."

He made a noncommittal sound and fell silent. It was a long drive to Fairbanks, and he didn't intend on passing the time with idle chitchat. He couldn't remember how to engage a woman in conversation. The less she spoke, the easier it would be to ignore her. He could keep his mind—and his eyes—on the road.

A part of him wanted to look at her. A part of him wanted to do more than look. He'd been living like a monk for three years. He'd isolated himself in Alaska for a reason. He'd abandoned every comfort, including female company. He couldn't imagine dating again. He almost couldn't imagine a single night of pleasure.

Almost.

He knew she wasn't offering. She wasn't a lot lizard, and he didn't prey on vulnerable women, regardless. The man he used to be, the man who'd been a good husband and conscientious police officer, would never have considered taking advantage of her desperation. The man he'd become was numb. He had no moral high ground. He was a shadow of his former self, frozen in grief. He suddenly longed for some release from the monotony of his existence. He longed for human touch.

He glanced at Jenny's smiling picture on his dashboard. Her guileless expression never changed. She wouldn't have approved of his reclusive lifestyle or his current predicament. But she was dead, and had no say in the matter. He moved his gaze to the windswept lanes ahead. His heart felt like a stone inside his chest. He didn't say anything to put his passenger at ease. He just kept driving, into darkness.

Chapter 3

Tala regretted asking him if he was a cop.

She should have just shut up and let him drive. He'd threatened to call the police, but he hadn't picked up his phone or CB. He hadn't pulled over and told her to get out. He'd questioned her safety, like any conscientious person would, and she'd panicked.

She couldn't tell him what happened at the diner. He'd take her to the nearest police station and insist that she report the crime. She had no intentions of falling into that trap. No, she was going to run until she felt secure.

Running was what she did. It was what she knew.

She slunk lower in the passenger seat, feeling nauseated. She wished she'd never come to Alaska. She wished she hadn't fled Canada like a thief in the night. Now she was in a bind, and she had no idea how to get out.

She snuck another glimpse at the man behind the wheel. She hadn't lied when she'd said he didn't look like a trucker. There was something different about him, beyond his handsome face. She couldn't put her finger on what. He was rugged and outdoorsy enough to fit in with the locals. He wore flannel shirts and steel-toed boots. He had dark brown hair that curled around his collar and a well-trimmed beard that suited his features. She got the impression that he didn't smile or laugh much. He had thickly lashed, soulful brown eyes.

He was built more like a logger than a trucker. His broad shoulders and lean physique added to his appeal. He looked stronger than most homesteaders. He could even pass for one of those elite mountain climbers who came to summit Denali. He was a man in his prime. He was also married. He wore a plain gold wedding band on his left hand. She hadn't noticed it when he'd visited the diner.

The diner. A fresh wave of memories assaulted her. She could never go back there. Thoughts of Walt trickled in, making her heart clench. She hadn't stopped to consider the danger to him. He'd been asleep inside the office. What if those men had shot him? Guilt and shame and fear struck all at once, overwhelming her.

"What's your name?" the driver asked.

"Tala."

"Tala? Is that Native American?"

In her distress, she'd forgotten to lie about her name. She'd been Abigail Burgess for the past six months. She massaged her forehead, wincing. "We don't say Native American in Canada."

"What do you say?"

"First Nations."

"First Nations," he repeated, glancing at her. "You're from Canada?"

She nodded. Now that she'd screwed up, she might as well be honest. "I was born in Yellowknife."

"They have ice roads in Yellowknife."

"Yes."

"Have you been on them?"

"No. Have you?"

"I've always wanted to. I've been on the Dalton, which has an ice road section near Prudhoe Bay."

She hadn't realized he was an ice-road trucker. Maybe that was why he reminded her of a mountain climber. Both endeavors required nerves of steel. Only the most daring truckers would drive over a layer of ice with arctic waters flowing underneath.

"I'm Cam, by the way. Cameron Hughes."

"Nice to meet you," she said automatically. It felt odd to have a normal conversation after what she'd been through. "Where are you from?"

"Tacoma, Washington."

"When did you come to Alaska?"

"Three years ago. I needed to…get away."

She could relate. Unless he meant he needed to get away from his responsibilities. Maybe he'd left a wife and children behind. He didn't seem like the deadbeat-dad type, but she didn't know him. She couldn't judge his personality on polite manners and generous tips. His nice-guy vibe could be deceiving. After Duane, she didn't trust easily.

The short exchange ended, revealing the extent of his curiosity about her. She was relieved by his disinterest. She didn't want to talk.

The sun rose over the horizon as they continued north on the highway. Warm rays penetrated her window. A few hours ago, she'd been convinced she was going to freeze to death. It had been unbearably cold in that dark space. She'd pounded her fist on the cab for help. If he hadn't pulled over to investigate, she might have died.

She moved her gaze to the side mirror. She didn't think they were being followed. The road behind them was clear. The killers must not have seen her flee. She was safe—for now. Thanks to Cam, she was warm and dry.

She folded his jacket and set it aside. Then she removed the blanket. Her stockings were ruined, her knees scraped. She had bits of gravel embedded in her skin. Her palms were raw, too. She needed to wash up.

"I have a first aid kit in the glove compartment. There's a toilet in the back. Make yourself at home."

She glanced over her shoulder. There was a narrow bunk and a mini-fridge in the berth. "Do you sleep here?"

"When I have to."

With his long legs and rangy build, he didn't look like he'd fit. She rose to her feet and ventured into the space. A sliding door led to a closet-sized bathroom. It was cramped, but clean. She washed her hands at the sink before inspecting herself in the mirror. Her hair had come loose from the bun. She combed her fingers through the tangled strands to smooth the disarray. Then she returned to the front of the cab. Taking a deep breath, she helped herself to the contents of the first aid kit. After she cleaned the minor wounds with alcohol, she applied antibiotic ointment and stuck on some bandages.

"There are drinks in the fridge," he said. "And sandwiches."

She grabbed a bottled water. "Do you want something?"

"I'm good."

He drove for several hours without speaking. It felt odd to sit next to a stranger in complete silence, but she made no attempt at small talk. Sharing personal information with him seemed unwise.

She felt self-conscious in his presence. She wished he wasn't so handsome. She couldn't pretend she hadn't noticed his rugged good looks, and the last thing she wanted to do was get caught staring. Many truckers, even the married ones, wouldn't hesitate to proposition a female hitchhiker. Cam hadn't given any indication that he expected sexual favors from her. He didn't have a creepy-predator vibe. She sat very still and tried not to imagine the worst.

He gestured to the radio. "You can change the station if you like. Or I have audiobooks."

"Audiobooks?"

"Books on tape."

She nodded her understanding. There was a device plugged into his port. She picked it up and browsed the files. A Stieg Larsson book was at the top of the queue. The other options were horror, murder mysteries and true crime. Disturbing stories of violence and mayhem.

"Is this what serial killers listen to?"

He frowned at the question.

"Sorry," she said awkwardly. "That was a joke."

He changed gears, glancing her direction. "I guess my selections are pretty stark."

"They're fine."

"I choose books that will help me stay awake. It's a trucker trick."

She set aside the device. "I've never listened to an

audiobook. I don't think they make them for the books I like."

"Why not?"

"I read graphic novels. They have pictures." She flushed at the admission, as if it was something to be ashamed of. Duane always said her "comics" weren't real books. But Duane never read anything, so what did he know?

"Where do you get graphic novels?"

"I've bought a few at a used bookstore, but they're hard to find. In Canada, I checked them out from the library. I don't have a card here."

"How long have you been in Alaska?"

"Six months."

He didn't ask her why she'd come. She wouldn't have told him.

"What's Canada like?"

"Cold."

He smiled at her answer. "Were you a waitress there, too?"

"I was before I got married."

"You're married?"

She searched his face for judgment and found none. "It didn't work out."

"Is he the one you're running from?"

"None of your business."

A muscle in his jaw ticked with displeasure, but he dropped the subject. She crossed her arms over her chest to hide her trembling hands. Although she wasn't naturally meek or shy, she'd learned to avoid conflict with men. She'd managed to escape Duane and his hair-trigger temper. This morning, she'd stumbled into more danger. Witnessing a murder hadn't improved her opinion of strangers. She half expected Cam to lash out at her.

When he didn't, she released a slow breath. Her first instinct was to apologize again, but she squelched it. They had to establish some boundaries. Certain topics were off-limits. She couldn't tell him why she was running.

To his credit, Cam took her prickly attitude in stride. He didn't interrogate her further. He continued driving, steady as a rock. He didn't exceed the speed limit or take unnecessary risks. They entered Denali State Park, which offered spectacular views. She looked out the window and watched the rugged landscape pass by.

They stopped for lunch around noon. Cam gave her a sandwich and a drink from the mini-fridge. Then he put on his jacket and went outside to check his load. She was surprised by how hungry she was. She bit into the sandwich with relish.

He came in from the cold, his cheeks ruddy, and they hit the road again. He ate his sandwich on a long straightaway.

Tala thought about the last man who'd given her a sandwich: Walt. He'd always been kind to her. The day she'd walked into his diner, he'd hired her on the spot. He'd fed her and offered her some pocket money at the end of the shift. His generosity reminded her that there were good men in the world. Men like her father, who'd raised her to be strong, to fight back, to take care of herself. She wondered if he'd have been disappointed in her, had he lived.

Cam seemed like a good man. Maybe a little too good, with his healthy eating habits and unflappable demeanor. It occurred to her that he might call the police after they parted ways. If something had happened to Walt, Cam would hear about it. He'd want to help. He would tell them everything. Her name, birthplace, nationality. It was more than enough information to identify her. She'd fled the scene of a crime. She could be arrested just for that.

Trying not to panic, she nibbled the edge of her thumbnail. Maybe he wouldn't go to the authorities. He was a trucker, not a Boy Scout. She sensed a certain amount of detachment in him, which made sense for a married man who wanted to stay true to his wife. He was giving Tala a ride to Fairbanks, nothing more. When they got there, she was on her own. She had no idea what she'd do.

She didn't know anyone in Alaska, other than Walt, her landlady and her coworkers. She had no family here. She hadn't seen her mother in years. She'd been closer to her father, who'd died almost a decade ago. She still missed him.

Blinking away fresh tears, she pushed her anxieties aside and focused on the present. There were majestic mountains in the distance. She hadn't seen much of the state in her short time here. She'd passed by Denali once on her way toward Anchorage. It was a sight to behold, immense and breathtaking.

Her father had been an avid outdoorsman. He'd shared his love of the land with her. Traveling through this beautiful country reminded her of him. *Live simply*, he'd always said. *Take only what you need.*

She closed her eyes and held those thoughts for as long as she could. When she opened them, she was strong again.

Chapter 4

Fairbanks, AK
65N
2 degrees

It wasn't a pleasant drive from Denali.

Another rig had jackknifed on the icy road before McKinley Peak, causing a major pileup. Traffic was stopped for miles in both directions. There was no way around the wreck, no alternative route. Cam had to sit and wait for several hours. Tala didn't complain about the delay. She didn't say a word. The sun set early and daylight faded. They reached the outskirts of Fairbanks in the evening hours.

"Where should I drop you off?" he asked.

"Anywhere is fine."

He didn't feel right about abandoning her on a street

corner. It was getting late. "You have family around here?"

"No."

"Friends?"

"I can get by on my own."

He wanted to ask how, even though it was none of his business. She appeared to have no belongings, other than a serviceable parka and a cheap waitress uniform. She wasn't carrying a purse or backpack. If she stood out in the cold, she'd get another ride. That much was certain. Someone would pick her up. Someone with ill intentions, most likely.

"I'll find work."

"What kind of work?"

Her eyes narrowed at the question. "Not the kind you think."

"You need a change of clothes before you go job-hunting."

She fingered the torn fabric at her knees, sighing.

"I don't want to leave you on the side of the road."

"I'll be fine. Don't worry about it."

That was the problem: he was worried about it. He'd assumed a certain amount of responsibility for her when he'd agreed to give her a ride. He'd decided not to call the police, against his better judgment. Now he couldn't just walk away. He was standing between her and danger, whether he liked it or not. He felt obligated to see her off safely. If he didn't, he'd think about her all night. He'd obsess over worst-case scenarios. He'd imagine her climbing into a stranger's car. Or freezing to death.

He hadn't been able to save Jenny, and he'd never recovered from the loss. The helplessness. The soul-crushing futility.

He didn't have to *save* Tala, per se, but he could at least offer her shelter for the night. He could give her a few bucks for clothes in the morning. She could find a job tomorrow. She was young and resourceful. She'd survive. It was no hardship for him to dig into his pockets, and it might make all the difference in the world for her. A minimal cost and effort on his part could keep her from doing something desperate.

"Are you hungry?" he asked.

She moistened her lips, not answering.

"I have to deliver this load first. Then we can grab some dinner."

"You don't have to buy me dinner."

"I know."

Her eyes narrowed with suspicion. "Why are you being so nice to me?"

"Not the reason you think."

"No?"

"No."

She crossed her arms over her chest, still wary. "What would your wife say about this?"

He gave her a puzzled look. "My wife?"

"Aren't you married?"

"No."

"You're wearing a wedding ring."

He rubbed the band on his left hand absently. He'd forgotten it was there. "I'm not married anymore."

"What happened?"

"She died."

Her lips parted in surprise. Then her features softened with sympathy. "I'm sorry."

"It's okay," he said, clearing his throat. Saying the words out loud wasn't easy, even after three years, but he'd learned to swallow the pain. Then the numbness returned to his chest and he could breathe again.

Maybe Tala felt sorry for him, because she didn't reject his dinner offer. He continued to the stockyard to deliver the trailer. He'd get a new load tomorrow morning before he traveled north on the Dalton. The Dalton Highway was both his savior and his nemesis. The route wasn't for the faint of heart. It was a death-defying stretch of snowpack, black ice and whiteouts, with avalanche-prone areas and roller-coaster turns. He relished every mile.

He'd come to Alaska to be an ice-road trucker. Nothing else got his blood pumping like the Dalton. There was nothing more exciting, more addictive, or more life-affirming. Except maybe sex. It had been so long since he'd had any, he couldn't quite remember. He'd stayed true to Jenny's memory. He still wasn't ready to move on.

He hadn't lied to Tala about his intentions. He wasn't being nice to her in hopes of getting laid. She was incredibly attractive, but he couldn't imagine hooking up with her. Even if he was in the market for female company, she wasn't an appropriate choice for a one-night stand. She'd had a close call this morning. She was on the run from someone. She needed protection, not seduction.

He unloaded the trailer and returned to the cab, invigorated by the chill in the air. It was perfect ice-road weather, with temperatures dropping below zero. He climbed into the driver's seat and pulled out of the yard.

There was a good burger joint off the main drag, so Cam headed in that direction. It was crowded with customers, despite the late hour. Tala kept her hood on as they entered the building. She chose a back booth in the corner, glancing around warily. Cam knew they hadn't been followed from Willow. He'd checked his rearview mirror at regular intervals. He figured her skittishness was a side effect of past trauma, not an indication of current danger, but he made a point to stay alert.

The waitress arrived quickly. He ordered a salmon burger, iced tea and french fries. Tala asked for chicken strips and a strawberry soda. After the food was delivered, he offered her some of his fries, because he had a mountain of them.

"You like to eat healthy," she said, grabbing a fry.

"I do."

"That seems unusual, for a trucker."

"I grew up on a farm in upstate Washington. My parents made me learn about sustainable agriculture and organic produce. We ate food we grew ourselves." He shrugged, picking up his salmon burger. "It stayed with me."

She nodded her understanding. "We ate food my dad caught."

"Was he a fisherman?"

"He did a little bit of everything. Fishing, trapping, hunting. It was hard in the winter, but we got by."

Cam swallowed the bite he'd taken. "You lived off the land exclusively?"

"Yes."

He couldn't hide his surprise. He thought his childhood had been atypical. Eating fresh farm produce instead of junk food was nothing compared to eking out a meager existence in the Northwest Territories.

"He died when I was sixteen. He was only forty at the time."

"Jesus," Cam said.

"He had a good life," she said. "Short, but not wasted."

"Is that what you want?"

She shook her head. "I'd rather take after my grand-mother. She lived to be eighty. She used to say my dad used up all of his spirit in half the time because he never sat still. He never stopped working."

"How old are you?"

"Twenty-five. You?"

"Thirty-four," he said gruffly.

"That's a good age," she said, grabbing another fry.

Cam tried not to be captivated by her, and failed. She had a slight accent that sounded woodsy and pleasant to his ears. She was interesting, as well as beautiful. A wave of sexual awareness washed over him, heat-ing his blood and kicking up his pulse. He felt mildly alarmed by his response to her. He needed to pump the brakes, and stop asking so many personal questions. This wasn't a date.

She stuck a straw in her soda bottle and took a sip, drawing his attention to her mouth. Tulips in spring.

"What about you?" she asked.

"What about me?"

"Would you rather have a short life or a long one?"

He made a noncommittal sound and kept eating.

"You're an ice-road trucker, so I'm guessing short. Then again, you eat healthy and take care of your body." Her gaze traveled over him. "You work out, right?"

He flushed at her perusal. "I don't work out to live longer."

"No?"

"I sit in a truck all day. I'd get stir-crazy if I didn't exercise."

"It's not natural to spend so much time inside a vehicle."

Cam couldn't argue there. The lack of activity didn't bother some truckers. They each had their own vices. Chain-smoking and snacking were common ways to stay awake. The long hours of limited movement were difficult, but it was part of the job. He embraced the restrictions as much as the freedoms. He relished the danger and the solitude. He hadn't become a trucker to take it easy. He'd done it to disconnect with the rest of the world, and from himself.

He also didn't exercise just to combat inactivity. He did it to assuage his grief, to punish himself for living, and to sleep at night. The more grueling the workout, the better. He'd become obsessive. He'd made an effort to cut down last year, after pulling a muscle in his thigh. Overdoing it wasn't healthy, either.

They were almost finished eating when a pair of uniformed officers walked in. Cam watched them dispassionately, reminded of his former self. Tala rose from the table after the officers paused at the front counter.

"I have to go to the bathroom," she said.

Cam paid the check while she was gone. The waitress came and went. So did the police officers, who ordered their coffee to go. Cam drummed his fingertips against the table. It dawned on him that Tala had taken her parka with her, which was odd.

He wondered if she'd ditched him. It wouldn't be a big shock. She'd wanted a ride to Fairbanks, and here they were.

Curious, he went looking for her. The women's restroom was at the end of the hall. An emergency exit on the opposite side of the restaurant offered the only escape. He paused outside the door, listening for a moment. Then he pushed it open. There were two stalls and two sinks under a big mirror. "Tala?"

No answer. Just a sharp intake of breath.

He waited another beat. "The officers are gone, if that's what you're worried about."

"I'll be right out."

Frowning to himself, he shut the door. What had he gotten himself into? It was one thing to risk death on the ice roads, quite another to risk arrest by harboring a female fugitive.

She emerged from the bathroom a second later, feigning innocence. They walked into the night together and approached his rig. He glanced in her direction, noting she was tight-mouthed and ghost-pale. He didn't ask her why she'd been hiding from the police. She probably wouldn't tell him, and he wasn't sure he wanted to know. He couldn't afford to get wrapped up in whatever trouble she was in. He had to leave tomorrow.

She paused in the parking lot, her breaths visible in the frozen air. "Thank you."

"I haven't done anything."

"You've done a lot. I won't forget it."

He realized she was trying to say goodbye. He shook his head in protest. "Come with me. I know where we can stay for free."

"Where?"

"Ann's Cabins."

"Why is it free?"

"I split wood for her every time I'm in Fairbanks. We trade services."

She searched his face for hints of deception. He was stretching the truth a little. Ann gave him a discount, but he hardly ever stayed at the cabins. He split wood because he liked doing it, not because he cared about saving money.

"Are we trading services, too?" she asked.

He laughed, rubbing a hand over his mouth. Then he realized it was a serious question. She wanted to know what he expected of her, and she was smart to be cautious. Very few men would offer her a bed without intending to share it.

He held her gaze. "No. We're not."

She stared at him with undisguised curiosity. "Why are you helping me?"

An icy fist of grief squeezed around his heart. He couldn't answer her question honestly. He couldn't bear to talk about Jenny and his inability to save her. He opened his passenger door. "I didn't bring you in from the cold just to let you freeze somewhere else."

She didn't appear satisfied with the response, but she climbed inside his truck. She must have trusted him more than another stranger. The next trucker she met might not be a gentleman. He might demand sexual favors in exchange for a ride. If she said no, he could leave her stranded on the side of the road. Or worse.

Cam got behind the wheel and started the engine. Ann's was within walking distance of a major shopping center. Tala could rest tonight and look for work tomorrow.

The cabins were quaint and secluded. Romantic, even. Although it wasn't a trucker hangout, it was known to truckers because the owner was a trucker's widow. Her husband had died on the Dalton a few years ago, in an avalanche. Cam had heard chatter about it on the CB last winter. The truckers pitched in to help Ann with odd jobs. One of them said she needed someone to chop firewood for her. Cam had jumped at the task.

Turning off the main drag, he drove toward the cabins. He parked in the back of the lot and went inside the office while Tala waited in the truck.

The front desk was empty, so he rang the bell. Ann came out to greet him. She reminded him of Mrs. Claus, with her round-framed glasses and curly white hair. "If it isn't my woodcutter," she said with a smile. "How's the season going?"

"It's good. I'm keeping busy."

"Have you been on the haul road?"

"I'm heading that way tomorrow."

"You be careful out there."

"I will."

She toggled the mouse on her computer to check him in. "The only cabin left is a double. My singles are under remodel, so they're all closed."

He took out his wallet, considering. Would Tala stay with him in one room?

"I'll give you a double for the single price, if it's just you."

His neck heated with embarrassment. "I have a guest, actually."

Ann gave him his discount and handed him the key. If she was curious about his companion, she was discreet enough to pretend otherwise. "Ring me if you need anything," she said, winking.

He left the office and approached cabin 4, which was at the end of the first row. He opened the door and turned on the lights. It was a cozy room with two beds, a fireplace and a bathroom. Tala got out of his truck and walked across the parking lot, her parka hood obscuring most of her face. She didn't object to the sleeping arrangements. Maybe she hadn't anticipated having her own space. He followed her inside, his heart racing.

She sat down on the far bed. She bounced on the mattress to test its firmness. "This is nice."

Cam glanced around for something else to look at. His gaze settled on the fireplace. There was a bin full of logs he'd split. The evidence of his last good deed unsettled him. He crouched down to build a fire with shaking hands. He didn't know what he was so nervous about. They were here to sleep, nothing more. He wasn't going to touch her. Even if he was capable of a clumsy seduction attempt, which he doubted, he wouldn't try anything. He might be numb and emotionless, but he wasn't a liar. He'd given her his word.

She stood, shrugging out of her parka. "I'm going to take a shower."

He watched her disappear into the bathroom. She locked the door behind her with a click. He turned his attention back to the fire. When he had it blazing, he got up and dusted off his hands. Then he moved to the far corner of the room, by the window. There were logs stacked up near the chopping block. He considered going outside to split wood. Tala might appreciate the privacy. He turned his attention to the bathroom door, picturing her naked. Wet, dark hair. Warm, soap-slick skin.

His blood thickened with arousal. He could feel that, if nothing else. He was still capable of desire. He scrubbed a hand over his eyes, but the images didn't cease. He was ten steps away from a nude woman. He could hear the water running, streaming over her body. Erotic thoughts filled his head, fantasies and memories combined. He remembered how it felt to join a lady in the shower. To lift her up against the tiles and take her. To drink water droplets from her skin.

His hands curled into fists and his groin tightened to a painful degree. He didn't know what to do, or where to look. Staring out the window didn't help. It was as if his brain had short-circuited from the sensory overload. He was afraid she'd emerge from the bathroom and see him standing there with an erection.

He sat down on the edge of the mattress, his heart pounding. He tried to think unsexy thoughts, but it was no use. He was too wound up. He took deep breaths, fists clenching and unclenching. Unfortunately, his arousal didn't ebb. He'd denied himself pleasure too long. His body was staging a full-on revolt. He needed to get out of here.

Springing to his feet, he walked outside, into the frigid air. He gulped it into his lungs, staring at the clear night sky. It was bracingly cold. He felt better. He wanted to stretch his legs, so he started jogging. He did a few laps around the neighborhood, his breaths puffing out in the black night.

After he regained control of his body, his thoughts cleared. He returned to the chopping block outside their cabin. There was a stack of heavy logs beneath a covered awning. The ax was in the shed. He placed a log on the stump and brought the ax down, splitting it in one strike. He repeated the process over and over, until his mind was numb.

Chapter 5

Tala ducked into the bathroom and locked the door.

Even though Cam had made it clear that he didn't expect her to sleep with him, she couldn't stop her heart from racing. She shouldn't have come here. Now she felt trapped. She was at his mercy.

What if he made a pass at her? He might think she was fair game for a one-night stand, despite his reassurances. The poor guy's wife had died. He was lonely. He was young and strong and healthy. It was only natural for him to seek out female company, and he liked her. She could see it in his eyes. When his gaze settled on her, awareness sizzled done her spine. Because she liked him, too.

She studied her anxious expression in the mirror, feeling conflicted. She wished she'd asked him to take her to the airport. She could have spent the night on the benches. It wouldn't have been comfortable, but she'd endured worse. At the airport, there were multiple exits. If she needed to, she could run.

Cam wasn't holding her against her will, of course. She'd agreed to stay with him. She didn't think he was a physical threat. It wasn't so much that she was afraid of him. She was afraid of men, period. She was afraid of letting down her guard, and of getting attached. She hadn't escaped Duane to become reliant on another man. She couldn't make that mistake again. She had to take care of herself before she could feel safe with anyone else.

She turned away from the mirror and stripped off her clothes. As she stepped into the shower, memories from this morning crept up on her. She started shivering again, even though the water was piping hot. When she closed her eyes, she imagined the scene in the parking lot. Blood spraying from the gunshot wound, spreading from the body in a dark circle. She scrubbed at her skin, as if the trauma had sullied her.

After she rinsed off, she felt lightheaded and slightly nauseated. She stepped out of the stall, wrapping a towel around her body. She didn't have anything to wear besides her uniform, which wouldn't double as pajamas. Her tights were ruined, so she tossed them in the trash. Then she washed her underwear in the sink. They were nylon, so they'd dry by morning. She hung them on the hook behind the door.

She was reluctant to leave the bathroom without clothes on, but whatever. She'd have to climb into bed in her towel. Maybe Cam wouldn't notice. Maybe he wasn't that interested. She'd been told she was pretty often enough, but she'd also been told otherwise. Duane had yelled at her to shut her ugly mouth, or move her skinny ass. She didn't think she was ugly, and she definitely wasn't skinny, but his criticism had eroded her self-confidence.

Tension welled up inside her. A part of her wanted Cam to find her attractive. She just didn't want him to do anything about it. She hoped he wouldn't consider her near nudity a sign of encouragement.

Taking a deep breath, she opened the door and ventured out. She tried not to worry about Cam's reaction, or overestimate her appeal. With her tangled hair and skinned knees, she wasn't some irresistible femme fatale. He might not look twice at her.

As it turned out, Cam didn't look once. Because he wasn't there.

She clutched the towel to her chest, bewildered. He must have gone outside. There was no reason to run for cover now, so she stood in front of the fireplace. It was crackling with new flames, bright and warm. If Cam didn't return, she'd spend the night in the cabin and figure out her next step in the morning. She'd have to look for work at another café or diner. While she fingercombed her hair, letting it dry, she became aware of a familiar sound. Someone was splitting wood. She approached the window and peeked through the curtains.

It was Cam. He swung the ax in powerful strokes, bringing it down hard. When he had a nice stack of split pieces, he carried them to the shed. Then he started over. He set a punishing pace, his brow furrowed. She didn't know what demons were inside him, or why he worked so hard for physical release, but she enjoyed watching him. His strength was impressive and his tortured-soul expression captivated her imagination. She assumed he was still grieving. He was still in love with his late wife.

That was why he didn't want to "trade services" with Tala. That was why he seemed so detached and alone.

She left the window, her heart heavy, and sat down to fix her hair. She made two braids and secured the tails. She hadn't worn her hair like this since she'd left Canada. She hadn't wanted to look Indian while she was hiding out in Alaska, but she was proud of her heritage. The blood of her ancestors flowed strong and true inside her. Unlike her self-esteem, it could never be weakened or changed. It could never be beaten.

Cam came in from the cold, breathing hard. His face was flushed from exertion. He had a duffel bag in his hands. He did a quick scan of her towel-clad form. Then he unzipped the bag and took out a red-checked flannel. He thrust it at her, averting his gaze. "You can wear this to sleep in."

She accepted the shirt with gratitude.

"I'm going to shower," he muttered, and ducked into the bathroom.

After the door closed, she brought the flannel to her nose and inhaled. It smelled nice, like cozy man and laundry detergent. She put on the shirt, securing the buttons. Then she climbed into bed and stared up at the log-beam ceiling. Her thoughts whirled around and around before settling on the obvious. She pictured Cam naked in a soapy lather. She wondered if he was hard-muscled all over, or if he carried most of his strength in his arms. Was he hairy, with a thick pelt on his chest to match his beard? Maybe he had ugly feet. She smiled at the thought. Surely he had flaws. He was just a man like any other.

When he emerged from the bathroom, she had to revise her opinion. He was shirtless, in a pair of gray sweatpants. She couldn't find a single imperfection. Splitting wood had brought his muscles into sharp definition. His shoulders were broad, his stomach tight. His biceps looked as hard and crisp as McIntosh apples. The smattering of hair across his chest didn't qualify as a pelt, but it added to his rugged masculinity.

He turned off the lights and headed toward the other bed, ignoring her. She watched him get settled under the blankets. They were quiet for several moments. She listened to the wood crackle and pop in the fireplace.

It became clear that he wasn't going to try to climb into bed with her. She didn't have to worry about him demanding sexual favors in exchange for the ride to Fairbanks. Maybe she'd mistaken simple kindness for desire on his part.

Maybe he didn't want her.

She should have been relieved by his decency. She could relax now that she knew where she stood with him. For some reason, she felt sad and restless. Although she was exhausted, sleep wouldn't come.

She turned toward him in the dark. The light from the fire didn't reach his face. Although she couldn't see his features, she sensed his tension. The reason for it eluded her. He hadn't seemed anxious before they entered the cabin. Something had triggered him. While she showered, he'd gone outside to chop wood in a frenzy. "Are you awake?"

"No," he said in a clipped tone.

She smiled at his curt response.

"Do you need something?" he asked.

"I don't want to bother you."

"I don't mind."

"What happened to your wife?"

He paused for so long she thought he wasn't going to answer. Then he said, "She was in an accident. Hit-and-run. They rushed her to the hospital and tried to save her. She was in a coma for a few months."

"She never woke up?"

"No. She didn't."

Her heart constricted with sadness. "I'm sorry."

He didn't say anything.

"Is that why you came to Alaska?"

"Yes."

"You needed to get away from the bad memories."

He shifted on the mattress, seeming uncomfortable. "I thought if I kept moving, I could...move on."

"Did it work?"

"What do you think?"

"I think you're too hard on yourself."

He fell silent again.

"It's okay to grieve, even for a long time."

"Let's talk about you," he said.

"Me?"

"You're on the run for a reason."

It was her turn to be quiet.

"You won't tell me about it?"

"No."

"You don't trust me?"

That wasn't it. Right now, in the dark of the cabin, with flames crackling in the fireplace, she trusted him. She didn't think he would hurt her or take advantage of her. But she also couldn't expect him to rescue her from this mess. She had to rescue herself.

"I don't want to involve you," she said finally.

"Why not?"

"It's not your problem."

"Maybe I can help."

She shook her head in denial. "I just have to lay low for a while. I've done it before."

He grunted at this admission, as if it didn't surprise him.

"I'll be okay. I can find a job."

"Where?"

"At a diner."

"A diner with no cops or truckers? Good luck with that."

"I'm not worried about truckers."

"You should be, because they'll recognize you."

"So?"

"They'll talk about you on the radio."

"They will not."

"Sure they will. They already do. I've heard them."

She moistened her lips, incredulous. "What do they say?"

"Complimentary things. Some of it's a little crude."

Those bastards. She curled her hands into fists. If truckers talked about her on the radio, she'd be in trouble. Anyone could listen to those stations, including the cops—and the killers. But maybe Walt was okay, and no one would come looking for her. Maybe no one would worry about a missing waitress.

"I'm sure you'll be able to find work on your back, if nothing else."

She sat up in bed, her eyes narrow. He wasn't insulting her to be mean. He thought he was helping her. "You're trying to scare me into going to the police."

"You should go to the police."

"Why do you care?"

He tucked his hands behind his head. "I don't know."

She settled back down and hugged a pillow to her chest. Cam meant well, but she didn't trust the police. She could take care of herself. Cam felt responsible for her because he'd given her a ride, and now she was like… his cargo. He wanted to deliver her safely. But she knew better than to expect him to stick around.

He was a trucker. He'd move on in the morning.

She closed her eyes and tried to rest. Visions of murder and violence plagued her. She burrowed deeper in the blankets. When she finally drifted off, the nightmares closed in. She was back at the diner. There was a bloody pile of innards sizzling on the griddle. She plated the mess and took it out to her customers. The killers were sitting at a table in the parking lot. She dropped the tray and started running, but her legs didn't work. She couldn't escape, so she climbed inside the dumpster to hide.

Walt was at the bottom. He'd been disemboweled.

She let out a terrified shriek, covering her mouth. A figure emerged from the shadows. It was Duane.

"I knew I'd find you in the trash with another man."

He struck her across the cheek, and everything went black.

Tala woke up screaming. Her skin crawled with creepy sensations, and blankets were tangled around her ankles. She kicked them aside to free herself, flinging out her hands. She connected with someone, but it wasn't Duane. It was Cam.

He put his arms around her. "Shh. You're okay now. I've got you."

She stopped struggling and went quiet. It was dark in the room. She could see the pleasant glow of the fire in the hearth. The only sound was her ragged breathing.

A sob rose up to her throat. The breakdown she'd been fighting all day caught up to her with a vengeance. She couldn't prevent the tears from coming, and they were long overdue. She hadn't cried since she'd left Duane.

Cam stroked her hair and made soothing noises.

She finally calmed down enough to speak. "Walt was in the dumpster. He was dead."

"It was just a dream."

"Duane was there, too. He hit me."

"Did he?"

She heard the edge in his voice and eased away from him. There were tissues on the nightstand, next to a bottle of cold water. She used a tissue and took a soothing drink. Little by little, her tears abated.

"Better now?"

"Yes."

"Duane is your husband?"

"He was."

"Are you divorced?"

"Not legally, but I left him."

"Because he hit you?"

Her stomach clenched with unease. It was a deeply personal question, but they weren't strangers anymore. They'd passed that point and entered another territory. He'd opened up to her about his wife. She'd wept in his arms.

She'd never told anyone about the abuse she'd suffered in her short marriage. She'd been too ashamed. Her father had raised her to be strong and proud. She wasn't the victim type. She was a survivor, and a fighter. Somehow Duane had taken that away from her.

Maybe talking about him would help her get it back.

He didn't deserve to be protected. She couldn't excuse his actions, and she was done keeping his secrets.

"He was abusive," she said, letting out a slow breath. "Mentally and physically."

"Do you want to talk about it?"

A cold calm passed over her, and she nodded. "He got more violent and controlling as time went on. It was so gradual, I almost didn't notice it. Or I didn't want to acknowledge it. Then he snapped, and I couldn't pretend it wasn't happening anymore."

"What do you mean, he snapped?"

"Well, he changed after we got married. It wasn't a huge transformation, because he'd always had a temper. He'd yell at me and act jealous and get drunk and stupid. I thought it was regular boyfriend stuff. Then we got married, and we moved to a very rural area. He started treating me like his property, instead of his wife. He'd have these dark moods that scared me. He didn't want me to leave the house without permission. One day, I snuck out to go to the library. When I got back, he hit me."

"What did you do?"

"Nothing. I was too stunned to move. He cried and begged me to forgive him. He said he'd never do it again."

"But he did."

"Yes."

"Is he a cop?"

She was startled by the question. "How did you know?"

"Just a hunch. Go on."

"We stayed together for a few more months. He flew into another jealous rage and hid my purse so I couldn't go anywhere. I realized things weren't going to get better. The next time he hit me, I hit him back."

"What happened?"

She touched her face, remembering. "I bloodied his nose. I don't think he expected that, and he got really mad. He knocked me out. As soon as I could move, I packed a bag. I left in the middle of the night while he was sleeping."

"How did you get to Alaska?"

"I stowed away in a trailer."

"You're kidding."

"No. I wasn't planning on leaving Canada. I thought the trucker was going south. Instead he went west, and here I am."

"Are you here illegally?"

She shook her head. "Have you ever heard of the Jay Treaty?"

"No."

"It allows First Nations people the right to come to the US from Canada and vice versa. There's really no such thing as an undocumented Indian, but I don't have my tribal card or any ID to prove my status. I left everything in Canada.'

"I'm glad you escaped."

"So am I."

She looked away, contemplative. Cam didn't seem to think less of her for having an abusive husband. She knew it wasn't her fault, but a part of her felt responsible for what had happened. She should have been smarter, and more aware of Duane's true nature. She shouldn't have rushed into marriage. She should have identified the threat sooner.

Tala closed her eyes to clear the bad memories. Her

relationship with Duane was over. She'd left him, and she'd never have to suffer his abuse again.

Unfortunately, she'd traded up as far as personal problems went. Now she had to worry about the other men she was running from.

Goose bumps broke out across her flesh. She'd kicked off the blankets in the throes of her nightmare. Her legs were bare and cold. So was Cam's chest, she realized with a start. She'd been too distressed to notice that before. The faint glow of the fire revealed an intimate scene. They were in bed together, close enough to touch. He was shirtless, his torso outlined against the pale sheets. She was wearing his flannel without a stitch underneath. She tugged the comforter back into place, flushing.

"I should let you sleep," Cam said.

"Don't go," she whispered. "Please."

He glanced in her direction, brow furrowed. He seemed uncomfortable with her proximity, and was possibly confused about what she wanted from him. Tala struggled to pinpoint it herself. She knew he was hung up on his wife, and not interested in sex. Or not interested in her. Whatever his reasons, she felt safe with him.

She wouldn't drag him into her problems, but she could ask him for one small thing. "Will you...hold me?"

He drew in a ragged breath, as if tortured by the thought.

"Just until I fall asleep," she said, to make her wishes clear. "Nothing more."

"I don't think that's a good idea."

She searched his features in the dark, uncertain what he meant. His eyes glinted with something she'd seen before. Something he'd been trying to hide. The desire she'd sensed earlier flared between them, like a new spark.

He wasn't so disinterested.

She altered her request. "Can I hold you?"

After a short hesitation, he rolled onto his side, facing away from her. She hugged his back, spoon-style. It was the best of both worlds. She could cuddle him and enjoy the simple pleasure of human touch without worrying about him getting aroused. He could lay there and be her teddy bear, no strings attached.

She slipped her arm around him and closed her eyes. He was warm and hard-muscled. Solidly built, like a protective shield. She could feel his heartbeat under her palm, strong and sure. He covered her hand with his and linked their fingers together. Her throat tightened with emotion. She hadn't felt peace or contentment in such a long time. His presence filled an empty place inside her she hadn't known was there.

She savored him for as long as she could before she fell asleep.

Chapter 6

December 12
65N
-5 degrees

Cam got dressed in the dark.

He pulled on his jeans over thermal underwear and shoved his feet into steel-toed boots. His long-sleeved T-shirt provided minimal warmth against the morning chill, but he didn't grab his jacket. He wanted to feel the cold bite of winter, and he did. It had snowed overnight. Powder crunched beneath his soles as he crossed the dark, deserted parking lot. Frosty air filled his lungs and penetrated his clothing.

He made his way toward the front office, which was open but unmanned. The smell of fresh-brewed coffee awaited him. He helped himself to two cups. He didn't know if Tala liked cream and sugar, so he grabbed packets of both.

"There's oatmeal," Ann said, emerging from another room.

He glanced at the cooking pot next to the carafe. His stomach growled with interest, but his hands were already full. "I'll come back for it."

"I can deliver two bowls to your cabin."

A flush crept up his neck at the thought of Ann coming to his door and catching a glimpse of Tala in his bed. He felt like a teenager who didn't want his mom to find out his girlfriend had slept over. "No need."

Ann smiled at his quick response. "Thanks for splitting logs."

"I enjoy the work."

She nodded, and he escaped the cozy space in a hurry. He had no reason to be embarrassed. He hadn't done anything wrong. He'd slept next to Tala without crossing the line. Even if their night hadn't been innocent, so what? Surely Ann had seen worse in her days as innkeeper. Drunken hookups, seedy affairs, hard partying. She wouldn't blink an eye at Cam's pretty young guest. Unless she assumed he was married, which might be the case. He was still wearing his wedding ring.

He winced at the oversight. He'd put it on again a few weeks ago, after a disastrous Thanksgiving at his parents' house. His mother had invited one of Jenny's friends—one of her *single* friends—in a clear attempt at matchmaking. He'd left as soon as possible, claiming he had an important delivery.

Women had flirted with him before, and he'd felt nothing. No whisper of temptation. No need to armor himself with proof of his lack of availability. This time was different. He hadn't been interested in Jenny's friend. He'd thought of the waitress at Walt's Diner, someone he hardly knew, and he'd been struck by a wave of intense longing, mixed with sorrow. It hit him like an avalanche, knocking him off-balance. He'd found his ring and slipped it on. He'd needed a protective shield, because his attraction to the waitress had triggered new pain. His grief had felt staggering, insurmountable.

That was the problem with moving on. It hurt more than standing still.

He took the coffee to the cabin and set the cups down on the mantel by the fire. He poked the ashes and added some wood. Tala stirred at the sound. She sat up in bed with an abruptness that suggested she'd forgotten where she was. Her gaze connected with his, and recognition dawned. She returned to a reclining position, her trepidation fading.

She trusted him not to try anything sexual. Which made sense, he supposed, because he'd kept his hands to himself all night. But if she could've read his thoughts in the wee hours of the morning—or right now, for that matter—she wouldn't look so relaxed. Because he wanted to climb into bed with her. He wanted to kiss away the hurt her husband had caused and show her how a real man treated a woman.

Heat crept up his neck at the thought. Of course he wasn't going to make a move on her. He wasn't ready for that kind of intimacy. He was still wearing his wedding ring. The only way to stay numb was to keep his distance.

"I brought you a coffee," he said. "Do you want oatmeal?"

She nodded, rising to her feet. She looked rumpled

and sexy in his flannel shirt. Her eyes were sleepy, her legs a mile long. When she tugged on the fabric to make sure she was covered, he averted his gaze. He knew she was bare beneath it. He'd seen her pale blue panties hanging in the bathroom. He'd touched them this morning—to see if they were dry. To feel the silky material and imagine it against her skin.

After she went into the bathroom, he released a slow breath. He needed to get a grip before he embarrassed himself. He cleared his throat and left the cabin, sucking in the cold air. There were two servings of oatmeal in disposable cups with lids at the front desk. He carried them back to the room, plastic spoons in hand. Tala was sitting by the fire, sipping coffee. They shared a simple hot breakfast in silence.

He wasn't eager to get on the road again, despite his discomfort in her presence. He wanted to make sure she was safe before he left town. He hadn't expected to be so concerned about her welfare, but they were in an unusual situation. They'd spent the past twenty-four hours together. They'd shared personal stories. They'd even *held hands*.

Cam might be numb, but he wasn't dead. His protective instincts were working overtime. So was his libido, if he was being honest.

"Do you have another load to deliver?" she asked.

He nodded. "I'm supposed to pick it up this morning."

"What direction are you headed?"

"North, on the Dalton."

It wasn't a trip she could take with him. The Dalton Highway was the deadliest stretch of road in Alaska. There were almost no facilities, and constant obstacles. Whiteouts, avalanches, ice patches, snowdrifts.

"You could stay here," he said, on impulse.

"In Fairbanks?"

"In this cabin."

Her lips parted with surprise. She hadn't expected him to make this offer. That made two of them.

"I know the owner of this place, like I said. She might hire you."

"To split logs?"

"Or for lighter work."

"I can handle heavy work."

He believed her.

"The owner is a woman?"

"Yes."

"How well do you know her?"

Cam rubbed a hand over his jaw. "Her husband was a trucker. He died on the Dalton. Since then, I've been coming around to do chores for her."

"Do you really trade services?"

"She gives me a discount. Also, I like it."

"You like helping women?"

"I like splitting logs."

She studied his face with skepticism. "Is there anything else you enjoy doing for her?"

He smiled at her question. "Like what?"

"You know what."

"She's pushing seventy. My generosity doesn't extend quite that far."

Tala set her coffee mug aside. "These cabins aren't cheap. Even if she hired me, I couldn't afford to stay here."

"I can afford it."

She shook her head in refusal. She wouldn't allow herself to depend on him, or anyone else, and it pissed him off. She had no belongings, no money, no job, no resources. She didn't even have a change of clothes. But she'd rather strike out on her own than kick back in this cozy cabin on his dime.

What was wrong with her? What was wrong with *him*, for that matter?

He should never have given her a ride in the first place. His contract prohibited picking up hitchhikers. She was clearly in trouble with the law. He should be cutting her loose, not trying to keep her around. He didn't understand what he was doing. He'd made a series of bad decisions upon meeting her. Emotional decisions that threatened his current, stark existence. He'd brought her inside his rig to get warm, and warmed himself in the process.

If he wasn't careful, the protective layer of ice he'd been hibernating under would thaw. Then the real pain would come.

"At least let me buy you a change of clothes," he said. She had nothing to wear. He wasn't leaving her on a street corner without any *pants*. "I have to go to Walmart and get some supplies anyway."

She nodded her agreement and ducked into the bathroom to get ready. She had to borrow his sweatpants. Even with the drawstring tightened, they rode low on her hips. Her black waitress shoes were for indoor use only. She needed warm clothes and winter boots no matter what her future plans were. She couldn't job-hunt in her old uniform, or his pajamas.

The big-box store was about five miles away. He parked on the outskirts of the lot and accompanied Tala inside. He grabbed a cart, swamped by memories of

Jenny. Their Sunday shopping trips. Rainy mornings in Seattle. They'd been good together. They'd been content.

He headed toward the women's clothing department, where Tala browsed the racks. She selected black leggings and an oversize sweatshirt. When he gestured for her to continue, she added a pair of jeans to the cart. They strolled through another section with packages of socks and underwear. She chose basic white cotton, seeming embarrassed.

"That's all you want?" he asked.

"You don't have to buy the whole store."

"This is Walmart. Everything's cheap."

"I'm going to owe you."

"Consider it a gift."

"No," she said, her face solemn. "I'll pay you back."

Warmth suffused his chest at her assertion. He admired her pride, even though he cursed her stubbornness. The thought of reuniting with her after he returned from the Dalton appealed to him—and not because he wanted to collect on a debt. He'd like to see her again, despite his wariness toward women, and his general misgivings about the trouble she was in.

"You should let me introduce you to Ann," he said.

She continued walking alongside him, not answering. It was a good sign, he supposed. She hadn't refused outright. They found the shoe racks. He left his cart at the end of the aisle and accompanied her on the search for practical footwear.

"You know what you said about moving on?" she asked.

"Yeah."

"I have to do that, too. I have to keep moving."

"You're running away from your problems."

"And you aren't?"

He didn't answer. Of course he was. They both were.

"If you stay in the same place, your past catches up with you." She turned to study the opposite side of the aisle. "When I first came to Alaska, I went from town to town. I hitchhiked here and there. I didn't feel safe unless I was on the go. It took me almost a month to settle down in Willow."

It was on the tip of his tongue to tell her that she didn't have to run anymore. He could help her. He used to be a cop. His brother was still a cop. Cam could make some inquiries about her husband. He could probably have the guy arrested, with or without Tala's cooperation. Cam didn't extend the offer, because he sensed it wouldn't go over well. She didn't trust the police, obviously. She wouldn't trust him if she knew he'd been a patrol officer.

He also had his own issues with faith and justice. And family, for that matter. Calling his brother would open him up to uncomfortable questions. He'd disconnected from everyone in Washington. He hadn't spoken to Mason since Thanksgiving.

He massaged the nape of his neck, feeling guilty. It was better to keep his secrets and protect his privacy. Stay distant. Stay numb.

She reached into a large box on a lower shelf and fished out a pair of sturdy black boots. They looked warm and practical, with faux fur trim. She sat down on the floor to try them on. "They fit."

He grunted his approval. "What else do you need?"

She walked back and forth to test the comfort of the boots. Then she removed them. "This is more than enough, Cam."

"You don't have to pay me back."

"I want to. How long will you be on the Dalton?"

"Three days, maybe."

"Do you have a cell phone?"

"Of course, but there's no service. You can leave a message."

"Give me the number."

He handed her a business card with his information. She tucked it into the front pocket of his flannel.

"You can go to the cabin anytime. I'll tell Ann to run a tab."

She nodded, avoiding his gaze. He didn't press, because he was afraid to scare her off. Maybe she'd call him in a few days. Maybe she'd rethink his offer to stay at the cabins. She had nowhere else to go, after all.

They headed toward the front of the store together. She added a couple of travel-size toiletries to the cart, along with a simple canvas backpack. He didn't really need any supplies, but he grabbed a few boxes of snacks. The store was busier now, at the start of the morning rush. He paid for the items in cash.

"I'll change here," she said, gesturing to the restrooms.

He went to wait for her near the entrance. There was an in-store restaurant with a café. He sat down at an empty booth. A mounted TV in the upper corner displayed local news. He listened to the weather report with interest. There was snow in the forecast, as usual. Then a photograph of Tala flashed across the screen.

Cam's blood froze at the sight. Newscasters launched into a story of a missing waitress from Walt's in Willow. The photo of Tala appeared again. It had been taken at the diner, probably by a patron. Tala was standing at the counter next to Walt.

The caption under her face read "Abigail Burgess."

Viewers were asked to call a number for the Willow Police Department if they had any information. The segment lasted sixty seconds at the most. He blinked and it was gone, like a figment of his imagination.

Abigail. *Abigail?*

He tried to remember hearing her name in the diner, or over the radio. The other truckers used terms like "honey" or "cutie" for an attractive waitress. Tala was a distinctive name, and he wouldn't have forgotten it. She must have lied to him. He was disappointed, but not particularly surprised, by the realization.

Cam pondered this latest development. There was no mention of a crime committed, by her or anyone else. She didn't have any family in the area to report her disappearance, and she'd only been gone twenty-four hours.

And yet, her story had made the morning news.

What the hell had happened at Walt's? He got the feeling it was something more serious than a brief sighting of her ex. She'd woken up screaming last night. She'd mentioned a dream about Walt in the dumpster. Dead.

He glanced toward the restrooms, uneasy. She was taking too long to change clothes. Either she'd ditched him to avoid saying goodbye, or she'd run into some more trouble. The first option was far more likely, and it filled him with dark emotions. He hadn't been able to say goodbye to Jenny because she'd never woken up. He couldn't bear to relive the moment his wife had slipped away.

He had issues with saying goodbye. Major issues.

Stomach roiling, he rose to his feet. Women who weren't Tala breezed in and out of the restrooms. Had she walked by him while his eyes were glued to the television screen? No. She couldn't have left the store, unless there was another way out. He spotted a garden section in the opposite corner.

Damn it.

Cam strode past the potted plants and fertilizer. Sure enough, there was an alternate exit at this end. He moved forward and shoved through the doors, searching the dark for a wolf-quick girl in a fur-lined parka.

There.

She was in the parking lot—and she wasn't alone. A man had his hand locked around her upper arm. He appeared to be leading her away by force. She looked over her shoulder at Cam. Their eyes met for a split second. Then the man, who must be her abusive ex, jerked her forward. She stumbled and almost fell.

Cam's vision went red. He was already on edge, filled with angry tension. The sight of her being manhandled made him completely snap.

He rushed toward them, intent on introducing himself with his fists.

Chapter 7

Tala had checked her reflection before she went out to meet Cam.

The form-fitting jeans flattered her figure and the oversize sweatshirt was cozy. Her dark eyes glittered with a mixture of emotions. Fear, excitement, hope. She liked Cam, but she couldn't accept his offer to stay in the cabin. It wasn't the right place to lay low. She needed a cheap, anonymous hotel where no one asked questions. Also, her instincts told her to keep moving. She had to run until she felt safe.

She wanted to be cautious with her heart, as well. She didn't know Cam well enough to trust him, and what she did know gave her pause. He was still in mourning. He was quiet and reserved. He wanted her physically, but he might change his mind about that. She wouldn't be surprised if he started to have second thoughts about her as soon as they parted ways. He wasn't ready to let go of his wife's memory.

There was also the small matter of Tala being on the run from the law. Cam wasn't the kind of man who would disregard her suspicious behavior. He'd continue to ask questions. He'd insist on helping.

She tugged on her parka, her spirits low. She didn't want to say goodbye to Cam yet. He made her feel sexy and tingly and warm inside. More importantly, he made her feel safe. Tearing her gaze away from the mirror, she picked up her backpack and left the bathroom. She searched the crowd for Cam and found someone else.

The police officer from Willow.

He was in plainclothes, but she recognized his face. He was standing less than twenty feet away, blocking her path to the exit. His mouth stretched into a menacing smile. Pulse racing, she whirled around and headed the opposite direction. She rushed through the garden section, trying not to panic. It was filled with indoor plants and herbs. Alaskans liked to grow stuff, even in the dead of winter.

She spotted another exit sign in the corner. She started running toward it. She knocked over a garden gnome and kept going. Then she was outside in the cold, dark morning. The parking lot lights beckoned. She didn't see Cam's truck, but it didn't matter. She needed to escape without involving him. She sprinted away from the danger, picking up speed with every stride. Running had always come naturally to her. She'd won several medals for her college cross-country team.

Unfortunately, she got tripped up before she could reach the road. A man jumped out from behind a parked car and pushed a shopping cart directly into her path.

She couldn't hurtle it, and she was going too fast to stop. She avoided the cart, but collided with the man. They both went sprawling.

When she tried to scramble away, he grabbed her by the arm. He was skinny, but strong. He rose to his feet and dragged her upright. She recognized him as one of the killers from the diner. With his free hand, he brandished a wicked-looking knife. When he twisted his wrist, the blade glinted in the dark.

She stopped struggling.

"Walk," he ordered.

She moved forward, swallowing hard. A glance over her shoulder revealed Cam emerging from the garden section. He bolted toward them. She didn't want him to get hurt, but she needed his help. Her captor pulled her along, wrenching her arm painfully.

Five.

She counted down the seconds until Cam struck.

Four.

The man at her side continued walking, staring straight ahead.

Three.

Cam was almost on them.

Two.

She jerked her elbow from the man's grasp and dove to the ground like a bomb was about to go off. And it kind of did. Cam was the bomb. He exploded with brutal force, punching her captor in the back of the neck. The skinny man staggered forward and dropped his knife, which clattered to the asphalt. He looked stunned, but he didn't fall down. He turned to fight, raising his fists protectively.

Cam punched him again, in the jaw, and that was all it

took. The man spun around and crumpled to the ground like a leaf. Cam kicked the knife away. He said a few choice words, his mouth twisted with fury.

Tala stayed down, afraid to move. She thought Cam might continue his attack. He stood over his opponent, as if evaluating his condition. Then he left the guy alone and came to Tala. When he offered her a hand, she took it.

"Are you all right?"

She stood, testing the strength of her knees. "Yes."

The parking lot wasn't deserted. There were cars driving past, people coming and going. She glanced around for the police officer, her legs shaky. He wasn't there, but someone else emerged from the shadows. It was the man who'd leered at her at the diner. His jacket was open. He had a revolver tucked into his waistband.

Cam used one arm to move Tala into the space behind him.

"What's the trouble?" the man asked.

Tala gripped Cam's elbow, terrified. Cam didn't answer. A car passed by in the next lane, its headlights illuminating the scene. The man closed his jacket. He squinted at the curious onlooker in annoyance. Then he nudged his friend with the edge of his boot.

"Get up."

The skinny man rose to his feet slowly. The man with the gun helped him stagger away. He shot Cam a threatening look over his shoulder. Then they both disappeared into the dark recesses of the parking lot. An older-model SUV, maybe a Ford Bronco, took off in the opposite direction. There were other vehicles in motion. It was difficult to tell which one held the men who'd attacked her.

Cam picked up her backpack. "We have to go back inside to call the police."

Fear spiked through her. "No. We can't."

"Why not?"

"There was another man in the store. He's with them."

His eyes narrowed with suspicion. He glanced toward the front entrance. "Okay, we'll call from my truck."

She didn't argue, because she wanted to get out of sight. They crossed the parking lot in long strides. Cam unlocked the door for her. She climbed in, taking the backpack from his hands. He walked to the driver's side and got behind the wheel.

"Please," she said. "Let's just go."

A muscle in his jaw flexed. He fired up the engine and left the parking lot. A delayed reaction to the close call struck her. She started shaking uncontrollably. Tears flooded her eyes. She drew her knees to her chest, making a tight ball with her body. She thought about Duane, the last man who'd been violent toward her. He'd said he was going to kill her once. She didn't know if he meant it, or if he was capable of murder. He seemed pretty tame compared to the men she was currently running from.

When she lifted her head, they were parked on the side of the street, in front of an auto repair garage. There was a café and a bookstore across the street. Cam turned off the engine and gave her a measured look.

"I have to call the police," he said again.

Fresh tears filled her eyes. She blinked them away. "I won't talk to them."

"That guy pulled a knife on you."

"He'll deny it."

"Was that your husband?"

"No."

"Which one was?"

"None of them."

"None of them?"

"Cam, you shouldn't get involved. The police won't help me. If anything, they'll arrest you for assault."

"That's bullshit."

"You struck first."

"I had cause!"

She flinched at his vehemence. She hadn't meant to put him in danger, but she had. Now he was on the killers' radar. They knew his truck. They'd seen his face. She shouldn't have gone shopping with him. She shouldn't have let him get so close, or shared so much personal information. She grasped the door handle, ready to bolt.

His gaze searched hers, missing nothing. He didn't reach for his CB. She didn't move. It was a standoff. After a long moment, he broke eye contact with her and squinted into the distance. He wasn't the type of man who casually disregarded the law. She was asking him to go against his natural instincts.

"I want to help you," he said. "But you need to tell me the truth."

"I wouldn't lie to you."

"Wouldn't you, *Abigail*?"

She drew in a sharp breath. "Where did you hear that?"

"It was on the news when you were in the bathroom. Missing waitress from Walt's Diner, Abigail Burgess."

"Was there any news about Walt?"

"No."

She twisted her hands in her lap. She hoped Walt was okay. She had to tell Cam her story, or at least part of it. He was already involved, and he needed to know what they were up against. But if she said too much, he'd call the police for sure. "When I first came to Alaska, I didn't have any ID, and I couldn't get a job. So I stole one from a lady's wallet. She was about my age, with dark hair. She was Abigail Burgess. My real name is Tala."

"Who were those men?"

"I don't know," she said. "They came into the diner yesterday."

"Do they work for your husband?"

She stared out the window, across the dark stockyard. Snow flurries had begun to fall. Cam had unwittingly given her the perfect lie. Of course he thought Duane was behind this. A girl could only have so much unrelated bad luck.

"How did they find you?"

"They must have followed us from Willow."

"No one followed us from Willow."

She moistened her lips, nervous. The killers would have looked for her outside the diner. She'd left the trash gate open and the keys dangling. They knew what she'd seen, and could guess where she'd gone. The truck stop was the only option. Since then she'd been in several public places with Cam. "Maybe someone talked about us on the radio."

"You don't have a cell phone they can track?"

"I had a cheap one, but I left it in the diner. I left my purse, keys, everything."

He fell silent, his expression skeptical.

"You don't believe me."

"I believe that you have an abusive ex, and that you're in trouble. I don't understand why you haven't gone to the police."

"I told you. He *is* the police."

"In Canada. Not here."

"I have a criminal record," she said, with reluctance.

"For what?"

"Civil disobedience."

He arched a brow. "Civil disobedience? That's it?"

She stayed quiet.

"Do you have priors?"

"No, but I missed my court date. Now there's probably a warrant for my arrest."

"So you think you'll be extradited to Canada if you file a police report? You think you'll go to jail instead of him?"

"Yes, I do," she said, frowning at his incredulous tone.

"That's crazy."

"It's not crazy, Cam. He's a white man who works in law enforcement. They'll believe him over me."

He deliberated for a moment, giving her point the weight it deserved. "They won't believe him over *me*. I'll give a statement about what happened in the parking lot. I'll make sure you're protected."

Tala was touched by the offer, but she couldn't accept. She didn't trust the police in Alaska or anywhere else. Even before she met Duane, she'd been wary of law enforcement. Her people had a history of being targeted unfairly in Yellowknife. She'd learned to avoid men in uniform at a young age. She didn't know why she'd ever trusted Duane. She'd been lost and alone, after the deaths of her father and grandmother. She'd been flattered by the attention. She'd made a mistake.

She hoped she wasn't making another one with Cam. He seemed like an honorable man. He'd been kind to her, and he'd come to her rescue without hesitation. She shivered at the memory of his brutal use of force in the parking lot. He could certainly handle himself in a fight. But did he have a dark side, like Duane?

"I'm sorry," she said, shaking her head. "I have to take care of this on my own."

He massaged his right hand, contemplative. His knuckles were scraped and swollen.

"You need ice."

"I'm fine. I'll put some snow on it in a minute."

She felt guilty for dragging him into this mess. He'd gotten hurt because of her. He could have been shot. Those men were clearly willing to kill again. They'd come all the way to Fairbanks to eliminate her as a witness.

"You can't stay here," Cam said.

She murmured an agreement.

"Where will you go?"

"I've thought about heading to Montana. I have family there."

"You'll be safe with them?"

"I think so," she said. Her mother and two half-brothers lived on reserve land, with her stepfather. The tribal police would protect her. She doubted the killers would be able to track her that far. They didn't even know her real name.

"How will you get there?"

"I'll hitchhike."

His jaw clenched with displeasure. "That's a stupid idea."

"Do you have a better one?"

"Yeah, but you shot it down."

"I could go with you."

"On the Dalton?"

"Why not?"

"It's too dangerous."

"And staying here isn't?"

"The weather is extreme. The roads are treacherous. There are constant storms, avalanches and snow drifts. It's white-knuckle all the way. If you break down or crash, you can freeze before help arrives."

"I'm from the Northwest Territories, Cam. Cold doesn't scare me."

"Cold is an understatement."

"I understand that, and I can handle it. My people have been thriving in polar climates for thousands of years."

"Not in eighteen-wheelers, they haven't."

"They lived in sod houses with no heat. Your truck is a four-star hotel compared to those lodgings."

"Did you live in a sod house?"

"No, I grew up in a two-bedroom trailer. But I've camped in the snow before. My dad was an outdoor expert. He taught me all sorts of winter survival skills. I can handle rough weather."

He raked a hand through his hair, sighing. She could sense his capitulation. He didn't want to leave her behind, alone and unprotected. And maybe he wanted someone in his bed, to help him forget about his wife. His eyes traveled down the length of her body. "I can't afford to get distracted on the road."

"I won't be a distraction."

"Right," he scoffed, his gaze searing.

"I'll ride in the back. I won't make a sound."

"And when we return? Then what?"

"I don't know."

"I can't take you to Montana."

"I didn't ask you to."

"I'm contracted to work exclusively on the Dalton for the next few months. I'll be hauling loads to Deadhorse and back."

"I'll figure something out," she said, more confident now.

He tightened his grip on the wheel. "Okay," he said, letting out a huff of breath. "You can come with me on one trip. You'll have to stay out of sight as much as possible. We'll spend the night at the basecamp in Coldfoot. It's rustic."

"I like rustic."

"There are separate bunks for men and women. We won't be together."

She nodded her understanding.

He turned on the ignition, his jaw clenched. He seemed irritated about the arrangement. He was bringing her along and not getting anything he wanted out of the bargain. She didn't promise to make it up to him. The tension between them was already high. There was no reason to fan the flames of their attraction.

"I have to get my truck worked on," he said, digging into his pocket for a few dollars. "Buy yourself a cup of coffee while you're waiting. I'll keep an eye out for trouble."

She smiled in relief. Leaning toward him, she kissed his bearded cheek. "Thanks, Cam. You're a good man."

He grunted his response, his neck ruddy. She climbed out and shut the door, zipping up her parka to ward off the chill. The temperature would climb after sunrise, but only a little. Winter days were cold and short. She inhaled the brisk, snow-laden air. She didn't see any other vehicles on the road.

Cam pulled forward, gravel spitting from his tires.

He drove the short distance to the entrance of the auto repair shop. Tala headed the opposite direction, toward the café. Coffee was huge in Alaska, and she liked it as much as the next girl, but the lights in the bookstore beckoned. She bypassed the café and headed inside. An elderly man in glasses muttered a greeting as she walked in. He was immersed in a taxidermy project. There were stuffed puffins and other frozen birds scattered around.

She strolled up and down the aisles, her hands in her pockets. After a few minutes of browsing, she found a small stack of graphic novels on a bottom shelf in the back of the store. She spotted a book that Duane had ordered for her last Christmas. She plucked it off the shelf, her throat tight. Fresh tears flooded her eyes and her knees went weak. She sank to a sitting position on the floor.

Her marriage to Duane had devolved into a prison of intimidation and abuse, but it hadn't started that way. She wouldn't have fallen in love with him if he'd been cruel every moment. They'd had good times, especially in the beginning. The man who'd abused her seemed like a different person than the man she'd married.

She felt guilty about her attraction to Cam, which was ridiculous. Duane didn't deserve her loyalty. She was angry with him for hurting her, and angry with herself for choosing him. She should have run at the first sign of trouble. She should have seen the darkness inside him before it closed in on her.

Her father had warned her that some people weren't what they seemed. Some men were wolves in sheep's clothing. She hadn't remembered his advice until it was too late. She wouldn't forget it again.

Her fingertips skimmed the novel's dusty cover. It

was one of her favorites. The artwork depicted a man with horns and a woman with a baby at her breast. Duane had torn her copy to shreds in a jealous rage one day.

Blinking the tears from her eyes, she set the book aside and chose another.

Chapter 8

Cam pulled into an empty space in the garage, letting the engine idle.

His rig needed a few modifications before he could drive it on the ice road. The adjustments would take almost an hour, and Cam didn't need to watch the process. He could have joined Tala in the bookstore. He could have brought her into the shop, for that matter. The company mechanic wouldn't report him for having a female companion in Fairbanks. On the Dalton, it was another story. He wasn't allowed to transport a passenger without permission and a liability waiver. If a safety supervisor spotted Tala with him, he'd be screwed.

He didn't know why he'd agreed to bring her along.

Okay…he *knew* why, but he couldn't believe he was doing it. He'd become infatuated with her, against his better judgment. He was letting his emotions take over.

He hadn't been himself since he'd found Tala in his hitch space. Every decision he'd made after that moment had been questionable. He wasn't usually a rule-breaker, but he'd been numb for so long. She made him feel alive, and he wanted to hang on to that feeling. He wasn't ready to let her go.

If he left her behind, he'd lose her. He felt it in his bones. She'd run away from Fairbanks and he'd never see her again. He'd never get the chance to save her. He'd never know what might have been.

He studied the smiling photograph of Jenny. He was forgetting her, little by little. Her face wasn't as clear in his mind as it used to be. Her voice didn't pop into his head as often anymore. He didn't hear echoes of her bright laughter.

After a long moment, he removed the photo from the dash and put it in the pocket next to his seat. Then he worked the ring off his finger, tucking it away with the picture. Before he could rethink his actions, he grabbed his cell phone and climbed out of his rig. He nodded at the mechanic as he left the garage. Snowflakes drifted down in soft flurries, adding to the fresh powder on the ground. The knuckles on his right hand throbbed.

He hadn't brought Tala to the garage because he needed space. He wanted to cool down and clear his head. He also wanted to have a conversation without her listening in. His older brother, Mason, was a detective with the Seattle Police Department. Cam scrolled through his short list of contacts. Then he bit the bullet and called him.

Mason answered on the second ring. He didn't sound happy, which wasn't a surprise. "Cam," he said simply.

"Mason."

"Where are you?"

"Fairbanks," he said, looking up at the bleak sky. "Do you have time to talk?"

"You want to talk now? Really?"

Guilt speared through him. He fell silent, because he deserved Mason's vitriol. He also figured that letting his brother vent was better than trying to forge ahead as if he'd done nothing wrong.

"You didn't want to talk in Tacoma."

"I felt ambushed."

"Give me a break," Mason scoffed. "Nobody ambushed you. Mom invited a friend of Jenny's and you freaked out."

"It was a setup," Cam said.

"So what? You didn't have to leave early, or treat the girl like the goddamned plague. You made Mom cry."

Cam swore under his breath. "I'll send her some flowers."

"Who, Jenny's friend?"

"No, *Mom*. I'm not interested in Jenny's friend, or anyone else Mom tries to throw at me. I know she means well, but she needs to back off."

"Stop living like a recluse and she will."

"I didn't call for a lecture."

"You think you're the only person in the world who's ever lost someone?" Mason continued, undeterred. "You're the only one grieving? The only one whose life didn't work out the way you expected?"

Cam tried to tamp down his anger, and failed. "Don't compare yourself to me, brother. Your wife is still alive. She just doesn't want you anymore."

It was a low blow, and Cam regretted the words as soon as he spoke them. Mason's silence indicated that the barb had hit its mark. Their conversations tended to be contentious, which was why Cam avoided calling. He wished there wasn't so much animosity between them. They used to lift each other up, not tear each other down.

"I'm sorry," Cam said gruffly. "That wasn't fair."

"You're an asshole, you know that?"

"I need your help."

Mason made a heavy sound into the receiver. But he didn't hang up. "With what?"

"I met a woman."

"You met a woman," Mason repeated in a flat tone.

"She was stowed away behind my cab, so I gave her a ride to Fairbanks."

"You're high, aren't you? You're on trucker drugs."

"I'm not high," Cam said, rolling his eyes. He told an abbreviated version of his adventures with Tala, omitting the overnight stay in the cabin. That was too personal to share. "I think she's in trouble, and I want you to look into it."

"What's her name?"

"Tala."

"*T-A-L-A?*"

"I guess."

"I need more info than that, Cam."

He gave as many details as he could remember, including the Abigail Burgess alias. "She's from Yellowknife, in Canada. She has family in Montana. Her husband is some kind of cop named Duane."

"What's her description?"

"She's about five-nine, maybe one hundred and forty pounds, long black hair, brown eyes. Unusually pretty."

"How old?"

"Twenty-five."

Mason grunted with derision.

Cam rattled off short descriptions of the two men in the parking lot.

"Why are you asking me to do this?" Mason asked. "You can call the local cops anytime."

"She doesn't want me to call them."

"That's a red flag, Cam. A big red flag."

"Maybe the local PD is in on it."

"Maybe she's a liar."

"I don't think so."

"Want to know what I think?" Mason didn't wait for a response. "I think you've gone off the deep end. You've been teetering on the edge for three years, and now you've tipped right over."

"I've been doing the best I can."

"Have you?"

Cam didn't answer.

"This girl could be a criminal, or a teen runaway—"

"She's not a teen runaway. I haven't gone that far off the deep end."

"Why are you ordering a background check, if you trust her?"

"I want to help her," Cam said, raking a hand through his hair. "I like her."

"She's unusually pretty, with a hot body?"

"I didn't say that."

"I'm glad you're not dead below the waist, Cameron. I'm just concerned about your mental state."

Cam scowled at the phone. "Are you going to run her or not?"

"I'll do it on one condition."

"What?"

"Come home for Christmas."

Cam smothered a groan at the request. Christmas was in the middle of the ice-road season, and the holidays were the most difficult time of year for him. Going home always reminded him of Jenny. She'd died the last week of December.

"Well?" Mason prompted.

"You're killing me," Cam said.

"You're killing Mom."

Cam told Mason to screw himself, and Mason said it right back. It was just like old times. "Okay, you rotten bastard. I'll come home."

"Lay off the crystal meth, too."

"It's hard to be the ugly brother, isn't it?"

"I wouldn't know. How's sitting on your ass all day working out for your metabolism?"

"You tell me, desk jockey."

Mason laughed, taking no offense. For most of their lives, they'd been close, with good-natured teasing between them instead of deep rancor. "I'll meet you on the basketball court and we'll see who's getting slow."

Cam smirked at the challenge. "I won the last round."

"Only because you cheated."

He shook his head in disbelief. Mason was such a sore loser. They'd been battling on and off the court since they were kids. "Text me the details as soon as you can. I'll be on the Dalton, so I might not be able to reply right away."

"Whatever," Mason said. "Stay safe."

"I will," Cam said, and hung up. He pocketed the phone, his spirits lighter. He'd expected Mason to be surly and judgmental, and he had been, but he'd also agreed to help. Their conversation had ended on a positive note. His brother had sounded almost jovial. They'd laughed together, like they used to. Maybe Mason was getting his divorce. Maybe, in time, Cam could get over Jenny.

He scooped up a handful of snow and covered his knuckles, hissing at the sting. Then he walked inside the lobby to wait. He could see the bookstore and the coffee shop from the front window. The stockyard was less than a mile down the road. Although the trucking company had several mechanics on site, they were always swamped with repairs. Cam preferred this place. Whenever he could avoid a crowd, he did.

As he iced his hand, he mulled over his brother's criticism. Mason exaggerated a little, but he didn't lie. Cam *had* overreacted at Thanksgiving. Their mom was a classic meddler, unable to accept Cam's withdrawal from society. She wanted him to come back to Tacoma, settle down with a nice woman and live happily ever after.

She wanted the same for Mason, who'd disappointed her as much as Cam, if not more. Last year his brother had been the target of her matchmaking efforts. She'd invited Lisa to her Thanksgiving celebration in an obvious attempt to reunite the estranged couple. It hadn't worked. Shortly after their separation, Lisa had started dating a firefighter. Mason had feigned indifference, but Cam knew better. His brother hated losing, and the dissolution of his marriage had devastated him.

Cam still didn't know why Lisa had left. Mason wouldn't talk about it, and Cam was basically a ghost at family functions. He'd been a shadow of himself since Jenny died, buried in his own grief. Disconnected from everyone who cared about him.

He felt guilty about abandoning his brother in a time

of need, but his guilt hadn't spurred him into action. It was another weight to carry, another feeling to escape.

He turned his thoughts to Tala, whose troubles offered a refreshing diversion. He didn't have to face his problems when he could focus on hers. She was pleasant company, beautiful to look at and interesting to listen to.

Cam understood his brother's concerns. Her story didn't add up. She was hiding something, refusing to answer certain questions. Her husband had sent a couple of thugs after her instead of coming himself. That seemed odd. Cam wondered if the guy was a dirty cop with sinister connections, not just a run-of-the-mill abuser.

Cam didn't really care how dangerous her ex was. Cam didn't need anyone's approval. He liked Tala, and he wanted to help her.

The snow melted on his knuckles and dripped from his fingertips. The physical discomfort added to a growing sense of unease. Mason had always been critical of Cam's decision to come to Alaska. Cam's family hadn't understood his need to withdraw. They didn't approve of his chosen profession. Maybe he wasn't doing his *best* here, but he'd been working steadily. He'd been surviving, one day at a time.

If he wasn't moving forward…at least he was moving.

No one could convince him to come home, because home offered no comfort. Tala did. One night with her had changed something inside him. He couldn't deny that he wanted her. He wouldn't pursue a relationship with her, however. Whatever happened between them, he couldn't afford to get attached. It would only lead to another heartbreak. Falling for her could send him over the edge Mason claimed he'd been teetering on. But maybe that was what Cam was seeking. Total ruin, instead of cold apathy.

They couldn't bunk together in Coldfoot, so he didn't have to worry about curbing his baser instincts tonight. Beyond Deadhorse was Prudhoe Bay, an industrial wasteland filled with scientists and oil riggers. There were several hotels. They could share a private room at the end of the ice road, on the outermost edge of civilization.

When his truck was ready, he drove back to the spot where he'd left her. She was sitting in the café with a cup of tea and a stack of books. She turned toward the door when he came in. She seemed relieved to see him.

"I spent some of your money on books," she said, tugging on her parka.

"Find anything good?"

"Yes."

She held the books protectively, as if she thought he might try to take them away. Her eyes looked red and swollen. "Are you okay?" he asked as they walked outside. She'd taken a spill in the parking lot earlier.

"I'm fine."

"You still want to come with me?"

"Of course."

He didn't try to talk her out of it again. If they were heading toward disaster, so be it. "I'm going to the stockyard now to pick up the load."

"What are you delivering?"

"I don't know. I'll find out when I get there." He opened the passenger door to let her in. She crawled into the berth with her stack of books. She'd have to stay back there until they left Fairbanks.

A trailer filled with building supplies was waiting

for him at the yard. He signed the paperwork and secured the load, pleased with the assignment. He'd hauled worse. Oversize loads, hazardous chemicals and cargo that exceeded recommended weight limits weren't uncommon. All of it had to be delivered to the drop-off zone as fast as possible, in order to facilitate the lucrative work on the pipelines.

Oil was big business in Alaska, and black gold flowed in any weather. The coldest months of the year were among the busiest, because the ice roads made it possible to drive the short distance from Deadhorse to Prudhoe Bay. When the ice melted, the route was closed. Goods for the pipeline and its employees had to be delivered by air or sea. It was that remote and inaccessible.

Cam filled up his gas tank before he headed out of town, toward the Dalton. It was about a hundred miles west of Fairbanks. The entire length of the highway could be traversed in one long day, if you started early enough and the weather cooperated. Cam was getting a late start, by trucker standards, and the snow flurries reduced visibility. He'd be lucky to hit Coldfoot, the halfway point, by early evening.

Tala stayed in the berth, reading one of her graphic novels. She closed the book after about thirty minutes. "Can I come up front?"

"Sure," Cam said, shrugging. No one would be able to see her in the snowy dark. Most drivers kept their eyes on the road and minded their own business, regardless. Cam wasn't that worried about getting reported by another trucker.

She settled into the passenger seat. "Should I duck if we pass someone?"

"Nah."

"What about after the sun comes up?"

"I'll let you know. If it keeps snowing, we're okay."

She gave him a tremulous smile. "Good. I'd rather sit beside you."

He searched her face, which looked a bit pale. He hoped she didn't get carsick, because the Dalton was twisty as hell. He focused on the drive, saying nothing. Her eyes darted to the side mirror to check the highway behind them. It was the same thing she'd done on the ride from Willow to Fairbanks.

"You think they'll follow us?" he asked.

She seemed startled by the question. "Can they?"

"They could try. There's no checkpoint or regulations."

"So anyone can drive on the Dalton?"

"They can, but they don't. It's too dangerous. You need special modifications so your engine parts don't freeze. We might see a tourist bus, or some smaller vehicles that belong to safety officials. Otherwise, it's just ice rigs."

She nodded her understanding. "How far is it to the entrance?"

"Sixty miles."

They fell into an uneasy silence as dawn broke over the horizon. It was almost ten o'clock, but they only had about six hours of daylight here. In Deadhorse, at the end of the road, there would be less than two.

Cam was on a long straightaway when a black SUV appeared behind them, moving fast. He straightened in his seat, squinting into the rearview mirror. He had a handgun in a locked box in the berth, out of reach. It was a memento from his cop days, packed away carefully with his photos of Jenny.

He considered asking Tala to grab it for him as the SUV veered into the passing lane. Then he dismissed the idea, because trading gunfire on a snowy highway at this speed would be stupid, even in self-defense. If they got shot at, he'd have to run the SUV off the road.

Tala followed his gaze, her expression wary. The driver moved into the space beside him. Cam got a glimpse of two young faces as the SUV surged ahead and crossed over the broken yellow line. Snowboarding stickers covered the back bumper. They were teenaged boys, not the men from the parking lot. Not a threat.

Cam glanced at Tala, who was visibly shaken. "You okay?"

She moistened her lips. "I'm fine."

"I can pull over."

"No. Just drive."

He didn't argue. She sounded defensive, as well as rattled. Maybe she was worried that he'd change his mind about bringing her along if she showed any weakness.

"I didn't use to be like this," she said in a low voice.

"Like what?"

"Afraid of everything. Jumping at shadows."

His chest tightened with empathy. "It takes a strong person to admit fear."

"I don't feel strong right now."

"You were just attacked. Give yourself a break."

She nodded, taking a deep breath. "What are you afraid of?"

"Nothing," he joked.

She laughed, which broke the ice a little. He'd forgotten how much he enjoyed hearing female laughter, and she had a great smile. She was stunning. He pulled his gaze away from her, clearing his throat.

"I'm serious," she said.

"I'm afraid of getting attached."

"To another woman?"

He shrugged, though she'd nailed it. He was afraid of women, dating…feelings.

"You're afraid to let go of her."

It was an uncomfortable insight, impossible to deny. Of course Jenny was at the crux of the matter. If he found someone else, he'd have to move forward. He'd have to get over the loss, instead of wallowing in it. "You're right."

"Do you want to talk about her?"

"No."

She gave him a chiding look. "That's no way to move on."

He didn't want to move on, especially if it meant baring his soul. He was more interested in physical release than an emotional overhaul.

"Tell me something easy."

"Easy?"

"A nice memory, you know. Not sad."

He mulled it over. "Okay, I have one."

She clasped her hands together in anticipation. Most women wouldn't be so eager to hear about an ex. It occurred to Cam that Tala saw him as a friend, nothing more. She hadn't cuddled him last night because she wanted his body. She'd needed comfort.

Cam felt reassured by the thought. It would be easier to resist temptation if she didn't give him any encouragement. He wouldn't try to cross the line with a woman who wasn't attracted to him. She could keep her secrets, and he could hold on to his grief, like a shield to hide behind.

"She was a teacher," he said.

"Primary or secondary?"

"Fourth grade, so nine- and ten-year-olds."

She waited for him to continue, her lips pursed.

"During her first year of teaching, one of her students got sick. He was admitted to the Seattle Children's Hospital, and his family needed financial help, so she decided to do this fund-raiser. It was a mud run."

"What's a mud run?"

"It's 5K run with a challenge course. She talked me into going with her. We had to wade through mud and climb over walls, stuff like that."

Her expression grew wistful. "Sounds fun."

"It was. We had a good time. Jenny promised to jump in the mud pit if she raised a certain amount. She met her goal and then some, because she was the kind of person who could get everyone involved. She had that infectious enthusiasm thing." He paused, glancing at Tala. "You know what I mean?"

"Yes."

"Anyway, at the end of the course, she really went for it, like completely submerged herself in the pit. When she came out, she was unrecognizable. Just blue eyes and white teeth. I took a photo so she could show her class."

"Did they love it?"

"They did," he said, his throat tight. The happy memory morphed into another one, steeped in sadness. "They came to her funeral."

"Her students?"

"The boy she'd raised money for came with his family. He'd recovered by then. All of the students from her current class came. They brought handwritten sympathy cards." Cam remembered standing there like a statue while weeping kids presented him with their heartfelt letters, colored in crayon.

"That must have been difficult," she murmured.

His chest ached with the same agony he'd felt three years ago. He gripped the steering wheel until his knuckles went white. After a few deep breaths, he could speak again. "This is why I don't talk about her."

"Because it hurts?"

"Yes."

"If you keep your feelings bottled up, they cause more pain."

He made a noncommittal sound. Bottling up his feelings was a defense mechanism, necessary for survival. He couldn't just open up and release his emotions like a jar of butterflies. They were a nest of hornets, ready to sting.

"I have another idea," she said. "Tell me about her bad side."

"She didn't have a bad side."

"Surely she had flaws. Did she leave her towels on the floor, or drink milk out of the container?"

"That was me."

"She was perfect? You never argued?"

"We argued."

"About what?"

He sighed, shaking his head. "Stupid things. I wanted her to spend more time at home. She was too busy with her students and colleagues. She had a lot of friends. Everyone liked her. *Men* liked her."

"That bothered you?"

"Yeah, it did. She was…flirtatious."

Tala's eyes widened with interest. "Really?"

"She was always touching some guy's arm, or laughing at his jokes. She flirted with my brother a lot."

"What did he do?"

"Nothing. He enjoyed it, that bastard."

She laughed at his disgruntled expression. Cam didn't laugh with her, but he felt the heavy weight of sadness slip away. He hadn't thought about Jenny's flirty nature in ages. It had been a minor issue between them, easily forgotten.

They'd argued about more important things, too. Private things, like when to start a family. Cam hadn't been ready. He'd wanted to *travel*, which was ironic. Now all he did was travel, without getting anywhere.

The entrance to the Dalton loomed in the distance. Once they started down that road, there was no turning back.

"This is it?" she asked.

"This is it."

She grasped the armrests at her sides, as if bracing herself for a roller-coaster ride. She seemed committed to the journey, if only because she thought coming with him would be safer than staying in Fairbanks on her own.

For both their sakes, he hoped it would be.

Chapter 9

The first fifty miles on the Dalton were uneventful.

Tala shifted in her seat, watching the tree-lined snow-banks pass by. It wasn't picturesque, like Denali National Park. She checked the side mirror every few minutes. Even though Cam had expressed doubt over anyone following them, she wanted to stay alert. The killers were intent on hunting her down. They'd already tracked her from Willow to Fairbanks. They wouldn't be easily deterred.

She turned her gaze to Cam, her gallant rescuer. He drove with his right arm extended and the heel of his hand resting on top of the steering wheel. His knuckles didn't appear to be bothering him, so he must not have broken any bones. He was wearing a gray thermal undershirt with a navy blue flannel. His beard was the kind that real men grew, thick and dark and dense, without any patches.

"What did you do before you came to Alaska?" she asked, studying him.

He kept his eyes on the road. "I did a lot of different things."

"Such as?"

"I had a job in public service."

"Doing what?"

"Road safety, traffic control, stuff like that."

"Like a construction worker?"

"Sort of. Before I graduated from college, I worked on the farm."

"You went to college?"

He scratched his jaw. "Yeah."

"What did you study?"

"Sociology."

She gaped at his answer. "Sociology?"

"Why is that so hard to believe?"

"Because you're a truck driver. I can't think of a more antisocial job."

"You've got the wrong idea about truckers."

"Do I?"

"We aren't antisocial. We interact on the radio all the time. We have our own lingo, our own network. It's a tight-knit community."

His radio was on, at a low volume. She'd heard some chatter, but she hadn't paid much attention to it, and he hadn't picked up the receiver once since she'd been with him. "Do you talk to the other truckers?"

"Sure."

"What about? Cute waitresses?"

He shook his head. "I try to keep it professional. There are female truckers who listen in. Some guys don't care, but I do."

"Would you speak freely if it was just men?"

"Probably not."

"Who do you talk to about personal stuff?"

He fiddled with the controls on his dashboard, seeming reluctant to answer. He didn't want to speak about his ex-wife, or his former profession. She got the impression that he'd be quite happy to drive all day in silence.

"You're not close to anyone?" she pressed.

"My brother."

"Older or younger?"

"He's two years older."

"Is he your only sibling?"

"Yes."

"Where does he live?"

"Seattle."

"I have three brothers," she said. "Two half-brothers and a stepbrother. They're in Montana with my mom. I haven't seen them in years."

"Why not?"

"It's a long story."

"It's a long drive."

She tucked her legs under her body, getting comfortable. Maybe it would be easier to have a conversation with him if she did all the talking. "My parents got divorced when I was ten. They weren't happy together. My dad was Yellowknife Dene, and my mom is Plains Cree, so they were kind of a mismatch from the start."

"How do you mean?"

"Well, my mom is from Stony Plain, near Edmonton."

He gave her a blank look. "Is that in Canada?"

"Yes. Edmonton is a big city in Alberta. It's nothing like the Northwest Territories." She tried to think of an analogy he would understand. "Imagine a New York City girl marrying an Alaskan from the bush."

"Oh," he said, nodding. "Got it."

"They met at college. My dad only went for one semester, but it was long enough for him to fall in love with my mom. They got married and he brought her to Yellowknife. I guess she expected to have a different kind of life. My grandma said she was the prettiest girl in Stony Plain. She had a lot of admirers."

"Does she look like you?"

"People say that."

He grunted an acknowledgment.

"We went to see her family about once a year. At some point she reconnected with an old boyfriend, and she decided to leave my dad for him. He told her she could go, but she couldn't take me with her."

"Did you want to go?"

"No. I loved Yellowknife, and I loved my dad. I loved hunting and trapping and living off the land."

"So you stayed."

"I stayed. My mom moved to Montana and started a new family. I spent a month with them every summer."

"How was it?"

"It was hard," she said honestly. "I felt abandoned and forgotten, and I didn't get along with my stepdad. I hated him for taking my mom away, and I resented my little brothers for having a mother when I didn't. The only one I liked was Bear."

"Bear?"

"My stepbrother," she said, her cheeks heating. "I had a crush on him."

Cam arched a brow. "Did he encourage you?"

"Not at all," she admitted. "He ignored me. One day

my mom caught me spying on him, and we both got in trouble. My stepdad yelled at Bear, even though he hadn't done anything. My dad wasn't happy about it, either. The next summer, he let me stay home. Then he died, and I went to live with my grandma. She passed away three years ago. My mom and brothers came to her funeral. I haven't seen them since."

"Are you still in touch?"

"I send my mom messages on Facebook, but we don't talk much. I haven't told her I left Duane."

"Why not?"

"I don't know," she said, tugging on one of her braids. "I was so angry with her for leaving me and my dad. I pushed her away for years. It seems hypocritical of me to reach out to her for help now."

"It's not hypocritical," he said, his gaze steady.

"I judged her pretty harshly."

"You were just a kid. How were you supposed to feel?"

She tried to put her thoughts into words. "What I went through with Duane changed my perspective. I realized it wasn't fair to lay all the blame on my mom for their divorce."

"Sometimes it *is* fair to lay all the blame on one person."

She looked out the window, pensive.

"Your ex, for example. He hit you. That's not a mutual failing. It's totally on him."

"I could have done some things differently."

"Like what? Ducked?"

She frowned at his sarcastic tone. "I'm not making excuses for Duane. I'm just saying that I'm more sympathetic toward my mom than I used to be. I know what it's like to marry the wrong person and feel trapped."

Cam focused on the highway, his mouth tight. She got the impression that he wouldn't mind meeting Duane in a dark alley, but he didn't say it out loud, and she was glad. She'd had her fill of violence.

Tala wasn't sure she could mend the relationship with her mother. She wished she hadn't been so rebellious and resistant. Her little brothers were teenagers now. Bear worked in law enforcement. Her stepdad was a large, intimidating man. She might not feel like part of their family, but she'd be safe with them.

They passed a sign that said Coldfoot 289 miles.

"How long will it take to get there?" she asked.

"About eight hours, depending on the weather and road conditions. It's possible to drive all the way through in sixteen hours, but we're not supposed to."

"Why not?"

"Anything over fourteen consecutive hours is a code violation."

"So you're required to stop in Coldfoot?"

"We're required to take breaks, and Coldfoot is the only place with services."

"Where is the final stop?"

"The end of the gravel road is in Deadhorse. From there to Prudhoe Bay, it's pure ice."

"Will we go on the ice?"

"Probably. They have to test the thickness every week. If it's safe, you can drive on it."

"What if it's not safe?"

"Then they restrict access."

"And you have to take the load back to Fairbanks?"

"Not this early in the season. You can leave it at the

yard in Deadhorse and someone else will deliver it after the conditions improve. Supplies pile up there. Last year I spent a couple of weeks going back and forth on the ice road. When it turns to slush in spring, they shut the whole thing down."

She went quiet for a few minutes, staring out the window. They passed by a sparse forest of spruce trees. A slow climb, followed by a series of hairpin turns, caused her pulse to kick up a notch. She gripped the armrests, trying not to show fear. They entered a straight section that was incredibly narrow. Trucks going the opposite direction flew by at a breakneck pace, as if they were on a roomy highway instead of a thin ribbon in the snow.

"How are you doing?" Cam asked.

"Fine," she said, releasing a pent-up breath.

"This is the easy part."

"Where's the hard part?"

"Atigun Pass is coming up. It's a steep incline along a sheer cliff."

"Sounds great."

He smiled at her sarcasm. "We have an hour before it starts, so you can relax."

She peeled her hands off the armrests. As they gained elevation, the landscape changed into a winter wonderland with snow-speckled trees. Rugged mountains loomed in the distance, promising sharp turns and dizzying plummets. The road followed the same path as the pipeline, which bisected the entire state of Alaska. The Trans-Alaska Pipeline had caused a boom to the economy and contributed to several unnatural disasters.

"I've heard of Prudhoe Bay," she said. "It's on the list of places with frequent oil spills."

He didn't seem surprised by this news. "Are you an activist?"

"I used to be. I started getting into it after my dad died."

"What happened to him?"

She glanced at the snowy tire tracks in the road. There were no markers, fences or telephone lines to guide their way. At least they had the bleak light of day. She didn't know how Cam would drive after sunset. "He got in a sled accident. He was cutting across a frozen river on a section of land that had been closed off due to arsenic contamination from the gold mine. It was discovered in the drinking water. They've been trying to clean it up for decades. They were testing some geothermal equipment, which taps heat from deep in the ground and brings it up to the surface. The process was melting the ice at the mouth of the river, but they didn't post a warning, because no one was supposed to be there."

"He broke through?"

She nodded. "The mining company gave me a small settlement. I used it to pay for college in Edmonton."

"What did you study?"

"Earth science. I was in my third year when my grandma got sick. She'd lived in Yellowknife for most of her life. The doctors said that stomach cancer is a side effect of low-level arsenic poisoning."

He made a sympathetic sound. "I'm sorry."

"I didn't get angry after my dad's accident," she said, thinking back. "Maybe I was too young, or too numb. But my grandma's death hit me hard."

Cam downshifted as they reached another sharp curve. She tensed in anticipation of a sideways slide into the embankment. He navigated the space with confidence, clearing a turn that appeared impossibly tight, before continuing uphill.

She released a shaky breath.

"Go on," he said, glancing her way.

"I'd been researching the impact of pollution on native communities, and I started getting involved with local protests. I actually met Duane at a rally. He was there because he hated the government, not because he cared about First Nations people or the environment, but I didn't realize that until later."

Cam flipped a switch overhead. His dashboard looked like the controls for an airplane. There were lights and dials and toggles everywhere.

"What's wrong?" she asked.

"Nothing. I turned off my jakes."

"What are jakes?"

"Compression brakes. I don't need them on an ascent."

She catalogued that into her mental files and checked the side mirror, which revealed an empty road behind them. So far, so good. Cam hadn't lied about the difficult driving conditions. It was unlikely they were being followed. "Where was I?"

"You'd just met Duane."

"Right," she said, moistening her lips. "Are you sure you want to hear this?"

"Why wouldn't I?"

"It's kind of a heavy topic."

"So?"

"We don't know each other that well."

"We're getting there."

She gave him an assessing look. If he wanted to avoid getting attached, they shouldn't be sharing so much personal information. Maybe he wasn't as afraid of intimacy as he claimed. Or maybe his only goal was to bed her, and he wouldn't have any trouble moving on after the deed was done. Either way, she felt obligated to tell him about herself. He'd risked his life to help her. The least she could do was make conversation, and part of her longed for a deeper connection. Her attraction to Cam went beyond physical needs. The emotional comfort and closeness he could offer was incredibly tempting.

She didn't just want to be touched. She wanted to be *held*.

"Duane was angry and rebellious," she said. "I liked that. I was mad at the world, and so was he. We both wanted to burn everything down. But he also had a sweet side, if you can believe it."

"I can."

"He gave me gifts and constant attention. He was obsessive. At the time I thought it was romantic."

"How old were you?"

"Twenty. We'd only been dating six months when he got stationed in Carcross, in Yukon. He asked me to come and live with him. I said no, because we weren't married. He bought a ring the next day."

Cam arched a brow, but didn't say anything.

"We moved too fast."

"I'm not judging."

"Did you and Jenny wait a long time before you got married?"

"We dated for a couple of years, but I knew she was the one right away. I could have asked her sooner."

She cleared her throat and continued. "With me and Duane, it was rocky from the beginning. He was unhappy with his assignment in Carcross. We didn't know anyone in town. He drank too much and didn't sleep enough. I wanted to hike and ride sleds and raise animals. Instead I ended up hiding in the bedroom whenever he was home."

"How long were you married?"

"A little over three years. I found a job as a waitress, just to get out of the house. There weren't a lot of women in the area, and Duane treated every man we encountered like a rival. Sometimes he accused me of encouraging them. He'd come to the café and sit in the parking lot, watching me. I finally had to quit."

"He knew you were out of his league."

She crossed her arms over her chest, considering. Duane hadn't been ugly. Not on the outside, anyway. But he'd been insecure and accusatory, even paranoid. "Maybe that's what he thought, but he didn't say it. He said mean things."

"About your looks?"

"Yes."

Cam studied her for a moment before turning his attention to the road. "You're beautiful. If he said otherwise, he's a liar."

Her cheeks warmed at the compliment. She believed he meant it. Admiration flashed in his eyes when he glanced at her, along with a sincere interest in her as a person. He cared about what she was saying. Men had complimented her before, Duane included, but she couldn't remember the last time one had made her feel special.

Waitresses didn't get a lot of respect. Some customers stared at her body as if she was on the menu, or demanded smiles for a tip she'd already earned. She wouldn't do it. Smiling for no reason didn't come naturally to her.

Cam didn't smile much, either. He seemed intent on holding on to his grief, as if letting go would insult his wife's memory. He'd resigned himself to a life of solitude on the road. Never staying in one place, but never truly moving on. Her gaze fell to his right hand, knuckles scraped from defending her.

"You took off your ring," she said, startled.

He flexed his fingers absently, as if they were sore. She'd remind him to ice his knuckles the next time they stopped.

An hour later he pulled over at the base of a steep incline. Snow flurries reduced visibility, which was probably a good thing. She didn't want to see too much. "I have to put on my chains," he said.

"Do you need help?" she asked, hopeful of a chance to stretch her legs.

"You're supposed to stay out of sight."

"Right," she said, shifting in her seat. She'd love to get out. Sitting still had never been her strong suit. "No problem."

He smiled at her answer, as if he knew she was getting antsy. He shared her need for physical activity. If he didn't, he wouldn't be so eager to chop wood for lonely widows. "Put your parka on."

"Really?"

"You can walk around on the passenger side. That's it."

She made a little squeal of excitement, reaching for her parka. She didn't bother to zip up, because she wanted to feel the invigorating chill. He didn't wear a parka at all, just gloves. He kept the engine running while he worked. She walked up and down along the snowy roadside. She hopped and jumped and twirled in circles. Then she watched him tug the heavy chains into place. She enjoyed the sight of his strong shoulders and hard-muscled arms. He winced as he placed the last set.

She scooped up some snow, striding toward him. "How's your hand?"

"Fine," he said gruffly.

"Let's see."

He removed his glove to show her. His knuckles were slightly swollen. She covered them with snow and lifted her gaze to his face. Although it was cold, he looked hot. His cheeks were ruddy, his eyes bright. The strenuous task had warmed his blood.

She held the snow in place for as long as she could. After it melted off, she brought his knuckles to her lips for a soothing kiss. His gaze flared with heat, and her pulse throbbed with awareness. Maybe he'd taken off his ring because he was ready to move on—with her.

"What are you doing?" he asked sharply.

She released his hand, flushing. "Nothing."

Or…maybe not.

Another truck came barreling down the hill, emerging from a snowy fog. Despite the speed of travel and thick air, she could see the faint outline of the driver. Which meant the driver could see them.

Cam stepped forward and grasped her waist, cursing. He crushed her against the passenger side and held her there. Her breaths puffed out in the chill air above his shoulder. Her parka was open, allowing him entry. His torso pressed tight to hers. When the tension drained from his body, she knew the danger had passed. She glanced up at him, moistening her lips. A muscle in his jaw flexed, but he didn't ease away from her. Her heart thumped with excitement, from the close call, and his close proximity.

Ready or not, his desire was clear. It glimmered in his dark eyes and radiated between them. He needed this, and so did she. He seemed uncertain about how to proceed with her, however. She wondered if he knew the attraction was mutual, or if he was waiting for her to give him an overt signal. Something even more obvious than kissing his knuckles.

She twined her arms around his neck. His gaze dipped to her lips. Then his mouth descended.

Yes.

She threaded her fingers through his hair as he kissed her. He started with a soft touch, his lips warm. The snowflakes in his beard melted on impact. She opened her mouth for his tongue, tentative. He groaned and deepened the kiss. It was an explosion of heat, tongues tangling. His hands gripped her hips and her back met the metal door. She made an encouraging sound, wanting more. He gave it to her. More tongue, exploring her hungry mouth. More hands, roving lower. He cupped her denim-covered bottom with a low growl. His erection swelled against the juncture of her thighs.

He broke the kiss and stepped away. Cold air filled the space between them. His eyes still smoldered, his breaths puffing hot.

"Get in," he said, opening the passenger door.

She climbed the metal steps, disconcerted. She engaged in a brief fantasy in which Cam followed her inside and pushed her down on the bed in the berth. There was hardly room for him, let alone the two of them, but they could make it work.

He slammed her door and walked around to the driver's

side. When he got behind the wheel, his jaw was clenched. She shrugged out of her parka, her cheeks warm. Everything was warm. Her breasts felt full, her mouth swollen. She slumped in her seat, embarrassed by her runaway desire. The seam of her jeans tugged at her tingling sex. She wanted to rub herself there to ease the ache.

His eyes traveled down the length of her legs and lingered between them, as if he could sense her arousal. She squirmed at his perusal, her pulse throbbing.

"Get in the back," he said in a low voice.

"Why?"

"I need to focus on driving."

"I won't bother you."

He gave her a look that said she was already bothering him, after she'd promised not to. She'd wanted to leave the cramped confines of the truck. She'd wanted him to kiss her. It was his fault as much as hers, but this issue wouldn't have arisen if she'd stayed in Fairbanks, so she didn't argue. She climbed out of the passenger seat and entered the berth.

Lying down, she found it even more difficult to ignore her physical needs. She hadn't been touched in a long time. She hadn't touched *herself*, either. Her body had gone into hibernation after she'd escaped her abusive marriage. Cam had brought her back to life. She'd forgotten how it felt to enjoy a man's attention.

She reached for one of her graphic novels as they ascended the steep cliff. She didn't like not being able to see the road, but maybe ignorance was bliss. The incline felt alarming, the engine shuddering from exertion.

It occurred to her that Cam had been angry with her for tempting him, and angry with himself for surrendering to temptation. Maybe he was angry about not being able to finish what they'd started, too. Either way, he hadn't yelled at her or done anything violent. He hadn't blamed or belittled her. He'd accepted the situation as it was, and found a solution that allowed him to continue driving.

He was calm and in control. That was comforting.

The book in her hands offered another level of comfort. She concentrated on the story, the illustrations, the characters. Despite the precarious road conditions, she felt safe and cozy, as well as highly desired.

Cam wanted her. He wanted her so much that he had to remove her from his sight in order to do his job.

Smiling, she turned the page.

Chapter 10

December 12
67N
-1 degree

Atigun Pass was as nerve-racking as usual.

Cam had to increase his speed steadily in order to make the climb. Slowing down meant risking a dangerous backwards slide. If his rig stalled or malfunctioned, he couldn't pull over. The weight of his load would cause the wheels to slip. It was a recipe for a jackknife—or worse. One wrong move could send them hurtling over the edge. Other truckers had taken that icy path before. They'd plummeted down the snowy cliff. There were no survivors in these accidents.

He was glad Tala had agreed to ride in the back, because this stretch of road demanded his total concentration. Through no fault of her own, she was a distraction. He couldn't afford to sneak glances at her luscious mouth or fantasize about their kissing session. He had to keep his mind calm and his thoughts clear.

She wouldn't have enjoyed the view, anyway. She'd seemed nervous on easier sections of the Dalton. It was better for her to sit tight in the berth. Reading her comics, or whatever she was doing.

When he reached the summit, he breathed a sigh of relief and flexed his fingers, which had been clenched around the wheel. A glance into the back revealed Tala, lying on her stomach on his bed. He couldn't see all of her, just the midsection.

She had a body made for blue jeans. Long, lean legs. Her curves were lovingly cupped by snug denim. The twin pockets seemed designed to lift her pert bottom in invitation. They had silver studs and gold thread. He imagined climbing on top of her, gripping her hips and pressing himself against her.

Swallowing hard, he returned his attention to the road. He'd drifted slightly off-course. He corrected in a calm, practiced motion.

Jesus.

This woman was dangerous in more ways than one. He'd risked his life to rescue her from two assailants this morning. Now he was lust-struck after a single glance. If he wasn't careful, he was going to veer into a snowbank.

For the next few hours, he concentrated on driving. The technical difficulty of navigating a loaded rig in inclement weather kept his thoughts occupied. He could hear subtle movements in the berth. The whisper of turning pages or shifting limbs. She switched positions often. He wondered if she was struggling to stay focused on her book. If she was distracted by memories of their kiss, and imagining other, sexy scenarios.

His neck flushed with heat. Now that he knew she felt the same desire he did, it would be harder to resist her. He'd assumed she wasn't attracted to him. He'd been wrong. Over the course of the day, he'd started to notice some signs of interest. She looked out the window a lot, but she also looked at him. She studied his body as if she wanted to touch him. She studied his hands as if she wanted *him* to touch *her*.

He hadn't been absolutely sure until he'd kissed her. The way she'd responded had removed all doubt. She'd moaned and clutched at his hair and devoured his mouth.

He tried not to think about her physical reactions, or possible sexual frustration. He tried not to wonder what kind of panties she was wearing, or if they were damp. Gritting his teeth, he cracked his window to let in a cold blast of air. It worked to clear his head. As the sunlight faded into another early evening, she set her book aside.

"You can turn on the lamp," he said.

"I'm okay."

"Are you hungry?"

"I can wait."

He didn't tell her that they were still hours from Coldfoot. Like most truckers, he preferred to drive as long as he could without stopping, and there weren't many places to pull over on this section of the Dalton.

She curled up with his wool blanket. It obstructed his view of her body, which was probably for the best. Darkness enveloped the cab. Her slow, even breaths told him she'd drifted to sleep. A warm feeling settled in the center of his chest. It was part satisfaction, part tenderness. She didn't trust easily, but she trusted him enough to take a nap in the back of his truck. She trusted him to protect her.

He wasn't sure if he deserved the honor, or if he could keep her safe in the long term. He balked at the responsibility. There were too many emotions, too many entanglements involved. He couldn't afford to get attached to a woman in jeopardy. He didn't want to control her fate, or make any life-or-death decisions.

He'd done that with Jenny, and it had almost killed him. Everyone had agreed that the breathing machine was prolonging the inevitable. Everyone had been ready to say goodbye—except him. He'd preferred limbo and false hopes to that soul-crushing end.

Tala slept peacefully for more than hour. He made good time in some tricky sections, charging over bone-white roads with nothing but vague tracks to guide his way. Snow flurries danced in his headlights. He expected storms and delays on the Dalton, but the weather was supposed to hold steady tonight. He hoped it wouldn't take a turn for the worse. All he needed was a blow, or a full-on blizzard, to trap them in Coldfoot. When visibility was nil, truckers had to pull over and wait for the conditions to improve. Sometimes they closed the road altogether until the storm passed.

It would be difficult to stay a single night at Coldfoot Camp with Tala. He'd have to keep his distance and pretend they weren't traveling together. If they got stuck there by bad weather, the ruse would fall apart. She wasn't a woman who could go unnoticed for long.

While he considered ways to address this problem, she stirred in her sleep. She mumbled something unintelligible and kicked her legs, as if running away from a threat. Then she sat upright with a start. Her eyes were wide, lips parted in distress.

"You were dreaming," he said helpfully.

She drew in several ragged breaths. "Yes."

"Everything's fine. You're safe."

"Is anyone following us?"

"No."

Wrapping the blanket around her shoulders, she held it clutched tight over her chest. "How far to Coldfoot?"

"Another hour. You can come up front."

She brought the blanket with her to the passenger seat. After she buckled up, she shot him a curious look.

"We need to discuss your story."

"My story?"

"You can't tell people you're a stowaway or a hitch-hiker."

"Why do I have to tell them anything?"

He smiled at the question, which he understood on a visceral level. He'd spent the past three years avoiding social interactions whenever possible. "It's better to have a story ready. Someone might ask if you're a trucker."

"I don't look like a trucker."

"No, you don't. More importantly, you don't talk like one. You don't know the lingo."

"What else can I be?"

He mulled it over. Tourists visited the Dalton on occasion. Mostly the road was populated with truckers, oil rig workers and engineers. "Keeping it close to the truth is easier. You can say you're a waitress, and you've got a job lined up at a hotel in Prudhoe Bay. They're always desperate for help."

"Okay."

"We'll see how busy it is when we get there. If it's

crowded, we might be able to come in without causing a stir."

"Why would we cause a stir?"

He arched a brow.

"Because I'm a woman."

"You're a young, beautiful woman, in a place where there are only men."

She fell silent, watching the snow-packed road. Then she turned her gaze on him. "You're a beautiful man."

He tensed at the compliment. He'd been called handsome before, but never beautiful. The term didn't fit him.

She studied his face with interest. "Do they hit on you?"

"Who?"

"The other men."

"No," he said, flushing. "Hell, no."

Her lips curved into a smile. "Maybe you cause a stir all by yourself."

"I don't think so."

"Are you sure? Some of those truckers could be pining away for you."

"If they are, I don't want to know."

She laughed at his reaction, seeming pleased with herself. He realized he didn't have any idea how it felt to be the object of unwanted desire. As a waitress, she'd probably dealt with lewd behavior and grabby hands, not just crude comments on the radio. After escaping her abusive husband, she must have been wary of strange men. Even so, she'd served them with calm efficiency. He admired her grit. It took a lot of courage to stare down truckers and pour their coffee with a steady hand.

"What if it's not crowded?" she asked.

"Then I can't pretend we didn't arrive together."

"Will you get in trouble?"

"I doubt it."

"But you'd rather not attract attention."

"Exactly."

"I get it."

He shifted into a lower gear as they climbed another steep slope. As soon as he was clear of the danger, he glanced in her direction. "I didn't mean to offend you by saying you'd cause a stir."

"I wasn't offended. I'm used to it."

"Used to what, being stared at?"

"But not really seen."

He nodded his understanding. He knew what other men saw when they looked at her—long legs and long hair and pretty lips. Obviously, he noticed her surface beauty, but he saw other things in her. Strength, determination, vulnerability. A fighting spirit.

"I see you," he said, after a pause.

She smiled at his simple statement. "I know."

Before they reached Coldfoot, the snow flurries turned into a swirling whiteout. Visibility was reduced to almost nothing. He crept along at a snail's pace for the last stretch, grateful it was a straight shot to their destination. By the time he pulled over in the camp parking lot, it was late evening, and he was dead tired.

Luckily, the lot was full. Several other trucks had just arrived. The rustic restaurant was packed with hungry men. Cam's stomach growled for a hot meal. He grabbed his parka and removed a few bills from his wallet.

"Here's the plan," he said, giving her some cash. "You pay for a bunk and get settled while I buy dinner. I'll bring you a plate."

"How will you know which room I'm in?"

"There's a separate hall for women. I think it's just one room with a few bunks. I'll knock on the door."

"Where will you eat?"

"At the counter."

Although she didn't appear pleased with the arrangement, she said nothing. She understood the need for discretion. She put the cash in her pocket and pulled her hood up, obscuring her face. Then she caught sight of a tour bus pulling into the space next to his rig. "Arctic Adventures" was written across one side.

"Tourists spend the night here?" she asked sharply.

"Only on weekends," he said, stroking his jaw. He'd forgotten it was Saturday. "They travel to Coldfoot and back."

"Anyone can sign up?"

"I guess so."

Her brow furrowed with unease. They hadn't been followed by her assailants—at least, not in the usual sense. Cam hadn't seen any standard vehicles on the road, and every trucker required special paperwork. There was a lengthy permit process, drug testing and other regulations.

Tourists, however, could hop on a bus without much trouble. If there were seats available, tickets would be sold on the spot. Her pursuers could have paid for a tour this morning. He drummed his fingertips against the wheel as about a dozen people piled out of the bus. He couldn't see most of their faces. They were all bundled up in hooded jackets and appeared to be headed toward the restaurant.

"What do you want to do?" she asked.

"Stick to the plan. You pay for a bunk and get out of

sight. I'll sit down at the restaurant. If I spot your friends, I'll let you know."

"They're not my friends."

"Whoever they are."

She didn't ask what their options were. There wasn't anywhere else to go tonight. In an emergency, they could sleep in his rig. He'd have to keep the engine running all night, or they'd freeze to death. She pressed her lips to his bearded cheek, leaving a trace of heat and softness. "Be careful."

"You, too."

She grabbed her backpack and climbed out of the cab. There was a door nearby with a glowing Vacancy sign in the window. The bunkhouses were basically a series of connected trailers crammed with narrow beds. Although most of the space was designated for men, there was a private room for women behind the front office.

He waited a few minutes before shutting down his dashboard and making his exit. The restaurant was half-full, even at this late hour. Dinner service appeared to be winding down. He took a seat at the counter, studying the faces in the crowd. They looked like regular truckers and tourists to him. He didn't see the lowlifes they'd tangled with earlier. If they were here, they were blending in.

Cam snorted at the thought. Those guys were thugs. They didn't blend in. Subtlety wasn't their strong suit. They'd tried to kidnap Tala from a public parking lot.

He ordered two plates of pasta with grilled chicken and broccoli, one to go. He knew from experience that the food here was good. Truckers had hearty appetites, and when they were sidelined by a snowstorm, there wasn't much else to do. There was no cell service or

Wi-Fi. A single television mounted in the corner offered news and weather reports. Cam caught up on the forecast while he waited for his meal. It was going to be cold and clear.

He took his phone out of his pocket to check for texts from Mason. Sure enough, his brother had come through with a cryptic message.

Call me. Important info.

Cam frowned at the words on the screen. Mason knew Cam couldn't call from here. If the information was so goddamned important, why hadn't he texted it? Sighing, he rose from his seat and approached the register. There was only one phone in the joint, and access wasn't free. Cam paid for a ten-dollar card to call his brother in Seattle.

"Who's this?" Mason answered.

"It's me."

There was a scrambling sound, as if his brother had dropped his phone. Then a whisper of sheets and a feminine murmur.

"I'm returning your call," Cam said.

"Hang on."

Mason's footsteps padded across a hardwood floor. He lived in a drafty old loft in a run-down area near the red-light district. It was an unusual space, straight out of a horror movie. He called it "industrial." Everyone else called it creepy.

"Do you have company?"

"No."

"I thought I heard a voice."

"It was the TV."

"You don't have a TV."

"I have internet. Livestreaming."

"Livestreaming? Is that what they call it now?"

"I'd explain, but you've been in Alaska too long to understand technology."

Cam grunted his disbelief, shifting the phone to his other ear. "I only have five minutes. What's the info?"

"I found Tala Walker in a criminal database. She has a record."

"I know."

"Funny, you didn't mention it."

"She said it was a minor offense."

"Not quite."

Cam waited for Mason to continue, his stomach clenched with unease.

"She was arrested nine months ago at a rally in Whitehorse, Canada. A few hundred people were protesting a pipeline expansion project by a local oil company. It started out peaceful, but ended in chaos. Riot police were brought in to handle the more aggressive activists, and they clashed."

Cam didn't automatically assume the activists were to blame. He'd worked crowd control before. Some protests attracted unpredictable weirdos and violent extremists. But there were also overzealous officers who added fuel to the fire, and inexperienced rookies who didn't know how to defuse tense situations.

"According to the report, your girlfriend assaulted an officer."

"How?"

"She broke a beer bottle over his head. He had to get stitches."

Cam squeezed his eyes shut. Damn.

"There's more," Mason said.

"I'm listening."

"She spent a night in jail and was released on her own recognizance. Then she missed her court date, which was a huge mistake. If she hadn't skipped bail, she might have ended up with a slap on the wrist. Now she's basically a fugitive. She's got warrants for her arrest."

"Was her husband involved in the altercation?"

"I don't know. I haven't gotten that far in the background check. I actually have better things to do than assist you on your latest foray into self-destruction."

Cam squinted at the harsh words. "Foray into self-destruction?"

"That's what I said."

"You sound like a depressed poet."

"I'll jot that down in my black notebook."

"What better things do you have to do, besides that stranger in your bedroom?"

"She's not—"

Cam pounced on the bitten-off protest. "She's not a stranger? Or you're not doing her?"

Mason sighed into the receiver. "Are you going to ignore the information I gave you?"

"No. I'm taking it seriously."

"So you're done with this girl?"

"I didn't say that."

"Cam, I get it. I've seen her photo. She's hot. By Alaska standards, she's a supermodel. But she's a wanted criminal, not an innocent victim. She's on the run from the law."

"Did you find anything on the husband?"

"Duane Laramie, age twenty-six. He's a customs officer stationed in Carcross, near the US-Canada border. No record, but he's got an extensive gun collection. Seven registered weapons. Some hunting, some home-protection."

Cam didn't like this news any more than he liked the report on Tala. "What about the diner in Willow?"

"Oh, yeah. I talked to a sheriff's deputy about that. Said I was looking into another missing girl case. He told me there was no indication of foul play, but the waitress left her purse at the scene."

"That didn't raise any red flags?"

"It raised some red flags about her being a thief. She had a stolen ID in her wallet."

Cam dragged a hand down his face. "I have to go. My time's almost up."

"What's your plan?"

"For tonight?"

"And tomorrow."

Cam didn't answer. He had no intention of ditching Tala, no matter what his brother said. Maybe she was nothing but trouble. It didn't matter; he still wanted her. When he looked at her, he didn't see a liar or a criminal. He saw a beautiful, desirable woman. Every time they touched, his heart thawed a little more.

"Cam?"

"I haven't decided what to do," he said finally.

He needed more information from Tala. He'd ask her some questions and gauge her responses. If she wasn't honest with him, he'd have to rethink this whole arrangement.

He should probably keep his distance, regardless. She was a terrible choice for a no-strings fling. The man he used to be wouldn't have entertained the idea of sleeping with a fugitive who assaulted cops. That man wouldn't have considered an affair with a desperate stowaway, either.

The man he was now didn't even feel ashamed.

He felt alive.

"Be careful," Mason said.

"I will," Cam lied.

Chapter 11

Coldfoot, AK
67N
-9 degrees

Tala stepped inside the empty room and looked around.

There were four narrow beds, spaced a few feet apart from one another. A single nightstand with a lamp sat in the center. She locked the door behind her and set her backpack on the nearest bed. Then she inspected the bathroom. It had a toilet, sink and shower stall. She didn't see any towels, just a stack of washcloths.

The space was chilly and lacked ambience. Thin carpet, drab walls, beige bedding. She crossed her arms over her chest, shivering. It wasn't much, but she'd stayed in worse places, and she didn't mind the cold. She'd roughed it in the Yellowknife wilderness more times

than she could count. Once she'd spent the night in a
hole her father had dug out of snow, after they'd been
forced to take shelter from a sudden blizzard.

Tears welled in her eyes at the memory. She didn't
miss Duane, but she missed home. She'd left all her personal belongings in Carcross. Priceless artifacts that had
been handed down from generation to generation. Tools
her father had made with his own hands. Her grandmother's blankets and furs.

She spent the next ten minutes curled up on the narrow bed, feeling sorry for herself. Then she pushed
aside her sadness and got up. She rummaged through
her backpack for a change of clothes. She could wear her
leggings and sweater as pajamas. A hot shower would
be nice, if she could find a towel.

She searched the dresser, which had nothing in it except a Bible. She ducked into the bathroom anyway. Her
hair didn't need washing, and there was no shampoo or
conditioner. She stripped quickly and stepped into the
shower stall, securing her braids at the nape of her neck.
The water was pleasantly warm, which made her wish
for a longer soak. Eyes closed, she let the warmth flow
over her bare shoulders. Then she unwrapped a tiny soap
to lather her body. Her hands swept over her breasts, lin-
gering on the tight points of her nipples. The flesh between her legs pulsed with arousal. She bit down on her
lower lip, trying to ignore the sensation. She considered
stroking herself to climax, for the comfort and release.

Instead of giving in to the urge, she finished washing and turned off the water. Cam's hot kisses and smol-
dering looks had left her wanting. The book she'd been
reading this afternoon hadn't helped. It had been surprisingly explicit, with a series of sexy scenes. One image

featured a topless woman lying on her back in the hero's bed. She was a typical male-fantasy character—perfect breasts, slim waist, flowing hair. Her face was contorted in ecstasy. The hero wasn't in the frame at all. Tala had puzzled over that for a moment before she realized he was going down on her. It was a beautiful drawing, despite the subject matter. Or because of it. Tala wasn't sure. She'd never experienced that particular pleasure.

After she'd set the book aside, squirming, the image continued to haunt her. She wondered if the act itself was as enjoyable as the artist's depiction. Duane hadn't attempted that kind of foreplay, and she hadn't asked him for it. Near the end of their relationship, she'd avoided his touch as much as possible. His lack of finesse in the bedroom had been the least of their problems.

Cam struck her as a generous lover. Eager to please, willing to go slow. He probably wouldn't hesitate to kiss her wherever she wished. He might even do it without any prompting. Her cheeks flushed at the thought.

She stepped out of the stall and dried off as well as she could with two washcloths. The chilly air gave her goose bumps, but that was okay. She needed to cool down. Shivering, she tugged on fresh panties, socks and leggings. She didn't bother with a bra under her sweatshirt. She let down her hair and combed the waves with her fingers. As she finished dressing, she heard a noise outside the bathroom.

Voices.

Tala froze, listening to shuffled footsteps and low murmurs. Someone was in the room. More than one person, by the sound. She swallowed hard, gathering her belongings to her chest. There were no windows in the bathroom, no escape routes. Nothing to use as a weapon. There were only washcloths. Two damp, two dry.

She opened the door and looked out. Two female strangers stared back at her. One had dark hair with purple and blue streaks. The other was older, with short gray hair. They both wore black leather vests with patches on the front. The older woman offered Tala a tentative smile.

"Hello," she said. "I'm Fran, and this is my daughter, Lily."

"Tala," she replied, nodding hello. She walked toward the bed she'd claimed earlier and started rearranging her backpack. She felt jittery and paranoid, though the women were clearly not a threat. She was glad she hadn't charged out of the bathroom with her fists raised. Fran and Lily didn't seem to notice anything amiss. They got settled on the opposite side of the room, chatting about their dinner plans.

"Are you a truck driver?" Fran asked Tala.

"No, I'm just tagging along with one." She told the story Cam had suggested about catching a lift to a waitress job in Prudhoe Bay.

"We're with the tour group," Fran said. She pointed to the patches on her vest. "Denali Devils Motorcycle Club. We ride the Dalton together every summer. This year we decided to check it out in winter."

Tala folded her jeans and tucked them away. "Is everyone on the tour in your motorcycle club?"

"Yep. The rest of the members are all men. Lily's the youngest in the club."

Lily rolled her eyes at her mother's proud announcement, but Tala thought it was sweet. She was also relieved by the information. If everyone on the bus was a

Denali Devil, the killers weren't among them. That was one less thing to worry about tonight.

"You should have dinner with us," Fran said. "Then you don't have to eat with the truckers."

"I don't mind truckers," Tala said.

A knock at the door interrupted their conversation. Tala went to answer it, but Fran was closer. The older woman opened the door to Cam.

"Hello, there," she said, blinking up at him. She seemed startled by the sight of a tall, broad-shouldered man in the hallway.

Cam nodded a greeting and looked past Fran. "I brought your dinner," he said to Tala in a gruff voice.

Tala moved forward to accept the offering. Fran smiled at her encouragingly. Instead of introducing him, Tala stepped into the hall and closed the door behind her. She knew Cam didn't want an audience for their conversation.

"Making friends?" Cam asked.

"The entire tour group is a motorcycle club. They're all together."

"Okay," he said, shrugging.

She studied his handsome face. He looked tense, and tired. His thick brown hair was slightly disheveled, his eyes bloodshot. There was something else in his gaze, a cold wariness she hadn't seen since Willow. It was as if he'd decided, in the hour they'd been apart, that she wasn't worth the trouble.

Her heart clenched at the thought.

She wished she could wrap her arms around him and stroke his rumpled hair. She'd soothe his fears and ease his fatigue. She'd kiss away whatever ailed him, and in doing so, heal herself. But she couldn't do those things, because they weren't in a private place, and she wasn't free to touch him.

"Are you going to bed?" she asked.

"I might hit the gym first."

"There's a gym?"

"There's a weight bench and a few barbells. It's not for you."

She didn't argue. She'd love to stretch her legs and burn off some excess energy, but she understood his position. He'd taken a risk by bringing her here. It was better if she stayed out of sight, as planned.

"We leave at six, sharp."

"I'll be ready," she said. "Sleep well."

He gave her a dark look and strode down the hall. He seemed irritated with her. Maybe he regretted getting involved in her problems. Maybe he just needed space. She went back inside the room, rattled by his brusque attitude. Lily and Fran wore curious expressions.

"Was that your trucker?" Fran asked.

"I'm riding with him, yes."

"Now I see why you don't mind truckers," Lily said.

Fran winked at Lily. "I wouldn't either, if they all looked like that!"

Both women laughed merrily. Tala didn't join in. She returned to her spot on the bed, feeling glum. She avoided eye contact, and they didn't ask her any more personal questions. After they left the room, she inspected the meal Cam had brought her. It was a tasty pasta dish with chicken and vegetables. She ate every bite. Then she brushed her teeth and crawled under the blankets, wide awake.

She shouldn't have taken that nap earlier. She was going to toss and turn all night. She tried reading, but she couldn't focus on the story. She kept flipping back to the sexy bits and staring at the bare-breasted woman.

Groaning, she buried the book in her backpack.

When Fran and Lily returned, she closed her eyes and pretended to be asleep. They were nice enough, but she didn't want to talk. She wanted to curl up with Cam and make them both feel good again.

Someone turned off the lights. It was dark and quiet. Tala couldn't stop thinking about Cam. His hot kisses and bold hands. The feel of his muscles beneath her fingertips. Heat built between her legs. She pressed her thighs together, unable to ease the ache. She couldn't touch herself with two strangers in the room.

After an interminable length of time, she gave up on sleeping. She rose from the bed, grabbed her shoes and tiptoed out the door.

There was nowhere to go, of course. She couldn't take a walk outside in swirling snow and below-freezing temperatures. The lights in the restaurant were dimmed. Lily had complained about the camp being "dry." There wasn't a bar or alcohol of any kind. There wasn't even internet or Wi-Fi.

Tala knew they had a phone in the front office. She imagined calling her mother and explaining her predicament. She'd have to spill all the details about Duane and admit that she'd made a mistake in marrying him. While she was baring her soul, she might as well say she wished she'd been a better daughter.

She rejected that depressing idea. There would be no tearful confessions tonight. She wasn't going to call her mother at this late hour. She wasn't going to break down and cry in the middle of the hallway, either.

She needed some other kind of release.

Cam had been clear in his instructions. Stay in the room, stay out of sight. She couldn't go around knocking on the doors to the men's bunks. What would she say if she found him? *Excuse me, I know you're in a bad mood, but could you please do page 36 to me?*

She choked on a laugh as she crept down the hall. There was a light at the end, beckoning her to explore farther. She moved toward it with silent steps. She could hear the sounds of clinking metal and ragged breaths.

The gym!

She paused at the end of the hallway, which split into a T. The light was coming from an open door on the left side. She continued forward, her pulse racing. When she reached the threshold, she peered inside.

Cam was there. He was alone, stretched out on his back on a weight bench. He lifted a bar away from his chest, arms fully extended. Then he lowered it, releasing a breath. His biceps quivered and glistened with sweat. Up, down. Up, down. It was mesmerizing.

He was wearing a basic gray T-shirt, despite the chill. Clearly, he wasn't cold. His legs were covered in a pair of charcoal gray sweatpants. Athletic shoes took the place of his steel-toed boots. His stomach clenched with every lift, drawing her attention to the flat muscles there. And lower, where he wasn't flat. The hem of his T-shirt had ridden up, and the elastic band of his underwear was visible at his narrow waist. With his feet planted on either side of the bench, powerful thighs spread, she had an unfettered view of his crotch. The soft fabric of his sweatpants did nothing to disguise his manhood.

Her mouth went dry at the sight. She'd never understood why some people objected to women wearing leggings in public, but not men wearing sweatpants. The second was more revealing, considering the outward projection of male anatomy.

On his next rep, Cam placed the bar on the rack and sat up. He used the edge of his T-shirt to wipe the sweat from his face, treating her to a glimpse of his washboard abs. He didn't look pleased to see her, but it was too late to retreat. She'd already been caught staring. She might as well stay and brazen it out.

"What do you want?" he asked.

Oh, boy. *That* was a loaded question. "I couldn't sleep," she said, venturing into the gym. It wasn't much of a gym. There was a weight bench, some barbells and a wrestling mat. One of the walls was mirrored.

He stretched out on his back and did another ten reps. She stood there with her arms crossed over her chest, trying not to ogle him.

"Isn't it dangerous to lift weights like that?" she asked.

"Like what?"

"Without a spotter."

He returned the bar to the rack. "I don't need a spotter for light reps. I'm not going to get trapped under a hundred pounds."

She nodded her understanding. His gaze trailed over her body, as if wondering how it might feel to get trapped underneath *her*. Although she weighed quite a bit more than a hundred pounds, she imagined he could lift her up and down with ease.

He arched a brow. "Is watching me work out going to help you sleep?"

"Probably not," she said, glancing around. There was a jump rope sitting in a plastic crate in the corner. She picked it up and started her own workout.

Jumping rope without a bra on was not recommended. She stopped after about two minutes, her cheeks hot. Cam's lips twitched with amusement, but he didn't say anything. He also didn't avert his gaze. She returned the rope to the crate and switched to yoga. Although it was a low-impact exercise, it wasn't easy. Holding the poses required strength and endurance. She tried not to feel self-conscious about twisting and bending over in snug leggings. Her sweatshirt rode up several times, exposing her belly.

Cam didn't sit idly for long. Nor did he continue smiling. Jaw clenched with irritation, he grabbed the jump rope and approached the mirrored wall. He did a Rocky Balboa routine that was almost as impressive as his weightlifting. He jumped with both feet together, lightning-fast, never tiring. The man was a machine.

A beautiful machine, with broad shoulders and a tight butt.

She moved into a challenging position and held it for as long as possible, eyes closed. Breathing in and out. She didn't achieve total zen, but she felt better when she was finished. She collapsed on the mat. Cam sat down on the bench again. They were both sweating. He didn't seem more relaxed, post workout. He was still on edge.

"Where did you learn yoga?" he asked.

"At the library in Willow. They had free classes several days a week."

He grunted in response, wiping his face with his T-shirt.

She hugged her knees to her chest. "Is something wrong?"

"You told me you were arrested for civil disobedience."

"Yes."

"Was that it? Nothing else?"

Her stomach fluttered with unease. "Why do you ask?"

"Because I'm taking a risk by traveling with you, and I have the right to know who I'm getting involved with."

His request wasn't unreasonable. She liked the sound of them "getting involved." Maybe a frank conversation would make him feel better and break the tension between them. He'd listened to her talk about Duane without judging. She could tell him this. "The charges were civil disobedience and assaulting an officer," she admitted.

"Did you plead guilty?"

"I told you, I never went to court."

"Were you going to plead guilty?"

"I wasn't sure. I didn't want to lie under oath."

"What do you mean?"

She swallowed hard. "Let me start at the beginning. I went to a protest rally in Whitehorse with Duane. He wouldn't let me go alone, and I was desperate to leave the house. I thought it would be good for both of us. Like old times."

"But it wasn't."

"No. He put on a black ski mask as soon as we got there, because he didn't want to be recognized. There was a big crowd, with military police in heavy gear. He started drinking heavily and acting really aggressive."

"More aggressive than usual?"

"Yes. I wanted to leave, but he refused. We were following a group of guys with their faces covered, like him. They were kicking over trash cans and breaking stuff. The police used smoke bombs, and most of the protesters dispersed. Duane bought me a beer, which I accepted to placate him. Then something set him off. I'm not sure what. He grabbed the bottle from me and chucked it at one of the officers. It hit him in the back of the head." She touched her own head, shuddering.

"What did Duane do?"

"He ran in the opposite direction. I didn't see him go, because I was walking toward the officer. I wanted to see if he was okay. When I knelt down beside him, two other officers tackled me and handcuffed me."

"Why did they think you did it?"

"I kept saying I was sorry, and… I was afraid to say anything else."

"You were willing to take the blame?"

"I didn't make a statement one way or another. I asked my public defender to file for a postponement, and she did. Duane said he'd lose his job if I told the truth, but if I pleaded guilty, I'd get community service."

"He's full of shit. No one gets community service for assaulting a police officer. Not even in Canada."

She narrowed her eyes at his certainty. "You're familiar with the law?"

"Yeah, I am," he said in a flat voice. "I used to be a cop."

Her heart plummeted. She scrambled to her feet, thunderstruck. Panic and betrayal washed over her in cold waves. She'd told him intensely personal things. Incriminating things. She shouldn't have trusted him.

"You lied to me."

He rose to his full height. "I didn't lie."

"I asked if you were a cop, and you said no."

"I'm not a cop anymore. I quit."

She shook her head in denial. He still acted like a

cop, with his protective instincts and Boy Scout attitude. Her gut reaction had been right. "You kept it secret for a reason. You knew I wouldn't stay with you if you told the truth."

"What about your secrets?" he shot back angrily. "You haven't been honest with me, either. You never said you were facing serious charges. I don't know what the hell is going on. I don't even know who you're running from!"

She swallowed a protest, even though the criticism felt unfair. She hadn't withheld information to deceive him. She'd done it to protect him, and herself.

"You're not as innocent as you pretend to be," he said.

She sputtered with outrage. "I'm not pretending to be *anything*."

He stepped forward, crowding her space. "I'm not a fool, Tala. I know you didn't come here to work out."

Her hand itched to slap him. He was making insulting accusations. They'd both been dishonest—and they were both suffering from the same malady. He wanted her. That was his real problem. She was upsetting his grieving-widower applecart. She was getting under his skin. "Why did I come here, then?"

"To torture me."

"You're delusional."

"Am I?"

"Yes," she said, shoving his chest. He didn't budge. "You think you're the only one who gets stir-crazy? I've been trapped inside a truck for two days, just like you. I need to move around, just like you. I feel restless, too."

"What I feel is sexual frustration, not restlessness."

"I'm aware of that."

"So you wandered over here to make it worse?"

"No. I wandered over here to make it better."

His eyes flared with heat. "Don't tease me."

"I'm not teasing."

She didn't touch him. She just waited for him to touch her, and he didn't disappoint. Thrusting his hands in her hair, he crushed his mouth over hers. She parted her lips eagerly, inviting him inside. He plundered her with his tongue, groaning. She wrapped her arms around his neck and reveled in him. His taste, hot and demanding. His hard chest and strong shoulders. The smell of damp cotton and warm man.

He took her mouth, again and again. His hands moved to her bottom, cupping her firm flesh and lifting her against him. His erection swelled at her belly and her unbound breasts flattened against the wall of his chest. She moaned, digging her nails in his skin. The heat between her legs became an intense ache. She'd never been this aroused before, and she desperately needed relief.

"Please," she said, biting his lip.

He glanced at the open door. Either the threat of discovery was low, or he dismissed it as unimportant. Instead of taking his hands off her, he backed toward the weight bench and straddled it, pulling her on top of him. Her soft sex met his hard length. She gasped at the sensation. His mouth covered hers again, tongue thrusting.

She moved her hips in a slow circle. His hands groped under her sweatshirt and found her bare breasts. He grunted in pleasure as his thumbs strummed over her nipples. She rocked faster, lost in sensation. There was no penetration or direct stimulation, but it felt too good to stop. Incredibly, she was close to orgasm.

She broke the kiss, uncertain. He stared up at her with half-lidded eyes. Lifting her shirt, he placed his mouth over her breast. The combination of heat, moisture and suction almost sent her over the edge. She whimpered, trying not to grind harder. His erection throbbed against her. He was impressively built, which added to her excitement.

But he seemed to know what she needed, even if she didn't say the words. He gripped her hips and slid her along his thick length. She made a strangled sound of encouragement, her hips jerking. Her breaths came in short pants and her stomach quivered. She strained toward climax, beyond embarrassment. Waves of arousal crashed over her, drowning out everything. There was only this moment, pure and raw and physical.

When she opened her mouth to scream, he thrust his hand in her hair and brought her lips down to his. She exploded in ecstasy, shuddering against him. He swallowed her cries with a thorough kiss.

Then it was over. She stared at him in awe, her head spinning.

"Wow," she said, panting.

The corner of his mouth tipped up. He was still unsatisfied, hard as a rock against her, his forehead lined with restraint. She slid off his lap like a wet noodle and moved into a kneeling position at his feet. He inhaled sharply, but he didn't object. He wanted this. Taut desire was written all over his face.

She wanted it, too. She wanted to touch him and kiss him and blow his mind. She untied the drawstring at his waist, giddy with anticipation. He stroked her hair softly. His hot gaze seared her parted lips.

The sound of approaching footsteps interrupted the moment.

His hand tightened in her hair. She froze, eyes wide.

"Get up," he ordered.

She scrambled to her feet. There wasn't a closet or a corner to hide in. She smoothed her sweatshirt and tried to look innocent. The intruder never arrived, thankfully. A door slammed at the end of the hall.

"He's in the men's room," Cam said. "Go now, before he comes back out."

She hesitated, reluctant to end their encounter. They'd just shared the most intense sexual experience of her life, and he hadn't even removed any of her clothes! He'd given her an orgasm that made her see stars. She didn't want to leave without returning the favor. She didn't want to leave at all. But she also didn't want to get caught, or land him into trouble. They couldn't afford to attract attention.

So she snuck out the door quietly. As she rushed down the hall, it occurred to her that she still wasn't sure where she stood with Cam. They'd been interrupted before she could give him pleasure, and they hadn't really finished their conversation. She'd accused him of deceiving her. He thought she'd done the same. They'd both been angry when they started kissing. But how did he feel about her now? His willingness to get physical didn't indicate a future commitment, or any tender feelings.

He knew she was a criminal, not just a victim. He was a former cop, not just a trucker. He might reconsider traveling with her. What if he took off without her tomorrow? She'd never see him again, and she couldn't do anything about it.

Her heart plummeted with distress. He might not have any tender feelings, but she did. She reentered the women's quarters and slipped into bed. She stared into the dark for a long time, too anxious to sleep.

Chapter 12

Cam squeezed his eyes shut and attempted to regain control of himself.

He hadn't meant to take things so far. He hadn't meant to touch her at all.

When she'd appeared in the gym doorway, he'd been mulling over the information his brother had given him. Cam hadn't wanted to listen to Mason's advice in real time. But after he hung up, doubt had crept in.

The world was a terrible place, full of terrible people. Cam knew that from experience. It was the reason he'd fled to Alaska. He couldn't accept the circumstances of Jenny's death. Someone had struck her with their car, critically injuring her, and driven on. They'd gotten away with murder.

The trauma of this loss had darkened Cam's soul forever. He wasn't capable of optimism. He'd disconnected from his emotions. Emotions were pain, and he'd had enough pain. He preferred staying numb.

Tala didn't fit into the cold life he'd carved out for himself. She was too young and hot. She had too much baggage. She'd been arrested for assaulting an officer. Cops, even former cops with no faith in criminal justice, didn't take such actions lightly. The fact that she'd fled the country was a bad sign. Innocent people didn't do that.

Cam hated it when Mason was right.

He'd considered confronting her in the hallway, but the space hadn't been private enough, and he didn't want to attract attention. He also wasn't sure how to broach the subject. He'd retreated to the men's bunks, weighing his options. Maybe he shouldn't interrogate her. Why should he delve into her problems? The less he knew, the better.

They didn't have to talk at all.

After staring at the ceiling for an hour, he'd gone to the weight room to burn off steam. And wouldn't you know it, Tala had walked in.

She hadn't come for a workout. Not with her hair falling in loose waves down her back. Not braless and heavy-eyed, her lips parted in invitation. She'd watched him lift weights hungrily. He didn't mind her appreciation of his muscles or whatever, but he preferred being on the other side of the equation. Watching her.

He couldn't enjoy the show for long before he became uncomfortable. In some positions, her sweatshirt rode up, exposing her flat belly and slender rib cage. Her breasts shifted beneath the fabric, nipples taut. She raised her arms high, then bent over and dipped her head low. Her leggings clung to her curvy bottom like they'd been painted on. They also failed to disguise her natural shape in front. He could see the faint outline of her feminine cleft. It wasn't polite of him, but his eyes kept dipping to that spot. He had to jump rope for twenty minutes to get rid of his raging hard-on.

He'd believed her story about Duane. He felt himself getting sucked in again. Instead of demanding more answers, he wanted to wrap his arms around her and make everything better. The thought of losing his heart to her scared him.

So he'd dropped that bombshell about being a cop. He had to tell her who he was. He'd turned his back on the law, but he still had a lot of respect for men and women in uniform. He wasn't stupid, or naive. He was just broken.

Somehow, he'd ended up kissing her. All roads seemed to lead in that direction for him. The argument got his blood pumping. He'd said something accusatory. She'd been defensive. Then they were all over each other.

He hadn't decided what to do with her yet. He was on the fence about…everything. Traveling with her. Sleeping with her. Letting himself feel again. He was tempted to lift her against the wall and go for it.

He'd held himself in check, just barely. Three years of abstinence had wrecked his self-control. There were certain lines he couldn't cross. If he slid his hand into her panties and felt her wet heat, for example—that would be his breaking point. It would be like tasting the frosting on a cake he couldn't eat.

He wanted to eat the cake.

So he didn't touch her below the waist. He'd still managed to get her off, under the false assumption that he could walk away after she was finished. Wrong. The sight of her in the throes of orgasm had undone him. He'd almost come with her. Then she'd dropped to her knees, and he'd lost his mind.

Maybe a stronger man could have said no. He couldn't.

He stayed on the weight bench after Tala left, breathing in and out. The stranger emerged from the bathroom and went back down the hall. Cam waited for several more minutes. His arousal didn't abate.

With a strangled groan, Cam got up and hobbled to the men's room. It was empty. There were two shower stalls. He stripped down for a quick shower. His soapy hand brought some much-needed relief.

He went to his room, crawled into a bunk and slept for six hours. The sleep of the dead, dreamless and deep.

He woke at 5:30, feeling rested. He was used to long days and short nights during the ice-road season. Most of the other truckers were already up, milling around the restaurant. There was a special on ham and egg sandwiches. Cam ordered two, with coffee.

While he sat at the counter, he watched the weather report. The temperature wouldn't rise above zero, and it wasn't even snowing. Welcome to Alaska. A short newsbreak followed the weather update. A ruddy-cheeked journalist in a heavy parka stood in front of yellow police tape on the side of the road.

"A man's body was found in this snowdrift on the outskirts of Willow last night," she said, gesturing to the scene behind her. "The sheriff's office hasn't released a statement about the cause of death, but they are investigating this incident as a homicide. The victim hasn't been identified. They believe he was killed elsewhere."

A chill traveled down Cam's spine as the newscasters

discussed the details. Willow was a small, quiet town, not a hotbed for violent crime.

"First a missing woman, and now this," the news-caster said. "We certainly hope the police find the an-swers they're looking for."

The photo of Tala appeared on the screen, along with the number for the sheriff's station. No mention was made of the alias she'd been using. They didn't give a name at all. Cam wondered if his brother had clued them in about her true identity.

If he hadn't, he would now. Mason was a homicide detective. He wouldn't hesitate to assist an investigation.

It occurred to Cam that Tala might have fled the scene of a murder. She was in more danger than he'd real-ized. He glanced around the restaurant, cursing under his breath. He hoped no one had gotten a glimpse of her in the hallways. The two women she was rooming with weren't in the crowd. He needed to get her out of here before someone recognized her as the missing waitress.

There had to be a connection between Tala and the homicide victim. She was probably a person of interest in the investigation. Maybe she'd witnessed the crime— or been an active participant.

What if the dead man was Duane? What if he'd at-tacked her at the diner, and she'd killed him in self-defense? She'd been rattled and half-frozen when Cam had found her. She looked like she'd seen a ghost. He didn't know how the body had ended up in a second-ary location, or who the other men following her were. There were a lot of things Cam didn't know, because Tala hadn't told him.

He should have tried to get more answers from her last night, but he'd lost focus the instant his lips touched hers. Instead of wringing the truth out of her, he'd wrung an orgasm. He couldn't say he regretted it, either. She had a powerful effect on him. Whenever she was near, his thoughts turned to sex.

Cam smothered a groan of self-derision. He was glad he didn't have cell service. Mason would be blowing up his phone with frantic texts.

Cam needed to talk to Tala before he decided what to do next. His first instinct was to protect her, not himself. He refused to put his own safety above hers. He didn't care about her arrest record. He didn't care about the risks involved. What he cared about was getting her out of Coldfoot, and into his bed.

It wasn't smart to be this obsessed with having her. He realized he was traveling down a slippery slope, throwing caution to the wind. But damn if it didn't feel good to make bad decisions once in a while. It felt good to pursue a desirable woman, after years of denying himself pleasure. He wasn't the same man he used to be, because her possible involvement in a homicide didn't dissuade him. If anything, it added an extra rush of excitement.

When his breakfast sandwiches were ready, he left the restaurant and went to Tala's door. She answered his quiet knock in seconds. Her hair was neatly braided, her face solemn. She already had her backpack on.

"Morning," he said.

She closed the door behind her. "I'm sorry about last night. I'll make it up to you."

He wasn't sure what she was talking about, but they didn't have time to chat. He had to get her out of here and back on the road. As they walked by the front desk, he put his body between Tala and the clerk to shield her from view. Bitter cold enveloped him in the parking lot. He grasped Tala's elbow and headed toward Ice Storm.

Her expression indicated distress, which concerned him. As much as he wanted this thing between them to be purely physical, it wasn't. He unlocked his truck and opened the door for her. Then he climbed behind the wheel, studying her face. She looked close to tears.

"What's wrong?" he asked.

"I was afraid you were going to leave without me."

He started the engine to let it warm up. Had she overheard the news report, and assumed he'd ditch her? "Why would I do that?"

"Because of my criminal record," she murmured. "Then we…you know, and we didn't finish. I mean, I did, but you didn't."

He gave her a curious glance. She didn't know about the homicide investigation. Cam decided not to bring it up. He had no idea how she'd react. "You thought I'd leave you stranded in the middle of nowhere because you came and I didn't?"

She nodded.

He didn't know whether to laugh or feel insulted. Her husband had been a real piece of work. He'd made her assume that all men were selfish and cruel. Cam hoped that Duane Laramie was the human Popsicle from the snowbank, frozen forever in hell. If he wasn't, Cam would like to send him there.

"I didn't mind. I enjoyed it."

Her brow furrowed. "You did?"

"Of course."

"Wouldn't you rather it be…mutual?"

He shrugged. "There's no crime in giving without taking. Haven't you ever done that?"

"Yes. Too often."

"Every time?"

She looked out the foggy window, not answering.

"For the record, I wouldn't leave without saying good-bye. And one orgasm is hardly worth keeping tabs on. When I make you come five or six times in a row, we can start worrying about me getting mine."

Her eyes widened in surprise. "You're kidding, right?"

He smiled, checking his gauges. He wasn't kidding. He was exaggerating a little, but he didn't doubt he could satisfy her. They had good chemistry. Rhythmic stimulation wasn't rocket science. Maybe her husband hadn't bothered to learn the basics, but Cam knew his way around the female body. Even so, he shouldn't be making any promises. He should be thinking about how they were going to get out of this mess. She couldn't run forever. He had to convince Tala to turn herself in before the law—or worse—caught up with her.

There were hundreds of miles between Coldfoot and Deadhorse, which led to Prudhoe Bay. They'd be together all day. Over the next ten or twelve hours, he'd find a way to get some answers from her. But he also had to tread carefully. She wouldn't be easy to interrogate. She had a fiercely independent streak, and she didn't trust law officers. She panicked every time he mentioned calling the police. She'd need a lot of convincing before she cooperated with an investigation. And she wouldn't be pleased to discover that he'd asked his cop-brother to do a background check on her.

He winced, massaging the nape of his neck. He couldn't change what he'd said to Mason. Cam regretted the deception, but not the actions.

They ate breakfast and drank coffee in silence. He enjoyed her company, as always. She had a quiet strength about her, even during moments of stress. He liked her voice, when she chose to speak. Her words carried weight, like her smiles. He wondered if he'd ever learn the truth about why she was running. She might refuse to talk to him. She might bolt at the first sign of trouble. His chest tightened at the thought.

"Maybe I should stay in Prudhoe Bay," she said out of the blue.

"Why would you do that?"

"If they're desperate for workers, it's not a bad idea. I could apply at one of the hotels."

"With what ID?"

She avoided his gaze. "Not every employer requires ID. Some people get paid under the table."

He knew what kind of job she could get "under the table," and he didn't approve. She'd have to make some seedy arrangement with a stranger who wouldn't have her best interests in mind. There were predatory men in Prudhoe Bay who'd take her up on any offer. Rough men who'd left civilization behind. Lonely men, like Cam.

"You're frowning," she said.

He touched his forehead to confirm her claim.

"You don't think I can find work?"

"That's not the problem."

"What is?"

"Prudhoe Bay is about 95 percent men."

"Walt's Diner catered to truckers. Mostly men."

"It's not the same."

"Why not?"

"You weren't trapped at Walt's Diner. Prudhoe Bay is incredibly isolated. If you want to leave, you'll have to buy a plane ticket or hitch a ride with a trucker during the ice-road season, which is only a few months a year."

"It's hard to get out, but it's also hard to get *in*. Maybe I'll feel safe there."

He made a noncommittal sound. They'd already talked about her beauty causing a stir with the truckers in Coldfoot. It would be the same situation in Prudhoe Bay, only worse. There were almost no other women. There were certainly no young, sexy women. She'd stick out like a sore thumb.

"What about your family in Montana?"

She looked away, not answering.

"I'm sure they'd like to hear from you."

"I'm not."

He dropped the subject. He hadn't meant to end the whole conversation, but his comment had that effect. She didn't speak for several hours. Which was fine, because he needed to concentrate on driving. The second leg of the Dalton was even hairier than the first. Avalanche Alley loomed in the distance. Cam had hit a moose on this precarious stretch last year. He was lucky he hadn't gone over the edge.

Most of the morning eked away and the sky brightened. Snow-heavy clouds draped the horizon, promising another blustery winter storm. He hoped for a swift commute and passable weather. The Northern Lights were spectacular in this area, when it was clear.

His thoughts kept returning to last night's furtive encounter. Despite the complications, he couldn't wait to touch her again. He didn't know if any romance could flourish after they tackled the following difficult topics: Did You Kill Your Husband? and Sorry, I Asked My Brother to Investigate You.

Cam raked a hand through his hair, uncomfortable. He could always take her to bed first and save the talking for later. That would be shady as hell, and he'd ruin the chance of ever sleeping with her again, but maybe that was a plus. He wasn't looking for a long-term relationship.

Cam had gone out of his way to help Tala. He'd rescued her from two attackers. If she wanted to share her body with him, why should he deny her? He'd give her pleasure. She'd be well satisfied. They didn't have to make any promises. There were too many secrets between them, too many obstacles to overcome. This was a hot affair, doomed to go down in flames. He might as well end it with a bang.

He didn't have to interrogate her, or convince her to go to the police. He was tired of doing the right thing. He wasn't a cop anymore. He wasn't the strong-but-sensitive husband who went to farmers' markets and charity fund-raisers. He was a cold, hard Alaskan now. He could engage in a one-night stand and walk away. There was nothing wrong with no-strings sex.

She glanced his direction as he shifted gears. "Can I ask you a question?"

"Go for it," he said, pulling his thoughts out of the gutter. They were on an easy stretch of road, with no obstacles in sight.

"Are you still in touch with your family?"

"Yes. They're relentless."

"What do you mean?"

"If I don't call, they badger me. If I don't visit on holidays, I never hear the end of it."

"Who do you call?"

"My mom and my brother."

"What do you talk about?"

He shrugged, evasive.

"You're not much help," she commented.

"You want tips from me on how to reconnect with your family?"

"Do you have some?"

He sighed, shaking his head. She was barking up the wrong tree. "I don't get along with them as well as I used to."

"What happened?"

"My brother and I were close, as kids. He was a typical big brother. He was good at everything. Sports, school, making friends, beating me up."

"He beat you up?"

"Sure. That's how brothers show love."

She chuckled at the assertion. "If you say so."

"I wanted to be like him. He was driven, competitive. He still is."

"Is that bad?"

"It's not bad. He's just sort of…rigid."

"He's rigid?"

"You think I am?"

"You're wound up pretty tight."

Cam considered her perspective. "I'm hard on myself. He's hard on everyone else."

"Ah."

"It's because of his divorce," Cam said. "His wife left him right after mine died. He didn't see it coming, and he doesn't like to lose. So he's been kind of an asshole for a few years, but I think he's getting better."

"Does he look like you?"

"Like me, but clean-cut."

"You're clean-cut. For an Alaskan."

"He wears suits."

She curled up in the passenger seat, tucking her knees to her chest. "What about your mom?"

"What about her?"

"Is she hard on you?"

"She has her moments."

"Give me an example."

"I went home for Thanksgiving a few weeks ago. She invited one of Jenny's friends over without asking me. It was like a blind date that I didn't agree to. She wants me to fall in love and get married again."

"What a monster."

He laughed at her dry response. "You're mocking me, but her guilt trips are legendary. I'm in the dog-house right now for not playing along with her match-making. Apparently, I was supposed to be charming, instead of sullen."

"Was she pretty? This friend?"

"She was okay."

"What was wrong with her?"

"Nothing. She reminded me of Jenny."

"Have you been with anyone else?"

"No."

"Not in three years?"

"I haven't even looked at other women. Until you."

"Why me?"

He glanced in her direction. She was young and beautiful, but that wasn't it. There was something else between them, a connection that went beyond physical chemistry. "You pour a great cup of coffee."

She rolled her eyes, smiling. "Is that all it takes?"

He mulled it over, trying to pinpoint the exact moment he became enthralled with her. "I was watching you at Walt's about a month ago. You were waiting on another trucker. Little guy with red hair. Kind of a jerk."

"Albert?"

Cam didn't know his name. "He reached for something while you were clearing his table and bumped into your arm. His coffee spilled everywhere. I thought he was going to start yelling. You calmly dropped a towel on the table, didn't say a word. You just stared at him. He wiped up the mess and apologized to you."

"It was his fault."

"Yes, it was. But most waitresses would have pretended otherwise."

"They get better tips than me."

"I like you the way you are."

Her lips parted in wonder, as if she was touched by the compliment. He returned his attention to the road, his gut clenched with unease. Yeah, he was in over his head. He needed to pump the brakes on this conversation. He'd just told her how much he *liked* her. That wasn't what you said to a woman you couldn't commit to.

"There's a rough section coming up," he said, avoiding her gaze. "You should get in the back."

She took off her seat belt and climbed into the berth to give him space. It didn't feel like much of a separation. He was still hypersensitive to her presence, aware of her every move. He thought about the unidentified dead body in Willow, frozen in a snowbank. He thought about Jenny, slipping away. The dark discussion he'd been dreading loomed like storm clouds on the horizon. Maybe Tala would clear her name with the police, and he'd move on with his heart intact.

Or maybe he was kidding himself, and it was too late for a clean break.

Chapter 13

December 13
69N
-11 degrees

Tala curled up on the narrow bed in the berth and tried not to panic.

She was getting dangerously attached to Cam. A former cop.

She was falling in love with him, in fact.

This was a total disaster.

She wished she could say she didn't know how it happened, but she did know. He'd rescued her and given her shelter. He'd been a perfect gentleman. He hadn't expected sexual favors. He'd been reluctant to put his arms around her because he knew it would result in his arousal—but he hadn't hesitated to hold her hand. The unselfish choices he'd made had set a series of events into motion, from their chaste embrace at the cabin, to his protective actions in the parking lot, to their sizzling encounter in the weight room.

He'd made her feel valued and respected from the start. He'd seen her as a person, not just a pretty server. He'd noticed something special about her before they even met. He'd admired her as a waitress. How could she resist that?

He was handsome and thrilling and he said nice things. He could control himself. He was capable of being kind and gentle.

But…he'd never love her. He was too hung up on his dead wife. He couldn't erase the woman he'd dedicated his life to and replace her with Tala. He wasn't ready to let go. It would take time for him to open up his heart again.

She didn't have time, unfortunately. She had three madmen chasing after her, threatening to silence her forever.

She closed her eyes and took deep breaths. She wasn't thinking straight. She couldn't trust her emotions right now, with all the stress she was under. Of course she felt attached to Cam, after everything he'd done for her. He was a good man. She was attracted to him. Maybe she'd confused desire and gratitude for deeper feelings.

The fact that she hadn't slept much last night didn't help. She'd convinced herself that Cam was going to leave her behind—or turn her in. He might not be a cop anymore, but he wasn't a typical trucker. He'd come to Alaska to be alone in his grief, not to settle down in a new place. She didn't think he'd make roots here. Maybe he'd go back home and work on the farm. Maybe he'd return to the police force. He wouldn't stay a trucker. He was too physical. He needed to get out and live.

And she needed a backup plan. She couldn't count on Cam to keep her safe, or even stick around. He wasn't ready to make a commitment. He wouldn't want to get tied down to someone like her. She could travel with him for as long as possible, and be ready to run. Or she could hide out in Prudhoe Bay, and be ready to fight.

She'd tossed and turned for hours, weighing her options. In the morning, she hadn't made a decision, but she'd bought herself some insurance. Actually, she'd stolen it. She'd stolen the identification from Lily's wallet.

Tala didn't look like Lily, but they were both dark-haired and the age was close. It would work in a pinch. If employers in Prudhoe Bay were desperate for service staff, they wouldn't question her ID.

She felt guilty about the crime she'd committed, which was another reason to cool it with Cam. He wouldn't approve. She had to stop mooning over him and face reality. They weren't going to ride off into the sunset and live happily ever after. They were going to spend a couple of nights together at the most. Then he'd move on, with or without her.

"This is Avalanche Alley," Cam said over his shoulder.

She sat upright to watch the road as they started a steep climb. There were snow-laden mountains on one side, sheer cliffs on the other. Now that it was full daylight, she could see every terrifying angle. "What do you do if there's an avalanche?"

"Not much you can do if you're in the direct path. Some trucks get swept off the road. Even if you see it coming, it's hard to stop in this area."

"Great," she said, swallowing hard.

"The maintenance crew comes out every week or so to blast the hillside. They create avalanches on purpose. It's the most dangerous job on the Dalton."

She glanced around for a seat belt and didn't find one. Cam continued driving steadily uphill, around hairpin turns. At one point his tires slipped on the icy surface. He cursed under his breath and made some adjustments to the controls to regain traction. After a long, nerve-racking ascent, they reached a flat stretch of road again.

"You can come back up front," he said.

She returned to her seat and secured the belt. "Are we out of the avalanche zone?"

"We're past the worst part. There's an easy section here, then it gets gnarly again after Nightmare Corner."

"Nightmare Corner?"

"Yeah. That's not for another hour."

She noted that the "easy section" was still flanked by steep cliffs, but the elevation remained steady and the road wasn't as narrow. There were places to pull over. After they passed an idling rig, Cam picked up his radio receiver. He had a short conversation with the driver that Tala didn't understand.

"Is he okay?" she asked.

"He's fine. Eating lunch."

"Do you ever pull over to eat?"

"Why, are you hungry?"

She shook her head. The twists and turns made her queasy.

"I don't stop on the Dalton unless I have to, and most other truckers do the same. We're superstitious."

"Of what?"

"There's a story about a trucker from the old days

who pulled over to take a nap. He froze to death. His engine died and he didn't wake up. Since then, everyone who stops between Coldfoot and Deadhorse seems to have some kind of trouble. Gears freeze or whatever. They blame it on Gary's Ghost."

"We had a spirit like that in Yellowknife. My father called him Nahani, the Woodsman. He told me not to wander too far, because Nahani was always in the woods, hunting for souls to take to the spirit world."

He arched a brow. "I don't know if Gary hunts souls, so much as causes delays."

She laughed. "Your spirits aren't as strong as ours."

"Did you believe in the Woodsman?"

"Oh, yes. My dad showed me his tracks one day. There was a set of footprints in the snow that suddenly disappeared. He said the Woodsman could leap to the tops of trees, or turn into a wolf or rabbit. I used to look for him, because I wanted to see how he did it."

He adjusted his gears and switches to accommodate for the level ground. "You weren't afraid of him?"

"I was, but I thought I could run away really fast if I saw him. One day I followed his tracks for several miles before I lost the trail. Then I turned around, and my dad jumped out from behind a tree. I screamed so loud I scared the birds out of the branches."

He smiled at her story. "Was he the Woodsman?"

"Maybe," she said, smiling back at him. "He was the best hunter and tracker in the area."

"Did he hunt alone?"

"He did. When we needed extra money he led hunting expeditions, but he didn't enjoy it. He wasn't into killing animals for sport. And he was a loner, especially after my mother left. He never got over her."

Cam grunted his understanding. He could relate to that problem. Tala wondered if her father would have been happier—and lived longer—if he'd found someone new to love. Her chest tightened with sadness at the thought. Spending time with Cam made her realize how important relationships were. What if she couldn't get over him? She might follow in her father's footsteps and pine away forever.

She fell silent, wishing she'd met Cam under better circumstances. She also wished she could smother her feelings for him.

"Hang on," he said, his brow furrowed. "There's a snowdrift."

She grabbed the handle above the passenger window to brace herself. Seconds later they hit a mound of snow in the middle of the road. It was a nasty surprise of a speedbump. Cam took the jolt in stride, as if these hazards were common. He held the wheel steady as they went over two more in rapid succession.

"Having fun yet?" he asked.

She released a ragged breath, shaking her head.

"Yeah, it's not for everyone."

"But you enjoy the danger."

"I don't mind it."

"Did you enjoy arresting people?"

He gave her a sidelong glance. "I was a highway patrol officer, so I didn't make arrests. I wrote tickets."

She went quiet again. The conversation had veered into uneasy territory, and the road was treacherous enough. Another rig appeared about a mile in the distance, barreling toward them. Her heart dropped as she noticed something in its path. It wasn't a snowdrift, which could be driven over, but a total obstruction.

Cam swore and reached for his radio as the other driver hit the mini-avalanche. Snow exploded over the rig's grill and front window. It was too late for the trucker to slow down, and he couldn't self-correct. Tala let out a terrified scream as the vehicle jackknifed, slid out of control and went plummeting down the cliff.

Cam shouted into the receiver to report the emergency. He pulled to a stop about a hundred feet from the obstruction. He reached for his parka before he climbed out. "Stay here," he ordered.

Tala didn't stay. She tugged on her own jacket before joining him in the bitter cold. The snow must have tumbled across the road seconds or minutes ago. She studied the mountainside on her right, wondering if another, bigger, avalanche might follow. She hurried to catch up with Cam.

He was on the opposite side of the road, standing above a sheer drop. He'd grabbed a heavy length of rope from somewhere. She looked down, her stomach roiling. There was a smoking, busted-up rig below. The windows were smashed, the cab filled with snow. It was half-buried, half-dangling, thirty or forty feet from the edge. It didn't look secure. She could easily imagine the wreck sliding further down the cliff and exploding in flames.

There was no movement but snow flurries. No sound besides the wind.

"I have to get down there," Cam said.

She gaped at him, incredulous. "How? There's nothing to tie a rope to."

He studied the area, his jaw clenched. There were no safety rails or natural features to use as an anchor. His truck was too far away, and there were too many hazards. The snow wasn't stable. Another vehicle could come around the corner any moment. Dropping the rope, he cupped his hands around his mouth and shouted down at the wreckage.

"Hey! Can you hear me? You have to get out! I'll throw you a rope!"

Tala was aware that help might not arrive anytime soon. They were in the middle of nowhere. If the driver was alive, he could very well die before emergency services responded. While she watched, breathless, fingers poked out through the broken window.

"He's alive," Cam and Tala exclaimed at the same time.

The fingers wiggled once, and stilled. They waited for more movement. Cam shouted encouragement until his voice went hoarse. It became clear that there would be no self-rescue. The man couldn't dig himself out of the snow-packed cab. He was going to suffocate.

"I'll go," Tala said, picking up the rope. "I can't hold your weight, but you can hold mine."

"No," Cam said, his eyes wild. "It's too dangerous."

"It's the only way."

He raked a hand through his hair, cursing. "You shouldn't even be out here. I told you to stay in the goddamned truck!"

"He'll die if we do nothing."

After a few seconds of watching her fumble with the rope, he took control and secured one end around her waist. He tied the other end to his own waist. Taking up the slack, he held it in a tight grip. "Whatever you do, don't get the rope caught on the wreckage. If it starts to fall, we'll all go down with it. You have to stay clear."

"I understand," she said. "You've got me?"

"I've got you. Go slow."

She had to brace her boots on the snowy rock face, which made a slippery surface, and lean back into the abyss. Cam gave her a few tips, but mostly he just shut up. His face was taut with worry, his mouth a hard line. Then she couldn't see him anymore. He lowered her with sure hands, steady as a rock. Seconds ticked by and her blood rushed in her ears.

She thought about her father, and how he'd died fighting. She knew he'd been awake after the crash. He'd swum to the surface and tried to punch through the ice. His knuckles had been broken from the effort. He'd needed help, but no one was there.

She couldn't save her father, but she could save this trucker. She could keep fighting.

When she reached the wreck, she fell to her knees on the hood and started scooping out snow with her bare hands. There was a limp arm to guide her. She freed him to the shoulder. His fingers twitched and tears rushed into her eyes. Redoubling her efforts, she tunneled a path toward his head. A weathered face appeared, with a gray mustache and unhealthy pallor. His eyes opened, bloodshot and confused.

"What happened?"

She sobbed with relief. "He's alive," she cried up at Cam. "He's alive!"

The man tried to move, groaning. Tala kept digging. She wept into the snow. After several more minutes, his upper body was exposed and he could breathe easier. He looked more alert, but they weren't out of the woods yet.

"Help me," she panted, tugging on his arms.

He strained forward. Together, they freed him from the snow-packed cab. The truck made an ominous creaking sound.

"Uh-oh," the man said.

Another rope got tossed down to them a moment later. She glanced up the cliff, disoriented. Her arms were tired from digging, her face and hands numb. There was a second figure next to Cam. Nahani, her mind whispered. The Woodsman.

"What's your name, girl?" the trucker asked.

"Tala."

"I'm Phil."

"Anything broken?"

"I don't think so."

She helped Phil loop the rope around his waist. He tied the knot himself. It looked secure. Collapsing on the snow-covered hood, she gave Cam a weak thumbs-up. She started shivering uncontrollably, and she didn't have the energy to climb.

Luckily, she didn't have to do anything. The other men lifted her to the top. Then she was in Cam's arms, warm and safe. He wrapped a blanket around her shoulders and pressed his lips to her forehead.

She didn't want to let go—ever.

But she had to, because their work wasn't done. The figure beside Cam wasn't the woodsman. It was another trucker named Robert. A third man arrived on the scene and offered his assistance. They brought up Phil slowly. He was heavier than Tala, and possibly injured, but leaving him down there wasn't an option.

Phil made it to the top safely. He seemed alert. He had a bump on his head, and some tenderness in his ribs. Tala gave him her blanket. After a short rest, he was able to stand up. He embraced Tala and professed his gratitude.

"You're the prettiest trucker I've ever seen," he said, and everyone laughed.

"I'm not a trucker," she said. "I'm a waitress."

Everyone laughed again, for no particular reason. They were all giddy from the close call and successful rescue. Cam had been right about truck drivers. They weren't antisocial. When someone needed help, they banded together.

"Are you sure you're not my guardian angel?" Phil asked.

"I'm just me."

Phil squeezed her shoulder. "I have a daughter your age," he said, his voice thick. "She wouldn't have a dad right now if it weren't for you. That was a very brave thing you did. I don't know why you did it."

"I told her not to," Cam said, and they all laughed some more.

Tala flushed at the attention, but she felt good about her actions. Phil wasn't exaggerating. He probably would have died if she hadn't dug him out of the snow. "I couldn't have done it without Cam."

Cam nodded an acknowledgment. His quick thinking in grabbing the rope, and his strength in holding her weight, had been essential to the rescue. "It was a group effort," he said, including the others.

Phil thanked everyone with handshakes and claps on the back. The rest of the men grabbed shovels and started clearing the road. They worked with brisk efficiency, part construction crew, part rescue team. Taking a break to help save a guy was no problem, but now they were all business. They had loads to deliver and deadlines to meet.

Tala stood on the sidelines with Phil. She watched Cam shovel until the formal "first responders" appeared. There were two EMTs in a modified ambulance, and a policeman in an SUV. She froze at the sight of the officer's navy blue winter uniform. Her panicked mind supplied the wrong face, morphing him into one of the killers. Then she saw Duane. She blinked to dispel the image, but she couldn't shake the bad feeling. She started shivering again, from a mixture of fear and stress.

There was no escaping an interaction with the authorities. If she tried to avoid them, it would look suspicious.

The EMTs escorted Phil to the ambulance to take care of him. They returned her blanket, which she held with numb hands. The policeman didn't stop to talk to her, which was a relief. She had no idea what to say to him. She'd told Phil her real name. Cam wouldn't lie for her. She was stuck.

While she stood there, trembling, Cam stepped forward to give a statement to the officer. She didn't want to tell a story that might contradict his, so she listened intently. Cam gave the details of the accident without embellishment. Just the facts.

The officer seemed surprised by her part in the rescue. He glanced over the cliff's edge. "She went down there to dig him out?"

Cam nodded.

"Whose idea was that?"

"Hers."

"So you lowered her toward the wreck?"

"Yes."

"How were you planning to get her out?"

"I thought I could pull her up. Then she and I could pull him up."

"That would have been extremely difficult."

Cam didn't argue. Tala hadn't thought that far ahead. They were lucky the two other men had arrived to help.

The officer brandished a pen and notepad. "What's your name, hero?"

"Cameron Hughes."

"And you, miss?"

"Tala Walker," she mumbled, her lips numb.

"Tara?"

"Tala. *T-A-L-A.*" If he returned to his vehicle and entered her name in his computer, he'd get a notification of her outstanding warrants. But maybe he wouldn't bother. As far as he knew, she hadn't done anything wrong.

"You're traveling together?" the officer asked Cam.

"Yes. That's my rig."

"I need to sit down," Tala said. "I feel lightheaded."

The officer shrugged, closing his notebook. "Go ahead."

Cam thanked him and grasped Tala's arm to lead her away. She stumbled forward on unsteady legs. She half expected the policeman to shout at them to stop, but he didn't. She glanced over her shoulder. He wasn't even watching them.

She made it as far as the passenger side of the truck. Then her knees buckled and everything went dark.

Chapter 14

Cam caught Tala before she fell.

He swept her into his arms as her eyelids fluttered closed. She made a moaning sound, resting her head against his shoulder. He lifted her into the cab and deposited her into the passenger seat with a grunt of exertion. It was warm inside, because he'd left the engine running and the heat on. He adjusted the blanket over her body to keep her cozy. By the time he got behind the wheel, she was awake again.

He handed her a bottle of water. She drank half of it and gave it back.

"Are you okay?" he asked.

"I'm fine."

"You fainted."

"I know."

"You also saved a man's life."

"I remember. Can we go now?"

The road was clear, but Cam wasn't in a hurry to leave. He took off his parka and used the restroom while they were stopped. She set aside her blanket and did the same, without help. He grabbed some snacks from the mini-fridge. He had fruit juice and whole wheat crackers. She accepted both.

He didn't think she needed medical attention. Her color looked better. He turned the heat all the way up. Then he put on his seat belt and pulled forward. The other truckers waved goodbye as they left the scene. Cam waved back.

"I guess the secret's out," Tala said.

"Which secret?"

"You're riding with an unapproved passenger."

"They don't know you're not approved."

"This story will get around."

He agreed that it would, and he didn't really care. If he was going to get fired for having a sexy, mysterious companion who rescued strangers, so be it. There were worse ways to go. "What you did was amazing."

"Stop," she said, nibbling on a cracker. "You're embarrassing me."

"I'm sorry I told you not to do it."

"It's okay. I wouldn't have wanted to watch you go down there, either."

He kept his eyes on the road, but his thoughts lingered on her. Her face, her actions, her uncommon bravery. "You were fearless."

"I wasn't fearless. I just fainted."

"That doesn't change anything."

"If you'd fainted, would you feel like a tough guy?"

He laughed at the question, shaking his head. He hadn't felt very tough while she was digging in the snow.

He'd been sick with terror and worry. If the wreckage had slipped, they might have all gone with it. He'd held the rope in a death grip, determined to hang on, no matter what. Letting go wasn't an option.

It still wasn't.

He came to the startling realization that he couldn't walk away from her. He'd been willing to risk his life for her. He wanted more than one night with her. A lot more.

The idea of getting seriously involved with anyone rattled him. He glanced in her direction, frowning. Her actions had been incredibly heroic. She was beautiful and exciting. He enjoyed talking to her, and he wasn't much of a talker. They were having a good time together, despite the circumstances. They'd just executed a daring rescue. Maybe he was high on adrenaline and temporarily enamored.

Yes. That explained it.

Relief washed over him, rinsing away the aftereffects of panic. Danger always heightened the senses. They'd bonded in the hotel room the first night. He felt a strong connection to her, and he still wanted her in his bed, but this infatuation would pass. Eventually.

"I told that cop my real name."

He flinched at her sudden words. "What?"

"I told him my name. Do you think he'll search me in the system?"

"Cops don't have time to run everyone without cause. They do it for a clear violation or suspicion of a crime."

"You said my picture was on TV."

He grunted an acknowledgment. Her photo had probably been distributed to every law enforcement agency in Alaska, not just the local news outlets. "If he recognized you, he would have said so."

She went quiet, huddled beneath the blanket.

Cam didn't tell her that her real name would appear in the police report. As soon as that information was entered in the database, it would trigger an alert about her outstanding warrants. Which might not attract much notice, all by itself. Many districts were understaffed and unable to hunt down every offender. If her name came up as a person of interest in a murder investigation, that was different. Locating her would become a high priority.

Cam felt guilty about the role he'd played in her evasion. Although he hadn't lied to the police officer, he'd kept her secrets and helped her slip away. He'd been reluctant to betray her confidence before he'd heard her side of the story. When they stopped at the hotel in Prudhoe Bay, they'd have a frank discussion. He'd ask her about the dead man in Willow. He didn't think she'd want to warm his bed afterwards. Which was probably for the best, considering his overwrought feelings. Sleeping with her wouldn't help him disconnect.

He noted that she was still shivering. "Are your clothes wet?"

"Just my jeans."

"Take them off. You can wear my sweatpants."

She went to the berth to get changed. He focused on the road, not watching her undress. She returned after a few minutes. He didn't ask her to stay in the back. It was warmer up front, and he could keep an eye on her condition.

Daylight faded quickly. North of Coldfoot, in the dead of winter, they got three or four hours of sun at the most. It messed with everyone's circadian rhythms. Sometimes Cam felt like a vampire, only half-alive. Before he met

Tala, he'd embraced the dark. Now he found himself wanting more light.

He rounded Nightmare Corner without incident and navigated the remaining obstacles. There were drifts and cliffs and narrow passages. Nothing he couldn't handle. While he drove, he thought about how lucky they'd been to witness that accident. If the other truck hadn't been coming toward them, Cam might not have seen the obstruction. It could have just as easily been him crashing into the snow mound and flying off the road.

And Phil would be dead right now, if not for Tala. Cam couldn't have climbed down to the wreckage on his own. Help hadn't arrived for ten minutes or more. Tala's quick thinking had saved the man's life.

There was some chatter on the radio about the accident, but not much. The story would circulate tomorrow. Once the truckers in Coldfoot Camp heard the tale, they'd spread it all over Alaska. Embellishments would be added. By the time Cam returned to Fairbanks, they'd be saying he'd sledded down an avalanche and picked up a guardian angel. The speculation about Tala would run rampant. He groaned, imagining the gossip. They'd assume she was his girlfriend, or his paid companion. Someone might realize she was the missing waitress from Walt's Diner. The trucking company would question him about the incident. If they frowned on his behavior, Cam wouldn't get any more ice-road contracts.

Which was a shame, because working on the Dalton had kept him alive for the past three years. The extreme danger had triggered his survival instincts. He'd needed a challenge as much as he'd needed solitude. But maybe he didn't need either as much as he used to.

The hours ticked by and the temperature dropped.

As he approached Deadfoot, he braced himself for a confrontation with the site supervisor, or even the police. His eyes felt grainy, his neck tight with tension. He pulled into the yard and parked, letting the engine idle. There were several other rigs in the area. Tala had fallen asleep in the passenger seat with her backpack clutched to her chest.

He picked up the radio to check in. "Hughes," he said, and recited the order number. Tala jerked awake with a start. Her backpack tumbled to the ground between them.

"You're clear to continue to Prudhoe Bay."

Cam replied an affirmative and ended the transmission. So far, so good. He hadn't been called into the office. No one had even mentioned the accident. Maybe they were too busy to deal with him right now. Truck yards were notoriously chaotic. Shrugging, he removed his seat belt and reached for his parka.

"What are you doing?" Tala asked. Her voice was husky from sleep.

"Taking off the chains. I'll be right back."

He climbed out, wincing at the cold bite of wind. He put on his gloves and removed the sets of chains. By the time he was finished, his face was numb. He hurried back to the cab to get warm. Tala handed him a cup of instant soup, which she'd heated in the microwave. He accepted it with gratitude.

"You don't need chains for the ice road?" she asked.

"It depends on the temperature and conditions. When it's really cold, tires have good traction, and the weight of the load helps them grip. The main danger isn't slipping so much as breaking through."

Her eyes widened in distress. Too late, he remembered the story of her father's death.

"Sorry," he said gruffly. "The ice gets slushy at the end of the season. Right now, it's rock-solid, and they test it every week."

She put another cup of soup in the microwave, avoiding his gaze.

"This section is the safest part of the route. It's wide and flat, and the speed limit is ten miles per hour. You'll be bored."

"I won't be bored," she said.

He sipped his soup instead of arguing. She went into the bathroom and slid the door shut. The motion caused her backpack to tip on its side. A book fell out, so he picked it up and flipped through the pages. He'd never read a graphic novel before. He'd expected it to be like a comic, with superheroes and action reels.

It had action reels. Just a different kind of action than he'd anticipated. There were several lovingly detailed illustrations of a couple having sex.

The microwave dinged, which startled him into returning the book to her backpack. He noticed an ID card inside. He was already snooping, so he glanced at the card quickly before putting it back. She emerged from the bathroom and retrieved her soup. They finished the meal in silence. His thoughts boomeranged from erotic art and hot memories to stolen IDs and frozen wastelands.

"Are you sure you want to come with me to Prudhoe Bay?" he asked.

Her brow furrowed. "What choice do I have?"

"There's a camp here like the one in Coldfoot. Separate bunks for men and women."

"Is that what you want? Separate bunks?"

"No."

"Then let's keep going."

He tossed his empty cup in the trash, feeling conflicted. A part of him wanted to confront her right now about the ID and everything else. Another part of him, centered below the waist, wanted to take her to the hotel and not talk at all. He drummed his fingertips against the wheel, searching for a good compromise.

"When we get there, we need to have a conversation about what happened in Willow."

She drew in a sharp breath and held it. For a moment he thought she might refuse. She seemed more comfortable with the idea of sharing her body than telling her secrets. Then she gave a terse nod.

He felt a mixture of relief and unease as he pulled forward. He hoped he hadn't negotiated himself out of her bed. Sleeping with her was a bad idea. It would cross a line he couldn't come back from, but he was willing to take that chance. He'd do anything to touch her again. He could sacrifice his ice road contract. He could even give up on staying numb and protecting his frozen heart.

The pages of her graphic novel had captured his imagination. It read like a window into her desires. Her reaction to last night's orgasm had been telling. She wasn't experienced in receiving pleasure. Giving her a taste of what she'd been missing was an irresistible temptation. If she let him, he'd show her how good it could be.

The ice road was as uneventful as he'd promised. At night, the frozen pathway looked like regular asphalt, tracked with snow. Broad daylight turned it into a sparkling mosaic, crystal blue in some places, foggy gray in others. There were clear sections that resembled glass, and you could see the ocean beneath it.

Ice crackled under his truck's weight as they traveled

toward the bay. It was a disconcerting sound, but normal. The ice shifted and moved with the weight of the vehicle, like a reed that would bend rather than break.

"Why do you have to go this slow?" she asked, gripping her armrests.

"Driving over ice causes waves to form under the surface. The faster you go, the more powerful the wave. When two opposing waves crash together, it creates a surge of energy, like an earthquake."

"So if two trucks go toward each other too fast, the ice cracks?"

"Yes. That's why the route is restricted to a few trucks at a time traveling at low speeds. There's no rush hour. No crashing waves."

"No ice-quakes."

"No ice-quakes," he agreed.

The information didn't seem to calm her nerves. She kept her eyes on the surface, as if searching for signs of trouble. Cam wasn't worried about the ice failing. All his fears and anxieties were focused elsewhere.

Time stretched into infinity on the way to Prudhoe Bay. Although the distance was short, the route was slow and arduous. It took over an hour to reach the construction zone, and another hour to unload the trailer. Then they were on the road again.

The best hotel in the bay was located between the sprawling oil fields and a small airport. It offered private, comfortable rooms for executives and engineers who could afford the expense. Truckers tended to choose the cheapest accommodations, so there were no other rigs in the parking lot. Cam paid at the front desk while Tala waited outside. Then they grabbed dinner in the empty café. He was too nervous to eat much. She nibbled on fruit, which drew his attention to her lips. Her braids were softly mussed, her eyes luminous. She wasn't the most beautiful woman he'd ever seen, but she was close. She was breathtaking.

It dawned on him that he couldn't remember every detail of Jenny's face anymore. When he conjured an image of her, it was from a photograph he'd memorized. She'd had a great smile. She'd laughed often, but he didn't hear the sound in his head. He couldn't picture her hand gestures, or the exact shade of her hair. He no longer felt the crushing pain of loss, either. Just a faint ache.

When they were finished, they went down the hall to his room. It wasn't as cozy as Ann's Cabins, or as rustic as Coldfoot Camp. The walls and carpet were a nondescript beige. A large bed with white sheets and a thick comforter took up about half the space. He set his duffel by the flat-screen TV. She placed her backpack in the only chair.

They stared at each other for a couple of seconds. He cleared his throat, trying to think of a conversation opener.

Then she ambushed him.

She rushed forward and collided with his chest. He made a sound of surprise as she wrapped her arms around his neck and pressed her lips to his. He didn't object to her kiss, though he recognized it as an attempt to silence him. The move worked like a charm. She touched her tongue to his and twined her fingers in his hair. Her mouth was hot and sweet and eager. He responded with an enthusiastic groan. He'd accept a frantic groping by a beautiful woman. His body didn't care about the reasons for her urgency. She was clutching his hair and rubbing against him. He responded predictably.

She kept moving forward until he fell back on the bed. He brought her on top of him, forgetting everything he'd meant to say. She straddled his waist, just as she had the previous night. The thought of repeating that sequence without clothes on exploded in his mind. His hands slid under her shirt, seeking warm skin and soft breasts. She was wearing a bra with lacy cups. His thumbs brushed over her taut nipples, making her gasp.

She stared down at him, lips parted. Tulips in spring. He imagined that mouth on his chest, trailing lower. He shuddered in anticipation. She rocked her hips back and forth, dipping her head to kiss him again. He felt deliciously trapped underneath her, and he liked it, but he needed to take control. If he let her set the pace, this would be over in minutes.

He wanted to undress her slowly and learn every inch of her body. He wanted to show her the consideration her husband hadn't.

Her dead husband.

Oof.

He broke the kiss, panting. He'd forgotten their talk, which really needed to happen now. Waiting until after wouldn't be gentlemanly. It would ruin the trust they'd built. He wished he didn't care, but he did. She'd thawed out his heart, and now he couldn't just bang her.

Very carefully, he lifted her off him and set her aside.

"What's wrong?" she murmured.

"We have to talk."

"Now?"

"Yes. Now."

She glanced at his erection, her gaze half-lidded. "I'd rather do something else."

Smothering a groan, he rose from the bed. "So would

I, but I have to say this first. You know that news report I told you about, with your photo?"

"Yes."

"There's been an update. The police found a dead body in Willow."

She swallowed visibly. "Oh?"

"Foul play is suspected. They ran your picture again without the fake name."

Her face paled as she digested this information.

"You're not just a missing waitress any longer, Tala. You're connected to a murder investigation."

Chapter 15

Tala's breaths quickened and her thoughts spun out of control.

She wasn't sure how to interpret this new development, or Cam's insistence on sharing it. Didn't he want to sleep with her? His body was clearly ready, and he'd responded to her kisses, only to push her aside and share this news.

Sure, she'd had an ulterior motive. She'd jumped on him to avoid this very conversation, but it hadn't worked. She wasn't sexy enough to tempt him. Her chest tightened with shame. Cheeks flaming, she stared at the carpet beneath his feet.

"Was it self-defense?" he asked.

Her gaze rose to his face. "What?"

"Did Duane come after you, and you defended yourself?"

She blinked in confusion. It dawned on her that he

thought she'd been an active participant in the murder. He thought the dead body in Willow belonged to Duane. She rose to her feet and crossed her arms over her chest, frowning. "When did you watch the news?"

"This morning, in Coldfoot."

"You saw it this morning, and you didn't tell me?"

He inclined his head.

"Why did you wait?"

"I didn't know how you'd react."

She gaped at him, incredulous.

"I thought you might freak out," he said, raking a hand through his hair. "I decided not to bring it up until we were alone and in a safe place."

"You waited until you had control of the situation, and I couldn't run away."

"That's not fair."

"Isn't it?"

"I could have waited until tomorrow morning," he said pointedly.

She would have preferred that. "Why didn't you?"

"Because I care about you," he growled. "I actually want to help you even more than I want to sleep with you!"

"Maybe you just want to ruin it," she shot back. "You're afraid to sleep with me. You'd rather avoid intimacy and stay true to your dead wife."

His eyes narrowed in warning. "We're not talking about my dead wife right now. We're talking about your dead husband. I'm not trying to ruin my chances to be with you. I'm trying to keep you safe. I'm thinking about the long term."

"The long term? Really?"

"You don't believe me?"

"You're not ready for that, Cam. You have to let go before you can move on."

"I'll work on it, if you meet me halfway. Tell me what happened in Willow."

"I can't."

"Why not?"

"Because you'll call the police. You were a cop. You know them."

"I don't know any cops in Alaska. I won't call them."

She sat down, twisting her hands in her lap.

"I want to protect you, but I can't do it blindly. I need to understand what you did and who we're up against."

"I didn't do anything."

"Come on, Tala. A dead body turned up the day after you went missing. You have to know something."

"You think I killed him?"

"I wouldn't blame you if you did."

He meant it. She could read the sincerity in his stellar brown eyes, along with strength and kindness. He wasn't perfect, but he was a good man. She wouldn't find a better person to share her secrets with. The prospect of reliving those dark details made her break out in a cold sweat. She took a deep breath, wondering if it was possible to explode from anxiety. "The dead man isn't Duane," she said finally. "I'd kill him in a heartbeat, but I didn't."

"Did he hire someone to track you down?"

"He wouldn't do that."

"Why not?"

"Because he's a loner who enjoys the hunt. He'd come alone. This has nothing to do with him."

Cam frowned at this news. "If it's not Duane, who is it?"

"A customer," she said, moistening her lips. She had to tell him the whole story. "He walked in the diner with two other men, first thing in the morning. They ordered breakfast. A cop came in around the same time. He sat at the counter by himself. There was a weird vibe between them, like they knew each other, but they were pretending not to."

"Were they regulars?"

"I hadn't seen any of them before."

"What kind of cop?"

"State police. He had a white squad car and a dark blue uniform."

"Go on."

She swallowed hard. "The three men ate breakfast and left. Two of them didn't finish their plates, which was a little strange. I took out the trash while they were still in the parking lot. When I heard the gunshot, I crouched down and hid. The cop stood watch while they loaded the body into the trunk of a car."

"What kind of car?"

"An old sedan. I don't know."

"Who did the shooting?"

"The blond one, I'm assuming. He had the gun."

"Was this same guy from the Walmart parking lot?"

"Yes."

"Why did you run?"

"Because the cop told them to clean up the mess and pointed to the diner. They went inside to get me. I waited until the cop left. Then I started running."

"Did they see you?"

"I don't think so, but I left the trash gate open. There was nowhere to hide. They must have figured I ran to the truck stop."

"The cop was the leader?"

"I guess."

"Shooting a guy in a public parking lot isn't a smart move."

Tala nodded in agreement. "The cop seemed angry about it. Maybe it wasn't supposed to go down like that."

"Something was supposed to go down. They were too nervous to eat."

"The victim ate."

"He didn't know what was coming," Cam said, pacing the room. "For whatever reason, they killed him on the spot. Then they had to deal with you. When you ran away from the diner, they knew you'd witnessed the crime. They probably saw my truck pull out of the lot and head north. So they dumped the body and came after us."

The succinct summary gave her chills. "And now I'm doomed."

"You're not doomed," Cam said. "We'll figure this out."

Tala took a few deep breaths to calm herself. He sounded optimistic, in addition to sympathetic. He hadn't questioned her story or acted suspicious. His faith in her was reassuring. She supposed the details weren't as shocking as he'd imagined. "Are you glad I'm not a murderer?"

"I'm kind of disappointed your ex is still alive, actually."

She smiled at his dark joke. His opinion mattered to her, because she cared about him. She was glad he hadn't judged her. He hadn't criticized her for running away. He'd believed her. She felt like a weight had been

lifted off her shoulders. She didn't feel alone anymore.
Maybe they could figure this out—together.

He stopped pacing and studied her. "I understand why
you don't want to call the state police."

"I don't want to call any police."

"What if we went to someone I trust in Seattle?"

"How would I get there?"

"I'll take you."

She stood, shaking her head. Talking to him was
one thing, but she wasn't ready to make a decision of
this magnitude. Going to Seattle with Cam meant stepping out of her comfort zone. It meant working with law
enforcement and trusting a justice system that hadn't
served her people well, historically. It meant opening
herself up to prosecution for her own crimes. It meant
that she had to stop running and hiding. That was a lot.

He waited for her to respond, not pressuring her.

"I'll think about it," she murmured.

"That's what you said when I offered to set you up in
a cabin in Fairbanks."

Her pulse kicked up a notch at the reminder. They
were still circling around the idea of sleeping together.
The comment he'd made earlier about giving her lots of
orgasms hung in the air between them. She wanted to
return the favor—and not because she felt grateful, or
obligated. She wanted to be with him for herself.

His gaze lowered to her lips and lingered there. Her
seduction attempt hadn't failed; it had been momentarily
interrupted. There was no lack of desire on his part. His
intentions hadn't changed.

Her cheeks suffused with heat. "I should take a
shower."

"Be my guest."

She grabbed her backpack before heading into the bathroom. It had clean white tiles, a small sink and a new-looking bathtub. She hadn't taken a bath in ages, so she filled the tub for a nice soak. She took the time to wash her hair and shave her legs. He was going to see her naked, up close and personal. She didn't know if they could be together "long term." If tonight was all they had, she wanted it to be special.

When she emerged from the bathroom, fresh-scrubbed and wrapped in towels, Cam was standing by the only window. The hotel wasn't fancy, and the oil fields in the distance didn't improve the bleak landscape, but the sky was spectacular. Northern lights trailed across the starry expanse, misty and ethereal.

His gaze wasn't on the view, however. It was on her flushed face, her damp hair and bare shoulders. He examined the length of her legs, taking the scenic route. His expression was taut with desire, his fists clenched. Male attention had often made her self-conscious, even afraid. Cam's gaze made her feel powerful and deliciously sexy. She wasn't afraid he'd hurt her. Anticipation sizzled across her skin.

He seemed eager to get started, but he didn't pounce on her. "Do you want me to shave?" he asked, touching his beard.

"No. I like you the way you are."

With a slow nod, he brushed by her and disappeared in the bathroom. She applied vanilla-scented moisturizer to her arms and legs while he showered. Then she sat down by the heating vent to comb her hair. He finished his shower and came out wearing only the sweatpants she'd borrowed. She'd left them in the bathroom for him. His hair was tousled and wet. He had a towel draped around his neck.

Her eyes traveled from his handsome face to his well-muscled torso. Last night, his sweatpants had molded to his male parts in a vaguely revealing manner. Tonight, she could see he wasn't wearing a stitch underneath them. His waistband rode low on his flat abdomen. He toweled his hair while she finished combing hers.

"Leave it down," he said, watching her.

She set aside the comb and put her toiletries away. Her heart was racing, her stomach fluttering with excitement. She was already aroused and he hadn't even touched her yet.

He moved to the edge of the bed and sat down. Letting her come to him. She went. She kept her towel clutched in a death grip, but she went. She stood before him, trembling. He rested one hand on the outside of her thigh, just above the knee. His palm was warm and strong.

"We don't have to do this," he said.

"I know."

"We could cuddle instead."

She was too nervous to laugh. He didn't want to cuddle, judging by his arousal. His sweatpants strained at the front.

"I have a condom in my pocket. Good?"

"Good."

"Maybe we should establish some signals."

"For what?"

"If you want me to go slower, you can tap my shoulder."

She touched his shoulder with two fingertips. "Slower."

He nodded. "What about stop?"

She placed her palm on his chest, as if preparing to push him back.

"Got it."

She slid her hand to his biceps and squeezed.

"What's that?"

"Keep going."

His lips curved into a smile. She gave his arm another squeeze. He took the hint and stopped talking. She liked his idea, but she didn't think she'd need the first two signals.

She twined her arms around his neck as he lifted his mouth to hers. He kissed her languidly, not rushing. She parted her lips for his tongue. He tasted like mint, clean and hot. Every stroke of his tongue seemed designed to melt her from the inside out. Her nipples pebbled against the damp towel and heat pulsed between her legs. She twisted her fingers in his hair, moaning. His hands moved under her towel, to her hips, and urged her closer. She straddled his waist eagerly. He reclined on his back with a low groan. His erection surged against her.

They kept kissing, and her towel fell away. She didn't feel embarrassed, even when he paused to look at her. She felt desired on a deeper level. He saw more than a sex object, and that made her want to show him everything. She arched her spine, putting her breasts on full display. He moistened his lips at the sight.

"I fantasized about this last night," he said, his breaths ragged. "I imagined you naked on top of me." His big hands skimmed her sides, settling on her rib cage and framing her breasts. "You're so beautiful."

"Touch me."

He cupped her soft flesh, pushing her breasts together to create a deep V between them. She groaned

as he stroked his thumbs over her nipples. He replaced
his hands with his mouth, sucking the taut nubs. She
squeezed his arm, because it was so good. Her hips
moved back and forth, seeking the same friction they'd
generated last night.

"Do you ever touch yourself?" he asked.

"Yes," she breathed, shuddering.

"Show me."

He rested his weight on his elbows, giving her space.
She moved her hands to her breasts. She used a softer
touch than he did, circling her wet nipples with her fingertips. Then she pinched them lightly.

His erection throbbed against her, and his jaw
clenched with arousal. He lifted her off his lap abruptly,
tossing her on her back. His gaze settled between her
legs. Her first instinct was to close them, but he didn't
let her. He braced his hands on her inner thighs, spreading her wider. "More."

She blinked at the command. He wanted her to continue the show. Maybe she did need those first two signals. They flashed in her mind like a safety net, available
if she chose to use them. There was comfort in knowing
she could stop him anytime she wished. But she didn't
want to stop. His eyes blazed with spectacular intensity.
She longed to please him, and herself. She slid her hands
down her belly. Her fingertips skimmed her sensitive
flesh. Shivering, she slipped one finger inside.

"That's it," he said.

She added another finger, pumping in and out. She
was very slippery and warm. He watched her movements as if mesmerized. When she removed her fingers
from her body, he grasped her wrist and brought them

to his mouth. He sucked one, then the other. Her stomach quivered at the erotic sight.

He didn't tell her to keep going, but she did. He didn't have to hold her legs open, either. She circled her clitoris, thighs parted wide.

"That's pretty," he said, his throat working. "That's so pretty. I'm going to come, just looking at you."

She moaned, stroking faster.

"Can I taste you?"

He already had, and she hadn't objected. She nodded her permission. A few minutes ago, she might have been too shy to ask for this, or even allow it. Now she was panting for it. When he settled his mouth between her legs, she clutched his hair and held him there. He smiled at her boldness, murmuring his approval. Then he touched his tongue to her. He sucked and licked her clitoris as tenderly as he'd kissed her mouth. He savored her as if she were a delicious treat. She'd never felt anything so heavenly. Pleasure rushed over her in endless waves. They rippled beneath the surface, gaining speed. She watched his tongue, warm and wet and precisely placed. He eased off the pressure, letting her teeter on the edge of orgasm.

She needed another signal, for Finish Me, please!

Animal sounds emerged from her throat and her head thrashed against the blankets. She fisted his hair desperately. He sucked her harder, and that was all it took. The wave broke in a brilliant surge of energy, crashing through her. She sobbed and shuddered and bucked against his mouth in helpless ecstasy. The immense power of it overwhelmed her. She'd never come like that on her own.

When she opened her eyes, he was watching her. She

released his hair, murmuring a vague apology. Languid satisfaction drizzled through her bones. She couldn't move. He seemed amused by her stupefied state. He wiped his smug mouth with one hand and rolled off the bed, heading to the bathroom. He filled a cup at the sink and drank. Then he brought the water to her. She sipped it.

He rejoined her on the bed. Instead of climbing on top of her, he stretched out on his back, tucking his hands behind his head. His erection jutted against the front of his sweatpants, proof of his desire. And yet, he waited patiently for her to recover.

He'd given her the best orgasm of her life, and he wasn't in a hurry to get his. The level of caring and generosity overwhelmed her.

Tears sprang to her eyes and her throat closed up. "I've never…"

He grasped her hand and held it. "I know."

He brought her knuckles toward his lips for a kiss. Tender emotions swelled inside her. She wanted to tell him she loved him, but she was afraid to ruin the moment. She didn't think he was ready for that level of emotion. So she showed how she felt instead.

She climbed on top of him and pressed her lips to his. His tongue penetrated her mouth in bold strokes, hinting at pleasures to come. She moaned at the thought. His erection felt huge and hot against her stomach. With another man, she might have been wary of his size. With Cam, she was excited. She needed him inside her, filling her to the hilt.

She broke the kiss and trailed her mouth down his chest. She touched her lips to his collarbone, his sternum, and lower. He threaded his fingers through her hair, caressing the long strands. She kissed his taut belly. He'd wanted this last night, and he wanted it tonight. His eyes blazed with hunger. But when she tugged at his waistband to release his erection, he groaned and stopped her.

"Next time," he said. "I won't last a second in your mouth."

"I don't care if you last."

"I do."

She reclined on the bed, acquiescent. He removed the condom from his pocket and took off his sweatpants. His arousal bobbed straight up against his belly. She moistened her lips in anticipation. He was long and thick, swollen with veins. It looked painful, and she longed to soothe that taut skin with her tongue.

He rolled the condom over his shaft. She parted her thighs in invitation. His nostrils flared at the sight. He stretched out on top of her, taking her mouth again. She slipped her arms around his neck and kissed him back. His latex-covered length slid along her swollen cleft, sending sparks of sensation all through her body.

He didn't rush to enter her. He feasted on her neck and breasts, flicking his tongue over her stiff nipples. She slid her hand between them and gripped his shaft. He inhaled a sharp breath, his gaze locked on hers. She guided him to her opening. With a low groan, he gave her what she wanted.

Although she was slippery from her orgasm, and eager to accept him, it had been months since she'd accommodated a penis. Never one this large. He pushed inside carefully, inch by inch. His arm muscles trembled from the effort of holding himself in check. When he was about halfway in, he had to thrust forward. She gasped at the intrusion, bracing her palms on his chest. He withdrew immediately.

It took her a moment to realize that she'd given the stop signal. He was breathing heavily, his stomach quivering.

Tears sprang into her eyes again and she kissed him, laughing a little. If she hadn't been sure of her feelings before, she was sure now. She loved him. She squeezed his arm and wrapped her legs around his waist. He seemed hesitant, so she whispered in his ear.

"I want you inside me."

He reentered her slowly, but he didn't need to. The twinge of discomfort she'd felt after his initial penetration was gone. She used her heels to urge him forward. He drove into her slick heat, making them both groan with satisfaction. She kissed him with an open mouth, squeezing his arms and neck and everything she could reach.

He buried himself in her, again and again. They kissed and touched and thrust together, limbs entangled. His mouth had been amazing, but this was even better.

This was pure ecstasy.

He reached between them to stroke her clitoris at regular intervals. His caresses seemed designed to keep her in a pre-orgasmic state. Tension built to an unbearable point inside her. She begged for release, sobbing his name. He licked his fingertips and made her come. She fisted her hands in his hair, screaming and shuddering.

He soothed her with a thorough kiss, still moving on top of her. Seconds later, he reached his own climax. His hips jerked forward in heavy thrusts. He let out a hoarse cry and drove deep inside her.

They collapsed together, totally spent. He didn't withdraw. She didn't want him to. She stroked his damp back for several moments. Finally, he pulled out, holding the condom in place, and went to dispose of it in the bathroom. When he returned, they crawled under the blankets. She cuddled up against him, drowsily satiated. She felt happy and safe and well-loved. Even if it was just physical for him, it wasn't for her.

She fell asleep and dreamed of a better future.

Chapter 16

December 14
70N
-17 degrees

The sun didn't rise until midmorning.

For the first time in years, Cam slept late. He'd stayed up half the night with Tala, reaching for her over and over again. Every time he touched her, she responded with enthusiasm. So he kept doing it. He'd probably *over-* done it, but he hadn't heard any complaints from her side of the bed. Her soft cries of pleasure had urged him on.

He finally got up, spurred by hunger and a niggling feeling of unease. He had no idea what to expect from Tala. They'd discussed the danger she was in and considered their options. He'd offered to take her to Seattle, but she hadn't accepted. He didn't know if they'd get stopped on the way. She was right to be concerned about state police.

He studied her nude form as he pulled on his sweatpants. She was curled up on one side, facing away from him. Her dark hair spilled across the white pillows, black as ink. Her vibrant skin made a pretty contrast with the pale bedding. Every inch of her was smooth and supple. The sheets were tangled low on her hips, exposing her elegant back and the upper half of her buttocks. His blood heated with arousal, despite the marathon of sex they'd engaged in. He entertained the idea of climbing back into bed with her. Kissing his way up her spine, taking her from behind.

A notification from his phone interrupted that fantasy. He retrieved it from his duffel with a frown. He hadn't realized there was cell service in this frigid wasteland.

Deadfoot was a dead zone, unsurprisingly. Prudhoe Bay was more of an industrial hub, so it made sense that they had cell towers. He'd never spent the night here, and he wasn't big on staying connected, anyway.

He rubbed his sleepy eyes and glanced at the screen. Mason. Of course.

Tension gripped him. Feeling guilty on several different levels, he ducked into the bathroom to check his messages. Mason had sent him a series of cryptic texts. When Cam tried to return his call, Mason didn't pick up. Cam silenced his phone and set it aside. He'd try again later. He realized that he hadn't told Tala about his brother or the background check last night. He winced at the thought of having that conversation this morning.

He studied his reflection in the mirror, contemplative. He looked tired but satisfied. Every moment with her was worth it.

Cam used the toilet and washed his hands quickly. Then he opened the door. Tala was still in bed, in the same position he'd left her. Her eyes were closed, her face serene. The heating unit next to her rattled and hummed with constant white noise. His movements hadn't woken her. Relieved, he tucked his phone away and climbed back into bed with her. He'd tell her about Mason…later. She made a sleepy sound when he touched his lips to her bare shoulder. When he slid his hands beneath the blankets to capture her hips, she murmured a faint protest.

"It's getting late," he said.

"You didn't let me sleep last night."

He pushed her hair aside and kissed the nape of her neck. "Mmm."

"Are you trying to keep me in bed or wake me up?"

"Lady's choice."

She groaned and pulled away from him, declining his offer. Which was probably for the best, since they were out of condoms, and he needed to get on the road as soon as possible. He also needed to call Mason.

She rose from the bed, stark naked. His breath caught in his throat at the sight of her. He hadn't seen her in the daylight before. White rays filtered in between the layers of curtains, illuminating her lovely curves. She was all dark hair and soft skin. Angelic, otherworldly…and achingly beautiful.

"Jesus," he said in a hushed voice.

She covered herself with her hands, self-conscious. His gaze rose to her face. "I can't get enough of you."

She moistened her lips. Her eyes were troubled, as if she had something important to say. But she ducked into the bathroom before he could ask. His stomach growled, reminding him that they'd skipped dinner last night. He rose from the bed and pulled on his clothes. He didn't want to leave the hotel yet. He wanted to stay in this room, with her, forever.

She emerged from the bathroom in a towel, with her hair caught up in a messy bun. He watched her rifle through her backpack, his chest aching. She started getting dressed. Her brow furrowed with discomfort as she tugged on her leggings.

"Are you okay?" Cam asked.

She seemed startled by the question. "I'm fine."

"If I hurt you, I want to know."

"You didn't hurt me."

"You're sore?"

"A little."

Guilt flooded him. He shouldn't have reached for her so many times. "I'm sorry."

"Don't be."

"I went overboard."

"And I loved it."

He groaned, wrapping his arms around her from behind. He pressed his lips to her head. "When you're ready, I'll kiss it better."

She squeezed his forearm. "You're insatiable."

"Only with you," he said, and meant it. He'd shared some special nights with Jenny, but they hadn't been like this. He'd been so young and green. He'd learned how to be a good lover with her, not before her.

Looking back, he hadn't been a perfect husband. He hadn't focused on her needs as much as he should have. He hadn't spoiled her with thoughtful gifts. He hadn't known their time together would be so short.

With Tala, he knew. He wasn't the same person he'd

been before. In some ways, he was less giving. Less accessible. He was colder and harder to reach. But he was also more aware of the casual cruelty of life, and better able to appreciate its shining moments.

Losing Jenny had torn him apart. Being with Tala made him feel whole again.

He was faced with another dilemma about what to tell her, and when. Yesterday he'd been reluctant to bring up contentious topics. Today the stakes were even higher. Last night hadn't been a one-off for him. It had felt like a new beginning.

His stomach growled again. "Are you hungry?" he asked, releasing her.

"Starving."

"We can eat breakfast before we leave."

She nodded her agreement. He put on his boots while she finished getting ready. They brushed their teeth side by side at the bathroom sink. It was quietly domestic, and he relished every second. She'd borrowed one of his flannel shirts to wear with her leggings. She had to roll up the sleeves. The hem reached her upper thighs. The outfit reminded him of the day they'd gone shopping together in Fairbanks. It seemed like weeks ago. They'd spent more consecutive hours together than some couples who'd been dating for months.

"I like you in my shirt," he said gruffly.

"It doesn't fit."

"That's why it's sexy."

She laughed at the claim, as if she didn't believe it. He felt the urge to scoop her up and carry her off to bed again. Instead, he let her slip away. He didn't want to scare her by coming on too strong. She'd escaped an abusive relationship less than a year ago. She'd witnessed a murder and been attacked by strangers. He understood why she'd be wary of entering a new relationship. He was willing to take things slow, but he was also ready to fight for her. She was in danger, and he would protect her by any means necessary.

That was one of the benefits of becoming a rough, tough Alaskan trucker. He could get uncivilized quick. He'd tear apart anyone who hurt her. He'd fall on them like a grizzly ripping into a salmon. Teeth bared, roaring.

But he couldn't let his caveman instincts take over with Tala. She needed space, not domination. She needed the freedom to make her own decisions. He'd been an animal last night. Today he would soften his approach. Instead of tossing her over his shoulder and declaring her his woman, he had to win her gently.

The hotel café was empty except for two other customers, single men at separate tables. One was reading blueprints. The other was focused on his plate, facing the opposite direction. Despite the late hour, there were some buffet-style breakfast items available. Cam piled a plate with turkey sausage and scrambled eggs. Tala had oatmeal and fruit. They both went for seconds. They'd worked up quite an appetite.

"What's the plan for today?" she asked.

He took a sip of coffee. "First the ice road, then the Dalton. I always try to drive straight through on the way back."

"We won't stop in Coldfoot?"

"Not if we don't have to. The return trip is mostly downhill, so it goes faster. When the weather's good, I can get to Fairbanks in fourteen hours or less."

She went quiet, glancing around the café. The airport runway was visible through a single window. He vaguely remembered hearing a few planes take off and land during the night. There was a mounted television in the corner displaying weather updates, but no news. It was a cold, clear day. Perfect for the ice road.

"Have you decided on coming with me to Seattle?" he asked.

She arched a brow. "Is that what you wanted me to focus on last night?"

"No," he admitted, raking a hand through his hair. "I didn't think at all."

He couldn't prevent the rush of male satisfaction her words inspired in him. He'd given her hours of mindless pleasure. He couldn't wait to do it again.

"I was hoping my performance had convinced you."

She swallowed hard and looked away. He didn't press her for answers. She wasn't ready for a long-term commitment. Maybe he wasn't, either. The physical component was more comfortable for both of them than exposing themselves emotionally.

Wiping his mouth with a napkin, he cleared their empty plates from the table. They returned to the room to gather their belongings. His bag was already packed. She still had some toiletries in the bathroom.

"I'll warm up my rig," he said. "Meet me in ten minutes?"

She nodded, picking up her hairbrush.

He left the hotel and crossed the parking lot in purposeful strides. Despite the brilliant sunshine, the chill in the air stole his breath away. He doubted the high would rise above zero. In the dark afternoon and early night, temps would plummet further. He'd driven in cold shots of –30 and –40 before, so he wasn't worried about freezing. Even if he broke down on the road, he had survival gear. He could handle the weather.

Tala was another story. She might be the death of him.

His phone rang, interrupting his thoughts. It was Mason.

"Hello?" Cam answered.

"Where the hell have you been?"

"On the road. You know I don't get service out here."

"Then how are we talking?"

"I'm in Prudhoe Bay. It's more developed."

"I've been trying to call you all morning."

"I had a late night."

Mason made a huffing sound. "I'll bet."

"Did you mention Tala's name to the local police?"

"Not yet, but the sheriff from Willow keeps leaving me messages. He wants to know why I was so interested in the missing waitress case. I have to return his call."

Cam dragged a hand down his face. "Can you blow him off?"

"No, Cam, I can't. It's regarding a homicide. I can't blow him off just so you can get blown by some hitchhiker."

"She's not a hitchhiker."

"Stowaway. Whatever."

"You've got the wrong idea about her."

"So you weren't drilling her all night?"

"That's none of your business."

"I've seen pictures of her, Cam. I understand the attraction."

"Maybe I just want to help her."

"If that's true, you have more issues than I thought."

"You know who has issues?" Cam shot back. "You have issues. You're so messed up over your divorce that you can't imagine spending time with a woman for any reason but sex. Angry revenge sex."

"Some women like angry revenge sex."

"Yeah? Do they come back for more?"

"They would if I let them."

Cam grunted his skepticism.

"I can't believe you're lecturing me about women. You've been avoiding them for years. You probably don't remember how to get one off."

"I remember."

Mason laughed in approval. "Good for you. Next time find a partner who isn't under investigation."

Cam headed back into the hotel lobby, which was deserted. "Did you call to heckle me or share information?"

"Both," Mason said. There was a sound of rifling papers, as if he'd made notes. "They found a dead guy in Willow with a receipt for Walt's Diner in his pocket. He was a hardcore criminal with an extensive record."

"Local?"

"From Anchorage."

"What else?"

"I talked to a detective in Whitehorse, where your girl was arrested. He had a vivid recollection of her. Everyone who saw her thought she was innocent."

"Why?"

"Pretty young women don't assault police officers very often. Her blood alcohol level was zero. The arresting officer said she seemed more afraid than defiant. She refused to give a statement, other than an apology. When her husband came to bail her out, he was a real asshole. They immediately suspected him."

"Why not drop the charges?"

"They were hoping she'd roll on him."

"Did they follow up?"

"They sent a unit to question the husband after she failed to appear. He claimed he didn't know where she was and declined to file a missing-person report."

"He doesn't want her found."

"Not by them, no."

Cam nodded in agreement. "This matches everything she's told me."

"Did she say he sent some thugs to kidnap her? Because that doesn't add up. Laramie's a scumbag, but he's a low-level scumbag. He doesn't have the money or power to hire professionals."

"She said he wasn't involved."

"Who is?"

Cam didn't answer. "Have you seen the case file?"

"No, I don't have access. But now this sheriff is breathing down my neck because I reached out first. I have to tell him something."

"I need more time," Cam said.

"More time to do what? Screw the truth out of her?"

"I'm trying to convince her to come to Seattle and sit down with you. She doesn't trust the cops here. She's afraid they won't believe her."

"What if I don't believe her?"

"You will."

"Cam, you're my brother, and I love you, but I can't do this. I can't stall for three days while you drive half-way across the country. You're asking me to ignore a direct request from a colleague while you continue to harbor a fugitive. And get laid."

Cam turned to stare out the lobby windows, searching for the words to convince Mason. His brother was a diehard skeptic on a good day. On a bad day, he was an unfeeling bastard. Cam had been numb for years, so he could relate. Accessing his emotions wasn't easy. Communicating them to Mason was damned near impossible. "I don't care about getting laid. I care about her."

"You hardly know her."

"You don't understand how I feel."

"I understand everything," Mason replied. "You couldn't save Jenny, and it broke you. That's why you went to Alaska, to be broken and alone and miserable. Now you have the chance to save someone else, and you're obsessed with playing the hero. It's not about her. It's about you, and your rescue fantasy."

Cam couldn't dispute any of Mason's observations. "Do you ever get tired of being the most cynical person on earth?"

"You brought me into this. You called me first, remember?"

"I wanted your support," Cam growled. "Not your judgment."

"I withheld judgment about your stupid ice-road job."

"No, you didn't."

"What do you expect me to say? I think you're making a huge mistake. You're putting your life in danger for a piece of ass."

"I already told you—"

"I know what you told me, so save it. I'm required to share information with other law enforcement officials unless I have cause to suspect corruption or negligence. I have to give them her name and let them investigate."

Cam cursed under his breath. He returned to the breakfast area and sat down at a quiet table. After a short hesitation, he told Tala's story. It was a betrayal of her trust, but he didn't have a choice. If he didn't share the details, Mason would cooperate with the investigation and they'd never make it to Seattle. He'd get pulled over in Fairbanks, or even sooner.

"You're saying that a statie is part of this crew?" Mason asked.

"Yes."

"Jesus, Cam. You need to file a report."

"With who? The state police are the only agency out here. There's nothing else for hundreds of miles."

"What about tribal police?"

"They don't have jurisdiction on the Dalton."

"You can call the FBI."

"I can, but I doubt Tala will talk to them, and what help could they offer at this point? A field agent wouldn't get here for days. They'll tell us to come to them. Until we get back to Fairbanks, we're on our own."

Mason didn't dispute him.

"If you give Tala's name to the sheriff, there's a chance he'll notify state police to be on the lookout."

"So what? They don't know she's with you."

"Yes, they do." He summarized the incident on Avalanche Alley.

Mason made an incredulous sound. "This girl is even crazier than you are."

"She saved a man's life."

"Is she an adrenaline junkie?"

"I don't think so. She fainted from stress afterward, and she doesn't like the Dalton."

"No one with common sense would like the Dalton."

"Thanks," Cam said, sarcastic.

Mason fell silent for a moment. "I have a bad feeling about this."

"You have feelings?"

"Maybe I can get on a late flight to Fairbanks."

"You don't have to do that."

"Yeah, I do. I'm your brother."

"Okay, but promise me one thing."

"What?"

"Don't tell Mom."

Mason let out a short bark of laughter and hung up. Cam stared at the screen of his phone for several seconds, smiling to himself. He couldn't dismiss Mason's concerns, but the remoteness of Prudhoe Bay added a measure of security. The police presence here was tiny. They'd already met a state trooper on the road, and they'd left a good impression on him. The danger of getting apprehended in this area was very low.

Once they returned to Fairbanks, he'd have to proceed with caution. Cam assumed the killers were still there, waiting for another opportunity to strike. His smile faded at the thought of a second attack on Tala. He couldn't let anything happen to her.

Here in Prudhoe Bay, the main challenge wasn't avoiding the bad guys. It was surviving the elements, and navigating the tricky space he'd entered with Tala. He hadn't convinced her to stay with him.

Tucking his phone away, he left the breakfast area. Tala still hadn't come down, so he went back outside and warmed up his truck. He'd get diesel in Deadhorse. He didn't need chains. His gauges looked good. When Tala didn't arrive to meet him, he started to worry. She didn't take that long to get ready.

He got out of his rig and glanced around. Miles of vast oil fields stretched toward the ocean in the west. On the east side of the hotel, a plane took off from the airport and accelerated with a low roar. The airport was within walking distance.

His blood went cold at the sight. While he'd been on the phone with Mason, he'd kept his back to the lobby. Had she quietly approached, without him realizing? Had she overheard his conversation?

"Son of a bitch," he said, turning off his engine. He rushed toward the front entrance of the hotel and ran down the hallway. He still had the key card, so he opened the door. The room was empty. He searched every inch of the space, frantic. He even looked in the shower stall. She wasn't there.

He couldn't believe it. She was gone.

Chapter 17

Tala found a laundry room with an alternative exit.

She snuck out the door, her heart racing. It opened to the opposite side of the building. Frigid air sucked into her lungs as she started running across the hard-packed snow. The airport was less than a block away, and she moved fast, but the distance seemed endless. She was completely exposed. Her light gray parka and dark leggings made a stark contrast to the blinding white tundra.

The cold soaked through her thin leggings and stung her cheeks. She didn't dare moisten her lips. Her breath huffed out in telltale clouds, like a flag waving over her head. She clutched her fur-lined hood with one hand and kept running.

Running was what she knew. It was her fallback.

What else could she do? She'd seen Cam on the phone in the breakfast room. He'd looked like he was trying to have a private conversation, which triggered her suspicions. Instead of making her presence known, she'd stood hidden in the doorway to listen. She couldn't hear every word, but she'd heard enough. He'd called someone, probably his police officer buddy in Seattle, and told her story.

She hadn't agreed to that. She hadn't even agreed to *go* to Seattle.

He'd betrayed her. She couldn't believe he'd shared her secrets. He'd argued about giving her name to the state police. She didn't trust the person he'd spoken with at all. She didn't know if she trusted Cam anymore.

Which was a real shame. Because she was in love with him.

Her chest seized at the realization, adding to her anguish. Less than twelve hours after she'd bared her soul to him—and her body—he'd broken her heart.

Tears froze on her face as she stumbled forward. She felt conflicted about leaving, despite his shady behavior. He'd given her the best night of her life. He'd been sweet and caring in the morning. His desire for her wasn't in question, and his feelings seemed sincere. Even so, he hadn't said a word about calling his contact. He hadn't consulted her.

He'd also searched through her belongings.

While she was packing up, she'd noticed some rearranged items in her backpack. Her book was in the inside pocket with the stolen ID. She was already upset about that invasion of privacy when she'd caught him on the phone.

She didn't look back as she raced toward the airport. She half expected him to stop her, or to call out her name. He must not have noticed her escape, because he didn't come after her. There was a twisted sort of irony in her actions. She was fleeing the hotel the same way she'd fled the diner. One hosted a love scene; the other, a murder scene.

She arrived, breathless, in the terminal. She didn't have any money for airfare. Even if she did, she was afraid to use the ID. She'd headed this direction on impulse. Instead of approaching a kiosk for ticket information, she sat down in an empty seat and bent forward with her head in her hands.

She had to think. Think.

She didn't feel safe in Prudhoe Bay. Cam had been right about the extreme isolation of the place. If she hadn't given the police her real name for the accident report, she might have been able to lay low here. That was no longer an option.

She glanced around the airport terminal warily. She could hide in the bathroom if Cam showed up. Her stomach clenched at the thought. She'd run away from the only person who wanted to help her.

Damn it.

She wished she wasn't in love with him. She wished he hadn't been so good to her. It was incredibly difficult to accept this turn of events. How could he spend the night in her arms, making her die with pleasure, and then go behind her back in the morning?

Maybe he'd been shady all along. Maybe he wasn't who he seemed. All she knew for sure was that he'd hurt her. When a man hurt her, she ran.

It occurred to her that he might not come looking for her. She'd mentioned staying in Prudhoe Bay to work. She'd left without saying goodbye. That was a big deal to him. Frowning, she rifled through the zippered pocket of her backpack. She had several quarters, and a business card with Cam's phone number on it.

She stood abruptly, taking a deep breath. There was a pay phone in the corner. She walked toward it and dialed a number. Not Cam's. Her mother's. After she inserted the required amount of change, the call went through.

"Hello?"

"Hi, Mom. It's me."

"Tala?"

"Yes."

"You haven't called in so long! I was getting worried."

Tala swallowed back a surge of guilt. Her mother sounded surprised and excited, not disapproving. She held the receiver in a tight grip, unsure what to say.

"How are you?"

"I'm okay," she hedged.

"How's Duane?"

"Uh… I don't know. I left him six months ago."

Her mother gasped. "Why?"

"He hit me."

"Oh, no," she said, as if it pained her to imagine. She repeated the phrase several times. Then, with resolve: "I'm going to send Clark."

"No, Mom."

"I'll send Clark *and* Bear."

Tears sprang into Tala's eyes at her mother's protective attitude. Tala didn't want anyone to beat up Duane on her behalf, but she appreciated the offer. "That's not a good idea."

"We'll all come. Where are you?"

"I'm in Alaska. Prudhoe Bay."

"What are you doing in Alaska?"

"It's a long story."

"Do you need anything? How can I help, *nitânis*?"

The term of endearment brought tears from her eyes. "I just wanted to hear your voice."

"It's nice to hear yours."

"I was wondering…did Dad ever mistreat you?"

"He never laid a hand on me. We just argued a lot."

"About what?"

"Oh, many things. We were so young when we got married. I thought it would be romantic to live in the wilderness with him. Instead I was cold and lonely and bored. I didn't have any friends. The other women hated me."

"Why?"

"Because they all wanted your father! He was the best-looking man in Yellowknife, and I was an outsider. A silly city girl."

"You weren't ever happy?"

"I was happy after you were born. I loved you so much, but I didn't love him. I couldn't forgive him for keeping you."

"What do you mean?"

"It was against tribal law for me to take you away from Yellowknife without his permission, and he wouldn't give it. I couldn't get full custody. Equal custody would have interrupted your schooling. You wanted to stay with him, so I had to let you go."

"I didn't know."

"You were little."

She wondered why her mother hadn't told her this before. Maybe, as a rebellious teenager, she wouldn't have listened. "I'm sorry."

"Don't be. It was better for you to spend those years with him. He was taken too soon. Now he's gone, but I

am here. You can come to Billings. There will always
be a place in my home for you."

Tala's throat closed up with emotion. "Okay."

"You'll come?"

She blinked the tears from her eyes. It felt good to
know her mother wanted her around. If Tala needed to
go to Montana, she could. This knowledge helped soothe
her overwrought feelings about Cam.

"Right now, I'm waiting for a ride to Fairbanks. I'll
call you after I get there. We can plan a visit."

"Be careful, *nitânis*."

She promised she would and said goodbye. She hadn't
expected her mother to be so sympathetic. She'd anticipated doubt and criticism. Living with Duane had brain-
washed her into assuming the worst of people.

Which brought her back to Cam. She had to give him
a chance to explain. He was her only way out of this
place, and she needed to face her emotions. She wiped
the tears from her cheeks, noticing a broad-shouldered
figure at the entrance. He opened the door and located
her in seconds. He looked relieved, and more than a little bewildered. She waited, heart pounding, as he strode
toward her.

She crossed her arms over her chest. Her hands were
shaking. She didn't like confrontations, but they needed
to hash this out. She deserved some answers, and he deserved an explanation.

"Why did you run?" he asked.

"I heard you on the phone."

He didn't make any excuses, or offer any denials.
"You could've asked me about it instead of taking off.
What were you going to do, stow away on a plane?"

Her cheeks heated at his sarcasm. "I called my mother."

"What did she say?"

"She said I could come to Montana."

"Is that what you want?"

She gave a stiff shrug.

"I can't believe you left without saying goodbye."

"I can't believe you talked to the police without my consent!"

"I was talking to my brother."

"Your brother?"

"He's a detective in Seattle."

She sat on the bench again, her knees weak.

He took the space next to her. "I should have told you about him. I was wrong."

She gaped at him, stunned by the admission. He'd actually said he was wrong.

"I called him after you were attacked in Fairbanks. You begged me not to call the police, so I called him." He raked a hand through his hair, seeming chagrined. "I asked him to run a background check on you."

The breath sucked out of her lungs. "You didn't."

"I was worried about you."

Tala struggled out of her parka, flushing. She remembered his pointed questions in the weight room. He'd interrogated her just like a cop. "You knew about my record and warrants. You knew before I told you."

He inclined his head.

"What else do you know?"

"I know the dead guy they found in Willow had a receipt for Walt's Diner in his pocket. He was a career criminal."

"Do they think I killed him?"

"I'm pretty sure you're not a suspect. You left your

purse at the scene. That indicates a terrified witness, not a cold-blooded killer."

She fell silent, trying to process the disturbing news.

"Look, I asked Mason not to give your name to the police. He needed a reason. That's why I had to tell him everything this morning." His steady gaze met hers. "It started off innocent, and sort of snowballed."

She hugged her parka to her chest. He'd lied to her, or at least misrepresented the truth. He'd promised not to call the police, but he'd called his brother, a detective. If she'd been thinking clearly, she would have anticipated this. Cam was a former cop, after all. She should have left him in Coldfoot after he'd admitted to his law enforcement background. She could have hitched a ride back to Fairbanks with that tour group. Instead, she'd stayed with him and let her hormones take over.

"I'm sorry," he said quietly.

"You took my choices away, just like Duane used to. You decided what was best for me, and now I'm trapped."

His jaw clenched with anger. "That's not fair."

"Isn't it?"

"No, it isn't. I'm not Duane. I'll *never* be like Duane."

"Did you search through my things?"

He flinched at the accusation. "Not really."

"Not really?"

"I saw the ID you stole, if that's what you mean."

"You invaded my privacy."

"You robbed someone at my place of work!"

She flushed with guilt. She shouldn't have done that, but two wrongs didn't make a right. She still felt betrayed by him.

"I'm not holding you against your will," Cam said,

lowering his voice. "You don't have to run away from me like you ran away from Duane. You want to go to Montana, go to Montana. Maybe you'll be safe there."

She heard the warning in his "maybe." He was trying to suggest the opposite, that she wouldn't be safe in Montana. She might be putting her family at risk by hiding there. It was a chilling realization. "You think I'll be safe if I talk to the police, but they won't protect me. They'll send me back to Canada and I'll go to prison."

"You won't go to prison. That's for longer sentences. If anything, you'll go to jail."

She leapt to her feet. "You're not helping, Cam."

He rose with her, grasping her arm. "All you have to do is tell the truth about what happened at the rally. They'll probably dismiss the charges against you and arrest Duane. Then he'll go to jail, where he belongs."

She pulled away from him in frustration. He didn't understand how difficult it would be for her to point the finger at Duane. The last time she saw her husband, he'd beaten her unconscious. It wasn't fair to ask her to make a statement that would infuriate him. Or one that would put her in the crosshairs of hardcore criminals, for that matter. She didn't have any faith in the system. When there were men like Duane in uniform, it was hard to believe in justice.

"You make it sound so easy," she said. "All I have to do is be honest and everything will work out."

"It's better than running forever."

"When are *you* going to stop running?"

His eyes darkened. "What do you mean?"

She gestured at the bleak landscape, visible through the terminal windows. "You don't belong here. You're not an Alaskan recluse, or a trucker. You came to escape, just like I did." She paused, studying him. "Or maybe you came to die."

"That's ridiculous. I don't want to die."

"Then why did you choose this job, above all others? Why this road?"

"It's not that dangerous."

She laughed harshly. "You're in denial. You should be saving lives at accident scenes or whatever you used to do. Instead you're courting death in hopes of getting reunited with your precious Jenny."

"I don't want to reunite with Jenny," he growled, closing the distance between them. "I want to be with you."

"For how long?"

His eyes darkened at the question. He fell silent, unable to answer.

She wasn't surprised by his reluctance to make promises. He was as gun-shy about relationships as she was. "Even if I clear my name and the police catch the killers, I'm still married. I'll have to go back to Canada and take care of my legal issues."

"Can we focus on the next few days?" he asked. "Let's make it to Seattle first."

She turned away from him, her heart aching. She couldn't imagine a happy ending for them. He was a former-cop-turned-extreme-driver. He liked her right now because they were on an adventure. He liked to chase danger, even if he didn't admit it. When the ice melted and the excitement died down, he'd lose interest.

"At the very least, come with me to Fairbanks," Cam said. "You can't stay here."

She couldn't argue with him anymore, so she stared out the terminal window. The oil refineries in the distance puffed out chutes of smoke, and snow flurries danced through the air like poisoned ashes. Polluted before they even hit the ground.

Cam wrapped his arms around her and pressed his lips to her hair. His embrace felt warm and reassuring. He was hard and strong and unyielding. She wanted to trust him. She wanted to forget her troubles, and escape into a fantasy in which love conquered all.

"I'll keep you safe," he said against her ear. "I promise."

She leaned into his chest, eyes closed.

"If you stop running, I'll stop with you. I'll fight for you, if you let me."

"Okay," she murmured, giving in. She couldn't resist him. She'd play along, for now. She'd hope for the best but prepare for the worst. She'd stay alert.

And if she had to run again—she'd run.

Chapter 18

They were back on the road by noon.

Storm clouds gathered across the sky, intersected with clear spots of blue. Brilliant sunshine shone through the patches, illuminating the slabs of ice beneath the spinning wheels. The road appeared to have been made from shards of crystals, crosshatched into a giant puzzle on top of a gently sloshing ocean. Later in the season the top layer would turn to slush.

Tala didn't speak while they were on the ice. She stared out the window, her face pale. Cam couldn't blame her. It was an unsettling experience.

He filled his gas tank in Deadhorse before they moved on. He didn't check in with the office for fear of being stopped and questioned about yesterday's accident. The possibility of getting pulled over by a supervisor truck or patrol vehicle loomed. There was nothing he could do to prevent it, so he focused on other things. His rig, the road, the weather, the woman beside him.

The woman he wanted, who didn't trust him.

He knew he'd screwed up this morning. He should have told her he'd been talking to Mason. He'd taken a gamble and lost. He'd apologized for the mistake, and she'd seemed willing to forgive him, but he wasn't convinced she would cooperate with the police. She might run away at the first opportunity.

He considered some solutions to her legal problems. He believed she'd be exonerated if she told the truth about Duane and the murder in Willow. She didn't have to stay in Canada. He had an apartment in Anchorage. She could live with him.

Cam stayed quiet about this option. It was too much, too soon. She'd rushed into a bad situation with Duane. She wouldn't be eager to tie herself down again, and they hadn't known each other long enough to take that plunge. Even so, the idea of sleeping next to her every night appealed to him. He wanted to spend as much time with her as possible. He wasn't going to change his mind.

For the rest of the day, they avoided contentious topics. He didn't press her about going to Seattle, or talking to his brother. He considered telling her that Mason was coming to meet him in Fairbanks, but decided not to worry her. They'd cross that bridge when they came to it. He was afraid of setting her off again.

Most of the hours passed in silence. She curled up in the berth and went to sleep. He drank coffee to stay awake. Twilight faded into endless night. He drove on and on, into the snow-laced dark. They passed Nightmare Corner and Avalanche Alley. Before he knew it, they were in Coldfoot. He'd made excellent time, and he didn't want to stop to rest. The other truckers would grill him about the rescue, and Tala. He decided to blow through camp and continue to Fairbanks.

"Wait," Tala said, before he passed by. "I have to return the ID."

"To who?"

"The front office. I can say I found it in the parking lot."

Cam had a better idea. "I'll put it in the mailbox."

She shrugged, so he went ahead and took care of it for her. They didn't stay in Coldfoot long. After a light dinner of soup and crackers, they were on the road again. When they were about two hours from Fairbanks, he remembered something important.

"My gun," he said.

"What gun?"

"It's in a locked box under the bed." He found the key and handed it to her. "We should keep it close."

"You think we'll need it?"

"I doubt it. I just want to have it within reach before we get to Fairbanks." He couldn't protect her without a weapon. The killers were armed. They might still be in the area, waiting for his truck to cruise down the main drag.

"Is it loaded?"

"No."

She retrieved the metal box and brought it up front. After fitting the key into the lock, she opened the lid. His 9 mm handgun was inside, under a pile of photos he hadn't looked at in years. The first was of Jenny frolicking at the beach in California. She was dripping wet and smiling in a skimpy striped bikini.

"Sorry," he said gruffly. "I forgot those photos were in there."

"Did you stare at these and stroke your gun?"

"Pretty much."

Her face revealed a mixture of sympathy and horror. Cam realized she'd been using "gun" in the literal sense.

"I mean, no," he said, flushing. "The gun is for protection only. I thought you were talking about…something else."

"Why are the pictures in here?"

"I locked them up so I wouldn't look at them anymore. I was spending too much time wallowing in grief."

She removed the gun and the clip, leaving the photos in the box without browsing through them. He was relieved. They weren't all sexy pics, but there were a couple of nudes mixed in with holiday photos and vacation shots. An embarrassing assortment. She studied the gun carefully before loading it.

"You know how to use that?" he asked.

"I've handled a 9 mm before. Where should I put it?"

"Here," he said, indicating the pocket next to his seat.

"I'll leave the safety on."

He grunted his approval. She tucked the gun away, where they could both access it easily. Making preparations for a shootout didn't brighten the mood in the cab. Or maybe it was the photos that caused tension. Either way, Tala stayed quiet, her face pensive. Cam didn't turn on the radio to break the silence. He let it echo between them. He wished he was better at making conversation. He wanted to know more about Tala. He wanted to hear her childhood stories. To share her hopes and dreams.

"What would you do for a living, if you could do anything?" he asked finally.

"Anything?"

"Anything," he repeated.

"I'd like to finish school first. I need at least another year to graduate."

"You're getting a degree in life science?"

"Earth science."

"Then what?"

"I'm not sure. Something outdoors. Maybe a wildlife biologist, or park warden."

"What's a park warden?"

"I believe you call them 'park rangers' in the US."

He arched a brow. "Are you aware that park rangers are law enforcement officers?"

"Yes," she said ruefully.

He didn't point out that she couldn't apply for that kind of job with a criminal record. She probably already knew.

"Don't judge me, Cam. You're a trucker with a sociology degree."

"Have you thought about search and rescue?"

"No."

"You'd be great at it."

"Why don't *you* do search and rescue?"

"We could do it together."

"Is that your fantasy?"

He mulled it over. "My fantasy is you and me in a cozy cabin with a fireplace. I'll chop some wood. You can braid your hair."

She smiled, a little sadly. "Sounds nice."

"What's your fantasy?"

"Freedom."

He couldn't argue with a fantasy. He wanted to give her whatever she needed, including freedom. Maybe she'd come back to him if he let her go. The idea disturbed him too much to contemplate, so he focused on the road. She took out her book, flipping sleek pages. He wondered how many of the images were sexual.

"I didn't realize graphic novels were so graphic," he commented.

Her lips parted in surprise. "You looked at it."

"I got a few ideas from the illustrations."

"You did not," she said, rolling her eyes.

He conceded her point. He hadn't needed any extra inspiration to give her pleasure. "Well, I enjoyed the art."

She closed the book abruptly. Her cheeks were flushed, as if she was picturing a similar scene from last night. He'd spent some quality time with his mouth between her legs—and he'd relished every second. If she left him, he hoped she'd think of that memory often. He could live with being the best she'd ever had. But he'd rather live with *her*.

"Why did you search my bag?"

"I didn't mean to."

"That's hard to believe."

"The book fell out. I glanced at a few pages and put it back inside."

"Then you saw the ID."

"Then I saw the ID," he confirmed. He didn't feel the need to apologize, because it had been an accident. But he tried to consider her perspective and respect her feelings. "Did Duane snoop through your things?"

"Yes. He always hid my purse so I couldn't leave."

"I wouldn't do that."

Her gaze searched his, as if gauging his sincerity.

"I wanted to look at the book, just to see what you were reading. I didn't mean to invade your privacy."

She nodded her acceptance. "I shouldn't have stolen the ID."

"Nobody's perfect."

"Most people aren't criminals."

"I like you the way you are."

Tears filled her eyes at the comment. "You said that before."

"It's still true."

"I like you the way you are, too," she said softly. "I'll never forget you, Cam."

His throat tightened with emotion. He couldn't deny his feelings any longer. He was in love with her. Head over heels in love with her.

And she was going to run away again, because she didn't believe they could be together. Because she was a petty criminal, and he was a former cop. Because the world was a terrible place sometimes. Because happy endings didn't happen every day.

He considered pulling over to talk, but they were on a downhill curve, and there was a bridge coming up. After he crossed it, he could find a quiet spot to park. He'd tell her he loved her and convince her to stay. If she wouldn't listen to his words, he'd show her with his hands. He would kiss her and touch her until she believed him. He had it all planned out.

Unfortunately, his plans were thwarted.

As he rounded the corner, shifting into a lower gear, he spotted a major problem. Someone had parked a white Chevy Suburban at an angle near the end of the bridge. It was obstructing both lanes, headlights beaming across the railing.

There was no room to maneuver. He couldn't get around the vehicle. He'd have to slow to a stop in the middle of the bridge. He engaged his jakes, cursing under his breath. That was when he noticed another vehicle parked on the side of the road beyond the bridge, barely visible in the grainy dark. It was a black SUV, lying in wait.

Fear spiked through him.

"This is an ambush," Tala said, her eyes wide. She was savvy enough to recognize the danger.

"If I stop, they'll shoot us."

She reached for the gun.

"Not yet," he said, easing off the jakes. "Get your head down and brace for impact."

With a muffled shriek, she bent forward and covered her head. He wasn't eager to get in a shootout against two or three armed men. They were already posted up. They could have a cadre of weapons, including long-range rifles. His 9 mm was no match for that kind of firepower, but his rig could do plenty of damage. The killers probably weren't expecting him to play demolition derby. They'd underestimated his survival instincts.

Instead of slowing down, he increased his speed, barreling toward the Suburban. Seconds from impact, a man jumped out of the vehicle and ran for cover. Cam wished he hadn't escaped, but the minor detail didn't change his trajectory. He smashed head-on into the side of the truck. The Ice Storm crushed the Suburban with brutal force. It was a jarring crash.

Tala screamed, cowering lower.

Cam anticipated some steering failures and other complications. He'd worried about losing control and jackknifing over the side of the bridge, but that didn't happen. His rig took the hit like a champ. There were no flames obscuring his view. The Suburban was stuck to his grill, bent and twisted and smoking.

He pressed on the gas and kept going. He hadn't done anything to even up the odds yet, except refuse to be a sitting duck. He needed to wreak some more havoc, or the ambush would succeed and they would die. As soon as he cleared the bridge, he veered to the right, where the other SUV was parked.

"Stay down," he said to Tala.

There were two men inside the second vehicle, and they didn't jump to safety like their quick-thinking friend. Maybe they didn't realize he was coming for them next. Maybe they wanted to stand their ground and shoot. Whatever. Bring it on.

He bore down on them like a freight train, unwavering. Bullets peppered the windshield, making Tala shriek again. Pain exploded in his left shoulder, so he knew he'd been hit.

Gritting his teeth, he wrenched the wheel toward the SUV and ducked his head. The Suburban stuck to his grill smashed into the SUV.

This time, there was fire. Not just bullets, but an exploding gas tank. The Suburban went up in flames, and his rig didn't fare much better. It jackknifed and rolled into a ditch, scraping across the frozen earth. He got slammed around inside the cab, despite his safety belt. Metal screeched and buckled. His shoulder burned and his leg twisted underneath him. Tala was still screaming, or maybe it was him.

His head cracked into the side window, and then there was nothing. No sound, no pain, no fire, no light.

Chapter 19

Tala couldn't believe what was happening.

She'd been worried about an ambush in Fairbanks, which was still a hundred miles away. It hadn't occurred to her that the killers would attack them on the Dalton. Cam had insisted that the road was too dangerous for regular vehicles, and she'd seen the evidence with her own eyes. She hadn't expected an early strike.

The killers had executed their plan with military precision and chilling foresight. They'd known when the Ice Storm was coming. They couldn't have set up on the bridge otherwise. She realized that as she braced for impact.

The first crash had been blindly terrifying. She wanted to lift her head to look, but Cam had shouted at her to stay down. Bullets peppered the front of the rig, and chaos erupted. They'd hit a second target. A gas tank exploded. That stupid metal box flew across the cab, slamming into Tala's elbow. Pictures of Cam's beautiful dead wife spilled out everywhere. For a surreal moment, they were suspended in the air. Frozen in time.

Then the action kicked into fast-forward. Flames and snow blurred together. She was jostled this way and that. Glass shattered inward, along with a cold blast of air. The world pitched sideways and came to a shuddering stop. Her seat belt jerked and held.

She glanced around woozily, trying to orient herself. The smell of smoke and gasoline burned her nostrils. An engine idled high, like a racecar before takeoff.

It was a bad wreck, and they were trapped inside it. The semi had rolled over onto the driver's side. Her seat belt held her in place, sort of dangling above Cam. He was slumped behind the wheel, motionless.

"Cam," she cried, grasping his shoulder. "Cam!"

He moaned in response. He was alive!

She reached out to turn off the engine. Panic gripped her in an icy fist. The front windshield was broken. Snow and cold seeped in, but her main concern was fire. They were dangerously close to two burning vehicles. And what about the inhabitants? She had no idea where the killers were. They could be inside the flaming wreckage, or roaming free. She couldn't see through the smoke. She couldn't breathe, couldn't think.

"Radio," Cam mumbled.

She grabbed the CB and pressed the button. "There's been an accident," she said in a shaky voice. "It's serious. We're on the Dalton Highway, near the bridge. I need an ambulance and police. Please hurry!"

She didn't listen for a response. She hung up the receiver and released her seat belt, promptly falling against Cam. He grunted in pain as she jostled him.

"Sorry," she said. "I have to get you out."

He didn't argue. She took off his seat belt and considered her options. He was a big, heavy man. She couldn't drag him far. The driver's-side door was blocked. The most expedient route was through the front window.

Decision made, she attempted to pull him toward her. He sucked in a sharp breath when she gripped his right arm. His shirt was torn and damp. She could smell the blood on him. Her stomach dropped.

"You're shot."

He seemed half-conscious, and not fully aware. His eyes drifted shut.

"Stay with me, Cam. Are you injured anywhere else?"

"Head...ankle."

"Maybe I shouldn't move you."

He wrenched his eyes open. "You have to."

She didn't want to cause him pain. She also didn't want them to burn to death, or get shot like fish in a barrel. She nodded her agreement. "This will hurt."

He gritted his teeth in preparation.

She put her arms around his waist and heaved. He helped her as much as he could. When she freed him from the cramped space behind the wheel, it was easier to maneuver. She crawled through the safety glass and over the hood, pulling him along. He used his good leg to push off. Then they were both clear, tumbling into the bitter cold.

She dragged him a few feet away from the wreckage. He collapsed there, his breaths ragged from exertion. She didn't think he could walk. The concussion was probably more of a factor than his busted ankle. The blood on his shoulder appeared minimal. She didn't see any other wounds, but he could have internal injuries.

Heart racing, she inspected their surroundings. It was a nightmarish scene. There were two bodies inside the black SUV. The Suburban looked empty. Maybe there was another corpse inside, buried under smoke and twisted metal.

"One got away," Cam rasped.

Tala swallowed hard. There was a killer on the loose, lurking in the shadows. She glanced around warily, unable to locate the threat. She felt the urge to flee, as always, but she couldn't take Cam with her.

"Go," he told her. "Run."

She ignored the order. She wasn't going anywhere. Her instinct to run couldn't compete with her love for him. She wouldn't leave him to die. He might die anyway, because of the cold. It was below zero, and he was injured, lying in the snow. They weren't even wearing jackets. They had no protection from the elements, and the flames from the wreck didn't warm them. Hypothermia would set in quickly—if the killers didn't finish them off first.

Cam didn't say anything else. Maybe he'd passed out again.

Running wasn't an option. She had to stand her ground and fight, for both of them.

She needed Cam's gun. In the chaos, she'd forgotten to grab it. Getting out of the truck had been her only focus. She studied the wreckage, noting that the fire had died down. Flames were no longer licking at the front of the rig. She didn't think it would explode if she went back inside. Either way, she had to risk it. She needed the gun and their jackets, too. She'd get both, save Cam and shoot whatever moved in the burning dark.

She didn't tell him about her plan. He wasn't in any position to object. She crawled across the hood with caution. Safety glass clung to her clothes and bit into her palms as she climbed into the cab. The gun was still in the pocket beside the driver's seat. She emptied her backpack and shoved it inside.

Her parka was easy to locate. She tossed it out the front window and searched for his. It was wedged against the driver's side door, caught on a piece of twisted metal. She yanked it free, panting, and threw it on the hood. Then she grabbed the sleeping bag from the berth.

When she returned to the front of the cab, the firelight shifted. Someone was standing outside, blocking the glow of the flames. He was a dark shadow, faceless and menacing. Her panicked mind supplied a picture of Duane. It was a nasty illusion, but reality was worse. The man tilted his head to the side to reveal his true features. It was the blond man from the diner. The rude roughneck with the gun.

"Look who we have here," he said, peering inside the cab. "It's that pretty little waitress from Willow."

Tala stared at him in horror. She clutched the sleeping bag to her chest. The heavy material would protect her from the elements, but it wouldn't stop a bullet. The gun she needed was in her backpack, out of reach.

He gestured to the burning vehicles behind him. "You did me a favor with those two. Now come on out and do me another."

She didn't move.

"If you cooperate, I'll make it quick. No suffering."

"Lay a hand on me and you'll be the one suffering."

He drew a pistol from his coat pocket. Metal glinted in the firelight, reflecting the menace in his eyes. She was about to lunge for her backpack when a flash of motion startled them both. Someone tackled the killer in a clumsy rush.

It was Cam.

She screamed in protest as Cam took the other man to the ground. He was too weak to win this fight. She couldn't believe he'd gotten up on his own. He was going to get shot again! He was going to die for her. She couldn't let that happen. She grabbed the gun from the backpack, her heart pounding with adrenaline.

Cam had risked his life for her, despite his injuries. He might not be able to move beyond the first strike—but that was all she needed. He'd given her an opening to save them both. She scrambled across the hood. Cam and his opponent were grappling in the snow. She disengaged the safety with shaking hands. The killer shoved Cam backward and raised his weapon.

Cam sprawled there, motionless.

A gun went off, but it wasn't the killer's. It was the one in Tala's hand. She squeezed the trigger twice in rapid succession. Two bullets struck her target in the chest. He slumped forward, dropping his weapon in the snow. Blood bubbled from his lips. He drew in a last breath and went completely still.

Tala inched forward, ready to fire again if he so much as twitched. He didn't. He wasn't breathing. She picked up the loose weapon and secured it in her backpack. Then she knelt by Cam's prone form. Flickering light illuminated his face. She hoped they weren't in danger from another explosion. Most of the flames had dissipated, and she didn't smell gasoline anymore.

"Did you get him?" he asked, eyes closed.

"I got him."

He grunted his approval. She retrieved both parkas, her throat tight. He was already shivering, his brow furrowed with pain. She couldn't imagine how he'd managed to stand, let alone launch an attack. Blinking the tears away, she inspected his shoulder. It appeared to have been grazed by a bullet. A small amount of blood seeped from the wound.

"Can you sit up? I need to put on your jacket."

With her help, he struggled into a sitting position. She eased him into his parka carefully, zipping up the front, before he reclined again. He had a bump on his temple. She scooped up a bit of snow and applied it to the tender spot.

"I had something to tell you," he said, wincing. "Before the crash."

"Shh," she said. "Rest now."

"It was important."

"We're alive. That's the most important thing."

He closed his eyes, his breaths labored. "I thought… he was going to kill you."

She donned her own parka, shivering. She was lucky Cam had intervened. If he hadn't, she wouldn't be here. Instead of dwelling on the close call, she grabbed the sleeping bag and covered them both. It was incredibly macabre to cuddle next to a dead man, with two other corpses burning in the background. She considered moving, but jostling Cam might exacerbate his head injury. Another trucker would come along soon.

"Why didn't you run?" Cam asked.

She reached out to hold his hand. "I couldn't leave you."

Two truckers arrived a few minutes later. Then the police came, followed by a fire truck and an ambulance. They didn't let her ride to Fairbanks with Cam. She watched as the EMTs loaded him into an ambulance. She'd barely stepped away before she was relegated to the backseat of squad car. Although she wasn't cuffed, she felt like a criminal. She wasn't given any updates about Cam's condition on the way. As soon as they arrived at the station, she was taken to an interview room, where she recounted the pertinent events in vivid detail.

Her statements were honest; there was no benefit in lying now. She'd been caught at the scene of the crime. If she didn't talk, she'd look guilty.

Guilt*ier*.

She told the truth about Duane, because her story didn't make sense otherwise. He was the reason she'd come to Alaska to hide. He was the reason for her arrest in Canada, and for her failure to appear in court.

She also told the truth about the two IDs she'd stolen, in the interest of full disclosure. She found out that she wouldn't be extradited to Canada because the charges against her weren't serious enough. Also, they confirmed she wasn't technically a foreign national. Full-blooded First Nations members were allowed entry from Canada to the US and vice versa. It was similar to dual citizenship. She had the protection of both countries. She was supposed to return to Canada of her own volition to take care of her warrants, but no one would be tracking her down with a dragnet.

Several hours passed in the interrogation room. Two detectives asked her a thousand questions, many of which were repetitive. She wasn't sure if they were trying to trip her up, or just being thorough. Either way, it was exhausting.

She received medical treatment for her minor cuts and scrapes. She was photographed, fingerprinted and given a hot meal. She was left alone to eat. She wanted to see Cam. They wouldn't even tell her where he was or how he was doing. He might be in surgery, or in pain. Her eyes welled with tears of anxiety.

She pushed aside the tray and buried her head in her arms. Moments later, a third detective appeared. He was younger and better-looking than the others. He had an athletic build and dark, close-cropped hair. His rumpled suit fit him well.

"Can I make a phone call?" she asked.

"I'd like to ask you a few questions first."

She wiped the tears from her cheeks, nodding her permission.

He took the seat across from her. His gaze moved over her in a measured sweep. She couldn't tell if he was assessing her feminine attributes or judging her mental state. He had a pretty good poker face. A good face in general, with strong features. There was something familiar about them.

"You're Cam's brother," she said.

"And you're his damsel in distress."

She didn't argue with the description, though it rankled. "Is he okay?"

Cam's brother passed her a card with his name on it. Mason Hughes, Seattle PD. "He has a concussion and a broken foot. The bullet wound isn't serious."

"He's conscious?"

Mason nodded. "He says you saved his life."

"He saved mine. More than once."

"He's a regular Boy Scout, isn't he?"

Tala didn't know how to respond to that. Mason's flat expression made her nervous. "When can I see him?"

"They gave him some pain meds. He'll be out for hours."

"I want to be there when he wakes up."

Mason studied her with interest. "My brother is infatuated with you. I'm sure he feels even closer to you now that you've braved death together, but I'm concerned about his judgment. Since he met you, he's been behaving erratically."

She bristled at the accusation. "Since he met me, or since he lost his wife?"

"He's had a hard time dealing with his grief," Mason acknowledged. "I'm glad you came along, because he needed a diversion."

First she was a damsel, now she was a diversion. She narrowed her eyes at his wording. Mason Hughes was trying to insult her without being too obvious about it. He was one of those psychological cops, trained to mess with people's minds.

"The problem is, he doesn't know you're a diversion. You're a beautiful woman, and he's been living like a recluse. He's not equipped to discern between psychical attraction and something deeper."

Tala just stared at him. She had her own poker face, and she could use it. He was an intimidating figure, tall and stern-looking. Before she met Cam, she'd gone out of her way to avoid men like this. Now she didn't feel so helpless. She'd regained a sense of her former strength. She didn't have to run from everything that scared her.

Mason leaned forward. "Do you follow what I'm saying?"

"You're saying that Cam is too broken to know his own heart."

"Exactly," Mason said, pleased with her comprehension.

"What do you want from me?"

"I want you to let him recover in peace."

"You think I'm disturbing his peace?"

"I think you have outstanding warrants and a crazy ex-husband." Mason drummed his fingertips against the table the same way Cam drummed his on the steering wheel. "Cam doesn't need that kind of stress right now."

She swallowed hard. "Cam can make his own decisions."

"I'll buy you a bus ticket," Mason said, undeterred. He removed several hundred dollars from his wallet and placed it in front of her.

Tala couldn't believe he had the nerve to bribe her in the middle of a police station. Shady deals like this were the reason she didn't trust law enforcement officers. The arrogance of his attempt galled her. "I don't want your money."

"Don't do it for the money," Mason said. "Do it for Cam. Don't drag him off to Canada to fight your battles."

She picked up the cash and threw it in his face. "Cam was right. You're an asshole."

Mason retrieved the loose bills from the ground, his brow furrowed. "Is that what he said?"

"He said you were bitter about your divorce."

"Well, he told me you're a firecracker in bed."

She drew in a sharp breath. "He did not."

Mason gave her an assessing look. "Okay, he didn't. But I bet you are."

"He's going to be furious when he hears about this."

Cam's brother returned the cash to his wallet. "If you don't tell him, I'll take you with me to the hospital. They won't let you see him without me. You're not family."

She nodded, curling her hands into fists. "Fine."

"Think about my proposal while we're there."

"I don't have to think about it. I wouldn't ask him to come to Canada, and I'd never pit him against Duane."

Mason shrugged, as if her intentions weren't important. He didn't seem bothered by her refusal to accept his bribe. Maybe he'd done it to test her loyalty to Cam—or to plant seeds of doubt in her mind.

Mission accomplished.

Was she foolish to believe that Cam wanted a long-term relationship, like he'd claimed? That he might, someday, love her with the same intensity he'd loved Jenny? She didn't know if she should stay and hope. She didn't want him to get hurt again.

Mason Hughes didn't think she was a good choice for Cam, and maybe she wasn't. Maybe she should leave him alone. He was injured. He'd suffered from a concussion. He didn't need any more grief or trauma in his life.

She followed Mason down the hall, her thoughts in turmoil. Mason was wrong about one thing; Cam wasn't broken. He was strong. He could decide for himself. She had to give him a chance to make up his own mind. She wouldn't give up without a fight.

And she wouldn't, under any circumstances, leave without saying goodbye.

Chapter 20

December 15
65N
5 degrees

Cam drifted in and out of consciousness for several hours.

Tala was there, holding his hand. She kissed his knuckles periodically.

Mason was there, too. He didn't do anything but lurk in the background and pace around. Cam appreciated his brother's presence, though he was hardly a calming influence. He wanted to tell Mason to relax, but he couldn't keep his eyes open.

When the drugs wore off, he woke to a bright room, a full bladder and throbbing pain. Mason was there, staring at him.

"Where's Tala?"

"She went to the cafeteria."

Cam studied his surroundings blearily. He was in a hospital bed, his busted-up foot propped on pillows. In addition to a gunshot wound, he had a sprained ankle and something called a "proximal fracture" in the bone on the side of his foot. Apparently those two injuries went together like peanut butter and jelly. They'd immobilized it with bandages and a medical boot. He wasn't supposed to put weight on it—or drive—for several weeks. He took the pain pill by his bedside with water. Then he gestured for Mason to help him. "Bring me those crutches."

"Why are you getting up?"

"I have to take a piss."

Mason gave him the crutches with reluctance. Cam managed to make it to the bathroom and back without falling down. His sutured arm didn't hurt as much as his foot, but it didn't feel good. Neither did his head, for that matter.

"I called Mom," Mason said.

Cam muttered a string of curse words.

"I had to. You're in the hospital, and you almost died."

"I didn't almost die. I have a broken toe."

"Metatarsal. It's attached to your toe."

"Whatever."

"Also, you were shot."

"You didn't tell her that, did you? It's a graze. It's nothing."

"She wants to book a flight. You have to call her and talk her down."

Cam changed the subject. "How's Tala?"

"She's fine," Mason said. "She answered all of the

questions they threw at her. The detectives found her very credible, and your story corroborates hers."

"They don't think she was involved?"

"No. They're more concerned about who the cop was working for. The guy they executed at the diner was a police informant. The cop might have been there to identify him for his buddies. Whatever they were up to, they're all dead now. You and your girlfriend don't have to worry about retaliation."

"Are we supposed to stay in town while they wrap up the investigation?"

"Nah. This is open-and-shut."

"What about her warrants?"

"She's supposed to take care of it on her own. They won't be detaining her. She's not exactly a menace to society. The guys at the station were falling all over themselves to get her a cup of coffee."

Cam was relieved by the update. He'd been interviewed in the ER early this morning, while he was waiting to get X-rays. He hadn't known for sure if Tala would talk to the police. This was a big step for her. She'd set aside her fears and told her story to strangers.

She'd also shot a man and killed him, to save Cam. It was surreal.

"I'm in love with her," Cam said.

"You're on drugs," Mason said. "Literally."

"I was in love with her before the accident."

"You were high on adrenaline then."

A nurse entered the room breezily to check his vital signs. Cam was glad for the interruption, even though she scolded him for getting up on his own. "You need to keep that foot elevated as much as possible. Don't make any major decisions today, because you're recovering from a head injury. The medication will make you sleepy. You can do as much activity as you feel comfortable with tomorrow."

"When will I be released?"

"Late afternoon or early evening."

She took his lunch order and left, smiling at Mason on her way out. Cam's phone was among the effects brought to him from the accident scene. He called his mother, who was "worried sick," and wanted to fly to Fairbanks immediately.

"Don't waste your money," Cam said. "By the time you get here, I'll be out of the hospital."

"Where will you go?"

"There's a hotel across the street."

"Why don't you come home with your brother?"

"I can't fly," he said. "I'm supposed to keep my foot elevated."

"For how long?"

"I don't know, Mom. I just woke up."

"Someone needs to take care of you, and Mason can't do it. You know he's a workaholic."

Mason, who could hear their conversation, rolled his eyes.

"I'll be fine. I can take care of myself." And if he couldn't, he'd ask Tala to help him. He couldn't wait to see her again.

"Are you sure?"

"Positive."

"When will I see you next?"

"I'll come home for Christmas."

She inhaled a delighted breath. "You will?"

"Sure," he said. He'd already promised Mason he would, and the holidays didn't seem like a big deal anymore. Maybe he could convince Tala to come with him. Then his family could interrogate her instead of him.

"Call me later and let me know how you're doing. I mean it."

"I've got to go, Mom. Love you."

"I love you, too, sweetheart."

He hung up on that positive note. Tala entered the room with two coffee cups. She handed one to Mason, who nodded his thanks. Then she approached Cam's bedside. Her hair was in loose waves, freed from the braids. He wanted to bury his hands in that hair and kiss her until they both lost their breath.

"Can you give us some privacy?" Cam asked Mason.

Mason took a sip of coffee and almost choked on it. He didn't refuse to leave, though he seemed annoyed by the request. "Remember your patient instructions," he said, glancing at Tala. "No major decisions."

"You're turning into our mother," Cam said.

Tala ducked her head to hide a smile. Mason gave them both a dark look and continued out the door.

"Has he been rude to you?" Cam asked.

She touched her lips to his, making a noncommittal sound.

"I'll tell him to cut it out."

"He's just being overprotective. He thinks I'm going to throw you in front of Duane."

"I wouldn't mind mixing it up with Duane."

"I'd mind," she said, holding his gaze.

He threaded his fingers through the rumpled silk of her hair. He wanted to immerse himself in it, and disappear in her. "You're a sight for sore eyes."

"How do you feel?"

"Better, now that you're here."

"What instructions was he talking about it?"

"I'm supposed to take it easy. No heavy lifting."

"Or heavy thinking?"

"Something like that."

"You called your mother?"

"Yes. I said I'd bring you home for Christmas."

Her mouth fell open. "You didn't."

"You're right. I didn't. But I'd like to."

She pulled away from him, her brow furrowed.

"You don't want to meet my family?"

"That's not it," she said, crossing her arms over her chest. "I just have to go back to Canada for a while. I have to get my life in order."

"Alone?"

She nibbled on her lower lip. "Maybe that would be best."

"Best for who?"

"You're injured, Cam. You can't even drive."

"I can sit next to you."

"You need to rest."

"Exactly. This is the perfect time for a vacation. My truck is totaled, and I can't work. We'll stay here in Fairbanks for a day or two. Then we can rent a vehicle and take a road trip. You can drive, can't you?"

"I can drive a sled, a snowplow and just about anything else."

"Then what's the problem?"

"I don't want you to feel obligated to come with me."

"I don't feel obligated," he said, grasping her hand. "I love you."

Her eyes filled with tears. "What?"

"I'm in love with you."

"You are?" she asked in a hushed voice.

He nodded, his throat tight. "I thought you were going to die last night. I know what that kind of loss feels like, and I can't survive it again. That's why I can't let you go. I want to spend the rest of my life with you, Tala."

She blinked the tears away. "I don't know what to say."

"You don't have to say anything. Just stay."

"Okay."

He smiled at her easy acceptance.

"You're not supposed to be making any major decisions," she reminded him.

"We can talk about it again tomorrow. I won't change my mind."

She pressed a kiss to his temple. The swelling had gone down, but it was still tender. "You should be resting."

"I am tired," he admitted.

"I'll let you sleep."

"Can you book a hotel room? They're releasing me this afternoon."

"Which hotel?"

"The one across the street. Take my wallet." He glanced around drowsily and located a large plastic bag in the corner. "Our stuff is in that bag. They brought it from the accident scene. If you need clothes or anything, it's in there."

She sorted through the bag, selecting a few items. She kissed him goodbye once more before she left.

He was asleep before her footsteps faded down the hall.

Chapter 21

Tala zipped up her parka as she exited the hospital.

It was a brisk winter day, cold and bright. She went snowblind for a few seconds before her eyes adjusted. Then she continued toward the hotel, which was less than a block away. It was nice to stretch her legs and get some air.

She paid for a room with one of Cam's credit cards. The first thing she did was strip for a shower. Her clothes smelled like smoke and gasoline. Maybe even burnt flesh. When she closed her eyes, she saw melting corpses. She imagined bits of gore in her hair, even though she'd made a clean kill.

Shuddering, she soaped and scrubbed until her skin was raw. She climbed out of the stall, feeling better. She found a hairdryer and used it on high heat. Then she got dressed in her wrinkled sweater and jeans. At least she had fresh underwear, and her body was clean. She scanned a laminated list of hotel services, noting that there was a laundry room on the first floor. She could wash their clothes tonight.

She didn't want to be away from Cam for too long, so she grabbed her backpack and headed out again. She felt restless and uneasy. She was still in shock from the series of traumatic events. Nothing seemed real to her. Had Cam's words of love been a sweet fantasy, or a lovely dream? She couldn't believe he'd offered to come to Canada with her.

His brother wouldn't be pleased. Mason clearly disapproved of their whirlwind relationship. Tala couldn't really blame him. They'd known each other less than a week. Her love for Cam defied explanation.

Amazingly, he'd said he loved her, too. She'd been so stunned that she hadn't even told him she returned his feelings! A little part of her, the part that she'd been trying to overcome since she'd escaped Duane, didn't believe he meant those words. Some things were too good to be true.

She zipped up her parka, shivering. She couldn't shake a vague stirring of doom. Her grandmother's voice echoed in her ears like an omen. She'd often spoken of ill winds and the calm *before* the storm.

What if they weren't out of the woods yet?

The sun had already dipped low in the sky, and the temperature had dropped to below freezing. She pinpointed several common-sense reasons for her anxiety. She'd spent the night in an interrogation room, after a harrowing near-death experience and several days of stress. She'd witnessed a murder. She'd shot a man, point-blank. No one would feel lighthearted and hopeful after what she'd been through.

Cam's brother didn't inspire any warm fuzzies, either. She hoped he wouldn't make any more trouble for her. She understood his concerns for Cam. They both needed time to recover. She'd nurse him back to health, and heal herself.

Deep breaths.

She put on her hood as she crossed the parking lot. The hairs at the nape of her neck stood on end. She hurried toward the front entrance of the hospital, her heart pounding. As she approached the double doors, they opened unexpectedly.

Duane was on the other side.

She froze in her tracks, stunned. This time, he wasn't a figment of her imagination. He was really there.

He strode forward, like a hunter with his prey in sights. Instead of calmly walking past him, into a public waiting room, she panicked and stayed outside. Gasping cold air, she retreated. Her first instinct was to cut and run.

She moved backward slowly, keeping her eyes on him. That was how she ended up in a deserted parking lot with her abusive husband.

He looked the same, for the most part. Handsome features belied his ugly nature. He was tall and lean, with disheveled blond hair and a short goatee. He wore his favorite hunting jacket, swamp-grass print with a sheepskin lining.

Something was different about him. Or maybe *she* was different.

She could see the physical qualities that had attracted her to him, along with the strength he'd used against her, but he didn't appear as intimidating as he used to. He looked pale and reedy. Cam was the bigger man in more ways than one, and he exuded confidence. Duane didn't. He had a scared-rabbit glint in his eyes.

She realized, with shock, that Duane was afraid of *her*. He was afraid of getting hurt. The knowledge didn't make her feel powerful or safe. Cornered animals were the most dangerous. He could still do terrible damage to her.

Even so, she stopped retreating. It was too late to flee. She could try to escape into the lobby, but he might grab her. She didn't want to trigger his predator instincts, and she was done running from him. Also, they had important matters to discuss. She might as well stand her ground and get on with it.

"How did you find me?" she asked, lifting her chin.

"I saw your picture on the TV. Missing waitress from Willow."

"This isn't Willow."

"You were on the news again this morning. Deadly accident near Fairbanks."

She crossed her arms over her chest to hide her trembling hands.

"I drove all night to get here. I thought you were hurt."

"I was hurt the last time you saw me. Remember what you did to my face?"

His mouth thinned with displeasure. He didn't like being reminded of his abusive ways. "It won't happen again."

"I know. I won't let it."

"You made your point, Tala. I was wrong to do what I did. You ran off to make me sorry. Well, I'm sorry. Are you happy now? Can we go home?"

She shook her head, incredulous.

"You got a new man? Is that it?"

"It's none of your business."

"I knew it," he said, spitting in the snow. "I knew you couldn't keep your legs shut."

"I'm filing for divorce."

"You won't get a penny."

She stifled the urge to laugh. Even if he had money—which he didn't—she wasn't interested in it. "I'll tell you what I want. Listen carefully."

"Why should I?"

"Because I'm pressing charges if you don't."

He made a scoffing sound. "You can't do that. You've got no evidence." He gestured to her unmarred face.

"Sure I do," she said. "I took pictures."

His eyes narrowed with suspicion.

"I'll show them to the police, and I'll tell them everything. I'll tell them what happened at the rally, too."

"They won't believe you."

"Yes, they will. It's the truth."

He glanced around the parking lot warily. "What do you want?"

"I want you to clear my name. Go to Whitehorse and confess to the assault."

"I'll go to jail," he sputtered.

"That's your problem," she said. "Hire a lawyer and submit a plea bargain, or do whatever you have to. When they drop the charges against me, I'll file for divorce and walk away. You won't have to worry about everyone knowing you're a wife-beater. But you really should get some help with that, Duane. You need it."

He stared at her for a long moment, his nostrils flared. "You goddamned bitch," he said through clenched teeth. "I loved you."

She recoiled in fear when he stepped forward. She'd

seen that look before. She'd seen his neck turn red with fury just before he struck. Duane's switch had flipped. He was beyond caring about making a scene now, beyond listening to reason. The urge to run gripped her again, but she didn't get the chance. She stumbled over a concrete divider and fell on her behind. Before she could scramble to her feet, Duane advanced. He loomed over her with a raised fist.

Then a man flew out of nowhere and knocked *him* on his ass.

It was Mason Hughes.

Her unexpected defender hit Duane with a right cross so well placed he spun around in a full circle before he went down. Duane stayed down, seeming stunned by the blow, but Mason wasn't finished with him yet. He straddled Duane's waist, lifted him by the collar and punched him again.

Duane's head rocked back against the snow-covered asphalt.

Mason drew back his fist a third time.

"Stop," Tala said, grasping his elbow.

"You want to take a shot?" Mason asked. "I'll hold him for you."

"No, I don't want to take a shot. I need him conscious."

Mason let go of Duane's collar, with reluctance. Duane gazed up at them blearily. Blood dribbled from his nose and continued down his chin.

"Remember what I said about confessing?" she asked.

"I remember."

"If you don't do it, I'll see you in court."

"And I'll see you in a dark alley," Mason said.

Duane grimaced, his teeth stained red. "I hear you. Now get your dog off me."

When Tala nodded her permission, Mason allowed Duane to his feet. Duane wiped his nose and spat blood in the snow. Then he started walking across the parking lot in angry strides. He didn't appear to enjoy being on the receiving end of violence.

"One more thing," she called after him.

"What?"

"Do you have my purse?"

He kept walking toward his truck. It was parked at the far edge of the lot, among a cluster of similar trucks and half-covered in new-fallen snow. She figured he'd brought her purse along. They couldn't cross the border without her ID. Sure enough, he tossed her purse out the window and took off in a squeal of tires.

She rushed forward to retrieve her purse from the ground. Her wallet was there, with her drivers' license and tribal card.

Victory.

She studied Mason with new eyes. He'd really grown on her in the past few minutes. "Why did you do that?"

He massaged his knuckles. "Do what? I didn't do anything."

"Thank you, all the same."

"It was my pleasure."

"I thought you wanted to get rid of me."

"Not that way," he said, watching Duane's truck until it disappeared. "Does he usually have a gun on him?"

"He keeps one in his truck."

Mason moved his gaze to Tala. Although he didn't say anything, his expression revealed his concern for Cam's welfare. This basic human emotion was much more effective than the bribe he'd attempted earlier. He'd asked her not to put Cam in the line of fire. She didn't think Duane would shoot anyone, but she couldn't be sure. He was a man scorned, and he wasn't known for handling rejection well.

Duane might confess to the assault at the rally. Not because it was the right thing to do, but to avoid the scandal of domestic violence charges. He might sign the divorce papers and let her go without a fight.

Or he might make her life hell, just because. She removed Cam's wallet from her pocket and handed it to Mason, feeling glum. Mason accepted the item in silence. They stood side by side in the snowy parking lot.

"I misjudged you," Mason said finally.

She was startled by the admission. Mason seemed even less likely to admit to a mistake than Cam. They were cut from the same stubborn cloth. She had her own stubborn streak, so she could sympathize.

"Cam says he's in love with you. I don't want him to get hurt again."

Her knees felt weak, so she sank to a sitting position on the curb.

"Are you all right?"

"I'm fine. I just need a minute."

He stayed right there with her, his arms crossed over his chest. She could tell he was cold. His jacket would suffice in Seattle, but it didn't have enough insulation for an Alaska winter. Now the adrenaline was wearing off, and he could feel the chill.

She took pity on him. "I'd rather be alone, if you don't mind."

He nodded curtly and walked away. Anxiety welled

up inside her once more. She wanted to be with Cam, but she also needed some time to herself. She needed time to think. Mason had helped her stand up to Duane. He'd asked her to leave Cam alone, and she felt obligated to consider his request.

So she did. She considered it very carefully.

It wouldn't be the end of the world to go to Canada without him. She could give him some space while he recovered from his injuries. She didn't have to leave forever. Just until the conflict with Duane passed. As much as she appreciated Cam's support, she could manage without him. She'd been doing it for months. She was an independent woman, capable of handling her own business. If Duane followed her suggestions and cleared her name, she'd come back to Alaska. If he didn't...perhaps it was best to stay away. Cam had been through enough heartache and struggle. He'd almost died trying to protect her.

Mason's concerns weren't unwarranted.

She rose to her feet, pulse racing. She understood Mason's perspective, but she had to consider Cam's needs, also. He said he loved her. He planned to introduce her to his family. He'd asked her to stay. She'd already told him she would.

Ultimately, this was her decision. If she wanted to go, she could go. If she wanted to stay, she could stay.

She studied the looming structure of the hospital, with its glinting windows and geometric shapes. She could walk inside and be with Cam right now, but the prospect of sitting in a quiet room with Mason Hughes didn't appeal to her. She couldn't take any more tension or stillness. She wanted space to move around. Physi-

cal activity would clear her head. She needed to run for
a little while.

She turned away from the hospital and headed toward freedom.

Chapter 22

Cam slept most of the afternoon.

When he woke up again, it was dark outside. His head felt better. His foot still hurt and his arm was sore, but he could endure the discomfort. He declined a second pain pill in favor of over-the-counter stuff. He wanted to stay awake.

Mason brought him some flannel pajamas to lounge around in. Cam decided to take a shower before he changed clothes. He smelled like blood and diesel and sweat. It would be easier to bathe here than in a hotel room, so he rose from his hospital bed. There was a safety chair in the shower stall, ready to go. The nurse gave him a plastic baggie to cover his foot. Sitting down to shower felt strange, but it was better than falling on his ass. He washed off, toweled dry and got dressed on his own.

He couldn't wait to get discharged. He was looking

forward to a night of snuggling with Tala. Maybe more, if he was lucky. When he emerged from the bathroom, Mason was sitting in the corner, reading a newspaper. He didn't look up.

"Where's Tala?" Cam asked.

Mason rattled his paper. "I don't know."

"Did she come back from the hotel?"

"She did. Then she left again."

Cam figured Tala didn't want to spend time with his surly brother. Cam didn't blame her. He pictured her reading one of her graphic novels in the lobby, or grabbing a cup of coffee. The nurse arrived with discharge forms, which he scanned quickly. She told him the doctor would come in to go over patient instructions.

"Do you want some ice for that hand?" she asked Mason.

Cam glanced at his brother in surprise. His knuckles were raw and swollen. "I'm good," he said, closing the newspaper.

The nurse said goodbye and exited the room.

Cam's gut clenched with unease. "What happened to you?"

"I ran into Duane Laramie."

"Where?"

"Right here, in front of the hospital. He was arguing with Tala."

"How did he find her?"

"I don't know," Mason said. "I didn't get the chance to interrogate him. I saw her fall down, so I intervened."

Cold fury enveloped Cam. "He hit her?"

"No. I got there first."

"Did you straighten him out?"

"I punched him a few times. I couldn't knock him

out because she wanted to talk to him. She threatened to take him to court if he didn't confess to assaulting that police officer."

Cam rubbed a hand over his mouth, contemplative. It was a better deal than Duane deserved. If he cleared Tala's name, she wouldn't press domestic violence charges against him. "Did he agree?"

"He'd be a fool not to, but he didn't say yes or no. After I let him up, he threw her purse out of his truck and drove away."

"Jesus, Mason. Why didn't you tell me?"

"You were asleep."

Cam grabbed for his crutches. One of them clattered to the floor. "She almost gets attacked by her ex, and you don't wake me up? You left her alone in the lobby? What the hell is wrong with you?"

Mason picked up the crutch for Cam. "I don't think she's in the lobby."

"Where is she?"

His brother shrugged, avoiding his gaze.

Cam's vision went red. He didn't know what Mason was up to, but he couldn't stay in the hospital another minute. He was leaving right now to find Tala.

"Where is she?" he repeated, his voice low.

"I don't know," Mason said. "She never came in from the parking lot."

"Did Duane take her?"

"I'm pretty sure she walked away on her own."

"Why would she do that?"

"I might have said something that upset her."

"You *might* have?"

"Okay, I did. I suggested that you'd already been shot once because of her—"

"I didn't get shot," Cam growled. "It's a *graze*."

"—and maybe she should leave you alone until things blow over."

"You son of a bitch. How dare you?"

Mason flinched at Cam's vehemence. "I'm your brother. I was worried about you."

"So you chase off my girlfriend? That's your way of helping me?"

"You've been racing toward death since you got here," Mason said, raising his voice. Now they were both shouting. "I thought you hooked up with her to accelerate the trip!"

Cam wanted to tackle Mason. He pictured them wrestling on the floor, knocking over trays of medical supplies. If he didn't have a broken foot, he'd have launched himself at his brother, fists flying.

"I wasn't racing toward death," he said curtly. "I was already dead inside. She makes me want to live again."

Mason fell silent for a moment. "I'm sorry."

"She's the opposite of whatever you're thinking. She's the best thing that's ever happened to me. She shot a man to protect me, for Christ's sake. You had no right to blame her for my injuries."

"I was looking out for you."

"I didn't need you to look out for me," Cam said. "I needed you to look out for *her*. She's a victim of domestic violence, and her abuser's in town."

Mason raked a hand through his hair. "Do you want to go after her, or yell at me?"

"Go after her," Cam said.

They didn't wait around to listen to the doctor's orders. Mason gathered Cam's belongings and headed out the door. Cam followed him down the hall, clumsy on his crutches. His foot throbbed and his arm burned as he loped along. He wanted to pick another fight with Mason in the elevator, but he saved his breath. They'd already spent too much time arguing. He had to focus on finding Tala.

They looked in the lobby, the gift shop and the cafeteria. She wasn't there.

"Maybe she went back to the hotel," Mason said.

"Let's check it out."

Mason brought his rental car to the front entrance of the hospital so Cam didn't have to maneuver across the parking lot. Crutches didn't mix well with snow and ice. Cam didn't thank him for the courtesy. He was too angry to speak.

"She returned your wallet," Mason said. "It's in the glove compartment."

Cam glanced in his wallet and found a key card with the room number. Mason drove the short distance to the hotel and pulled into a parking space. He hopped out to help Cam with his crutches.

"Be careful. It's slippery."

Cam offered a curt two-word response as he exited the vehicle. He wasn't in the mood for Mason's brotherly advice. They entered the hotel lobby and walked down the hall. Tala had booked him a room on the ground floor. She wasn't inside, but he noted the evidence of her presence. The scent of shampoo lingered in the bathroom, and a damp towel hung on the rack. There were no clues to her current whereabouts. She'd taken her backpack and clothes with her. The graphic novel she'd been reading was sitting in the middle of the bed.

He wasn't sure if she'd meant to leave it behind. Maybe it was a subtle hint that their erotic encounters

hadn't been important to her. They were fleeting pleasures, easily forgotten. Abandoned at the first opportunity.

He picked up the book and threw it against the wall,
very close to his brother's head. Mason ducked to avoid
the object, which wouldn't have hit him anyway. Pain
stabbed down Cam's arm from the sudden motion, and
one of his crutches fell to the carpet. He struggled to
maintain his balance.

Mason hurried to help him sit on the edge of the bed.
"Settle down, Cam! You're going to end up right back
in the hospital."

"I should put *you* in the hospital," Cam said.

Mason shoved him until he sat down. "Dream on, little brother. You can't even take me when you're healthy."

Cam considered punching his lights out. "I could take
you right now."

Mason leaned forward and pointed at his chin in offering. "Make my day. You think I won't hit you back
just because you're injured?"

Cam didn't really want to fight. Not in his current
condition. His entire body ached and his brain felt
scrambled. Hurting Mason wouldn't bring Tala back.
So he took a deep breath, trying to refocus. His crutches
were in a heap on the floor. He had a busted-up foot and
a bandaged arm. And his brother was still getting in his
face, taunting him.

Cam had to laugh at Mason's pugnacious expression.
"You're ridiculous."

Mason straightened abruptly. "You started it."

"Give me my crutches."

"Don't be stupid."

"We have to keep looking for her."

"You're in no condition to be out on foot in this kind of weather. You weren't even officially discharged."

"I'm fine," Cam said, his irritation rising again. "We're driving around, not climbing Denali."

"One of us should stay here in case she comes back. That's you."

It wasn't a bad plan, but Cam didn't trust his brother to find Tala. Mason was the one who'd scared her off. "She won't talk to you."

"She doesn't have to. I'll just make sure she's safe."

"Okay," Cam said, because he didn't really have a choice. They were wasting time arguing about it. "You'll want to check the airport."

"What about the bus station?"

"There's no bus service in the winter. This isn't Seattle."

"Where else?"

Cam raked a hand through his hair. "I don't know. She might go to a diner or a bookstore. She likes books."

"I see that."

"If all else fails, I can get on a CB and ask the truckers to be on the lookout. Do you know what her husband drives?"

Mason's eyes narrowed. "Yeah, I do."

Cam swallowed hard. He couldn't finish that thought, but he didn't have to. Mason knew the statistics for domestic homicides better than Cam did. If she'd been harmed, Cam would tear Duane apart with his bare hands.

"Stop mad-dogging me," Mason said. "She'll turn up."

"She'd better, or I'll kill you."

They stared at each other for a tense moment. Mason looked a little choked up. Cam glanced away, clearing his throat. His brother meant well, and he seemed sorry. It was difficult to hold a grudge against Mason. He had emotional issues, and not just because of his divorce. In his line of work, he dealt with unspeakable atrocities.

"Go on," Cam said. "I'll keep my phone handy."

Mason nodded and left the room, his gaze sharp with determination.

Chapter 23

Tala ran until her muscles ached and her lungs burned.

When she got off the treadmill, she was breathing hard, her skin damp with sweat. Her head was clear, and she felt better.

Much better.

She preferred running outdoors, but that wasn't an option in this nasty weather. The hotel gym was nice enough. She'd changed into her leggings before she left the hotel room. She ran barefoot on the treadmill, her muscles flexing. She ran off her tension, and her troubles. She ran without running away.

Then she started a load of laundry and waited for Cam. He'd said he'd get discharged sometime today. After she put the clothes in the dryer, she wandered down the hall and found an empty office area. There were a couple of desks for guests to work quietly. There was a cozy-looking chair and a phone.

On impulse, she settled in to call her mother. The hotel clerk charged the long-distance fee to Cam's room. Tala waited for her mom to pick up. Once again, she sounded happy to hear from her.

"When are you coming to visit?" her mother asked.

"I'm not sure."

"What about Christmas? Bear will be here."

"Oh, *now* you want me to hang out with Bear?"

Her mother laughed. "You don't have to."

Tala switched the phone to her other ear. "I met someone here in Alaska, but I don't know if it's going to work out."

"Why not?"

She struggled to find words for her feelings. "Maybe I'm supposed to be alone."

"Of course you're not. Why would you say that?"

"Dad didn't have anyone."

"He had you."

"That's not what I mean. He didn't have girlfriends. After you, he gave up on love."

"He didn't give up on love. He had a girlfriend."

"Who?"

"Helen Barclay."

"Mrs. Barclay? The music teacher?"

"That's her."

"She was married."

"Yes. That's why he kept it a secret."

"Where did you hear that?"

"There was gossip around town. They started seeing each other when you were eleven or twelve. It went on for years, until her husband caught them. He moved the family to Edmonton. Helen wanted to stay in Yellowknife, but your father told her not to. They had two little girls, and he didn't want to break up their family."

"She came to the funeral."

"Yes. She loved him."

"I never knew," Tala said, her voice breaking. "That's so sad."

"I didn't tell you to upset you, *nitânis*. I just wanted you to know your father had love in his life, even after me. He worked hard and he never gave up on anything. I think he learned not to be so selfish after what we went through in our divorce. He became a better man."

Tala was glad her mother had told her about the ill-fated affair. She wasn't sure if it brightened her outlook, but it did color her perspective. She said a quick good-bye to her mother, rising from the chair.

She'd always thought of romantic love as something beautiful and fleeting. It was the rainbow after the storm. It didn't last. Maybe she'd been wrong. Maybe love was the storm, too. Maybe it was the wind and the rain and the thunder. It wasn't a settled feeling, static and unchanging, but it didn't have to fade away. It could be calm one day and tumultuous the next.

Her mother said love was hard work. Tala had never been afraid of hard work. She loved Cam, and she was willing to fight for him.

She couldn't run away from love anymore.

She had to tell him how she felt, right now. She left the office and hurried down the hall, her heart racing. She had to get back to the hospital and confess her feelings to Cam. He'd said he loved her, and she'd left him hanging. She'd been afraid to say the words back to him. Afraid to put herself out there. Afraid to get hurt again. She was still afraid, but she couldn't let fear stop her from getting what she wanted. Maybe this time everything would work out. Maybe it wouldn't. Either way, she had to try.

She was her father's daughter. Unlucky in love, perhaps, but not a quitter.

Feeling giddy, she ducked into the laundry room to retrieve their clean clothes. Then she headed down the hall with her arms full. When she opened the door to the room, someone was inside, waiting for her.

She let out a startled shriek and dropped everything on the floor.

It was Cam.

Her heart couldn't take another shock, even a good one. She clutched the center of her chest and tried not to hyperventilate.

He stood, with some difficulty. He seemed as surprised to see her as she was to see him. He was wearing flannel pajamas, and he had crutches under his arms. His left foot was encased in a heavy black medical boot. He looked injured, but still strong. Still ruggedly handsome. Her chest swelled with love for him. She wanted to throw her arms around him and kiss him senseless, but she was afraid to knock him off balance.

"You came back," he said.

She closed the door and locked it behind her. They stared at each other for a taut moment. Emotions welled up inside her, spilling over. She rushed into the comfort of his embrace. He managed to hug her back without falling. He smelled like snow and heat and man. She closed her eyes, relishing his warmth. "I love you."

His body went tense. "You do?"

She pressed her lips to his neck. "I should have told you earlier."

"I thought I'd lost you," Cam said, hugging her closer.

"I've been here all afternoon."

He released her abruptly, his expression incredulous. "You've been here at the hotel? This whole time?"

"Where did you think I was?"

"I thought you ran away!"

"I didn't run away. I came here and ran on the treadmill. Then I called my mother and did some laundry."

He stared at her as if he couldn't fathom these ordinary things. "My brother said Duane attacked you in the parking lot."

"He did, but he's gone now."

Cam lowered himself to the edge of the bed. "How did he find you?"

She took his crutches and placed them nearby. Then she sat down next to him and told him the whole story. "I think your brother broke his nose."

"I guess he did one thing right," Cam muttered.

"It almost makes up for the attempted bribe."

Cam narrowed his eyes. "He offered you money to leave me alone?"

"Yes."

He dragged a hand down his face. "I'm sorry."

"Don't be. It's not your fault."

"He's out looking for you right now."

She laughed merrily at that turn of events. "Are you sure he wants to find me?"

"I told him I'd kill him if he didn't."

Her amusement died at this dark claim. "Cam, I don't want to cause trouble between you and your brother."

"You're not causing trouble. It's him."

"He doesn't want you to get hurt."

"I'm not going to get hurt," Cam said, stretching out his injured leg.

"You're already hurt."

He ignored this observation and took his phone out of his pocket. "Should I tell him I found you, or let him sweat a little longer?"

"Tell him."

She waited while he had a short conversation with his brother. They spoke to each other in grunts and monosyllables.

"He wants to apologize," Cam said.

Tala shook her head, grimacing.

"She's busy," Cam lied. He listened to Mason for a minute. Then he said goodbye and hung up. "Mason talked to the state police. They spotted Duane's truck in Delta Junction. It's halfway to the Canadian border."

"He's going home."

"Looks like it."

She was relieved by the news. She hadn't figured Duane would stick around to cause trouble with a busted nose. She'd stood up to him, and he'd run off with his tail between his legs. Good riddance.

Cam set his phone on the nightstand and stretched out on his back. She put a pillow under his ankle to prop up his broken foot. She retrieved the clean laundry from the floor and folded it. Then she cuddled next to Cam, enjoying his warmth. He had a great physique for snuggling. He was lean and solid. Steady as a rock.

"Do you want kids?" he asked.

"Right now?"

"Now, later, whenever."

"Why do you ask?"

"It's good to be on the same page about some things."

She considered the question carefully. "I'd like to be a mother."

"When?"

"Before I'm thirty, I guess."

He seemed to find this timeline acceptable.

"What about you?"

"I'm past thirty already."

"I know."

"Before I'm forty is good. I don't want to be too old."

"There are a few things we should discuss before we plan the next five years, Cam."

"Okay."

"I'm planning to finish college. You already know that. I'd like to go to school in Billings, where my mother lives. I want a chance to repair our relationship. We've spent too many years apart."

Cam pointed out the obvious. "I can't be an ice-road trucker in Montana."

"You could be a regular trucker."

He made a noncommittal sound. Maybe after the ice road, highway hauling didn't hold the same appeal. "What if I returned to law enforcement?"

"Would you consider it?"

He arched a brow. "I thought you hated police officers."

"That was before I fell in love with one."

Cam smiled at her answer. "I can look for work in Montana. I'll live wherever you want to live. When you're ready to get married and have babies, we'll do that. You want me to come home to you every night, I'm there. How does that sound?"

She smiled back. "Too good to be true."

"Maybe we've earned it."

"My grandmother used to say, 'After the storm comes the rainbow.'"

"Do you believe it?"

"I'm trying to."

He shifted into a more comfortable position. "We'll make it work."

"How do you know?"

"Because you're a warrior, and I'm your soldier. I'll do anything for you. Together, we can't lose."

She studied his handsome face, contemplative. Maybe he was right. Last night he'd dragged himself upright, half-conscious and bleeding, to tackle the gunman. "You're unstoppable."

He propped a finger under her chin. "So are you."

Tears filled her eyes. "I love you, Cam."

He touched his lips to hers. "I love you, too."

She kissed him until they were both breathless. His hands roved over her body, squeezing her waist and the curves of her bottom. She could feel his arousal swell against her hip. She gentled the kiss, reluctant to encourage him. He grasped her thigh and tugged, as if urging her to climb on top of him.

"We can't," she said.

He stared at her mouth intently. "Why not?"

"You need to rest."

"I need you more."

She kissed him again, biting his lower lip. "I don't want to hurt you."

"If you do, I'll give the stop signal."

She laughed at his eagerness. "No, Cam. Not tonight."

"Tomorrow?"

"Tomorrow," she promised.

She snuggled against his chest. He grasped her hand.

They fell asleep like that, fingers entwined and limbs entangled. Just the two of them against the world, united by love, unbroken and unstoppable.

Chapter 24

Big Sky, MT
45N
21 degrees

Three weeks later.

Cam's recovery went well.

He wasn't great at resting, but he tried to relax as much as possible. They lounged around the hotel for almost a week. Tala took care of his every need and then some. She even indulged him with exercise. He spent many quality hours underneath her. He thought he'd get bored with reclining positions, but he didn't. She had a knack for being on top, and he loved watching her. He loved every inch of her sweet body, sliding all over him.

While they were in Fairbanks, they did a few other

things besides making love. Cam submitted his resignation to Northern Lights Trucking Company, on their request. They weren't pleased about his unapproved passenger or the melee on the Dalton. They launched an insurance investigation, with predictable results. Cam had broken the rules of his contract, so he was liable for all the damages.

Cam could pay for his own hospital bills, but his rig was unrepairable. He had to sell it for parts. His ice-road trucker days were over. A month ago, he'd have been devastated by this turn of events. In his current state of sexual bliss, it was hardly a blip. He'd already decided to move on with Tala.

They'd hired a lawyer to help Tala with her legal issues. Although Duane hadn't caused any more trouble in Fairbanks, he hadn't taken the initiative to confess to the assault at the rally. Tala's attorney had to send him a letter of encouragement, along with the divorce papers. Duane responded by hiring his own defense. In the end, he'd cooperated with investigators. He pleaded guilty to disorderly conduct.

This outcome frustrated Cam, because it felt like another travesty of justice. Duane was a menace to society, a coward and an abuser of women. But instead of a stiff punishment, he'd gotten a slap on the wrist. Cam had to let it go, however. In addition to clearing her name, Duane had signed the divorce papers.

Tala was a free woman.

When Cam was cleared to travel, he rented an SUV and headed south. Driving was still uncomfortable for him, so Tala took the wheel. They visited Denali National Park. He was an expert on his crutches after the first week. After Denali, they passed through Willow.

She visited Walt at the diner. He'd managed to sleep through the excitement and remain unscathed.

For Christmas, they flew to Tacoma and spent several days on the farm. She didn't really warm up to Mason, but she hit it off with his parents. Tala enjoyed cooking and was genuinely interested in the land. They loved her.

Before they left, his mother pulled him aside and said, "Marry her."

"I'm working on it," Cam replied.

Their next stop was Billings, Montana. Although Tala hadn't seen her family in years, and her younger brothers hardly knew her, they accepted her with open arms. Her older stepbrother, the one she'd had a crush on, was now a sheriff's deputy in Great Falls. When Tala mentioned Cam's previous profession, Bear gave him a curious look.

Later, Bear approached Cam for a private talk. Cam thought he was going to get grilled about his intentions toward Tala. Instead, Bear told him about an employment opportunity in Big Sky. They'd offered Bear the position, but he didn't want to relocate to a sleepy mountain town. The sheriff there needed a deputy, and not some wet-eared rookie. He was looking for someone with enough experience and education to train for the sheriff's position. The current sheriff planned to retire in another year.

"I didn't mention it in front of Tala because I don't know how serious you are about her," Bear said.

Cam smiled at the brotherly comment. "I want to marry her."

"What does she want?"

"To finish school and be near her family."

"So you're staying in Montana?"

Cam nodded. "I told her I'd look for work here."

Bear seemed satisfied by his answers. "If you're interested in the deputy job, I'll put in a good word."

Cam thanked him with a handshake. He was interested—very interested. A sleepy mountain town sounded perfect after what he'd been through. He'd had enough excitement to last a lifetime. Now he wanted to settle down in a peaceful place.

He mailed in an application, listing his credentials with the Seattle PD and adding Bear Klamath as a reference. He didn't tell Tala about the opportunity. Big Sky was more than a hundred miles from Billings and he wasn't sure how she'd feel about living there. If he got an offer, he'd ask her to come with him.

They spent the next few days touring Yellowstone National Park, which was nearby. Cam had never been there, and Tala hadn't visited in winter. It was a snow-covered wonderland. He didn't need his crutches anymore, but he still had to wear the medical boot. He couldn't wait to take it off.

While they were at the Yellowstone Lodge, Cam received a message from Sheriff Dugan in Big Sky. It was a request for a FaceTime interview. Cam waited until Tala was in the shower to step outside and return the call.

Sheriff Dugan was a no-nonsense lawman in his late sixties. He explained that the job was physical, the weather was challenging and the terrain was rugged. He needed someone with patience, fortitude and stamina.

Cam liked the sound of the job. He told Dugan about his nine years on highway patrol and his recent stint as an ice-road trucker.

"Ice roads, huh? You must have nerves of steel."

Cam didn't agree or disagree.

"You're not afraid of extreme conditions."

"No, sir."

"How do you know Bear?"

"He's my girlfriend's stepbrother."

"Well, you look healthy enough to do the work and you have the right background. A degree in sociology is better suited to this position than criminal justice. You'll be keeping the peace more than investigating."

Cam wanted to pump his fist in triumph. "Yes, sir."

"We get tourists all year round. Summertime's the busiest. Lost hikers and vehicular accidents are common. It's mostly quiet, though."

"I like quiet."

"Good," Dugan said. "There's a cabin by the old sawmill that comes with the job. Drive out there and take a look before you decide. Bring your girlfriend."

"I'll do that."

Cam jotted down the address for the cabin. Dugan needed an answer within a few days. It was a great opportunity, but he had to discuss the details with Tala. He checked the directions to Big Sky on his phone. It was only an hour away from the lodge.

When Tala was ready to go, her hair blow-dried and bags packed, he drove them north. Big Sky was off the beaten path a little, about ten miles from a major highway. He suggested they have lunch there. Tala shrugged her agreement, nose in a book. He continued through the rustic little town, with its snow-covered roofs and chimneys chugging. There was a busy café with a Help Wanted sign in the window.

Tala perked up when she saw it. "We could eat there."

"We'll come back to it," he said, continuing past the

café. A few minutes later he found the cabin on Sawmill Road.

"Are we lost?" Tala asked.

"No," Cam said. "I wanted to surprise you."

He got out and opened the passenger door for her. She followed him toward the cabin. The key was under the mat, as promised. He unlocked the door and stepped inside.

It was a well-built cabin. The fireplace in the living room promised cozy nights. There was a small kitchen with modern appliances, a full bath and a single bedroom. Good lighting and sturdy hardwood floors. With some furniture and rugs and stuff, it could be transformed from an empty space into a quaint little home.

He glanced at Tala. "What do you think?"

"Is it for rent?"

"I got a job offer here in Big Sky. This place comes with it."

"A job offer? To do what?"

"Sheriff's deputy. I'd train to take over as sheriff."

She blinked at him in surprise. "I didn't know you'd applied for any jobs."

"Your stepbrother told me about the opening. It seemed too good to pass up."

"It is," she said, twirling around in a slow circle. Her attorney had arranged for her belongings to be packed and shipped from Duane's house to her mother's. Tala had told him about her grandmother's furs and other cherished items. She could keep them here. She could decorate however she liked.

"I don't have to take the offer," he said. "I came to Montana to be with you. If you don't want to live here, we won't."

She inspected the bathroom. "How far away is Bozeman?"

"Thirty miles."

"Montana State University is in Bozeman. I could go there."

"You would do that?"

She returned to his side and twined her arms around his neck. "As long as we're together, I'll be happy."

Relief and love overwhelmed him. "So will I."

"This is a beautiful town."

"It's two hours away from Billings. Ten hours from Tacoma."

"Some distance from family is good. Especially from your brother."

He laughed, hugging her closer.

"Maybe I'll apply to that café."

"You don't have to."

"I want to."

He lowered his head to kiss her. She kissed him back sweetly, threading her fingers through his hair. He couldn't believe his luck. A month ago, he'd been completely numb. Tala had thawed him from the inside out.

"Will this be exciting enough for you?" she asked.

"You're all I need for excitement."

"You said your fantasy was a cozy cabin."

"And yours was freedom."

"We got both."

"We did, didn't we?"

On impulse, he lifted her into his arms and carried her over the threshold into the bedroom. She laughed at his romantic gesture, which was no easy task with a healing foot. He set her down by the window. There were no furnishings, and it wasn't warm enough to get intimate, but he kissed her until they were both breathless.

"I love you," he said, his heart full.

"I love you, too."

"Always?"

"Always," she agreed, and kissed him again.

* * * * *

SUDDEN SETUP

BARB HAN

Many thanks to Allison Lyons, the absolute best editor. My enduring gratitude to Jill Marsal, the absolute best agent. I'm privileged to work with both of you and count my blessings every day.

Brandon, Jacob and Tori, nothing in my life would make sense without the three of you. Your smiles bring joy and light to every day. Bitty Bug—our fairy-light chats are the highlight of every evening.

Babe, how lucky am I? You make me laugh, lift me up when I cry and cheer me on every single day. If I could be granted one wish, it would be that every person could have this kind of love. I can only imagine how much better the world would be for it. I love you

Chapter One

Whoever said mistakes don't define a person didn't have a clue. Holden Crawford stood over the petite woman curled in his bed, figuring that helping her would cost him dearly. He shook his head at his own stupidity. She'd already been in and out of sleep for a day and a half, and he was beginning to worry that she'd taken a harder knock to the head than he initially assessed. As soon as she woke and he made sure she was all right, he'd drive her close to the sheriff's office. Then he'd disappear. Again.

Holden had recognized Ella Butler immediately when he saw her hiking. She was the daughter of the wealthiest man in Cattle Barge, Texas—a man who was helping Holden out while he needed a hand and a protected place to stay off the grid.

His daughter was trouble times ten. His best bet would be to leave her in the cabin with a few supplies and take off before anyone connected the dots that he'd been there. And yet, abandoning her while she was so vulnerable wasn't something he could do. Even someone as hardened as him couldn't walk away like this.

Holden ignored the annoying voice in his head that tried to convince him sticking around might be an option. His duffel was already packed and sitting next to the door.

He'd told himself that staring at the wavy-haired beauty as she hiked along Devil's Lid was for survival reasons and not because those long, silky legs of hers were highlighted perfectly in pale pink running shorts. He'd needed to see if she would detour to the cabin on the outskirts of her father's property where he stayed and expose his hiding spot. Hell, it had been his sanctuary.

Out of nowhere, her head had snapped to one side and then she'd lost her footing. She'd free-fallen a good ten feet before hitting the hard clay soil. She'd rolled another twenty before meeting an equally rough landing at the bottom of the gulch.

It had been no accident.

At that point, Holden had had two choices: help or walk away. Tracking the responsible party hadn't been a serious consideration, although Holden didn't doubt his own skills. It was more important to make sure she was safe first. But there was a problem with helping her.

Ella Butler was news.

If it hadn't been ninety-five degrees at eight o'clock in the morning, he would've cleaned her wound and then left her with a couple of water bottles for when she woke. August weather was too unforgiving to leave her stranded and the gash on her head was serious. Holden had had no choice but to bring her back to the cabin.

To complicate matters, she'd blinked up at him. He

had to know if she remembered him when she woke because if she could give his description to law enforcement, the real trouble would begin.

Holden walked another circle around the room.

Questions ate at him. First of which, what kind of fool hiked alone in one of the most remote and barren places of the Butler property? There were all kinds of dangerous creatures out there, and he should know because he'd found a scorpion in his boot yesterday morning and had crossed paths with a coral snake by lunch. He recalled the childhood saying he'd been taught to tell the difference between a coral and a harmless snake with similar markings: *red on yellow, kill a fellow; red on black, venom lack*. This part of the country had no shortage of venomous creatures.

There were other concerns about leaving her alone. Did she know there was no ready water supply? He'd had to hike for miles to locate a decent place to dig to find the lifesaving liquid when he first arrived. Making the trek had become part of his daily routine after morning push-ups and was the reason he'd seen her in the first place. His daily schedule had been the dividing line between life and death for Ella Butler.

Holden had kept an eye on her to ensure that she didn't get too close to his camp. The place sat on the westernmost boundary of the Butler property referred to as Tierra del Fuego, meaning *land of fire* in Spanish.

If he was being completely honest, he'd admit to being intrigued by Ella. He'd chalked it up to too many days without female companionship and his dread at realizing the time had come to move on from Cattle Barge.

He'd spent a little more than two years on the run. Two years of not speaking to another person. Two years of eating every meal by himself without anyone to share his life with. And yet in a strange way, Holden had felt alone his entire life.

Scouting a new location was a lot of work, but his diligence had kept him alive so far. He'd been on the move twenty-five consecutive months, never pausing for more than a pair of weeks in one spot. This was the longest he'd stayed in one place, and his instincts had told him that it was time to go even before he'd witnessed the assault.

The problem was that he liked Cattle Barge. Holden felt an unexplainable connection to the land. He'd let his emotions win over logic in staying on too long. He'd erred by not listening to his instincts. And there'd be a price to pay for that lapse in judgment, he thought as he looked down at her.

ELLA'S EYES BURNED as harsh light and a sharp pain in that spot right in the center of her forehead, like a brain freeze, nailed her. She blinked a few times, trying to clear the blur. The outline of a very large man looming over her came into focus, causing very real fear to surge through her. Ella tried to force herself awake but darkness pulled. Her mind screamed to get up and run. Her limbs couldn't comply and so no matter how hard she fought against it, her eyes closed and she gave in to sleep.

It was dark by the time Ella woke again. She vaguely remembered being helped outside to go to the bathroom once, or maybe it was twice, but then she might've dreamed the whole episode.

Glancing around, she tried to get her bearings. Her head pounded as she strained to figure out where she was. The bed was hard but comfortable. There was a blanket draped over her. It was clean and soft.

Instincts kicked in and she felt around to make sure she had clothes on. Movement sent shards of pain needling through her skin. A flicker of relief washed over her when she realized her shirt and shorts were on. The respite was short-lived. Her eyes were beginning to adjust to the darkness when she saw the silhouette of a man folded forward in a chair in the corner. Based on his steady breathing, she surmised that he was asleep.

Ella couldn't make out his face from across the room but a warning buzz shot through her at the sheer size of him. Questions raced through her mind but she couldn't bring one into focus. Exhaustion kicked in again and it felt like she'd run a marathon in the August Texas heat. All she could do was close her eyes and rest. So she did.

"What time is it?" Ella asked, unsure how long she'd dozed. She'd been awake for a few minutes, assessing whether or not it was safe to talk. The sun was up. Her thoughts had been engaged in a battle of good versus evil, debating the intentions of the stranger in the room. Eventually, logic won out. If this man had wanted to hurt her, he could've done so already. Still, she'd walk a fine line with him and make sure she didn't provoke him.

"You're asking the wrong question," the strong male voice said—a voice that sent electric chills up her back.

"What should I be asking then?" She tried to push up to sit but her arms were too weak. The male figure made no move to help her.

"It's Thursday." He turned his back to her in a surprising show of trust and picked up whatever was on his plate. He popped something into his mouth. It must be what smelled so amazing. Her stomach growled despite being convinced that she wasn't hungry.

She scanned the room for anything she could use as a weapon while he wasn't watching. Her vision was improving even though looking around still made her eyes hurt. She glanced at the door, hoping to find a baseball bat or something she could use if push came to shove. There had to be one around there somewhere, her head would argue because it felt like one had been used to crack it open.

The room was sparse. There was the makeshift bed in the corner that she was presently resting on. A very uncomfortable-looking lawn chair—the one he'd slept on last night—was pushed up to a table, which was nothing more than a piece of drift board propped up by stick legs tied off by rope. Either this guy was a survivalist or a former Boy Scout. She couldn't decide which one.

Ella remembered that the stranger had slept hunched forward on that chair made of lightweight aluminum and cheap material. Only a gentleman would give up his bed…right?

Embarrassment heated her cheeks as she recalled

him helping her outside to use the bathroom. If he'd wanted to take advantage of her, he'd had plenty of opportunity. And yet he wasn't being welcoming.

The plate the stranger ate from was some kind of metal, like she'd used for camping with her brothers and sister when they were old enough to set up a tent in the backyard. It had come in an outdoorsman kit, she remembered.

She performed a mental calculation that took longer than it should have and made her brain pound against her skull. "I've been out for two days?"

"In and out," the stranger said. She didn't recognize his voice at all and she knew she would remember such a deep baritone if she'd heard it before. There was an intense but calming quality and it sent a trill of awareness through her, which was totally inappropriate and unwelcomed. She chalked her reaction up to hitting her head too hard.

"I'm sorry, have we met before?" she asked, hoping to place him. Her mind was fuzzy and she was having a hard time processing information.

"No."

"Then can I ask who you are?" Ella racked her brain trying to figure out who he could be.

"No." There was finality to his tone that sent a different kind of shiver down her spine, an icy chill that said he was a man with secrets.

The thought of being alone with a person who wouldn't identify himself made Ella want to curl into a ball to protect herself. Her father was one of the richest men in Cattle Barge, Texas, and her life had turned upside down after being given the news of his death a few days ago. When she really thought about it, this man could be after her father's money. She was still fuzzy as to why she was here in the first place, and no matter how hard she tried she couldn't come up with a good explanation. She'd lost more than the last two days because she didn't even remember why she'd gone hiking in the first place.

And then it hit her. Had she been abducted?

"Good luck if you're trying to get ransom for me from my brothers," she said. "My father was killed and all of our money is tied up right now."

"I'm not interested," he said, his voice a low rumble. He froze.

If it wasn't ransom money he was after…then what?

Ella didn't want to go there with the physical thing. Besides, there was something strange in his voice when she'd mentioned that her father had been killed. He'd stopped what he was doing, too.

"I should go." She tried to force herself up on weak arms.

"That's not a good idea."

Icy fingers gripped her spine at his response.

"I'm perfectly capable of getting up and walking out of here and you can't stop me," she said with more indignation than she'd intended. It was the latent Irishwoman in her. Her mother had had the bright red hair to match, or so Ella had been told. Dear Mother had disappeared when Ella was too young to remember her and had never looked back. Ella took after her father with his honey-wheat locks and blue eyes. She had the stubbornness to match. She was also astute, and it didn't take a rocket scientist to realize the stranger was hiding from something or someone. And now she was alone in a cabin with him.

She had no plans to let her guard down.

"You need to hydrate. You wouldn't make it a mile in this heat in your present condition," he said.

"Do you live here?" she asked. He seemed to know the area pretty darn well and he was right. She wouldn't last long in the August heat without provisions.

All he did was grunt in response.

Ella looked around, trying to find clues as to who the mystery man could be. The place was tidy. There was no dust on the floor. Her gaze slid to the door where a makeshift broom was positioned. It had been made from hay that had been tied together at the base of a tree limb. Whoever this mystery man was, he'd set up shop with the intention of sticking around awhile. He had survival skills, too. Her mind immediately headed down a negative path… Who would want to be alone on the most remote area of her father's land? *A man who has something to hide*, a little voice answered. He could be a doomsday prepper, bank robber or—gasp—serial killer.

Her gaze darted around in an effort to find evidence as to which one he was.

To the other side of the doorway sat a duffel bag that had been zipped closed. She fought against her worst fears that there were torture instruments in there.

The stranger turned around and she could barely make out his features for all the facial hair. His build was football player big and he had to weigh in at well over two hundred pounds. He was pure muscle and his size was intimidating. That thought sent a trill of awareness skittering across her skin. Under different circumstances, she could appreciate the athletic grace with which he moved. Ella's five-foot-five-inch frame was no match for this guy. Working the ranch kept her strong and in shape but she was small by comparison.

The lawn chair scraped against the hardwood flooring, drawing her attention.

"You didn't tell me your name," she said.

Another grunt came in response as the large figure moved toward the bed. Ella scrambled backward—pain shooting through her with every movement—until her back was against the wall. She fisted her hands, ready to swing if he gave her any indication that his intentions had changed.

There was something in his hand as he moved toward her, the light to his back. His sheer size blocked out the sun rays coming from the window and bathed her in darkness. Her body was ironing board rigid.

"Be still. And relax. I'm not going to hurt you," he said, and he looked offended as his features came into focus.

"If that's true, why won't you tell me your name?" she asked, not ready to trust him.

"You're better off not knowing." His side was turned to her and his face was partially hidden. He didn't make eye contact. Up close, she could see that he would be quite attractive if he cleaned up that beard or shaved it off altogether. More than attractive, actually, she thought as her stomach did an inappropriate little flip when he turned and she could really see into his eyes.

The man was clearly hiding something and an attraction was so out of the question that she had to choke back a laugh. Her emotions were all over the map. How hard had she hit her head?

"I'll be the judge of that," she said, seeing how far she could push her luck.

The layer of blankets dipped where he sat.

Her heart pounded in her chest and it felt like there was glue in her mouth for how dry her tongue was. Her entire body was strung tight.

"Let me see that gash on your forehead," he said in his deep baritone. It had an amaretto-over-vanilla-ice-cream feeling and had that same warming effect on her insides. This close, she could see that he had deep-set, serious eyes that were the lightest, most pure shade of blue that she'd ever seen. A square jaw was covered by that dark beard. He had thick, curly hair the shade of a dark cup of coffee.

"What happened to me?" She inched toward him, not ready to give much more.

"I'm a man of my word. I already told you that I wouldn't hurt you and I won't. So move a little faster, will you." He sounded frustrated and impatient.

"Well, excuse me if I don't jump into the arms of a complete stranger when he beckons," she snapped back. Talking made her skull hurt. Could her brain be in actual pain? Speaking of which, now that blood was returning to her limbs, her entire body was screaming at her.

A smirk lifted the corner of the stranger's mouth. He quickly reeled it in.

"I have two pain relievers in my hand if you'll sit up and take them," he said, holding out his flat palm.

Okay, so he wasn't lying about the twin tablets. But who knew if they were OTC or not.

"What are those?" she asked.

"Ibuprofen," he stated. His tone was about as flat as stale beer.

She stared at them like they were bombs about to detonate.

"There's a bottle of water on the floor," he said, leaning toward her.

She let out a yelp that caused his entire face to frown.

"I've already said that I won't hurt you. I brought pain relievers and a wet napkin to clean some of the dried blood from your forehead so I can get a look at your injury. I didn't do it before because I didn't want you to wake with a stranger standing over you." He shot her a look of aggravation.

That actually made a lot of sense and was considerate when she really thought about it. She wasn't exactly ready to relax because he could still be a weirdo, and she was too weak to put up much of a fight. Besides, what was with the secrets? Sharing his name would go a long way toward winning her trust. Instead, he acted like a criminal. If he wasn't one, he needed to come clean.

"I'd apologize personally if I knew your name," she said, matching his level of irritation. He wasn't the only one who could be frustrated.

"What were you doing out here all alone?" the stranger asked.

"I don't know," she responded. If he wouldn't give out any information, neither would she.

He shot her a look that cut right through her.

"I was hiking. I must've lost my footing and hit my head," Ella said, pressing her fingertips to her temples. "It's all still a little fuzzy."

Brooding pale blue eyes examined her and she saw the dark circles cradling them. Whoever this guy was, he had a lot on his mind. There was something else there, too, but she didn't want to analyze it because it made awareness electrify her nerve endings. It also made her aware that if she'd been asleep for two days she must look like a train wreck and have breath that could wilt a flower.

Blue Eyes dabbed the wet cloth on her forehead above her right temple. She winced.

He muttered a curse and pulled his hand back. "That hurt. I'm sorry."

"It's okay." Why was she reassuring him? Reason took over, reminding her that he seemed intent on helping her. She was in a vulnerable state and while she couldn't exactly trust him, she also had no reason to think he had plans to hurt her.

He gave her an apologetic look.

"Best as I can remember, I was hiking pretty far out on the trail. Most of how I ended up here is fuzzy. Am I allowed to ask what you were doing out there?" Ella flinched again when the cold, wet cloth touched her skin.

"No more questions," Blue Eyes said. He made a move to stand.

Ella caught his elbow.

"Please don't leave. My father was killed and that's the last thing I remember. I have no idea what happened or how I got here. I'm not trying to be a jerk, but I've just been told that I've been out of it for two days. I have a gash on my head that I don't even know how it got there, and I'm so thirsty I could suck a cactus dry, and despite that, I really need to go to the bathroom," Ella said, letting all the words gush out at once like a geyser whose time to erupt had come.

"Can you manage on your own?" He motioned toward the door and there was a storm brewing behind those blue eyes at the mention of her father.

"I believe so," she said.

"Toothbrush and toothpaste are on the sink. Bathroom's outside." He turned and walked out.

Chapter Two

Holden needed air. He lifted his face to the sun. The Texas heat beat down on his exposed skin, warming him. Maverick Mike was dead?

For a split second Holden feared that he could be the reason, that the men who were after him had somehow connected him to his father's friend. But that was impossible.

This was a wake-up call. Helping Ella had been a knee-jerk reaction and Holden could feel himself sliding down a slippery slope with nothing solid to grab hold of. He owed her father for offering him a place to stay when Holden was at a low point, and that was the reason he'd told himself that he stepped in with Ella. Speaking of her father, the news still hadn't quite absorbed. Holden rubbed his chin through the overgrown scruff. How could Butler be gone?

The door opened and Ella froze as soon as she saw him standing there.

"I'll give you privacy," he mumbled. Someone needed to toss him a lifeline because the woman stirred feelings he hadn't allowed in longer than he could remember—feelings he never wanted to experience again. Then there was the obvious fact that he couldn't afford those feelings. They'd have him wanting to stick around and protect Ella Butler while they figured out who wanted to kill her. Holden reminded himself that he'd done his part. He'd kept her alive.

"Why did you help me? You could've walked away. Left me there. No one would've known any different." She positioned her hands on either side of the doorjamb.

"No, I couldn't have." He made a move toward the door to indicate that he was done talking. She didn't flinch.

"Sure you could. It would've been easy. My body would've been found eventually and no one would be the wiser that there was someone who could've saved my life." She stared at him for a long moment without saying another word. "Something tells me you know how to cover your tracks, so there must've been some reason."

"You're welcome for saving your life," he said, debating whether or not he should tell her everything. She needed to know that her fall had been no accident, but he'd keep the part about his connection to her father to himself. "Now that you're up and around, I'll drop you off in town tonight."

"And then what? You'll disappear?" Her gaze zeroed in.

She shouldn't care what happened to him because she needed to be concerned about herself.

"Don't worry about me," he said.

"Too late for that." She issued another pause while

staring at him. There was something about her corn-flower blue eyes that he couldn't afford to notice. "I'd like to properly thank you for what you've done to save my life. Any chance I can convince you to come back to the main house with me?"

"Sweetheart, I've been taking care of myself for a long time. I really don't need—"

"Obviously, you need a place to stay." She glanced around as if for emphasis. "We're always looking for a good pair of hands around the ranch. It's clear to me that you'd make a good addition and we need more men like you."

"You ought to be careful who you go offering jobs to," he stated.

"I trust you."

"That's a mistake," he said plainly.

"No, it isn't. But even if it was, it wouldn't be my last." One of her balled fists was on her hip now. She had a lot of sass for someone in such a vulnerable position. He'd give her that.

This conversation was going nowhere so Holden did what he did best: went silent as he stared her down. She should be more afraid of him than she was acting. She had been earlier when she'd opened her eyes, and as much as he didn't like it at first, her reaction was for the best. What had he done to make her so comfortable now?

"You want coffee?" he finally asked, shaking his head. She was as stubborn as the stories he'd heard about her father.

"That would be amazing, actually," she said with a small smile.

"Then get out of my way."

She twisted her mouth in a frown at his sharp tone but stepped aside. He walked straight past her without making eye contact even though she stood there expectantly for minutes afterward. And then she slammed the door shut. Not only was Ella stubborn but she had a temper. The nuances of her personality were none of his business. Period.

Holden refocused on the facts. Ella Butler had been missing for two days. His position at the cabin had been compromised from the moment he'd witnessed the attack, and he could see now that it was a miracle no one had shown up. The situation was declining. Fast.

There'd be a search underway by now. The news that "Maverick" Mike Butler was killed would be enough to create a full-scale media circus in Cattle Barge. Add a missing heiress to the equation and Holden couldn't begin to wrap his mind around how out of control the coverage would be. He'd been so far off the grid that he'd missed all of it.

The news that her father had been murdered before an attempt had been made on her life sat in Holden's gut like he'd eaten a pack of nails. The media attention surrounding her disappearance—and that would be big news—must be the reason the person who'd chucked that rock at her hadn't returned. Holden had been watching out for the culprit.

She needed to know that the blow to her head wasn't an accident. He wasn't sure how she'd react, especially given the fact that she'd just lost her father. Normally, he'd suspect someone close to her, a family member. Money or greed would be motive for murder, and especially when considering the amount Maverick Mike had amassed. His fortune was legendary but so were his antics. He had a lot of enemies. Holden wanted to ask about the circumstances surrounding her father's death but decided against it for the time being. He shouldn't show too much interest in the Butler family. Once he settled into a new location far away from Cattle Barge, he could find out what had happened. Mike Butler's death would be all over the news, so it would be easy to find.

Holden glanced at his watch. Ella had been gone a full ten minutes. Should he check on her?

A thousand thoughts rolled through his head. Adjusting while in action had always been Holden's strong suit. He told himself this time would be no different. The door opened at about the time he'd made up his mind to mount his own search. She looked at him boldly.

"Coffee's getting cold," he snapped. She needed to be afraid. He set her cup on the table that he'd made by hand after he arrived last month. The cabin was the first place he'd bothered to put together anything that resembled furniture. His thinking had always been "get too attached to any one place and leaving would be that much more difficult."

His plans had really gone south in Texas—but then he was beginning to see why the place was so appealing with its wide-open skies and thousands of stars at night.

Ella moved to the table and picked up the tin mug.

She cradled it in her hands like it was made of pure gold when she sipped. A little sound of pleasure drew from her lips. "This is really good. How did you do this?"

"You haven't had any for too long. Muddy water would taste good to you right now." Holden kept the part that he liked giving her that small moment of happiness to himself.

"I promise the coffee's not this good at the main house." She paused and then her eyes brightened. "I don't know what I've been thinking. My brothers and sister are probably frantic with worry right now. There's no chance you have a working cell phone, is there?"

"No." He was completely off the grid. There was no way to track him using technology.

"I need to reach them and let them know that I'm okay. I know what I said earlier about our money being tied up, but if you're in some kind of trouble I can help." The determined set to her jaw said she meant it.

Holden shook his head. The less she knew about his circumstance, the better.

"I'm more concerned about you right now," he said. "Besides, you're news and that's bad for me."

"You're on the run from something." She had part of that right.

More like *someone*.

Her gaze penetrated deep into him. "You know who I am, don't you? You've always known."

He nodded.

"And you're not out to hurt me. So far, from what I can tell, you've been helping me," she continued.

"I want you to listen carefully to what I'm about to

say. What happened to you out there was no accident," he warned.

She gasped. "Not *you*…"

"No, it wasn't me. But someone did that—" he motioned toward the gash on her head "—on purpose."

He let the revelation sink in for a minute.

"It wasn't you and it wasn't an accident," she said so quietly that he had to strain to hear.

Holden handed her another cup filled with beans he'd warmed in the fire. "You're used to better food, but this is protein and it'll keep your stomach from growling."

Ella took the offering with trembling hands as his message seemed to be taking seed. "Who would want me dead?"

He didn't like that momentary lost look in her eyes.

"I'm telling you because you're going to want to be careful from now on. Take necessary precautions and don't wander off alone." Holden leaned his hip against the counter.

She took a bite of food and chewed.

"You said that your father was killed," he continued.

"Yes."

"You'll want to look at people who stand to gain from your death after his to start. Scrutinize those closest to you," he said, figuring with her money she could hire proper security who could keep her safe until the law found the man trying to kill her.

"I have no idea. I mean, I think what you're saying is that my brothers or sister might want me dead to get me out of the way or take my share of our inheritance, but I trust them with my life," she said.

"What happened to your father?" he asked. The look he shot her must've been interesting.

"He was shot twelve times while he slept naked in the spare bedroom attached to his office in the barn," she informed.

"No one heard anything?" he asked, thinking that someone had wanted to make a point. An act like that came across as anger motivated.

"The barn isn't near the main house. Dad liked to keep home and work separate," she said.

"Which is difficult, considering you do live your work when you own a ranch," Holden said. "Your family would know everyone's sleeping patterns and where your father would be on a given day."

"He spent a lot of nights in the barn. What makes you so sure it's one of them? Did you used to work in law enforcement?" She turned the tables.

"No." Holden had no plans to elaborate on his background. The less she knew, the better for both of them.

"We leave as soon as the sun goes down," he said, closing the bag to the coffee grinds.

ELLA REALIZED SHE'D been gripping the coffee mug so tightly that her knuckles were white. She reminded herself to breathe as she tried to absorb the reality that had become her life. Her brothers would not try to hurt her. For one, the Butler kids had had each other's backs since childhood after their mother had taken off and left them with their father. They'd had to. Their father wasn't exactly skilled in the parenting department. He'd loved them in his own way, Ella thought defensively. She'd always felt the need to protect her father. But he wasn't the problem this time.

Thinking made her brain cramp.

Ella eyed the stranger carefully. By nightfall, she'd be done with him. He'd be out of her life forever. She should be happy about that, and yet the thought tugged at her heart. Maybe it was because she'd lost so much already with her father's death. Or it could be her soft spot for lost causes. There'd been countless stray animals that she'd made space for in the barn only for her father to tell her they had to go. Usually, they were injured and she knew they'd never survive on their own. Her brothers or sister would come to her rescue and help her keep them hidden until she'd manage to nurse them back to health and then find a new home.

A few were worked into the menagerie of pets on the ranch. Oftentimes one of the hired hands would end up with a new pet to take home to his family. And many of the employees at Hereford Ranch covered for her to help with her causes. No one went against Maverick Mike's wishes directly, but everyone pitched in behind the scenes to help Ella.

Looking back, it was probably difficult for them to turn away such a persistent little girl. Ella had been told more than once that she had the campaigning abilities of a politician.

Her gaze drifted to the wounded person standing before her with no name. If anyone needed to find his way, it was the man across the room. She told herself that was the reason she felt an unexplainable draw toward the mystery man and it had nothing to do with the inappropriate surge of attraction she felt every time she glanced his way.

"What will you do once you drop me off? You can't stay here anymore, can you?" she asked.

"You need to worry about yourself. Use some of that money you have to hire extra security," he snapped.

Ella bristled.

His voice softened when he said, "You're in danger and you owe it to your father to be careful."

"Why do you care?" she asked.

"I don't," he said. "But you should."

A noise sounded outside and Blue Eyes dropped into a crouching position in half a second flat. The remarkable thing was that he made no noise with his movement, and that made her think he might have a military background.

His gaze locked onto hers and the look he shot her warned her to be quiet. She froze, fearing that whoever had tried to kill her was back. Would they have returned to verify that she was dead and then go hunting for her when they didn't find a body?

Her pulse raced.

With effort, she slid off the chair and made herself as small as she could on the floor. Movement hurt despite the couple of pain relievers he'd supplied earlier. Ella knew Blue Eyes had this under control. And it struck her as odd that she felt safe with the stranger.

Thinking about the attempt on her life made her realize that there could be others coming to town to get a piece of her father's will. Hadn't his attorney, Ed Staples, warned that there could be a lot of surprises forthcoming? Even though he couldn't possibly have meant this, Ella was beginning to fear that the actions of her father would haunt her and her siblings long after his death.

When the silence had stretched on for minutes, Blue Eyes moved to the window and checked outside. Without speaking a word, he slipped out the door.

Ella moved to the window to get a look for herself, watching as he moved stealthily. There was a certain grace about him.

Despite his untamed appearance, his muscles gave the impression he maintained a disciplined workout schedule. In fact, looking around the room, it was obvious that he liked things tidy. Something had made him want to drop out of civilization for a while. He couldn't be a doomsday prepper because he seemed to have on hand only what he needed for a couple of days. She wanted to offer him some type of reward for saving her life but he'd already refused work. What else could she do? Offer a reward?

Ella thought about her two brothers, Dade and Dalton, and sister, Cadence. She wasn't kidding before. They'd be frantic with worry about her by now. Even though her siblings had left town to escape the media circus in Cattle Barge, one of the employees would've contacted them about her disappearance. She'd been out of communication for two days...and with a total stranger. He could've done anything he'd wanted to her. A shiver raced through her. But he hadn't.

For that reason and a few others that she didn't want to overanalyze, Ella intended to figure out who this man was and why he was running.

Chapter Three

Blue Eyes walked back into the cabin, glanced around and then picked up his duffel bag. "Finish your coffee. We're leaving ahead of schedule."

"Everything okay outside?" Ella asked.

He didn't respond.

"Is someone out there?" Her heart rate jumped a few notches higher.

"Not now. There will be," he said and mumbled, "I should've gone a long time ago."

That statement implied he wouldn't have been around to help her and she didn't appreciate the sentiment. "Well, I, for one, am glad you outstayed your welcome. I wouldn't be alive otherwise."

She was getting indignant. She couldn't help herself. He wouldn't tell her anything about himself and she wasn't trying to take advantage of him or turn him in to the FBI. All she wanted to do was find a proper way to thank him. The guy was working her last nerve and her head still pounded.

"Why don't you come to work for me on the ranch?" she asked while watching him pull out bleach wipes from his bag. He wiped down the dishes before placing them inside the duffel. Now he really had her curiosity heightened.

"I already said that I don't need a job." For the irritated sound that came out of his mouth next, she would've thought she'd just asked him to scrub the toilet with his toothbrush.

Ella made a production of glancing around. "Are you being serious?"

He shot her a warning glance. It said to tread lightly. She ignored it.

"Because as far as I can tell, you very much need a paycheck. And a decent place to sleep." She waved her hand around.

"I had one until you came along and messed it up for me," he quickly countered.

"You can't be serious," she said.

"Try me."

"Is that a threat?" She planted her balled fist on her hip. It was probably the fact that she'd almost been killed that was giving her this new bravado. She didn't care. The guy had some explaining to do and he was squatting on her family's land.

"No. If you haven't figured it out already, I'm trying to help you," he said, opening up a knife and cutting the rope he'd used to hold together the table. The metal sparkled in the light. He wiped down each leg.

"Why won't you let me return the favor?" she asked.

Another frustrated noise tore from his throat. "You don't have anything I want."

That sounded personal. She tried not to take offense.

"I'd like to offer a financial reward. Surely, you could use some money."

He didn't look up but waved her off.

"At least tell me your name," she persisted. Why was he being so obstinate? Was it really that difficult to give her something? Granted, she was used to getting what she wanted and with enough persistence she was sure that she could wear this guy down, too. She didn't have the luxury of time and she wanted to send a proper thank-you or reward for his help.

"I've already told you that's not a good idea." He broke one of the legs in half and then tossed it into the fireplace.

"I disagree." She stood there, fist planted.

"You always this stubborn when you're wrong?" he asked, breaking the second leg and tossing it on top of the last.

"I'm usually right," she said. Ella glanced around. It wouldn't be dark outside for hours.

"Since you're feeling better, I'll take you to town. Go to the sheriff and tell him what happened. I'd appreciate it if you left me out of your statement. That's how you can thank me for saving you." Another broken table leg, more tinder for the fireplace.

"I thought we weren't leaving until the sun went down," she said, a moment of panic crushing her. Her father was gone. Nothing at the ranch would be the same without him. She hadn't even begun to deal with his murder. An attempt had been made on her life. Of course she would go to the sheriff but she wasn't quite ready to return to town and the unknown waiting there.

"Plans changed."

"You won't tell me why? I mean, I realize that we heard a noise but everything's okay now, right?" She was still trying to figure out why she was arguing for more time with the man who wouldn't even tell her his name. Logic be damned. Ella needed to know he was going to be all right. At least, that's what she tried to convince herself and not that there was something magnetic about this man that was completely foreign to her.

"Being seen anywhere near you is dangerous for me."

"What have you done wrong?" she asked, figuring she might as well go for it.

"Nothing that concerns you." He broke the final leg and tossed it into the fireplace. She might not understand his way of life but she appreciated his self-sufficiency.

"Then tell me what you're running from," she said in a last-ditch effort to get him to talk.

A moment of silence passed between them as they stared each other down.

Okay, he won. Ella wasn't in a position to bargain and this stranger seemed intent on keeping his secrets. He'd helped her and she was grateful.

"I probably haven't sounded like it so far, but I really do appreciate everything you've done for me," she said as she moved toward him, toward the door.

She paused before crossing over. For a second, time stopped and they just stood there, staring at each other. A sensual shiver goose bumped Ella's arms. The stranger had the most amazing eyes, piercing eyes. Eyes that she could stare into for days. As odd as it sounded even to her, the moment felt intimate.

The attraction she felt caught her completely off guard. Rugged mountain men had never been her type. It was probably the mystery surrounding him that held so much appeal and the fact that all her senses were on full alert.

Ella broke contact as she heard the *whop-whop-whop* of helicopter blades in the distance.

"Let's go," she said.

HOLDEN SAT AT the counter of the diner in neighboring Rio Suerte. Another couple of hours and he'd be out of Texas altogether. He'd dropped off Ella Butler two blocks from the sheriff's office. She could retrieve her Jeep near Devil's Lid once she gave her statement to law enforcement. Ella was smart enough to take it from there. He'd done his part, repaid his debt to Maverick Mike.

Time to move on, he thought with a heavy sigh. He hadn't thought about the murders he'd been accused of for two days while he was with Ella. The initials, HA, hadn't haunted him. He'd discovered them etched into the bottom of a chair leg at his father's place—the chair where his father had been tortured and killed.

Holden shook off the bad memory. He was no closer to figuring out what had happened then he'd been two years ago.

The restaurant was a typical off-the-highway food stop and seemed like the place frequented mostly by truck drivers. Holden had befriended more than his fair share while crossing the country, making his way to Texas. The diner was shaped like a train car. There was one row of booths behind him matched by a long counter with bar stools for single travelers. Two families were in the booths, no doubt stopping off for a quick meal while on a road trip.

There was only one truck driver in the building. Bathrooms were to Holden's left, near the end of the counter where the cash register was located. There was one cook in the kitchen and only one waitress on duty. The cook was significantly shorter than Holden, bald, with thick arms. He bench-pressed. The man was in his early fifties with a cook's belly. Holden dismissed him as a threat. He fell into the same category as the dads. One drove a minivan, the other a Suburban. Holden could tell they were from the suburbs based on their clothing—one was in jeans and a polo shirt, the other wore warm-ups and a T-shirt. They had that haggard look that came with long road trips with young kids.

The truck driver was substantial in size, mostly fat from spending his days seated. He looked strong, though. Holden could see his arms in the sleeveless flannel shirt he wore. The man couldn't be ignored as a threat. If Holden assigned levels, five being the highest, the dads were ones and the truck driver was a two and a half, maybe three.

There were exactly two exits in the building: the front door he'd come through and the one in the kitchen. Holden was used to memorizing every detail, looking for every possible escape route. Doing so had kept him alive. Was he really living?

Holden dismissed the thought as going too long without human companionship. His brief run-in with Ella Butler reminded him of everything he didn't have. He'd been alone for a very long time, focused on staying alive, staying one step ahead of the men who were after him. They were good. He was the best. And that was precisely the reason he was still breathing.

The waitress approached. Her metal-plated name tag read Deena.

"Make up your mind?" Deena asked, motioning toward the menu. She was in her late thirties and had early wrinkles around her eyes and mouth. Her neck was the biggest giveaway of her age.

"Chicken-fried steak with mashed potatoes and gravy, carrots. More coffee when you have a chance," he said.

She wrote down his order on the ticket with a smile, a nod and a wink. "Sam makes the best."

"I'm counting on it," Holden said, returning the smile. He excused himself to the restroom. He wanted to splash water on his face and wash his hands before he ate. He didn't sleep much while he'd been taking care of Ella.

As he stood in front of the bathroom mirror, he was shocked at the stranger looking back at him. Furry face. Dark circles under his eyes. His thoughts snapped to Ella Butler and her initial reaction to seeing him. No wonder she'd been so afraid when she'd first opened her eyes. Hell, he would be, too.

He pushed those unproductive thoughts aside.

Holden splashed cold water on his face before washing his hands. Maybe it was time to shave the over-growth. He hardly recognized himself anymore, and he certainly looked more animal than man. It was easy to do while he'd been mostly living off the land. And yet his reflection had caught him off guard.

Walking out of the restroom, he scanned the room. The situation was the same. The threat potential was low. He reclaimed his bar stool and did his level best not to look at the TV mounted in the corner of the room. A cursory glance revealed the channel was set to local news.

Holden picked up his fresh cup of coffee, ignoring the screen. He didn't treat himself to a restaurant meal often. This was a delicacy he had every intention of enjoying.

And then he made the mistake of looking up.

There was a picture of the Butler ranch on the TV screen. The story was about an heiress's life being in danger. Holden gripped the cup and waited…

Another attempt had been made on Ella's life. A witness had seen a man trap a woman between two vehicles on a residential street one block from the sheriff's office. The woman managed to fight off her attacker before slipping around an SUV and disappearing between two houses as at least one shot was fired. The witness, who would only agree to speak anonymously, recognized Ella Butler but was too frightened to get close enough to get a description of the heiress's attacker. There was a lot of blood at the scene and a manhunt was underway for a gunman wearing a ski mask. He was considered dangerous and authorities cautioned people to keep a distance and call law enforcement immediately if he was spotted.

Holden could think of a few other things he'd like to do to the guy besides turn him in.

He released a string of curses under his breath. It was his fault for taking her to town in the first place. He'd left her there without transportation or a way to escape. Damn it. This was on him.

Anger roared through him along with an overdose of guilt.

He listened for any other news about Ella and sighed sharply when he learned she was missing and believed to be injured.

"I need my check," he said to Deena.

Chapter Four

Ella rolled onto her side, ignoring the pain shouting at her. She could feel her pulse pound in her thigh where she'd been shot and pain gripped her in between the temples. She was losing blood, which was not a good sign. At least she'd managed to fight off her attacker and run. She'd poked her fingers through the ski mask he wore and had managed to knock him off balance. Then she'd bolted. It had all happened so fast. The blast. The cold, wet feeling spreading through her thigh.

Who would want to hurt her?

The stranger's warning hadn't been an overreaction. Her life was in danger. She'd been in such a fog earlier that she hadn't even thought to ask any of the right questions. Could Blue Eyes have identified the rock thrower?

She crawled into the front landscaping of the modest home on Sixth Street, gasping. How long could she stay there unnoticed? A few minutes? Hours? The night?

It was getting late. She'd barely escaped the gunman. If only she'd been able to get a look at his face. And now she was hiding, on the run from someone determined to get her out of the way. She searched her mind for a name, anyone who would want her gone. Could this be related to her father's death? Or was the timing a coincidence?

Her father had enemies and plenty of people didn't like him, but it was as if he'd been made of Teflon and she could scarcely believe that someone had managed to get to him. Her heart fisted and grief shrouded her, weighing down her limbs. Her larger-than-life father was gone. She was hiding in someone's landscaping and she had nowhere to go.

A sob released before she had time to force it back. Tears brimmed but she couldn't allow herself to cry. Not now. Let that dam break and the flood might just leave a trail big enough for her attacker to find her. Start crying and she might not be able to stop.

A branch snapped. She glanced around, afraid to breathe in case the gunman was closing in on her.

Hope that the noise could've been the sheriff or one of his deputies—anyone who could help—fizzled when she saw the bobcat winding through the front landscaping. He was fairly small and definitely not a threat. But it reminded her that there would be others. Soon.

Ella needed a plan. Her thoughts shifted to the compelling stranger in her father's cabin. He was strong enough to defend her. She told herself that was the only reason he entered her thoughts and not because of something deeper, something like missing him. Missing a stranger sounded ridiculous, even to her. How much blood had she lost? She had to be delirious if she was thinking about Blue Eyes.

One thing was certain. If she surfaced in the open,

she'd be killed the second her chaser caught sight of her. The shotgun that had been fired at her shot real shells, as evidenced by the blood on the outside of her thigh where shrapnel had grazed her. Speaking of which, she needed to clean her wound before it got infected.

She couldn't go home. There was too much chaos going on since news of her father's murder broke and she'd be an open target.

She had no idea what the person targeting her wanted. Ransom? Revenge?

She and her siblings were close-knit. They'd had to be since it was generally up to the four of them to handle things at home. Their father had been tougher on the twins. She'd been protective of Dade and Dalton when they were young. They'd long since grown into men who could take care of themselves and everyone around them. Ella and the twins had always looked after their younger sister, Cadence.

Speaking of her siblings, she needed to warn them but had no way to contact them. Thankfully, they were tucked away, far out of town, having left immediately after news broke of their father's murder. They'd decided to get away from Cattle Barge until this whole mess blew over and life returned to normal, whatever that would be now that their father was gone. With his unconventional lifestyle, she and her siblings had feared people would come out of the woodwork to claim stakes in his vast fortune. Based on the traffic she'd seen coming into town and the resulting chaos, the others had been smart to leave. Someone had to stick around and make sure the ranch was still running, and Ella had convinced them it should be her.

But being in town was dangerous. So was the ranch. She didn't suspect any of the workers who'd been around for years. There were a few new hands. She couldn't rule out the team her father had put together even if she doubted he'd put anyone questionable to work on his ranch. He loved his family and was fiercely protective of them even if their relationships with him were highly individual and complicated. He'd never knowingly put them in jeopardy. *Knowingly* might be the key word. Could her father have put his trust in someone who'd duped him?

Her brain hurt. Her body ached. And some of her memories were patchy thanks to the blow she'd taken. At present, she was exhausted, hungry and bleeding. Her mind was going to places that she wouldn't normally consider. She knew exactly where she needed to go so she could take a step back and think this through but had no idea how to get there. Her Jeep was parked near Devil's Lid, which wasn't doing her a lot of good. Blue Eyes had ridden her into town on his motorcycle.

There was no way she could make it to the sheriff's office. The person who was after her could be watching. If she got anywhere near—

A hand clamped over her mouth. Ella gasped. She tried to bite but whoever was behind her was too fast at securing his grip—and it had to be a man. His hand was huge. He'd been stealthy, too. She hadn't heard a peep. Her pulse pounded and adrenaline caused her body to shake.

"Be quiet and I'll get you out of here," said the familiar voice—the voice that belonged to Blue Eyes. "Can you walk?"

Her pulse raced from fear mixed with another shot of adrenaline. She nodded and his other hand slipped around her. A second later, she was being helped to her feet.

"I'm shot," she said and could feel the physical impact of those words. No matter how much Blue Eyes tried to deny he cared about what happened to her, his body language belied his words when his muscles pulled taut with the news.

"How did you find me?" she asked as the initial shock began to wear off while they were on the move.

The motorcycle was parked at the end of a quiet street.

"I saw the news story about the attempt against your life," he responded without missing a beat. "I recognized this area as close to where I dropped you off and tracked you by the blood trail I found."

He made it sound easy but it couldn't have been. How had this stranger become so good at hunting down a person? She decided this wasn't the time to ask. By all accounts he was helping her…but he was so secretive before and it had her imagination churning against all logic. She didn't like the confusing feelings she had toward him.

"How do I know you're not going to hurt me?" she asked.

A frustrated-sounding grunt tore from his throat. "Seriously?"

Now all her defenses flared. "Yes. I'm a woman. I'm injured. Basic survival instincts kick in at some point. I have no idea who you are. I don't even know your name."

"If I wanted to hurt you, I would've already done it." That deep voice reverberated through her, sending a trill of awareness coursing through her. "We've already covered that."

Okay, she could concede that point.

"Who are you?"

"My name is Holden Crawford. Now that you've heard it, forget it as fast as you can. Knowing my name will only end up hurting you more," he said. "That's why I didn't tell you before now. It's not because I'm trying to hide something from you or don't trust you. I haven't had a real conversation with someone in more than two years. So I'm guessing by your reactions to me that I'm pretty bad at it. Can't say I was especially good with idle chitchat before, so…" He shrugged massive shoulders. "And the last person I really cared about ended up dead."

She gasped.

"Not telling you my name has been my way of trying to protect you," he continued. "Your father was good to me, offered to let me stay on his land, and I figured I owed him one for it. That's the reason I helped you and didn't walk away. I'm not that good of a person to stick around for pure reasons. It was a debt. One that has been paid."

"Sounds like you're a better man than you want to admit," she said.

"Me? Nah. I know exactly who I am, what I am, and it's not good for someone like you," he stated. "You're better off without me."

A frustrated grunt tore from her throat.

He turned to face her.

"I'm sorry about that." He glanced at her thigh and a trill of awareness blasted through her, which was unwelcomed. There was something primal and magnetic that pulled her in when she was near Blue Eyes. Sex appeal over standard good looks? "That was my fault, and I came back to make it right."

"You're on the run from something you didn't do."

"That's what I said." He held out a helmet and waited for her to make a decision.

"Maybe I can help you," she offered.

The look on his face said he doubted it.

"It's now or never, sweetheart. The choice is up to you. Go with me and I can't take you to the law."

Ella figured her options were pretty limited at the moment. She had no idea who was after her. Going to the sheriff was logical, but getting there safely wasn't guaranteed and the man who was after her would most likely expect her there. Striking out on her own wasn't even a consideration. She was injured and had none of the necessary skills to survive. Go back to the ranch and she couldn't be certain that she'd be safe.

"Let's go," she said, taking the offering. "And my name is Ella, so you can stop calling me sweetheart."

She slid onto the seat behind him. He took her hands and wrapped them around his chest.

"Hold on," he said, like there was another option.

Ella turned her head and pressed it against his strong back as wind whipped around her.

Adrenaline had long since faded by the time they reached the cabin and exhaustion made it difficult to lift her leg over the motorcycle. Holden helped her take off the helmet and then he secured it to the back of the seat, mumbling something about needing to get another one. Texas didn't require one by law, but most riders seemed smart enough to take the precaution.

Ella stared at his face. Beneath all that wild facial hair was an attractive and capable man, and she ignored what the revelation did to her stomach.

"Did you get a look at who did this to you?" he asked.

"No. He had on a ski mask and it was dark outside, so I couldn't get a good look at his face," she said.

A disgusted look crossed his features. "This is my fault. I shouldn't have left you there and especially not without a vehicle."

She leaned her weight on him as he put his arm around her waist, hoping she'd feel less vulnerable if she knew a little more about the stranger who was helping her. More electricity fizzed through her as he walked her inside the cabin, and the overwhelming feeling that she was safe for now settled over her.

"Sit still," he said as he retrieved a bottle of water and poured it over her thigh. "I have something that'll help with the cut on my bike."

He brought in medical supplies and attended to her wounded leg.

"Who are you *really*?" she asked, staring up at him.

"A man defined by his mistakes." He stepped back

but maintained eye contact, holding a second too long. The dark lines of his serious expression said he meant every word of that. Fire shot through her when she realized the implication of what he said.

"You think helping me was a mistake?" She scoffed. Anger had been building and she'd explode if she held it in any longer. "Well, then, I'm sure glad you went against your *superior* judgment or I'd be dead."

"Twice," he said through clenched teeth as he stood. His breath was a mix of mint and coffee. An infuriating part of her wanted to see what that tasted like. He raked his fingers through thick, wavy hair.

"Now that you've saved me again, why not just leave? My Jeep isn't far from here. I'll head north, away from the ranch, until I figure out who's doing this to me," she said with more anger than she'd intended.

He took a threatening step toward her, closing the gap between them even more, and this close she could almost sense what his skin would feel like pressed against hers as she stood.

Ella blew out a frustrated breath. She thought the same curse that he muttered when she said, "Mistakes aren't the only things that define a person."

Holden caught her gaze again and she felt the moment her anger turned to awareness. Awareness of his strong, masculine body so close to hers. Awareness of how much he turned her on even though she fought against it. Awareness of how good it would feel to have his hands on her, roaming her skin.

"Do tell," he said, and there was so much sexual undercurrent running between them.

"We're also defined by our choices," she said.

"Fine. This is one of mine." He dipped his head and kissed her.

His lips, pressed to hers, sent a current of need rippling through her and heat pooled inside her thighs. She'd never been *this* aroused *this* quickly in her life, but then a sexual current had been building between them since she'd first seen him.

He tensed, like he expected her to fight back, but all she could do was surrender to the out-of-control wildfire spreading through her. She stretched her fingers out and smoothed them across his chest as she parted her lips. His tongue dipped inside her mouth and she could feel the groan rumble from deep in his chest.

The realization she was having the same effect on him that he had on her was satisfying. A frustrating and intense sexual draw stronger than anything she'd ever experienced enveloped her. That strength of an emotion could be dangerous. Holden was dangerous.

Instead of pulling back, which would be the most sensible move, Ella wrapped her hands around his neck and deepened the kiss.

His arms looped her waist and he hauled her body against his. She could feel his heart pound inside his chest at a frantic pace. Her breasts strained against her bra as they pressed flush against his muscled chest.

How on earth was it possible to feel so much heat in one kiss?

Holden's strong, flat palm slipped inside her shirt and her nipples pebbled. He hesitated at the snap on her bra and then all of a sudden her breasts were freed. He released a guttural groan as he took one of her full breasts in his hand. He teased the nipple, rolling it between his thumb and forefinger, and her stomach fluttered.

He pulled back long enough to search her eyes. He seemed to need reassurance from her that all of this was okay.

Was it?

Ella didn't want to think. For once, she wanted to go with what her body craved…and right now, that was the blue-eyed stranger.

He pulled back. "See what I'm talking about?"

She studied him.

"I've needed to do that since you woke up the other day," he grumbled. "And it's a huge mistake."

He had that right, she thought, as anger flared through her.

"Don't worry. I'll make sure nothing like it ever happens again," she said.

Chapter Five

Ella could not, under any circumstances, allow Holden Crawford to affect her. She moved away from him and onto the makeshift bed, grateful that he'd left it intact. She needed…something—physical space, maybe—to clear her mind. What she wouldn't do for a strong cup of coffee right now.

"I need to get a message to my family and make sure they're okay. Whoever is doing this to me might also be targeting them," she said, needing to redirect her thoughts and gain control of her overwrought emotions. Her attraction to him could be explained in simple terms. She'd almost been killed. Twice. He'd saved her. Twice. The magnetic pull she felt was nothing more than primal urge.

Holden studied her for a long moment. He had that wrinkled-forehead expression that made her believe he wanted to speak his mind. He seemed to decide better of it.

"Where are the twins and your sister?" he asked.

Ella couldn't mask her surprise. She was going to have to get used to the fact that this stranger knew more about her than she did about him, reminding herself that he was one of her father's many acquaintances. But then, it seemed like everyone knew her father or at least believed they did. She also realized that for all his antics, her father wouldn't help someone who broke the law. Maverick Mike was many things, but he wouldn't harbor a criminal and especially not anywhere near his beloved family or ranch. Despite complicated relationships, family was everything to Maverick Mike. His property was a close second. Her father had loved his land and everything about Texas was sacred to the man. She'd inherited his zest for family, the ranch and her home state.

"I don't know exactly. They disappeared to get away from the media circus surrounding Dad's death and I didn't think to ask," she said. "We all have places we go when we need time away."

"Why did you stick around?" His gaze narrowed and his lips thinned.

"Someone had to stay in order to keep an eye on the business," she stated. "An operation as big as Hereford doesn't run itself."

He gave her a look of concession. "Your brothers didn't see it as their jobs?"

"As a matter of fact, they did," she said, a little indignant. "They wanted to stay but I convinced them that they should take some time away."

"Your arguing skills aren't in question but I'm still surprised they agreed," he said with a shake of his head.

"Well, they put up a good fight. But I managed to

convince them." That was putting it lightly. She'd almost had to physically force them off the property.

She looked at Holden, who seemed not to believe her.

"You may not realize it, but I can be pretty convincing when I need to be," she defended.

"On second thought, I shouldn't doubt that you know exactly how to get what you want," he said with a tone she decided to ignore rather than explore. Mostly because it sent more of those unwelcomed shivers up her arms.

"What about you?" she asked, realizing that he wasn't saying more than two words about himself.

He didn't answer.

Shocking.

"What's next?" she asked. Adrenaline must've worn off because she was starting to feel every ache and the pain was taking the fight out of her. Besides, the chemistry constantly sizzling between them was exhausting.

Holden paced. She waited.

"You make a choice," he finally said. There was so much frustration and warning in his voice.

"I can't go back to Hereford until I know who's trying to kill me," she stated. "I have no idea if this person has access to the main house, but he's made his intentions clear."

"It's best to assume he does, and especially after what happened to your father on the property. I can keep you safe while the sheriff investigates the attempts on your life. Or we can figure out a better way to get you to law enforcement."

She was shaking her head before he finished his sentence.

"If you accept my help that means going off the grid. You have to follow my rules and cut off all communication with everyone but me," he said, and the look in his eyes said he meant every word. "You already know what it's like to be around me. This is what you'll be stuck with until this...*issue* is resolved."

"I'm aware of your magnetic personality," she shot back. She was also aware that he was the only one who seemed capable of keeping her alive. He might not be one to talk much, but it was obvious that he knew how to hide and a piece of her—a piece she should probably ignore—felt safe when he was around.

"Good. Being angry with me will keep us both from making another mistake like the one we made earlier," he said, and his gaze dipped to her lips. He refocused on the patch of wall behind her head.

Did he have to keep reminding her?

"If I can't speak to anyone else, how will the sheriff know what's happened?" she asked.

"I'll arrange for you to give a statement, but it won't be in person," he said. "Then we'll disappear."

She could hire a security company to keep her safe, but there was no time. She needed protection *now*. And it was too risky to give up her location to anyone before she could thoroughly vet the agency's employees. This wasn't the time to chide herself for not thinking of having a security team ready to go sooner. She hadn't needed to consider it before now. Security on the ranch had always proved up to the task until her father...

Thinking about him caused tears to threaten.

Going to the ranch was out. Again, her father had been murdered at home, so someone had slipped past security. Either way, returning to Hereford might not prove good for her longevity.

Her father had trusted Holden Crawford. And that was saying a lot.

"I want your help," she stated. "There are reporters everywhere in Cattle Barge and apparently—" she blew out a frustrated breath "—I'm news. If I surface anywhere, then my face will be all over the internet, on live feeds, and that will lead whoever is after me to my location. I can't afford to be seen right now, and since you seem very good at staying under the radar, you're my best chance at staying alive."

His lips thinned and his gaze narrowed.

"I was afraid you'd say that," he ground out as he walked right past her and out the door.

HOLDEN STALKED OUTSIDE and paced. The room had felt confining, like he was strapped in a straitjacket. Being in the Texas night air always gave him perspective.

Maverick Mike was dead. He'd been killed in a manner that was meant to make a statement. Sure, the man knew how to have a good time. Holden's own father had always gotten a look of appreciation when he'd talked about his poker buddy from Texas. The annual secret game that had happened at Hereford every year was legendary but rarely spoken about. Holden was unclear as to how his father had been included, but he'd been making the trip since Holden could remember. Thinking of Pop brought a wave of anger to the surface. Holden should've been there to stop it. His fists clenched and that familiar sense of frustration bore down on him. Beating himself up over Pop's death again wouldn't change the past.

The door squeaked open behind him. He turned to look at Ella and his heart hammered against his ribs a little harder. The tension of the day was written in the worry lines bracketing her mouth, and Holden had an overwhelming urge to kiss her again. Self-control was normally second nature to him, so his reaction to her threw him off balance.

"Do you think the guys who are after me had anything to do with my father's death?" she asked, and he was grateful for the change in subject.

Was someone planning to systematically kill off the Butler family?

The question was worth considering.

But his noncommittal shrug had the effect of a raging fire in her eyes.

"I'm sorry about throwing my problems in your lap, but why volunteer for this since it's so obvious that it pains you so much to help me?" The spark in her eyes lit something else inside him that he couldn't allow. Holden couldn't go there to that place where he cared about someone again. Not when the two people closest to him were dead because of him.

"There's no need to be sorry," Holden said, unsure of what else he could say in this situation. He'd been away from people for too long and she wasn't making it easy to keep her at arm's length.

The breath she blew out could've put out candles lit across the entire Lone Star State.

Good. Maybe her anger would warn her to keep a safe distance from him.

"You may not realize what it's like for your father to be killed practically under your nose," she said.

Those words lit a fire inside him that no amount of reasoning could extinguish. He stalked toward her until her back was against the wood structure and her lips weren't five inches from his.

"Don't you ever mention my father again," he ground out. "Do you understand me?"

There should be a look of fear on her face because he could damn well be intimidating when he needed to be and he'd released only a tiny portion of what he was capable of. Most people would be shaking right now. Not her. Not Ella. Instead of flinching, her face was soft with compassion. Her arms were at her sides, her hands open.

He planted his palms to either side of her head and practically growled at her.

"I'm sorry for your loss," she said quietly as her cornflower blue eyes rose to meet his. Her honey-wheat hair fell around her shoulders in loose curls. And with that one look, he almost faltered.

Holden, dude, get a grip.

He pushed off the wall and took a couple of steps in the opposite direction. He needed to steer the conversation away from his problems and back to the danger at hand.

"Earlier you said that your father was shot and he

was na—" he shifted his gaze back toward her "—not wearing clothes."

"Yes, that's right."

"The sheriff most likely already made the connection that the murderer was making some kind of statement," he said and could see that her mind was clicking.

"Or seeking revenge," she said.

Holden nodded. "I see it like this. Someone wanted the whole world to know that they could access him at his home while he slept." He started pacing again. He could see out of the corner of his eye that she was nodding.

"Did he have a girlfriend?" he asked.

A harrumph noise tore from her throat. "Several, but he seemed to be getting serious with one, Andrea Caldwell."

"Did she know about the others?" he asked.

"Yes," she replied.

"Since a male attacked you, it's probably safe to rule her out," he said.

"Right after my father's murder the sheriff asked for a list of employees, family, friends who might've been there that night. We were putting it together when the room started spinning and my mouth felt dry. I had to get out, to go take a walk," she said. "He was gone by the time I got back."

Holden ignored the fact that he'd felt the same way a few minutes ago. *Almost ignored*, a little voice reminded—a voice he tamped down the second it made itself known. That her stress reaction was similar to his had registered. Fine. The knowledge would help him memorize her habits and reactions, and that could mean the difference between life and death at some point. Holden filed away those facts with others he knew about Ella. She was strong, independent and intelligent.

"Did you ever complete that list and turn it in?" he asked.

"May, our housekeeper, was still working on it with me," she said and then a different kind of emotion lit behind her eyes—concern. "She's probably worried sick after my disappearance and then the news story about my attack. I need to contact her and let her know that I'm okay."

And now Ella was pacing, too.

"Out of the question," he said.

"I wouldn't tell her where I am. Just that I'm safe," she defended.

"We don't take any unnecessary risks. The man who tried to shoot you meant business and I won't—"

Her hand came up as if to stop him and her gaze dramatically swept down across her thigh. "Save your breath. I already know that."

Holden didn't want to look at those long legs of hers.

"She's looked after me since I was a baby. She's like a mother to us. Please figure out a way to get a message to her and let her know that I'm not lying in a ditch somewhere because that's what she's thinking. She's getting older and I can't stand the thought of her worrying herself sick," she said with eyes that pleaded.

And it was working. He thought about Rose, the friend of his father's who Holden had known all his life. He hadn't been in contact with her since he'd been on the run, and now he wondered how many sleepless nights she'd spent worrying about him.

Hell, he was beginning to see how Ella managed to get her way with people. It was a combination of her arguing skills, concern for others and passion. She gave the impression that she cared deeply about others and that was compelling. Those eyes didn't hurt either.

"No." He needed to see that she would listen to him even when she didn't agree. Not even Holden could keep someone alive who was determined to work against him.

She balked and her cheeks reddened with anger, but to her credit she didn't continue to argue her point.

"And don't get any ideas about going behind my back," he said, testing her further. "I'll know."

"How?" she blurted out.

"Trust me. I will," he stated.

Ella stalked past him again, wearing a path in the dirt.

"Fine," she said. "But when are you going to start actually trusting me?"

Chapter Six

Holden had no response. No one had ever been able to read him that well, and especially not someone who barely knew him. Never mind that he felt a deeper connection to Ella Butler than anyone he had ever known. He pushed it out of his mind and chalked it up to them being in similar situations.

Ella's hand came up. "I get it. This is real and you need to feel like you know me. I'm not going to betray you. In case you haven't already figured it out, I need you right now more than you need me. So I won't mess up and risk forcing you to walk away for your own safety's sake. I get what's on the line here for both of us."

Well, those words did a lot toward building a tentative bridge of trust.

"Whatever has you on the run has also caused you to stop believing that you can rely on people," she continued.

He begrudgingly nodded. She was intelligent and observant. He could use that to their advantage.

"Even if it means nothing to you right now, I give you my word that I'll do whatever you ask. Whoever is after me could also be targeting my brothers and sister. They're safely out of the public eye right now, and I'll do whatever it takes to protect them," she said with a defiant sparkle in her eyes.

"Family blood runs thick. I get it," he started.

"Do you really?" she asked. "Because I'm beginning to think that all you know is how to be alone."

He started to tell her that his personal life was none of her business but thought better of it. "What about you? Where is your boyfriend in all this because I need to know if someone else is going to interfere?"

"I don't have one," she admitted. Her cheeks flushed.

Relief washed over him and he chalked it up to the kiss, not wanting to admit how truly interested he'd been in her answer.

A thought struck him. She needed to see that he trusted her with information and he could give up a little. "My mother took off when I was little and I wouldn't know her if she walked past me. I don't have biological brothers or sisters. At least, none that I know of."

He had no plans to elaborate further.

"But I understand and appreciate your loyalty to yours." His comfort zone had been shattered twenty minutes ago, but she'd been painfully honest with him and he figured he owed her something in return. "And your loyalty to me until this mess is untangled is your best chance at staying alive."

"We're in agreement," she said.

Holden remembered her telling him that she'd been good at campaigning for what was important to her. He could hand it to her. She'd gotten more out of him in the little time he'd known her than any other human had gotten out of him in months. He wasn't much into sharing.

He could also admit to admiring her inner strength as much as he could appreciate that she was a beautiful woman. Okay, where'd that last part come from? *The heart*, that annoying little voice supplied. Time to shut it down and turn it off—whatever *it* was. Holden refused to think that he could have real feelings for her, for anyone, and especially not someone he barely knew. He didn't believe he could be that cruel to another person again. And he needed to get this conversation back on track and off this slippery slope of feelings.

"Earlier, you mentioned the list," he said. "Did any of the names stick out to you?"

"Not really." She blew out a breath and it was like a balloon deflating. "My father was well liked and just as well hated, I guess. Depends on which side of the fence you stand on. If he was your friend, there was no one better. If you crossed him, he would have nothing to do with you. He was dating a few women but he seemed keen on Andrea. I got the feeling that he was getting close to making a real commitment to her."

"Could she have gotten tired of waiting?" he asked.

"I suppose. But she's a good person. And, like you said, she couldn't be the one who attacked me." Her proud shoulders were starting to curl forward and dark circles had formed underneath her eyes. A good look at her said she was exhausted.

"Let's finish talking about this inside," he said and wasn't surprised she didn't put up a fight.

Ella accepted the arm he held out. Her grip was weakening, so he wrapped his arm around her waist to absorb her weight. It was probably a mistake for their bodies to be anywhere near this close to each other. Heat sizzled between them despite the amount of energy it took for her to walk.

"Thank you, by the way. Again. For saving my life," she said quietly.

"Not necessary," he said.

She gave him a look and he quickly added, "It's the least I can do for someone who needs a hand up. Our fathers knew each other and that's how I know yours. When I reached out, he didn't hesitate to help me. I owe him for that."

That seemed to ease her stress and she rewarded him with a warm smile. He helped her inside and to the bed in the corner. "I have a few supplies on my bike. I'll be right back."

She winced as she scooted her back against the wall in obvious pain.

Holden retrieved his pack from his motorcycle. He had several clean rolled-up T-shirts that he positioned as a pillow for Ella. The bed might be hard but she could at least put her head down on something soft. "This is a far cry from what you're used to on the ranch."

"If you really think that then you have no idea how I spent my childhood," she quipped, and he could see a flash of humor in her eyes. She quickly reeled in her smile but he liked the curve of her lips when she was happy, fleeting as it might've been.

"And how was that, exactly?" He went to work on

her leg, cleaning the area with wipes and dabbing the ointment generously. Being prepared for the possibility that he'd have to patch himself up at some point, he was grateful for the medical supplies he kept on hand. He used a patch of white gauze and medical tape to cover the wound.

"In a tent in the backyard," she said. "More bluebonnets than you could count in the spring and we'd come in with more bug bites than should be allowed. But we liked being outside and when we got old enough, Dad would let us build a fire." She shook her head before curling on her side. "May would be so furious with him that she'd sit up half the night in the screened-in porch watching over us. Dad sure didn't make her job easy."

"Sounds like a good way to live if you ask me," he said. But before they could get too far off course and mired in nostalgia he added, "I'm guessing security is lighter around the barn area of the property."

"Dad liked his privacy. He didn't want anyone, and that included his security team, too entangled in his personal affairs," she stated. "He liked to be able to come and go as he pleased without his extracurricular life part of our dinner conversation."

He could appreciate that a single man wouldn't want his children waking up to a stranger in the house. He also didn't need to say out loud that was a mistake that had cost her father gravely. He could see that she'd made that connection by the look in her eyes. "The person who did this to him wanted to make a statement with his death."

"I know that we ruled out a woman, but could it be?

Someone whose heart he broke?" she asked and her voice was almost hopeful.

"Maybe one of the others figured out he was about to cut them loose and decided to show him," he said without conviction.

"He wanted to create office space for me, my sister and twin brothers. He'd been dropping hints to me that he was at least thinking about retiring from the day-to-day operations of the ranch," she said.

"I can't see a man like Maverick Mike retiring from anything," Holden pointed out.

"True. I got the impression he had other plans. Maybe he was thinking of doing something different. Ever since he'd turned sixty-five he'd been acting strange."

"How so? Like midlife-crisis, go-out-and-buy-a-corvette strange?" he asked.

"Not really. My father never really denied himself cars or much of anything else he wanted. It was more like something was stirring. There was a new excitement in his tone that I hadn't heard in a few years." She shrugged. "At the time I thought it had something to do with Andrea. Maybe he was considering his legacy."

"I owe an apology for what I'm about to say, but from what my father said about yours, Maverick Mike didn't seem the type to wax altruistic. Don't get me wrong, he was a good man on many counts." Holden figured she was remembering her father how she might've wanted him to be instead of the man he was, flawed. He'd done the same with his own father, who also happened to be a good man. It was so easy to forget the imperfections of someone who was never coming back.

"I can see why outsiders would feel that way about him," she said. "But Dad had another side to him that even I rarely ever saw."

"A side that makes you think it's possible for a scorned woman to wiggle her way into his heart and then try to destroy him?" he asked.

"I learned a long time ago not to put people in boxes, Mr. Crawford," she said as she stared right at him.

He could concede that point. He'd seen himself in the mirror at the diner—the person he'd become—and yet she trusted him, his word. Despite what his appearance might've cautioned her. Having seen it for himself, he was shocked at the transformation. A shave didn't sound like the worst thing.

Maybe it was time to clean up.

"Morning will come early," he said after giving her a protein bar and finishing one off himself.

"Good night, Holden," Ella said before rolling onto her other side so her back was to him.

He shouldn't like the sound of his name on her tongue. Hell, he shouldn't be thinking about her tongue at all.

ELLA WOKE THE next morning thinking about what Holden Crawford had said to her last night. There were so many possibilities roaring through her head as she blinked her eyes open to find an empty room. She pushed up onto her elbows to get a better view and panic roared through her when she realized he was gone.

The makeshift pillow he'd placed underneath her head was still there. She forced herself to stand on shaky legs and ignored the pounding at that spot on her fore-head between her eyes. A little bit of rest was almost worse than no sleep. She moved to the door to check on his motorcycle. Relief washed over her when she saw it.

Holden Crawford. She liked the sound of his name.

There was a bottle of water on the kitchen counter and something bright yellow positioned next to it. She moved closer to get a good look—a toothbrush. Funny how little things mattered so much when everything was taken away. Being able to wash her face and brush her teeth, things she took for granted literally every day, suddenly felt like gifts from heaven. Ella brushed her teeth in the sink using water from the bottle and used one of the rolled-up shirts that she'd slept on as a wash rag. She doused it and washed her face. The cool liquid felt so good on her skin. Next, she poured water into her hair and then finger-combed it, figuring that was better than nothing.

The door opened and Holden walked in, balancing two tin mugs of what looked like coffee.

"It's strong," he said, holding out the offering.

"Good. I need it," she replied, taking the cup and wasting no time sipping. Seriously, this was heaven in a cup. "How do you do this? It's amazing."

"Let's just say I've had a lot of practice," he said with a look that seemed so lonely and yet so resigned at the same time.

"Why is it you have two cups?" she asked. "Being that you've been alone for a while."

He chuckled and it was a low rumble from deep in his chest. "I always have a backup for the important things. I never know how quickly I'll have to abandon a place. Plus, one's always clean and ready to go."

"Makes sense," she said after another sip of the fresh brew. "This is the best coffee I've ever had."

He produced another protein bar.

"In your condition, boiled mud would taste good." He laughed a low rumble from his chest and it sent goose bumps racing up her arms.

"I doubt it," she countered, taking the offering and finishing it in a few bites.

"There's something about coffee brewed over an open fire that makes it taste better," he conceded, rewarding her with a smile.

"Not better. Heavenly," she said, returning the friendly gesture. "I've been thinking about everything that's happened to me, my father."

"What did you come up with?" he asked.

"My father's murder seemed planned and, as you already said, like someone wasn't just making sure he was dead. He or she was making their frustration known."

Holden nodded, listening. For someone who, by his own admission, wasn't great at talking, he excelled at listening.

"My attacks seem just as calculated. And so we have to decide if these two could possibly be linked," she continued. "Maybe he planned my father's murder and now wants to get rid of his heirs, or doesn't feel the need to take extra precautions with me. Maybe this person is just interested in taking me out and possibly my siblings next. We don't know if the others have been targeted and won't until I make contact." She brought her hand up. "Which I won't do unless you say it's okay, and besides, I don't have a phone. But if we figure out who killed my father, then we might be led to the guy who's after me and possibly them. And I'm making myself sick with worry about what might happen next. What if they get hurt or worse because I didn't warn them? How could I live with myself?"

He waited until he seemed sure she was finished.

"I understand if you want to search for the person who killed your father," he said. "The sheriff is already on the case and could have an answer soon."

"I keep going back and forth in my mind, but there must be some link, right?"

He shot her a look that said he wasn't convinced. "I recommend focusing our energy on who's coming after you."

"I guess I'm not much good to my father's investigation if I'm dead," she conceded.

"Won't happen on my watch," he said, and she believed that he meant it. She wished for half of his confidence. "It'll be best if you call in your statement to the sheriff. He might offer to arrange witness protection and you should consider it. After all, you're a high-profile case and you're being targeted. The feds will most likely offer assistance."

"What about you?" she asked, a little stunned at the suggestion.

"I can't go near anyone in law enforcement," he said emphatically. "And I need you to leave it at that."

Ella stopped herself from asking why. "I won't ask

for details you're not willing to give. But I'm curious why you think law enforcement wouldn't help you, too."

"Simple. Because the evidence they have makes them believe I'm guilty of something I didn't do." He looked at her dead on.

She did her best not to flinch at his last words. "There's more to the story, though."

"Hell, yeah. But they think they've done their jobs. All I have to contradict the investigation is my word and the knowledge that I'm innocent," he said, and she figured that was more than he'd planned to say by the way he leaned forward and placed his elbows on his knees. That was a move reserved for people who felt exposed.

Ella took a sip of coffee, and it was pretty much a stall tactic so she could think hard about her next words. She didn't want to anger the man who was helping her or offend him. But she'd always been bad at holding her tongue. "You don't strike me as the kind of person who would just check out and give up so easily." He started to say something but she held out her hand, palm up. "Hold on. Before you get upset with me. Hear me out."

He nodded but she could tell there were a whole string of words backing up on the tip of his tongue. Lucky for her, he bit them back.

"You've put yourself in jeopardy twice to save me, and I'm someone you've never met." She made eyes at him. "Granted, you knew my father but he's gone. You didn't have to come back that second time. So as much as you want me to believe otherwise, you're not a bad person."

He opened his mouth to speak but she pointed her index finger at him.

"You're about to mention my father," she stated, already figuring out his next argument based on the look in his eyes.

Holden nodded this time, making a frustrated-looking gesture about being forced to hold his tongue.

"I know what you're thinking and it's not true. You already repaid the debt to him," she said. "You didn't have to come back even if you blamed yourself for dropping me off. You're a decent man no matter how much you blame yourself for whatever happened in the past. I understand why you refuse to go there with a stranger. You say it's because you're afraid for me, but it's so much more than that."

"Oh, yeah?" Holden crossed his massive arms over his chest. "Enlighten me."

"From my point of view, you're afraid to let anyone else in," she stated. She was finished so she steadied herself for his argument, bracing herself against the counter.

Except now, Holden Crawford really was mute.

Chapter Seven

"Since you know me so well, tell me, what's our next step?" Holden asked the woman who left him scratching his head. She was perceptive and thought she'd figured him out. She was wrong. Keeping her at a distance was more for her benefit than his. It was the best way to protect her and keep her safe.

Wasn't it? Or was there a shred of truth to her words?

"We find a way to tell the sheriff what happened last night," she stated, interrupting his thoughts. "In order to do that, we have to leave here. How's that for starters?"

"Obvious but decent," he responded.

"Okay, so where will we go? You've been successfully hiding in rural areas for a while, so I'm guessing you'll stick to what you know. We'll stay somewhere around here." She had a self-satisfied grin and just enough defiance in her eyes to rile him up.

"Sorry. No dice," he stated. "We leave Texas. That's a given. I have a contact in New Mexico who will put us up. I want to stay close and keep my ear to the ground for a few days but we need to stay on the move. We'll head south for an hour and then stop to make the call to the sheriff. Then we can retrace our steps and head west. If the sheriff is going to catch this person, his best chance is while the trail is still hot. If he hasn't made progress in a few days, a week, then we'll have to find a way to get answers ourselves. Interfere too soon and we might hamper his investigation."

"Is this New Mexico person you're referring to a woman by chance?" Ella asked, and there was a mix of emotion playing out behind her eyes that he couldn't quite pinpoint.

"As a matter of fact, yes. Why?" He couldn't wait to hear the answer to this.

She shrugged him off but he could've sworn that she'd bristled. "Curious."

And then it hit him. She was worried they were about to be on their way to see a woman he'd *spent* time with. "She's—"

"None of my business," Ella stated.

"A friend of my father's," he continued. It was important to him that she knew the truth for reasons he didn't want to analyze. "She was sixty-seven on her last birthday."

Ella's cheeks flushed and he forced himself not to think about how attractive it made her, how attractive she already was.

"Finish your coffee. We need to get on the road," he said, harsher than he'd intended.

An hour south, he stopped off at the first megaconvenience store and bought a cell phone with prepaid minutes before returning to Ella outside. "Using this will keep us under the radar. If the call is somehow tracked, which should be impossible, we'll take the precaution of tossing it away as soon as we're done. Do you know the numbers of your brothers or sister?"

"Without my cell?" Ella shifted her weight to her left foot and her gaze darted up and to the left. "How sad is it that I tap on a name when I want to call someone and don't remember phone numbers anymore?"

"What about the ranch?" he asked.

"That one I know. It hasn't changed since we had to memorize our phone number and address in elementary school," she stated. "Are you saying I can call home?"

Holden handed over the cell and nodded.

After punching in numbers and listening for someone to pick up, her face lit up.

"May, it's me, Ella." Her excitement was barely contained. The sparkle in her eyes matched.

Holden dropped his gaze to the ground and listened.

"I'm fine, but please don't tell anyone that I called other than my brothers and sister." She paused for a beat. "I promise that I'm okay. Do I have your word?" Another few seconds passed. "So you have heard from all three of them? And they're okay."

Ella looked at Holden, so he brought his gaze up to meet her gaze. She nodded and smiled. The relief in her expression detailed just how much she loved her siblings.

"The next time you talk to them, tell them to stay out of sight until the sheriff figures this out," she said into the phone. "And tell them I'll do the same." Another beat passed. "No, tell both of my brothers to stay put. I'm nowhere near the ranch and I won't be. I appreciate that they want to stop whoever's doing this but they can help me more if they stay out of the media and away from danger."

Good. She was giving the right direction.

"Tell them it won't matter because I'm not coming back until this is over," she stated, and there was conviction in her voice—conviction that would keep her brothers alive and she seemed to know it. "Just tell them that I love them both and I'm safe. No one can hurt me because they'll never find me."

Holden had every intention of making sure she kept that promise.

"I'm good," she continued, "and, more important, safe." She glanced up at Holden. "I'm in good hands, May. But that's all I can say right now."

May seemed to accept Ella's answers.

"I need to call the sheriff and give a statement now, so I have to go." Her face morphed and gave the saddest look Holden believed he'd ever seen. It caused his chest to clutch.

"I will," Ella promised. After a few more affirmations into the phone and an almost-tearful goodbye, Ella ended the call. She looked away and Holden gave her a little time to gather herself.

Missing a home like Hereford had to be hell. Holden and his father had moved around during his childhood. His father had served in the military and Holden had signed up the day after graduating from high school. There was no place that made him feel like Ella's Hereford.

Ella spun around and took in a breath. "Okay. I'm ready to call the sheriff now."

The conversation was brief. An all-too-familiar anger rumbled in Holden's chest as he listened to the details of Ella being ambushed and then hunted while she bled. He could hear the fear in her voice as she recounted the scene and her vulnerability made him want to put his hands on the man who was trying to kill her. His own past, the horror that his girlfriend, Karen, had endured, filled his chest with rage. The image of the crime scene flashed in his thoughts—an image that had replayed a thousand times in his nightmares for the past two years. Karen splayed across his bed in a pool of blood, her pajamas torn half off her body. The blade of his KA-BAR jammed through her heart.

"Holden," Ella's voice caught him off guard, breaking through his heavy thoughts.

"Yeah?" he responded, even though his clenched jaw had fought against movement. His hands were fisted at his sides and his muscles pulled taut.

She stood there, examining him, and her penetrating gaze threatened to crack through his walls.

"Are you okay?" she asked.

"I will be." He handed her the helmet and threw his leg over the bike. "Ready?"

BY THE TIME they reached Rose's place near the Texas border in Ruidoso, New Mexico, the desert air was cold and Ella shivered. Eight hours on the back of a motorcycle had seemed to take a toll on Ella, but she didn't complain.

He'd stopped off three times for bathroom breaks but had barely spoken to her. Talking about himself had dredged up memories. Remembering his pain was good because being around Ella made him want to forget, to move on. Karen was dead. His father was dead. Holden had been accused of the murders. Those were the only facts that mattered.

"Rose Naples is an artist who specializes in Southwest art," Holden said to Ella as he parked his motorcycle behind her rustic brown log cabin with a green tin roof. "She's lived here most of her life and she and my father went to elementary school together. They stayed in touch but very few people ever knew about her. She leads a quiet life. We'll have food and shelter."

"After eight hours on a bike, all I need is a hot shower and a soft bed," Ella said. She no doubt picked up on the change in him. Good. She needed to stay at arm's length. "I take that back—the bed doesn't even need to be soft."

He started toward the door and she put her hand on his arm. He ignored the fission of heat that was like a lightning bolt to his heart.

"She'll be safe, right?" she asked. "I mean, us being here won't put her in jeopardy, will it?"

"I wouldn't be here if I thought there was the slightest chance," was all he said as he linked their fingers. "It's best if we act like a couple. And to be safe, we can't stay long. A day or two should give us enough time to let the sheriff do his job or come up with a plan."

The word *couple* sat sourly on his lips. He thought about Karen. It had been two long years since she'd been killed, and that same old rage filled his chest when he thought about not being able to bring her killer to justice. Instead, the coward had framed Holden and gotten away with murder. Twice.

Holden picked up the blue cactus pot and located the spare key Rose kept there for him. The sun dipped below the horizon and his stomach reminded him that it had been a while since lunch.

No one should be able to track them to New Mexico. No matter how dire his situation had become, he'd avoided making contact with Rose. She was all he had left.

Best-case scenario, he and Ella could stay a few days. Worst-case, they would get a few hours and then divert to Big Bend National Park to camp out. It was August and he wasn't convinced that Ella would do well under extreme conditions and especially not with her injuries. She needed guaranteed access to clean water to keep the gashes on her head and her leg from becoming infected.

Holden listened at the door for any signs Rose was inside.

The pump action of a bullet being engaged in a shotgun chamber sounded.

"It's me, Rose. It's Holden."

The light flipped on and the door swung open.

Rose dropped the nose of the weapon and flew toward Holden. He caught her in time to give her a bear hug.

"Holden Crawford, you're alive." Shock widened her tearful green eyes. Droplets streamed down her cheeks even though her smile was wide. She was just as thin as he remembered, and her Southwest style of teal poncho, jeans tucked into boots and lots of turquoise jewelry was intact. "I didn't think I'd ever see you again."

"I couldn't risk getting in touch before now." His heart clutched as he noticed the deep worry lines in her face. "But I'm here and I'm okay."

"I'm so sorry about your father." She wiped tears as her gaze shifted from Holden to Ella.

She stepped back and focused on his companion. "I'm sorry. I promise I have better manners than this. I haven't seen this guy in two and a half years and thought I might never again."

"Rose, I'd like you to meet my girlfriend, Ella," he said. The word *girlfriend* sounded a little too right rolling off his tongue. He felt Ella's fingers tense and she radiated a genuine smile.

"I've heard so much about you," Ella said. "And normally I'd hug you but I don't want to offend you by my smell."

"It won't bother me," Rose quipped. "What happened to the two of you?"

"Lost my wallet camping and Ella came out with a pretty bad injury climbing," Holden said by way of excuse. Rose's narrowed gaze said she didn't buy any of it but she smiled anyway. "Can we bunk here for the night until I arrange a transfer of funds and find another place to stay?"

"Do you really have to ask?" Rose set a balled fist on her right hip and pursed her lips. He knew her well enough to know questions were mounting. And he knew her well enough to realize that she wouldn't ask until he gave her the green light.

"Thank you," Ella said, breaking the tension. "Could I trouble you to use your shower?"

"Of course, dear. Follow me," Rose said. She set her shotgun down and motioned for Ella to follow her. "I've got plenty of clean clothes if you need something fresh to borrow."

"I would love that, actually," Ella said.

The two disappeared down the hall and he poured himself a glass of water.

There were so many holes in Holden's plan to pretend he and Ella were in a relationship. He knew nothing about her and vice versa. The plan that he'd been living by to shut Ella out of his personal life was most likely about to backfire. Rose wasn't stupid and he wanted to tell her more. But Ella's secrets weren't his to share.

Rose returned a couple of minutes later and took a seat at the table in her eat-in kitchen.

Holden followed suit, taking the chair across from her at the round table.

"Where have you been?" She took his hand and squeezed.

"All over," he said.

"I know you didn't do it." She gave him a sincere look. "I've been following the story and there's no way you would've done that to Karen. I know you better than that and started to come forward, but before I could get on a plane I read about what they did to your father."

"I'm glad you stayed put and I appreciate your confidence in me." Gratitude filled Holden's chest.

"Sorry I couldn't attend your father's funeral," she said, twisting her hands. "I was sick about it but he wouldn't have wanted me to go and especially not after the way he was…"

She stopped as though she couldn't say the words.

"No, he wouldn't," Holden agreed. "For the record, that makes both of us."

"You couldn't be there either, could you?" She shook her head and her voice was filled with sadness. Like a heavy rain cloud before the first drop of rain spilled, he decided.

"Not because I didn't want to be," he said.

"Your father got a message to me after Karen was murdered. He said that I should tell you 1-9-6-4. I have no idea what it means. Do you? He also mentioned a place you used to fish but I can't remember where. Now it feels so important but at the time I had no idea."

He shook his head. The numbers didn't register as important or click any puzzle pieces together. "I'll have to think about it. Could be a year?"

"I thought about that, too. But why a year?" One of her brows spiked.

Rose picked up the saltshaker and rolled it in between her flat palms. Then Rose set it down and looked him straight in the eye. "Do you have any inkling why they were killed?"

"Other than to cover for someone who wanted Karen dead and set me up for murder? No," he admitted.

"He must've worried they'd come after him or he wouldn't have sent the message." She focused on the saltshaker. "Guess he thought he could handle them when they did."

"They got to him before I could," he said and then stood.

"Don't go," she said, and she must've realized how difficult it was for him to speak about the past.

He reclaimed his seat. Those same frustrations of getting nowhere with his own investigation enveloped him.

"Who's the girl?"

"My girlfriend." Could he share a little without endangering her?

"How'd the two of you meet?" Her gaze penetrated him.

"I didn't underestimate you, Rose. And you know I'd tell you anything that I could." The thought of defining his relationship with Ella or his need to help her spiked his blood pressure. "I was wrong to come here. We'll leave after she finishes in the shower."

"Maybe it was a mistake to come here because I can read you so well," she said. "I'm not concerned that you hurt Karen. I know that for the lie it is. But I know you, Holden, and there's something going on between you and Ella. You're not telling me every—"

"You're reading too much into it. She's a friend in trouble. Can we leave it at that?" Trying to continue the charade was going nowhere. Rose knew him too well. His father had brought him to New Mexico every summer. Sometimes they'd stay with Rose. Others they'd camp the entire time. But they always met her for a meal. The woman had watched Holden grow from a young child. It was Rose who had stepped in from afar when his own mother took off. He'd considered Rose a mother figure, if not his mother. And since she knew him so well, he needed to tread carefully when it came to Ella.

"All I'm saying is that I hope you can find a way to forgive yourself for the past—"

He started to argue but she waved him off.

"Two years wandering. Lost. Karen didn't deserve what happened to her, but neither did you. You didn't do anything wrong," she said, and an odd wave of relief washed over him. Strange that one person's opinion mattered so much to him. But it was Rose, and their relationship went way back.

"That means a lot coming from you," Holden said quietly. Was she right? Was he punishing himself by cutting himself off from the world?

"Promise me you'll try to forgive yourself, Holden," she continued.

"When I find the killer and bring him to justice."

She started to protest but he held up a hand.

"As far as she goes, can we leave it alone for now?" He nodded toward the hallway. "Keep up the charade for her sake?"

"My lips are sealed." She pretended to close a zipper over her mouth. "If and when you can talk about it without violating her trust, I'm here for you."

Holden thanked her again, drained his glass and poured another. "Any chance you have an extra razor in that guest bathroom of yours?"

A CLEAN BODY and fresh clothes borrowed from Rose did wonders for Ella's attitude. Holden had disappeared into the bathroom after redressing the bandages on her thigh and forehead. Rose was cooking up something that smelled amazing. Ella's stomach growled so loudly that her cheeks flushed with embarrassment. "Excuse me."

Rose turned and chuckled. She moved to the fridge and pulled out a container of what looked like homemade salsa. After, she poured tortilla chips into a bowl and set both down on the table in front of Ella. "This should help until the food's ready."

Ella immediately dug into the offering. It was good. So good. And nice to be in a safe place. "This is amazing. Thank you."

"I grow the cilantro fresh in pots out back," Rose said, looking pleased. "Makes all the difference in the world."

The older woman moved with grace, and her half dozen bracelets jangled in time with her fluid movements. Her all-white hair was pulled back in a neat ponytail. Turquoise earrings dangled from her ears. She embodied Southwest elegance at its best.

Ella was grateful that Rose seemed content to be together in the same room without the need for conversation. So much had gone on in the past few days that Ella could scarcely wrap her thoughts around it, and she was still trying to break through the fog. She dipped another chip in the homemade salsa, took a bite and savored the taste of the fresh tomatoes.

"Did you grow these, too?"

Rose nodded and smiled.

Ella thought about May. She grew her own garden

and said the same things with a similar look of pride. Ella's heart squeezed. She felt naked without her cell phone and she missed home more than she wanted to show. And so many questions loomed, keeping her away from everything she loved.

Why would someone come after her? So far, the others in her family were safe. Ed Staples, the family's lawyer, had promised May that he would help keep the ranch running while Ella was away. Ella had learned that during her phone call with May. He was a good man and close confidant to her father. She could trust him to hold up his end.

"I'll get you started eating." Rose interrupted Ella's thoughts. The older woman set a plate down in front of Ella and then motioned toward the chili peppers. "I wasn't sure which you liked, red or green, so there's both."

"That's perfect," Ella said, accepting the literally mouthwatering chalupa. She dug in immediately and the shredded chicken was tender beyond belief. The covering of homemade guacamole was smooth and creamy in her mouth. And she already knew the salsa on top was in a whole new class of Tex-Mex.

"It's Holden's favorite dish, chalupas." Rose went back to work, humming while she deep-fried what had to be his.

"He talks about your guacamole all the time," Ella offered, pretending she knew more about her "boyfriend" than she actually did.

"Really? He's been allergic to avocados since he was seven years old." Rose didn't turn around but her humming picked up.

Ella figured trying to save herself after that slip was futile, so she focused on her food. Her back was to the hallway, so she didn't see Holden when he first entered the room. She had a big bite in her mouth when she turned around and it took everything inside her not to spit it out. She covered her mouth as she finished chewing and swallowed. "Holden?"

He seemed almost embarrassed by her reaction.

"Sorry," she quickly added. "It's just... I've never seen...you look..." She could feel herself digging a hole as the right way to frame this conversation didn't hit her. What did strike her was how drop-dead gorgeous Holden Crawford was underneath all that untamed facial hair. She'd seen a hint of it before in his eyes—those bold blue irises. "Your face. You look...good."

"I thought you should finally see what you're getting yourself into," he said easily, and she realized that he was covering for her slip, her second mistake. There was a slight curve to his lips, not exactly a smile but a hint of one. He walked right over to her and kissed her on the forehead. The second his soft lips touched her skin, a thunderclap of need rocketed through her.

All she could do was look up at him, mute, with a dry throat. It suddenly felt like she'd licked a glue stick.

Holden had that strong square jaw that most women obsessed over, and she could admit that it looked damn good on him. She already knew he had a body made for athletics. He had stacked muscles that surfers, or anyone who wore very little clothing for their sport, would lust after. She had to force her gaze away from his lips. *Okay, come on.* This was getting a little ridiculous. It wasn't like Holden was the first attractive man Ella had ever seen. Of course, she'd never met one with his sex appeal and magnetism before. And she'd spent a few days with him already so she needed to pick her jaw up off the floor and get a grip.

Out of her peripheral she could see that Rose continued on with her work, ignoring the show of affection on display for her benefit, and for a split second she wondered if the woman was on to them.

Holden took a seat next to Ella, his right thigh touching hers, and the contact sent warmth to all kinds of places that didn't need to be aroused at the dinner table of such a kind stranger.

Ella needed to redirect her energy. She studied her chalupa as she dug into another bite.

"Do you grow your own chili peppers?" she asked Rose, and her voice came out a little strained.

"Is there any other way?" Rose quipped with a satisfied smirk.

"Your food is the best thing I've ever tasted aside from Holden's coffee," she said.

"Thank you." Rose had cleaned up the last of the dishes. "It's late, so I'll make up the guest room for you two."

Rose padded down the hall.

Right. Ella and Holden were supposed to be a couple and couples slept together. With his leg touching hers and the way he'd just looked at her, she almost believed the lie herself.

Ella finished up the food on her plate, surprised that she could eat a bite let alone empty the plate so quickly. "So, you're allergic to avocados?"

"No." He seemed confused at first but then he cracked another smile. "That what Rose told you?"

She nodded.

He shook his head. "She's a tricky one."

"A little too smart for her own good if you ask me," Ella said, feeling the burn in her cheeks. Or was that a simple reaction to the attractive man sitting next to her.

It didn't take long for Holden to finish the food on his plate, guacamole and all.

Rose reappeared in the hallway. "Leave the dishes. I'll take care of those."

Ella started to protest but Rose shut her down.

"Found a couple of unused toothbrushes in my cupboard. Leftovers from visits to the dentist over the years. I used to save them to use on trips but I haven't wanted to leave home in more years than I want to admit," the older woman continued.

"I can see why. You have a beautiful home," Ella said with true appreciation. The style of this place reflected that of its owner—elegant Southwest.

Holden stood, rinsed off their plates and linked his hand with Ella's as he led her down the hallway after Rose. She tried, rather unsuccessfully, to ignore the chemistry fizzing between them.

"I put fresh sheets on the bed, so you should be good," Rose said, stepping aside so they could enter the bedroom.

Ella wasn't sure what she'd been expecting to find. It was a bedroom after all.

But seeing one bed with turned-down sheets sent her pulse thundering.

Chapter Eight

"I can take the couch," Holden offered as soon as Rose disappeared down the hallway, figuring him and Ella alone in a bed might not be the best way to get a night of rest.

Ella stared at the bed for a thoughtful minute and then stepped inside the room. "It'll be best if we both get a good night's sleep and someone your size won't fit on the sofa. Plus, Rose will get the wrong idea about us being in a relationship. No reason to raise suspicion because that would be bad for her in the long run."

"I could always tell her we had a fight," he said, his gaze stopping on the base of Ella's throat where he could see her pulse pounding. And that wasn't helping matters for him one bit.

"It's okay," she said. "I trust you."

He hoped she wasn't making a mistake because he could tell she meant those words even though she'd said them so low he practically had to strain to hear.

She climbed into bed and turned onto her side, facing the opposite wall. She smelled like flowers and citrus, clean and like spring. Holden was already in trouble because he liked Ella Butler, and any kind of a relationship, no matter how short-lived it would be, was a slippery slope best avoided.

He pushed the covers aside and moved to the spot next to her. She rolled over and curled her body around his left side. Flat on his back, she nestled into the crook of his arm and rested her head on his chest.

Freezing up when a woman shared a bed with him was foreign to Holden, but then he'd never been in this circumstance before. In the past, a warm body beside him, hell, curled around him, meant two consenting adults who equally wanted to be there. Expectations were clear on both sides: great sex. This was not the same. The water was muddy with Ella. She wanted to be home, not there with him, but had to stay away in order to live.

Holden could hear her breathing and almost convinced himself that she was asleep until her eyes slowly opened and she looked up at him. That's all it took for him to do what he knew he shouldn't. He dipped his head down and claimed her mouth. Her lips parted and he delved his tongue inside, tasting her sweet honey. Her tongue teased him and she sucked on his bottom lip before gently biting. Need stirred from deep within. He wrapped his arms around her and hauled her tight against his chest. Her body fitted his, melding against him perfectly, and he could hear her breathing quicken.

Her hands were on his chest, her fingertips sliding along the ridges of muscles there. It would be so easy to let go with her…

Karen popped into his thoughts. Her lifeless body

lying in the bed they'd shared the night before, and his eyes shot open as he pushed up to his elbows. Ella was still partially tangled up with him so she repositioned, curling her legs around his midsection and balancing by digging her hands into his shoulders rather than spill off his lap.

"Not a good idea" was all he could manage to say.

Face-to-face, her minty toothpaste washed over him with every quick breath. She had that all-too-familiar hungry look in her eyes.

"Really, Holden?" she asked.

"This is getting out of hand," he said through ragged breaths. His body argued that a night of hot sex with Ella—and he was pretty damn certain it would rock his world—would be all he needed to get past his attraction to her and move on so he could focus on what was important: saving her life. And he could almost convince himself that once the mystery was gone, it would some-how become easier to be around her without so much sexual chemistry firing between them, distracting him. But that logic was as smart as pouring gasoline onto a forest fire and expecting to curb the flames. Laws of physics dictated a raging inferno.

"I'm confused," Ella said, and he could see the emotion in her eyes—eyes that were so expressive she was easy to read.

For lack of a real answer, he said, "So am I."

She crawled off his lap and curled onto her side again, hugging the edge of the bed. He mumbled an-other apology but she didn't respond. He repositioned onto his back and stared at the ceiling. He might be the dumbest man alive because not having sex with Ella wasn't exactly stopping him from thinking about the soft curve of her hips when they'd pressed against him. Nor did the intensity of their chemistry ease. Being with her was like sleeping with fireworks under the blanket.

Holden sighed harshly. If only he hadn't gone jogging at five that morning twenty-five months ago. Karen would be alive and so would his father.

By the time sunlight peeked through the blinds, he heard Rose padding down the hall toward the kitchen. Ella was still asleep based on her even breathing and he didn't want to wake her, so he peeled off the covers and slipped out of bed.

Rose was in the kitchen with a fresh pot of coffee brewing that he smelled from the bathroom where he stood at the sink brushing his teeth. His thoughts had bounced around last night. Most of them entailed how sweet Ella's silky skin felt against his body. The silhouette of her sweet round bottom had broken his concentration more than once. He dozed off in fits and starts because something was trying to break through. Something was bugging him. And he couldn't pinpoint what that something was. It was frustrating the hell out of him. He'd lost perspective and he needed to talk about it. He hoped a strong cup of coffee could clear his head.

"Morning," he said to Rose as he walked into the kitchen.

She nodded and caught his eye. "I haven't seen you this twisted up since you were in the eighth grade and that girl—what was her name? Tara—went off with your friend because she was convinced you didn't like her. And you did like her. But once you realized your friend did, too, you knew that you could never ask her out."

If only his problems could be that simple again, deciding between a hot girl and loyalty to his best friend. Holden had made the obvious choice—loyalty. But it had felt like a huge sacrifice at the time.

"I was awake chewing on something all night," he said. He could talk the basics of the case through without giving exact details or violating Ella's trust. "In a murder case, investigators always look to the people closest to the victim, to their inner circle, and work outward from there."

"True," she said, and she would know because her father had spent his entire life working for the Santa Fe Police Department. "Tell me more about this person's family. What are they like?"

"I couldn't say, personally. They seem to care for each other on the surface. There are twin brothers and a younger sister in this situation." He appreciated Rose going along with him without asking if they were talking about Ella.

"Does this have anything to do with what you're going through?" Rose studied him before taking a sip of coffee.

"No. This is different," he clarified. "There's no tie. This person's siblings seem to care. Both of her brothers had wanted to drop what they were doing and come to her but she'd convinced them that it would be too risky. They might lead the men targeting her right to her. Her sister shared a similar sentiment."

"So, let's rule out the immediate family," she said. "You've no doubt considered who stands to gain from her death."

"That's where things get complicated. Her father is wealthy. He was recently murdered and an attempt was made on her life almost immediately after," he said.

"She was the only one targeted out of four children?" A gray eyebrow hiked.

"The others left as soon as news of their father's death broke. She stayed to run the ranch," he supplied, holding back the fact that her father hadn't been gone for a whole week when she'd been attacked.

"All the siblings are out of town and that's not a convenient excuse?" she asked.

"I don't believe so."

"And that's where everything gets confusing, isn't it?" She picked up the spoon on the table and stirred her coffee absently. Rose always did that when she didn't have a good answer. There was so much comfort in knowing someone well enough to know their little quirks.

Holden had been away from civilization far too long. On balance, he had to consider if he was really living at all or just existing. Hiding. He raked a hand over his shaved chin, half expecting his beard to still be there and feeling nothing but exposed skin.

"Let's circle back then, to the actual attempt on the victim," Rose said. "What were the circumstances?"

"A rock was thrown at her head and she was left to die while hiking alone," he supplied.

Rose's eyes lit up. "That tells me whoever did this

wanted to make it look like an accident, so they have something to lose. It could be more than just status in the community."

"I thought that, too, until she was shot at on the way to the sheriff's office to give a statement a couple of days later," he said.

"Killer might've been expecting that. He goes back for the body where she was hiking. Doesn't find one, so he camps around the sheriff's office, figuring she might've gotten a good enough look at him to give a description," she said. "She shows and he figures he has to take her out. He's afraid to leave a possible witness."

"Good points." Holden reached for his beard again. Halfway there he realized he'd shaved and stopped as he held out his hand awkwardly in midair. "I suspect you're right and this person wants to keep his place in the community."

ELLA STRETCHED SORE muscles and pain rifled through her thigh. Her hand shot to the spot as she grimaced and blew out a breath. Contact was a bad idea even though all she touched was gauze and tape.

There'd most likely be some pain relievers in the kitchen and, more important, caffeine. More movement was going to hurt. *Time to suck it up, buttercup.*

Forcing herself to move her legs against all the resistance her body was giving seemed like the worst of bad ideas. Movement took every bit of effort inside her. Ella cursed under her breath and repeated the word a few more times as she pushed off the bed. Brushing her teeth was the first respite she had from the stabbing pain as she leaned her weight against the counter. Even her hip was sore. And all that screaming pain distracted her from the monster-sized headache raging between her temples.

After turning off the water, she heard the low hum of Holden's voice coming from the kitchen, and awareness trilled through her and her cheeks burned with embarrassment. She'd practically thrown herself at him last night and he'd stopped abruptly. She'd blame the entire episode on herself except that she'd seen that momentary flash of terror in his eyes that he tucked so masterfully behind that steel-jawed facade before rejecting her. She'd be angry with him for the rejection—and part of her was—but he'd said the last person he'd cared about ended up dead because of him, and she sensed that he couldn't go there with her and especially not under the circumstances.

He was right, though. Her life was complicated enough right now without adding to the confusion with a romantic entanglement with the man keeping her alive. Emotions were heightened. She needed to focus on being grateful to him and nothing more.

That's as far as she planned to allow her feelings for Holden Crawford to go.

Hopefully she'd be able to stick to her plan.

Chapter Nine

"We're leaving today. We'll pack up after breakfast," Holden said to Ella as she entered the kitchen. He barely glanced up.

"What's the rush?" Rose stood and moved toward the counter with the coffee maker. She looked to Ella when she said, "Have a seat. I'll get a cup for you."

Ella thanked her and sat next to Holden. The sexual chemistry between them zinged as intensely as ever and her stomach gave a little flip when her knee touched his thigh.

She must've also winced with movement when she sat because Holden stopped what he was doing and said, "You're in pain."

"A little," she admitted.

"I have something for that. I'll make something to eat first," Rose said, handing over a fresh mug. "Doc is always warning me about taking ibuprofen on an empty stomach."

"Thank you." Ella stared into the brown liquid before taking a sip. Anything to take the focus off how she felt whenever Holden was near and the assortment of aches and pains her body had racked up. She took a sip, enjoying the burn. "This is so good."

The breakfast burritos were equally wonderful.

"I have a few errands to run in town this morning," Rose said. "Can I pick up anything for you?"

Holden's gaze flicked up and held. "Do me a favor?"

She nodded. "Anything."

"Don't mention having houseguests." The concerned look on his face seemed to resonate with the older woman.

"Not a problem," she said before grabbing her keys off the counter and her purse off a hook positioned near the back door. "I'll only be a couple of hours. Will you be here when I return?"

"Yes," he said.

Relief washed over Ella as the older woman smiled and disappeared through the door. No way would she want to put Rose in danger but she had hoped they could stick around a few days. Being near her, in her calm presence, was comforting. Since Holden had already said they were leaving today, she sipped her coffee and tried not to think about having to get on the back of the motorcycle again.

"She'll be safe, right?" she asked Holden as he studied a laptop screen.

"As long as no one figures out we've been here, she will be," he said. "And I have every intention of ensuring that she is."

Shock reverberated through Ella as reality once again bore down on her. They were both on the run from dangerous men.

"Where do we go next?" she asked.

"That depends on how your leg's doing and how close the sheriff is to figuring this out." He didn't look up and she took it as a sign that he didn't want to talk.

The physical presence of him was difficult to ignore. He was big and imposing. *And sexy*, a little voice decided to add. It was an annoying little voice, like a fly at a picnic, buzzing around her face. She squashed that bug immediately. Holden Crawford was complicated. Danger practically radiated from his muscled biceps.

She drained her mug and pushed to standing, wincing as she tried to regain her balance, not yet steady on her feet.

"Don't do that," he said, rising to catch her. She had no intention of falling, pain or not.

"My leg is just sore. I need to walk it off," she defended, motioning toward her thigh.

"Mind if I take a look?" His gaze was on her now. The intensity of those honest blue eyes released a thousand butterflies in her stomach. Her throat felt like she'd downed a bottle of glue and her upper lip stuck to her top row of teeth when she managed a weak attempt at a smile. "Okay."

Ella took a seat again and showed him the injury.

Holden set up a few supplies, wipes and antibiotic ointment on the table next to her. She could've sworn he took in a sharp breath and muttered something that sounded like a swear word before he dropped to his knees in front of her.

She flexed her fingers when she thought about how deep the ridges in his shoulders were and how thick that dark hair of his was. Focusing her attention on the investigation would hopefully diffuse some of the sexual tension pinging thickly between them.

"We can't rule anyone out other than my siblings until we hear my father's will," she said.

"I have to consider everyone." His gaze was focused on the tape as he made a move to tear at one of the corners.

"So, what? The entire town is suspect? We'll never figure out who's responsible at this rate. We haven't ruled anyone out in your opinion, and I have no chance of going home anytime soon." She was frustrated and taking it out on him. In part because she needed to keep herself from thinking about doing other things to him. She clasped her hands and forced them on her lap. Thoughts of missing her father, of missing her family and of missing home struck a hole in her chest.

Holden tugged at the medical tape. A patch of skin pulled up along the tear line. As light as the touch might've been, she could've been hit by a bolt of lightning for the effect it had on her skin. A trail scorched from contact and her entire thigh warmed and zinged with awareness. Other places did, too, but she was determined not to think about those.

"Does this hurt?" His gaze flicked up to hers.

"That? No." There was so much going on inside her emotionally that the pain in her leg barely registered. She was having a difficult enough time fighting the barrage of tears threatening. Her thoughts were a jumbled mess spanning everything from his rejection to how much she wished life could go back to the way it was two weeks ago.

"Not the whole town, just people who would benefit from you disappearing." Holden went back to work.

"Like the people who work for us?" she asked.

"If they fit the bill. I was thinking more along the lines of projects you're involved in that impact other people." He dabbed antibiotic ointment along the gash, which looked like a crack in her skin.

"Ranch business impacts a lot of people, provides a lot of jobs directly and indirectly," she said.

"Any vendors who've been cut out of the pie recently?" He took scissors to a gauze pad, cutting it down to fit her wound.

"No. We've been doing business with most of our suppliers for years. Many are second- or third-generation owners." Thinking hurt. "We pay all our bills on time."

Ella must've made a face because he froze.

"Did that hurt?" He lifted the bandage slowly.

"No."

"I know you're upset and that's partly my fault. I let things get too far last night and I regret it," he started.

"Don't give me a speech about how there's nothing wrong with me. That you're just not attracted to my type," she quipped with more anger than she'd intended. "I'm sure you haven't been with a woman in a long time since you've been on the run."

His gaze locked onto hers.

"For your information, there've been plenty of women since I've been off the grid, just none that I could really care about. That doesn't happen often for me," he said, the intensity of his gaze washing over her like a rogue wave.

"Really? Maybe it's your magnetic personality," she bit out sarcastically, still fuming.

"Probably." He leaned back on his heels and placed his hands on his massive thighs, elbows out. "But the last person I cared about was killed by the men tracking me and I'm no closer to figuring out why now than I was two years ago. My father was also killed before I could get to him, which you already know but those thoughts keep rewinding inside my head."

His words sucked the wind out of her and all she could manage to say was, "Oh."

"So, yeah, I don't want to care about you and I'm frustrated because you're smart and beautiful with a body made for sinning on Sundays but none of that matters." His gaze was searing her skin as his eyes traveled her body. "Because if I allow myself to get soft enough to actually care what happens to you beyond blind loyalty to your father, you might end up dead, too. And I can't do that to another person. Not again. I wouldn't survive. There's enough blood on my hands."

"In case you haven't noticed, I don't need to worry about *your* men chasing after me. I seem to have attracted my own jerk intent on doing me harm all by my lonesome," Ella barked, ignoring the shivers racing up her arms with Holden this close. "I'm guessing someone wants to see my family suffer or has something to gain by targeting me after killing my father, but I have no idea what or who. So how's that for infuriating?"

"You should probably calm down," Holden said.

And that was like pouring gasoline on a fire. Ella pushed to her feet quickly.

"Because what? I'll raise my blood pressure? Have a heart attack?" She was really getting worked up now, like an out-of-control wildfire she couldn't douse, the flames roaring inside her. "In case you haven't noticed, I may not live to see tomorrow so I'll scream all I want."

Holden pushed up to his feet, too, and was standing inches away from her. She could see his chest rise and fall rapidly as his hands came up to cup her face.

"Because we'll make mistakes if we let emotions override rational thinking. It's best for Rose if no one knows we're here. I'm thinking about doing what's right for her, for you." There was something so calming about his physical presence. "Not kissing you is taking what little self-discipline I have left after last night, but I'm not doing it *because* I care about you. We'll figure out who's after you and I'll make sure the person responsible is locked away for a very long time or buried ten feet under. It'll be his choice. But, damn it, when this is over, I have every intention of walking away from you and never looking back."

His gaze had narrowed and his lips thinned.

Ella grabbed a fistful of his T-shirt, her knuckles meeting a wall of muscle.

"You may be able to stop yourself from kissing me but what will you do, Holden Crawford, when I kiss you?" she asked, locking onto his gaze. Her cheeks flushed against his hungry stare. And she might be baiting a bull, but she didn't care.

"It would be a mistake on your part," he said. His eyes had that dark, hungry look she'd seen moments before the first time he'd kissed her.

"What makes you say that?" she continued, knowing full well that she was enticing him.

"Because you don't have any idea what you're really asking for," he stated. And then he turned away from her and sat down at the laptop.

Neither frustration nor rejection would stop Ella at this point. She took the couple of steps toward Holden and straddled his thighs. He could ignore her once they were face-to-face.

"I'm a grown woman. You're a consenting adult male," she said, and she could see that he was considering her words.

He brought his hands up to grip her hips and her stomach quivered.

"Believe me, you don't want anything to do with me," he said before leaning forward to rest his forehead on hers. "It would be a mistake to think otherwise."

There was that word again. *Mistake.*

He seemed determined to avoid anything good that could happen between them. He couldn't let go of the past and she couldn't compete with a ghost. No amount of logic could change a man who was so strong willed.

Ella stood up.

"Mistakes don't define a person. Everybody makes those. It's part of how we learn. But choices do," she said before walking out of the room.

He could take it or leave it. Ella was done.

An hour had passed and Holden still hadn't found the right words to say to Ella about whatever was happening between them. He felt it, too. The current running between them was strong and powerful. And just like a power cord in water, dangerous.

"Why do you really owe my father?" Ella asked as she entered the room.

The question caught Holden off guard.

"I already told you." He didn't look up, didn't need to. She was watching him and he could feel her glare roaming over him. Yeah, she was giving him the signal that would normally make him react differently, but he didn't go into anything deeper than a one-night fling without both parties being completely aware of what they were getting into. Ella Butler was in over her head and had no idea.

He hammered the keyboard.

"No, you didn't. All you said was that you owed him a favor. Why?" she pressed.

"Maybe you weren't listening before in the cabin," he started, but she cut him off with a strangled noise.

"Don't say he put a roof over your head so you wanted to return the favor," she said.

"I wasn't going to. He did a helluva lot more. He could've turned me in with one quick call to law enforcement. He didn't. He knew what he was getting into and he had every right to turn his back. He didn't. Helping me put him directly in danger. I don't know the man from Adam, personally. He and my father were friends. Maverick Mike said he owed my father one and I didn't ask a lot of questions, considering how short on options I was," he said, studying a section of map on the screen, searching for a safe place to camp for a day or two. Exhaustion poured over him and he—once again—fought against it. If he had his druthers, he'd still be at the cabin on the Butler property, the place that had felt like his first real home in longer than Holden could remember. Virginia had never really been the place where he saw himself setting down roots. Although Holden had lived there going on five years before his world had come crumbling down around him. And Karen? He still couldn't believe she was gone. It had all happened so fast.

"Do you ever directly answer a question?" she asked, and he could almost feel the heat oozing off her.

"Yes."

The silence in the room stretched on for longer than he should've allowed. He shook his head and went back to work, scouting locations from the map on the screen. Not any closer to finding an appropriate place to go than he had been an hour ago.

Ella's earlier words kept winding through his thoughts. Was he afraid to let anyone in? No matter how much he wanted to continue to refute them, he couldn't ignore the shred of truth. And he was getting tired of the war raging in his head trying to keep her away.

"I owe you an apology. I'm going stir-crazy sitting around here. My mind is starting to think about all the things I need to do but I can't." Ella paced in the charming kitchen, wringing her hands together. Her chest squeezed thinking about how distant she felt from everything she'd ever known, everything familiar. Work was no doubt piling up. "I feel so disconnected. Normally, my cell is an extension of my hand

and I'm feeling panicked without it. My inbox is probably exploding. I guess there's no chance I can check email on that thing." She motioned toward the laptop.

"Your location can be traced back here based on the unique IP address if you access anything personal." Holden shook his head, twisting his lips in an apologetic look. "Nothing matters more to me than keeping you alive, finding out why you're being targeted and ensuring Rose's safety."

"I know we've discussed this before, but have you ruled out my father's killer trying to erase the family?" she asked.

"That's one possibility," he responded. "I'd like to explore a few others. Is anyone upset with you? Have you had any fallings-out with a friend?"

"None that I can think of," she stated. "But honestly, the days leading up to me going hiking are still a blur. I'd just found out about my father and this—" she motioned toward the covered gash on her forehead "—can't be helping."

"Was anyone jealous of you?" he asked.

"People like me overall, I think." She really thought about what he was saying. Could she have upset someone enough for a person to want her dead? The notion that someone she knew could be hunting her sent an icy chill down her spine. "I do a lot of work to give back to the community. I don't always agree with people's opinions and, sure, there are conflicts from time to time within pretty much all my charity work. Anytime you get ten or fifteen different people in the room there are going to be that many opposing views. We argue, debate and then eventually come to a resolution. Does everyone walk away happy? No. But what could possibly warrant this?" She heard her own voice rise defensively.

"It would be easier to pin down the responsible party if we could trace them to you instead of your father," he said.

"I don't know." Flustered, she paced.

"I'm not trying to upset you." He tried to reassure her.

"I know. And what you're saying makes sense," she said, wishing she could will her pounding pulse to calm down.

"What about your friends?" he asked.

"I have a few people who are close but between helping run the ranch and my work with organizations, I don't have a lot of time for happy hour." Hearing her life put in those terms sounded like a sad existence. She felt the need to add, "I spend most of my time with my family."

"You already said that you aren't seeing anyone special." His gaze intensified on the screen. "Are you dating around?"

"I can't see why that would be—"

"Before you get distraught with me I'm only asking to see if there could be a jealous guy in the mix," he added, and he still didn't look at her. "Someone who looks like you would attract a lot of interested men."

"I date a little." She shrugged. The compliment caused her cheeks to heat. "I love living on the ranch and Cattle Barge is home, but there aren't a lot of interesting men around. I grew up there and it's a small town so I dated around in high school and haven't looked back since college. Not a lot of new people move to town unless you count the men who work in the stable, and I would never date inside the ranch. It's bad business and someone would lose their job if things got awkward after."

The only truly good-looking person she'd seen in the past year was a new guy who'd moved to the outskirts of town and kept to himself. But she didn't mention him to Holden.

"And besides, I'm too busy with work and my charities to get out much," she defended. "I haven't been serious about anyone for a long time, and I've been thinking that I need to spend more time in Austin or San Antonio so I can meet someone."

Holden waited for her to finish. She was oversharing. Being nervous had her talking more than she should.

"I'm sure my life sounds awful to someone like you but—"

"Tell me more about your charity work." He leaned back in his chair and finally took his eyes off the screen.

One look from him caused her heart to flutter and she hadn't experienced that with anyone in too long.

"I pick projects that I'm passionate about, especially ones that need a helping hand," she responded, thankful for the redirection.

"What kind?" He folded his arms over a broad chest, and it was the most relaxed she'd seen him since they met.

"Mostly local stuff. Animal rights, various park cleanup and preservation initiatives, our local food bank and charities that serve the elderly in our community," she said.

"Sounds like a lot." His brows shot up.

"Does it?" She shrugged. "I don't know. I see something that needs to be done and I pitch in to help it along."

"The Butler name opens a lot of doors," he said, and she picked up on a hint of sarcasm.

"Yes, it does. If you expect me to be ashamed of it, you need to think again." Her shaky voice belied the confidence she was trying to project.

"I didn't mean anything by it. I'm sure it helps to have that name behind you," he said.

"It does. And I was born with a silver spoon in my mouth. There. Are you happy?" She went ahead and said it for him…for everyone who'd discounted her because her father had made a show out of giving her everything. Had it been too much? Yes. "If you think wearing nice clothes and being given lavish gifts makes you feel good about yourself or loved, you're wrong. A little girl needs to be held when she cries. Not handed an expensive doll and left alone in her room to sort through her emotions."

"So you're saying that giving a little girl everything she could possibly desire is a bad thing?" Holden asked. "Because if I had a daughter, I'd move heaven and earth to give her the world."

Her stomach gave a little flip at the thought of a newborn wrapped in a pink blanket in the burly man's arms. A thought struck her like a rogue wave…*their daughter*.

Before she tumbled into the surf with that one, she

made a couple of laps around the breakfast table. She stopped.

"How do I say this without sounding ungrateful?" She wished for the right words. "*Things* are nice. But there's so much more to bringing up a child than presents. All kids really need is love."

"Try filling a growing boy's stomach on that," he said.

"Everyone needs food. A child also needs to be comforted after waking from a nightmare. All the gifts in the world don't mean as much as hearing the words *I love you*." Ella hadn't planned to cry, so the stray tear rolling down her cheek caught her off guard. "I'm sorry. I know my father loved us in his own way. I didn't mean—"

"No, it's fine." Holden said. "Don't be embarrassed about telling me how you really feel. Believe it or not, I might've made the same mistakes as a father. All a man wants to do with a little girl is spoil her."

There was a quiet reassurance to his voice. A dangerous comfort under the circumstances. Ella couldn't afford to let her guard down around Holden and especially since he seemed too intent on keeping her at a distance, except in times like these when he was being her comfort while she was vulnerable.

And then he'd just push her away again.

Ella thought better of it this time.

"I'm tired," she said.

His brows drew together like he was confused.

"We're leaving later, right?" she asked.

"That's the plan." His gaze bounced from her to the screen and back.

Her sense of security with Holden was false. He hadn't opened up one bit. He'd been clear about one thing. She should keep her distance.

"Then I better get some more rest before we leave." She intended to listen this time even if her heart fought her on it.

"I'll think about what you said." Holden glanced up and it was like stepping into sunlight, being bathed in warmth.

"Great. Maybe you'll have this whole situation figured out by the time I open my eyes again." She managed a weak smile as she turned to leave.

"I'm not talking about that," he said. His voice was a low rumble in his chest. "What you said about choices earlier. You might have had a point."

She didn't dare turn around and let him get a good look at her face. She hadn't inherited her father's gift at poker. Her face was easy to read.

And she didn't want to be *this* attracted to Holden Crawford.

Chapter Ten

"It's time to go." Holden's voice was a whisper in Ella's ear. It took a second to register that she wasn't dreaming, and his soothing, deep baritone had her reaching for him. Until she realized she was awake.

"Okay." She pushed up to sitting, keenly aware of the strong male presence next to her on the bed. Thoughts like those were as unproductive as trying to grow grapevines in clay soil.

Ella tried to clear her thoughts. She'd dozed off after an exhausting afternoon. Exhausting because she'd basically done nothing but climb the walls all day and her exchange with Holden had her emotions all over the map.

There was no other choice but to be cooped up and she knew it. Still, she couldn't help but feel like a caged animal and her confusing feelings for Holden intensified everything. Beginning to feel better was almost a curse under the circumstances. She was well enough to move around but they had to keep a low profile or risk endangering Rose. There was no way Ella would knowingly put that sweet old woman in danger.

Every noise had had Ella feeling skittish. Constantly being on alert with no outlet for her energy had caused fatigue.

"I'll wait in the other hall," Holden said. And then she felt his weight leave the mattress. The heat in the room vanished with him.

Ella dressed using only the light from the moon sliding through the slats in the blinds. As much as she didn't want to leave *la hacienda*, putting Rose at risk by staying wasn't an option. And at least she would finally have something to do, a purpose, even if it was dangerous. She'd go stir-crazy if she stayed inside much longer.

Holden was waiting outside the door.

"Ready?" he asked as he took the duffel from her.

"I think so," she said. "Any chance we can wake her and tell her goodbye?"

Ella didn't have to ask to know that Holden had wiped the place clean. The smell of bleach permeated the air.

Her eyes widened at the sound of a motorized vehicle outside. Holden muttered a curse. "Stay right here unless I tell you to come out."

He dropped to the ground and instructed her to do the same. Pain shot up her right thigh at the quick movement. She swallowed her gasp, making no sound as she hit all fours and scooted behind a cabinet.

The kitchen door opened and closed so fast and so quietly it barely registered. Ella was reminded how little she knew about the man who was helping her. Why was he so adept at moving stealthily into the night? Had he served in the military? Or been in law enforcement?

The way he'd questioned her earlier gave the impression he might've been. Hadn't he said that he and his father shared similar professions? She wanted to know how it was even possible that her father had met the man. For reasons she couldn't explain and didn't want to analyze, she wanted to know more about Holden.

Another swish of the door and she realized she'd been holding her breath.

"It's all good," Holden said, reclaiming the duffel. He had a second helmet and she figured he must've left it at Rose's on a prior visit.

Ella followed him out the door, surprised at the stabbing pain in her chest at leaving. She'd lost so much already and Rose had managed to wiggle her way into Ella's heart in the short time she'd known her. Rose's eyes belied her smile. There was emptiness there, a hollowness that Ella couldn't ignore.

"I'd like to check on her when I get my life back," she said to Holden. "We have our annual fall festival coming up in a few weeks. Maybe she'd like to come."

"When this is over, you can do anything you want," he said. He wasn't arguing against the idea but he came off like he didn't care either way. Was he reminding her that they'd go on to live their separate lives by then? She couldn't see his face with his helmet on.

Leaving Rose was harder than Ella expected it to be. Her heart broke a little as she climbed onto the back of Holden's motorcycle. She was glad that he didn't notice the tears welling in her eyes at the thought of leaving Rose by herself.

The highway was long and empty when they first

started out. Traffic thickened as they headed east and neared major cities. After riding on the back of Holden's motorcycle so long Ella's arms felt like they were being dragged down by hundred-pound weights, they exited the highway.

Holden located a dirt path about a mile off the highway and Ella lost count of how many minutes they'd been on it until he finally stopped.

After Ella climbed off the back of the bike, Holden threw his leg over and hopped off.

"I thought we'd camp for a few days. I have camping gear in my duffel," he said. With his helmet on, visor down, she couldn't read his eyes.

Ella balked. "Seriously? Out here?"

"Sure. Why not?" He removed his helmet to reveal concerned, pinched eyebrows.

"Mosquitoes for one. They'll eat me alive. Showers for another. You won't want to be anywhere near me without one." She was getting nowhere and could tell by his tense expression.

And then his face broke into a wide smile, revealing near-perfect white teeth.

"You think this is funny?" She really was working herself up now and it seemed to amuse him all the more.

"Actually, I do." He turned and walked to a clearing where one of those tiny houses stood. He was jiggling what sounded like keys.

Ella blew out a frustrated breath as she watched him unlock the door.

"Coming?" he asked, and there was a contrite quality to his voice. "Or do you plan to stand out here and become mosquito bait?"

"Think you're funny?" she shot back with a look meant to freeze boiling water.

"I used to," he said under his breath.

And that made her laugh as she walked past him. She couldn't help herself. It was most likely the stress of the past few days and how out of control her life had become, but she laughed.

"I don't know what shocks me more. The fact that you made me laugh or used to think you were funny," she said as he opened the door.

A laugh rumbled from Holden's chest and it was sexy. Ella wanted to shut off her attraction to him. But it felt impossible at the moment. No matter how much she tried to hold it back, she couldn't. So she gave in and it was probably the stress that they'd been under more than anything else, but both of them laughed until she had to sit down.

"That felt good," she said, ignoring the feeling like champagne bubbling up her throat as she wiped tears from her eyes.

"It did." Holden stood at the door, leaning against the jamb, arms folded. "Life used to be…more funny."

"How long did you say you've been living like this?" she asked.

"Twenty-five months." His smile faded.

"That's a long time." She stood.

He nodded and she thought he said, "Too long."

"What about Rose? Will she be safe now that we're gone?" she asked.

"That's the idea. But if they figure out her connection to me…" He stopped as though he couldn't finish the thought let alone the sentence.

"Would she be safer at my family's ranch?" Ella asked. "I could have someone pick her up. No one would have to know."

"She's stubborn." He was already shaking his head. "There's no way she would leave her precious garden for more than a few days."

"What if I talked to her? Maybe she'd listen to me if I came up with a good argument."

"You'd be wasting your breath," he responded.

"It'd be worth a try," she argued.

"You really think you can change people, don't you?" Holden asked, and the question took her off guard.

"Why do you make it sound like a bad thing?" Her defenses flared.

"It's good." He shrugged. "Probably naive. You do realize that you can't save every stray."

"Maybe." She probably shouldn't speak her mind to the one person who seemed intent on helping her. Especially when she was about to send out a zinger. "But at least I don't quit."

That brought an amused smile to Holden's face. "And that's what you think I did?"

"Obviously. You got into trouble and you've been hiding ever since," she surmised.

"I'm sure it looks that simple from the outside." He picked up the duffel and brought it over to one of the chairs. The living room of the place was too small for a couch, but there were two reasonably sized, comfortable-looking chairs with a small table in between. The kitchen was more like a kitchenette with a microwave and a hot plate. Ella's dorm room in college had been bigger, and yet she was never happier to be in a space. There was a full-size bed on the back wall. It would be way too small for a man like Holden Crawford. And a closed door that she assumed led to an equally small bathroom, which was fine because this was so much better than being out there in the elements, exposed.

"How'd you know about this place?" His comments still stung, which meant there was a tiny bit of truth. Ella didn't believe in lost causes. Everyone could be saved. *Except those who refuse help*, a little voice reminded.

"Belongs to a friend of mine." He pulled out the makings for coffee.

She must've balked because he got a defensive look on his face.

"I have friends," he said, defensive.

She wasn't touching that statement. "Are you tired after that long ride?"

"Not really. Riding helps clear out the clutter in my head." He moved to the kitchen and held up a mug.

"Yes, please," Ella said.

"Our conversation is churning through my mind." He heated water on the small stove before filtering the grinds.

"Anything stick out?"

"I just got to thinking about your life, your activities and who might benefit from your death."

"No one, really. The ranch would continue to run.

Dad had a trust set up years ago in order to protect jobs in the event something happened to his kids. It's part of the reason his employees were always loyal to him. He looked out for them," she said. "Ed Staples, the family attorney, would oversee it and then he'd name a successor. There are a lot of controls built in so no one can override the document or successfully challenge it in court. I wish I'd paid more attention to that part but I honestly never thought I'd need to know. My dad was such a presence. I just never believed anything bad would happen to him."

Holden paused long enough to make eye contact before continuing. The look seemed meant to be reassuring.

"But we have no suspects and we're no closer to figuring out what happened than we were after the first rock to my head," she said, frustrated.

Holden handed over a mug of fresh steaming brew.

Ella took a sip and mewled with pleasure. "I will never tire of the taste of your coffee."

Her response netted another smile and she liked the way his lips curved.

"You figure out how to make do with what you have in your environment," he said.

"Where are we, by the way?" she asked, realizing it hadn't occurred to ask before now. She'd been too busy laughing and her stomach still hurt.

"We're in Texas," he said.

"I figured that much out," she quipped before taking another sip.

"A couple of hours from Cattle Barge," he said. "I

keep rounding back to the fact that we need to be near here in order to track down leads. We might be able to clear this whole thing up if you could talk to people."

"Agreed."

"Don't get any ideas because you can't go back home," he said. "It's too risky and we have to give the sheriff time to do his job. He has more evidence to work with now."

Ella got quiet for a long time. If she could stay alive, Sheriff Sawmill should be able to find the person after her, especially after that last attempt. "I know you make an amazing cup of coffee, and I mean pretty much anywhere with whatever's around. But I don't know much else about you."

Holden's gaze narrowed and his lips thinned, and for a long moment she didn't think he was going to respond. "I told you that I was set up for murder before. Doesn't that make you a little scared to be around me?"

"Why should it? You're innocent." She didn't hesitate.

"I am. But how do you know?" An emotion passed behind his eyes. Hope?

"I've been around bad men before. I'm not as naive as you believe. Dad taught me how to tell the difference a long time ago. Said he was protecting me. When a man's truly evil he has a dead quality to his eyes. A darkness that no light can fill. A man capable of murder, even if it was a passion killing, would have those eyes," she said.

"I was out jogging that morning when it happened,"

he said after a thoughtful pause. "Came back and found her stabbed to death."

There was an almost-audible thud in Ella's chest at the tight-clipped pain in his voice—pain that he'd held inside for too long. "What happened?"

"As in details? You don't want to know."

"Maybe that's true on some level. You haven't spoken to anyone in more than two years and I think it's time you got this off your chest," she said quietly.

Holden blew out a sharp breath, and for a minute she thought he'd change the subject. There was so much pain behind those pale blue eyes—eyes that had spoken so much to her when she'd first seen them while the rest of his face was buried underneath that beard.

He took in a sharp breath. "Her name was Karen. Blood was everywhere. I bolted over so fast that I didn't even look to see if anyone else was around. Everything moved in beats after that. One beat and I'm standing in the doorway in shock. In the next, I'm beside the bed. My field training told me that pulling the knife out of her chest would make everything worse. Her eyes were already fixed, open...blank."

Ella didn't speak, even when Holden looked like he might not continue. She just sat there, still, patient. Wishing there was something she could do to help ease his heartache.

"Another beat and I'm trying to stem the bleeding, performing CPR. None of my years in the corps mattered because I couldn't bring her back." He clenched his back teeth. "A few beats later, cops are there. Looking back, that part was strange because I never called them. Guess I just assumed one of my neighbors had heard her screaming. Another beat and EMTs arrived. The whole place was chaos by then. A few more beats and I'm in the back of a squad car being taken in to give my statement, and that should've been my first clue that something was off. Looking back, why wouldn't the cops have had a witness ride in front? And then the cop pulls off on this back road. I had blood all over me, my hands, Karen's blood. I was in shock so it took a minute to register that the cop wasn't heading toward the station anymore. I was in a fog. He orders me out of the back and pulls out his service weapon. Throws a cord at me and tells me to wrap it around my neck."

Holden paused. Ella touched his arm for reassurance. She was listening. She cared about the truth.

"Cop gave me two options. Wrap the cord around my neck or be shot. I told him he forgot my third choice." Holden looked high and away from her like he could see the past there. "Run."

"How did he react?" she asked.

"I dropped down and caught his leg as he tried to shoot me. He went over backward, landed pretty hard and started calling for help on his radio," he said.

"And that's when you got away," she finished.

"My father was tortured and killed a few days later and that's when I knew something big was going on. I still don't fully understand why I was set up to look like a murderer in the first place. I'd only been dating Karen for a few months when the whole thing went down. And, yeah, it was my blade, but I wasn't even in the house when it happened." Holden stared at a spot on the wall for a long moment and she could only imagine the horrors of what he'd witnessed.

"Wouldn't the evidence have cleared you?" she asked.

"If the officers in charge of the investigation had followed it, I would've been fine. They didn't. The officer who took me in supposedly to give my statement never intended for me to live long enough to say what really happened," he said.

Ella gasped.

"Within days of my disappearance reports started showing up about me suffering from PTSD, going berserk and killing my girlfriend and then my father." He made a disgusted face and grunted. "They were so off base and I was angry. But someone important was pulling the strings. Had to be, and I realized how far they would go the minute they killed Pop."

"I'm so sorry," she whispered.

Silence sat between them for a long moment.

"What did you do?" she finally asked.

"At first, I'll be honest. I thought I'd bide my time and then creep back into the shadows. Figure out who committed these crimes. Make them pay with their own lives. The thought of revenge kept me moving forward when I wanted to die," he admitted.

"And now?"

"I remembered a promise that I made to Pop once about looking after Rose if anything ever happened to him. We were fishing and I guess he was getting older. Started thinking about the day he might not be around any longer. She was his only friend when he lost his parents and had to live with a relative in New Mexico. He was kicked around from place to place after that, to whoever would take him. But he and Rose managed to get back in touch," he continued. "She was his North Star and helped him get his life together when it was falling apart. They kept their friendship a secret so none of his relatives knew where to look for him. He'd show up at her parents' place when life got too real and they'd take him in. I guess it never occurred to them to go public with their friendship once they were adults. When I was born and my mom took off, Rose urged him to join the military to straighten himself out. He did. We moved around a lot before settling in Virginia, where my father established a moving company, but we had each other and we had Rose. Pop might not have been perfect, but he did the best he could, and I respect that in a man."

Ella could relate to those feelings. She and Holden weren't so different no matter how much he wanted to be a man stranded on an island. At least he was talking to her, revealing something about his past and why he was in this predicament. She couldn't imagine walking in to find someone she loved—that word pained her to think about when it came to Holden and another woman—murdered. She shuddered at the thought. And then to find out that your father had been tortured and killed and you'd been blamed. The worst part was that she could see why Holden would hold himself responsible for all of it even though something else had to be going on. Would it really be any different for her?

There was a storm brewing behind Holden's blue

eyes as he spoke. He'd lost two people he cared about in a very short time and he held the blame for both. Two long years. So much pain.

"Were the two of you in love?" Ella surprised herself with the question.

"I thought I might have been at the time," he said.

"What changed?" She didn't look at him and scarcely registered that she was holding her breath, waiting for his response.

"My definition."

"How so?" she asked, still not able to look him in the eyes.

"I met you."

Chapter Eleven

Light peeked through before Holden seemed to quash it by turning away from Ella. When he looked at her again, he was all business.

Ella had no idea how to process what he'd just said, but she couldn't ignore how his words made her feel. Before she could gather her thoughts to speak, he said, "Tell me more about what kinds of projects you were working on leading up to the attack at Devil's Lid."

Ella stretched out sore legs and pressed her fingers to her temples, trying to make her head stop pounding. Refocusing might give her a chance to get a handle on her runaway emotions. "I'm on a committee that was formed to clean up the creek along Slider's Rock. Another to raise funds to build a bigger playground at the elementary school in town. Both of those met recently. And then there's our recycling program. We're always trying to drum up support and raise awareness of the benefits of recycling in schools and at parks. Let's see. What else?" It was hard without having her schedule in front of her to work from. "We're working on raising awareness for elder abuse and neglect. So many in our community don't have enough money to run AC in the summer or have to resort to eating canned dog food when their Social Security check doesn't stretch far enough."

"And these projects have opposition?" he asked, a dark eyebrow rose.

A frustrated half laugh, half snort ripped from her throat. "Every single one."

"Who could argue against preventing elder abuse?" Disdain brought down the corners of his lips.

"You'd be surprised," she said. "Anytime you draw a line in the sand, you separate sides. People may not disagree about educating others about the needs in our community, but everyone will have a different opinion about how to get it done. And I mean everyone. From the mayor to someone's uncle to the town's barber."

"When you put it that way, I believe it." Holden took a sip of coffee. "We should make a timeline of events and include every meeting you attended recently, especially those with heated debates. Also, I'd like to get the names of everyone who is involved in the organization and any persons who might have something to lose based on outcomes of your decision or decisions you heavily influenced on paper."

He moved into the kitchen and opened the few drawers until he pulled out a pad of paper and a pen. "This'll help."

AN HOUR AND a half later, Holden stood in the kitchen reading the long list of Ella's activities. "You're one busy person."

"I already said I was involved in the community," she said, and that solicited a grunt from Holden.

"Involved? Is there anyone else in town doing anything?"

Ella laughed. "I'm sure that I'm forgetting something. Like I said, the days following Dad's death are a little hazy and my head hurts when I try to overthink."

"You mean there's more than this?" He held up the paper. "When do you have time to do anything else?"

"Like what?" she asked.

"Date, for one," he said.

Ella laughed. "It'd be crazy to empty my schedule and wait for Mr. Right to waltz in when there's so much to be done. Besides, I already told you about my personal life."

It looked like a small smile crossed his lips before he took another sip of coffee. "The person who tried to kill you wanted it to look like an accident at first. I'm guessing they were expecting a headline that read Grieving Socialite Falls into Canyon Days after Her Father's Murder."

"Right. But the second attempt was out in the open."

"He could've planned to kidnap you and then set the scene once you were secured. No one had seen you since you'd disappeared at Devil's Lid, so he might've figured that he could kill you and stage it to look like an accident."

"Wouldn't someone notice the bullet holes?" she asked.

"True. The assailant did shoot but that was most likely out of panic."

"Now that I think about it, he shot when I fought him off and ran." She sighed. "Pretty much every household in this part of Texas has a shotgun on property. If not to deter criminals then to shoot predators stalking their herds, so that doesn't help us."

Holden nodded again as he examined the list. "There are a lot of names on here. What about friends? Any arguments with the people in your circle?"

"When do I have time?" she quipped. "I do charity work, which I'm passionate about, and I help run the ranch. I barely have time to eat and sleep."

"That's a choice," he said with a look.

"You're a man on the run and I doubt you've made time for *friends* in the meantime," she quipped. Yeah, she was being defensive. There was something about detailing the boring nature of her private life to a ridiculously handsome man that put her on edge.

Holden held up a hand in surrender. "I make no claim about being perfect. But I have a good reason to stay solitary. Everyone I get close to ends up dead."

She started to argue but he'd made a good point. Had she been pushing people out of her life? Keeping everyone at a safe distance? The short answer? Yes. Never knowing her mother and growing up with an emotionally distant father wasn't exactly the recipe for letting people in. She was as close to her siblings as she could be, but Ella could admit that she'd taken on a mother-like role with them since she was the oldest. At least until the boys were old enough to do what they wanted, and that came early for the independent-minded Butler men. Even now while her life was in danger she was focused on protecting them. Maybe she and Holden had more in common than they wanted to admit.

"Anyone stand out on that list you're holding?" she asked, figuring she'd done enough self-examination for one day. Her brain hurt and that wasn't helping her figure out whatever was pressing against the back of her skull. Something was there but she couldn't reach it, and that was frustrating under the circumstances. The stakes were high and it wasn't like she was trying to remember her shopping list. Trying to force it didn't help, though.

"I'd have to dig around and figure out the impact these decisions could make to know anything for certain," he said.

"Impossible out here with no laptop or Wi-Fi," she explained. "You already said contacting people is out of the question."

"When my choices are to keep you safe or investigate, I'm always going to choose the first," he said, and there was an emotion present behind his eyes that stirred something primal inside her.

Ella ignored it. Sort of. Her body trilled with awareness.

"We could talk it through over lunch," she said, her stomach rumbling. Had they eaten breakfast?

"I'll head into town for supplies," he said. "I don't like leaving you here alone but it'll be safer for you if we split up."

Holden pulled his Sig Sauer out of his duffel and set it next to Ella.

She glanced at the weapon before locking onto his

gaze. "I guess I should've seen this coming. This is the first time I've seen you with a gun."

"I didn't need it before now," he said, and she figured he had a military background by way of his commitment to everything being on a need-to-know basis. "You know how to use it?"

"I have experience with shotguns mostly, but I'll figure it out if I have to," she said with sincerity.

He nodded and that should've been the end of it. He should've walked out the door and gone for supplies. But he stood there like he couldn't move his feet. It dawned on her why he'd respond that way.

"I'll be okay. Go ahead," she urged. "Nothing will happen to me while you're gone."

HOLDEN WAS SURPRISED at how easy it was to talk to Ella. He'd never had a problem closing up and keeping everything locked inside until her. He shocked himself with the amount he'd wanted to share. He'd been a regular Chatty Cathy back there. He reminded himself to tread lightly. It probably had more to do with the fact that he'd barely spoken to a soul in twenty-five months than the possibility that he could have real feelings developing for someone he'd only known a few days.

Granted, there was something about Ella Butler that gave the impression they'd known each other for years, a familiarity he'd never experienced with another person. She was different from the women he usually dated. But this wasn't the time to get inside his head about it. There were more important issues to think about, like who was trying to ensure she took her last breath. And the issue of him still being on the run after two years in hiding, getting nowhere.

Holden thought about what Rose had told him. The numbers 1-9-6-4 still meant nothing to him and he'd racked his brain during the ride to the small cabin trying to find a connection. He'd first thought it referred to a year and then an address. Nothing came to mind.

Immediately after the murders he'd gone over his last conversations in his head a hundred times, and his thoughts became an endless loop. Looking back from a fresh lens, he thought about his relationship with Pop. How quiet he'd become in those last few weeks before the murders. People talk about intuition all the time. Had Pop sensed something was coming?

Holden parked his motorbike around the side of the country store and purposely kept his sunglasses on to shield at least part of his face. At his height, it was difficult to move undetected and he still felt exposed without a beard. He'd covered his face with one for two years—years that had felt like they'd dragged on for twice that amount.

Ella's words haunted him. Had he given up?

Holden pushed open the glass door and heard a jingle. The chipper cashier looked up from a magazine and welcomed him. He nodded but kept his face turned away in case there was a camera. Seemed like there was one in every store no matter how remote the location. Technology made it more and more difficult to stay off the radar.

He picked up a basket and loaded it with grilling supplies. Normally, he saved steak for a special occasion. In this case, he wanted to feed Ella a decent meal. Based on her devotion to her causes, she seemed like a good person and deserved at least that much.

Her situation haunted him.

The logical answer was that someone had killed Maverick Mike and had now set his or her sights on Ella. The responsible party had clearly wanted to make a statement with Mike's death, but something had changed when the person went after Ella. What? His thoughts kept rounding back to the same thing. *The person.*

He let that thought sit while he approached the cash register.

"This all for you today, mister?" the short brunette cashier chirped. She looked to be in her midtwenties and wore a green shirt and khaki-colored pants.

"Yep." Holden nodded and quirked a smile. He'd found a small gesture like that put people at ease around him. It wasn't difficult to find a smile when he thought about the simple pleasure of grilling a good steak and feeding someone he cared about.

Damn.

Ella's words kept cycling through his thoughts. He'd convinced himself that keeping to himself and staying so far off the grid that he'd become half animal, half man was to keep himself alive until he figured out who was behind Karen's killing. Losing her had been a blow. His father being killed so soon after had knocked the wind out of Holden. It had only been him and Pop since his mother had disappeared not long after he'd been born. Sure, Pop had made mistakes but the two of them had grown up together and Holden could easily forgive the shortcomings. Hell, he was far from perfect himself. When his old man was killed, a piece of Holden had died. His anger had turned inward and he'd retreated to nature, where he'd been trained to survive.

The cashier chirped an amount and Holden paid with cash. He'd cashed out his savings when he went on the run and had kept a low profile, sleeping in vacant cabins and trapping and cooking most of his own food. He took his bags with a thank-you and forced a casual-looking smile.

The cashier beamed up at him. The twinkle in her eyes said she was flirting. Holden wasn't the least bit interested. Being with Ella made him realize how far he'd drifted away from the man he used to be before his life had been turned upside down. That needed to change.

Holden kept his head down as he exited the store. Out of the corner of his eye he saw a white sedan with blacked-out windows fly past and a bad feeling took seed deep in his gut.

He broke into a dead run toward his motorcycle as his pulse galloped. His chest clenched at the thought of anything happening to Ella while he was away. He'd left her with his Sig for protection, not really expecting her to need it. Could she even use it on another human being? A moment of truth like that only came when confronted with the situation. He muttered a few curses after quickly securing the grocery items. He released the clutch and gravel spewed from underneath his back tire.

Ella should never be faced with a kill-or-be-killed

situation. Holden should know. He'd had to when he was in the service. And taking someone's life, even an enemy, wasn't something a decent man took lightly.

With the agility of his motorcycle, he caught up to the sedan in no time. As he neared, he heard music blaring. Teenagers?

He whipped around the vehicle in order to get a look at the driver. A strong honk-like sound caused him to look up in time to realize he was about to go head-on with a semi.

Holden zipped around the white car. In his rearview, he could see the driver clearly. He was male and too young to buy a real drink. Relief was short-lived. Holden needed to see Ella with his own eyes and know that she was fine. In the future, he'd figure out a way to take her with him when he left for supplies because being away from her, not knowing if she was safe, did bad things to his mind.

By the time he navigated up the drive, checking several times to ensure no one had followed him, his nerves were shot. She was waiting outside, sitting in the sun, when he parked behind the shack. Seeing her caused a jolt of need to strike him like stray voltage. Holden was done. Done biting down an urge so primal his bones ached. Done holding her back when she'd been so clear that she wanted the same thing. Done protecting her from him. She needed to know that she meant something to him. So he walked right over to her and hauled her against his chest. Her sweet body molded to his. Her fingers tunneled inside his hair as he pressed his forehead to hers. "We can't let this go any further, but I had to hold you."

This close, he could feel her body tremble and need welled inside him. The feel of her soft skin under his hands connected to a life he used to know only this somehow was better. Sexual chemistry crackled in the air around them. Sex couldn't happen but he was done fighting the need to be close to her.

She looked up at him with those cornflower blue eyes and he almost faltered. He reminded himself to keep a grip on his emotions.

"What happened?" she asked.

"There was a car…"

"And you thought it was coming for me," she finished when he paused.

"Yes." He closed his eyes to shut out the other possibilities, the ones that involved him not making it to her in time.

"Are you okay?" she asked, and there was so much concern in her voice.

"I am now," he said, and she didn't seem to need him to elaborate. She just leaned into him and wrapped her arms around his neck. The movement pressed her full breasts against his chest and for a half second he pictured them naked, tangled in the sheets in a place far away from here.

But that wasn't reality and Holden didn't do fairy tales.

He took in a sharp breath.

"I'll make lunch," he said.

Ella took a step back, away from him, seeming to

understand that he needed space. Damn, it was going to be difficult to leave her once this was all over.

For now, he needed to concentrate on giving her her life back. She had plans, meetings and causes to fight for.

What did he have?

A ghost of a life. No family to speak of. Yeah, his life couldn't be more opposite. Another in a long list of reasons he needed to maintain his distance. He would only bring her down.

He was cursed.

Chapter Twelve

Ella smiled as she took another bite of perfectly cooked steak. The potato with all the fixings was just as amazing. "I'm impressed with your cooking skills."

"Don't be. Coffee and steak are all I can do," he said with a crooked smile. She was grateful for the break in tension between them and even more so that her comment brought out a lighter side of him. He looked pleased with himself and like a different person than the one who'd arrived an hour ago. Ghost white with anger written all over his face, Ella could see beyond the mask to the absolute fear inside him.

And then he'd taken her in his arms.

Their sexual chemistry was off the charts and she figured mostly because it felt like death lurked around every corner. The thought that one of them could be gone in an instant when they'd grown to depend on each other solely for survival was odd considering that she hadn't even known the man existed a week ago. Yes, there'd been an instant attraction even before he'd shaved the beard. The feeling had intensified the more time they spent together. A small piece of her—a piece she didn't want to give too much consideration—needed to acknowledge that there was more to their attraction than proximity and circumstance. The rest of her realized that none of it mattered because he carried too much baggage from the past to let it go anywhere. And where would it go? He was wanted for murder and someone was trying to kill her.

When she thought about it in those terms—and really all she could do was laugh—they were quite a pair.

The feeling that something lurked in the far reaches of her mind that she couldn't access frustrated her. She told herself that was the only reason she was preoccupied with her feelings toward Holden.

"What?" he asked, breaking into her thoughts.

"Nothing." She shook her head.

"Whatever it is made you smile and then frown." He set his fork down on his plate. "You should smile more."

If only he knew that she'd been thinking about him.

"It's the food," she lied. "Even if you are a one-trick pony as you claim to be, it's a mighty fine trick."

That netted a genuine smile from Holden. He should do it more, too. She imagined a life before his world was turned upside down where he laughed easily, held cookouts in the backyard and perfected his coffee-making skills.

"What was your life like before…?" she asked.

He shrugged his massive shoulders. "The usual stuff. Opening-day baseball with Pop in the spring. No matter where we lived we always drove to Queens to watch the season opener."

"What was he like? Your father?" Ella figured

Holden would stop her if she touched on a subject he couldn't talk about.

"Quiet. Kept to himself mostly. He and my mother, if you can call her that, had me when they were young. Dear old Mom took off and Pop joined the military after Rose's urging. We moved around a lot, going from base to base. And he was gone for long stretches but the military was family and we managed to get by. Rose was like a mother to me."

"Did your father and Rose ever go out?" she asked.

He shook his head.

"Why not?" Ella toyed with the fork.

"Honestly? I don't know. Pop had feelings for her. I didn't realize that until I was grown, but it's obvious to me as a man." Holden glanced up. "Guess the timing was never right."

"Shame. He sounds like a wonderful man and Rose is amazing. Plus, you would've grown up eating her chalupas." Ella smiled even though her heart dropped when he'd made the comment about timing. It applied to them, too.

"Her cooking skills would've been a definite plus." Holden stood up and she figured that was his way of saying he was done sharing.

Ella had to admit she was surprised at the change in him since visiting Rose. He seemed calmer, more at peace. Rose would've made a great mother.

"Any chance we can go into Cattle Barge safely?" she asked as he offered to take her plate.

"It wouldn't be a good idea," he said as a hint of that earlier fear flashed in his eyes.

"This feels like a stalemate. How are we supposed to make progress if we can't ask people questions or poke around?" Ella followed him inside.

"I've been thinking a lot about that. We could head to San Antonio before sunrise. Do a little digging online at an internet café," he said. "I'd like to make a few calls, too. I might be able to get a little more information from your acquaintances."

"What makes you think that'll help?" she asked.

"I've been thinking about your charity work. We need to see if any of your projects could have had a negative impact on anyone," he said.

"Sounds like looking for a needle in a haystack," she stated.

"It is. But we have to start somewhere and talking about it might help you remember." Holden stretched his long muscular legs. "Have you thought more about those last few days before you went hiking?"

"Yes, but it doesn't seem to be helping. I end up with a headache." She frowned. "Will it be safe for you in San Antonio? It's a big city and people could be watching for you."

"We'll have to play it careful. The murders happened two years ago and in Virginia, so they shouldn't be top of mind anymore. I'd go back to Rose's but that would be too risky for her." He turned on the water in the small sink and hand washed the pair of dishes.

"I know a place we can go in San Antonio," she said. "It's small but has high-speed internet and everything we'd need."

"Any place familiar to you could put us in danger.

Whoever is tracking you might know about it," he said. "Since we don't have a clue who is behind your attacks, we don't truly know how close they are to you."

"I could call in a favor from a friend," she said. "I know people who would be loyal to me."

"That may be true under normal circumstances, but believe me when I say a persistent person can break down pretty much every barrier." He wiped water from the plates and stacked them. "Besides, you wouldn't want to put your friends in danger by giving them information that could lead to you."

"I hadn't thought about it like that," she said, realizing that was most likely all he'd thought about since being alone after his girlfriend and father had been killed. The past week had been hell for her being shut out from everything she cared about and disconnected from everyone she loved. She couldn't imagine living like this for two years and especially after losing two people he cared so much about. Other than Rose, they were all he had.

"There's something else," he said. "While we're there I thought it might be a good idea to do a little digging into my past. See what kinds of stories have been running about me since I disappeared. That might give me an idea of who's trying to find me and why. I never could figure out why local police were involved but enough time has passed now that it should be safe for me to surface and dig around."

"I think that's a great idea." Ella managed a smile. When she'd first met Holden, he seemed uninterested in trying to find the truth. His life had become about stay-

ing off the grid and surviving day to day. She saw this
as progress, good progress toward him reclaiming life.

"We'll grab a motel room in San Antonio," he continued. "See what we can come up with on a computer.
I have a few tricks up my sleeve and by the time anyone
figures out the IP address, we'll be long gone."

Ella nodded. "When do we leave?"

"Now," he said.

"MIND IF I stretch my legs before we sit on that bike for
a few hours?" Ella asked, those cornflower blue eyes
breaking down his walls.

"Not as long as I can go with you. I can use a walk,"
he said. Food was done, dishes were handled and he'd
wiped the place clean of fingerprints. He had no intention of letting her out of his sight again after the sedan
incident.

"It feels like we're a long way from answers." Ella
started toward the trees and he followed.

"Which is why we have to change our approach," he
said. Part of him wanted to hunker down right where
they were and take a minute to catch his breath. Their
luck wouldn't last forever. Ella Butler was big news and
it seemed like everyone had a camera and a social media
account ready to post news in a few clicks. He couldn't
leave her alone and taking her with him to get supplies
was risky. In the late-August Texas heat she wouldn't
survive for long, and if he took her completely off the
grid, they wouldn't know when it was safe for her to
come home. Unlike him, she had a life worth returning
to. Was that the reason he felt especially drawn to her?

It had been so easy for him to disappear. There was no one counting on him, no one expecting him to come back. No one except Rose, Ella would argue. She'd be right, too. He hadn't realized what this was doing to Rose until he'd seen the worry lines etched in her face.

As for Ella, she deserved to get back to her ranch and the land she loved so much. She was doing important work whereas he'd felt like a drifter since returning to the United States from the action overseas. Time had provided perspective and, looking back, he could see that he'd kept everyone at arm's length. Maybe his and Karen's relationship could've gone somewhere if he'd let her in. But that only made the guilt worse. She'd died because she'd been in his home at the wrong time. Holden knew there'd been a cover-up, but why? Questions he hadn't allowed himself to ask in two years started surfacing.

"Where are you from originally? You don't have an accent, so I can't place you," Ella said, breaking into his heavy thoughts as they walked.

"I'm from everywhere," he supplied.

She shot him a look.

"Military brat," he said.

"I already know that. You had to have been born somewhere," she countered.

"Colorado Springs," he said.

She responded by cocking an eyebrow.

"It's the truth," he said, holding his hands up in the universal sign of surrender.

She increased her pace, moving farther from the tiny

house that had felt like a temporary home. A little voice said it felt like that because of Ella.

"What?" he asked. "Am I doing it again?"

"Doing what?"

"I already told you that it's been a while since I've had a real conversation with another human being. I also plainly stated that I'm no good at it to begin with—"

This time her hands came up to stop him.

"You're doing better than you think," she said. "I wouldn't even be alive right now if it wasn't for you. Thank you for everything you're doing for me. I can see that it's taking you out of your comfort zone and putting you in danger and I just want you to know that I appreciate it."

Holden stayed quiet for a long time. A thousand thoughts raced through his head. He finally settled on "You're welcome."

Ella swatted at a bug as she stomped ahead with a smile. "Did you spend much time in Colorado?"

"Not really. We moved every couple of years, so I never really got attached to one place," he continued.

"That must've been hard in high school." She glanced at him.

"I managed to get out with a diploma. Although I'm not sure how. I got into trouble. Guess you could say I was a brat." Holden grinned.

"I doubt it," she said, rewarding him with another small smile that was sweet and sexy at the same time. "At least this partly explains why you're so self-reliant."

"All my self-reliance can make me difficult to get

along with," he warned, and she immediately made a sound.

"I have noticed that you can be—"

"Stubborn."

"Determined," she corrected. "But your skills and knowledge have been useful in keeping me alive, so I'm not about to complain. Even if you can be a little blunt at times."

Holden grunted. "Say what you mean. I'm a jerk."

Ella stopped and turned to look at him. She fisted her right hand and rested it on her hip as she seemed to study his features.

"Are you always this hard on yourself?" She stared into his eyes when he didn't respond. "Never mind. I can already tell the answer to that question. Yes."

"We should get on the road," Holden said. Talking about himself, opening up to another person, was foreign. Especially since it was so easy to do with Ella.

"Okay," she responded. "But first you should know that you always change the subject when I try to talk about you."

"There really isn't much to tell," he said, and she made another one of those harrumph noises that sounded like it tore straight from her throat.

"I could probably write a book about your experiences," she said. "And I'm pretty sure the least exciting thing in your life would be more thrilling than anything I've ever done."

Holden caught her stare and intensified his gaze. "I could tell you everything about my past. But then I'd have to kill you."

Silence stretched on between them in a checkmate. Until Holden burst out laughing and then she did, too.

"You didn't believe that load of nonsense, did you?" he teased as she swatted his arm.

"Only because I know you were in the military and I assume most of what you did there is classified," she said.

She reached out to swat him again and he caught her hand in his, ignoring her delicate, silky skin.

"At least you know I have a sense of humor now," he said, figuring touching her had been another mistake. His were racking up. He hoped it wasn't a mistake to dig into the past, too. This was the first time in two years he could let himself hope to find answers and bring justice to the person behind the murders.

"You call that funny?" She withdrew her hand.

"I thought it was," he said.

"You really have been alone for a long time." She looked indignant right before her face broke into a wide smile. "See. I can do it, too."

Holden didn't hold back his laugh. "We should head back and then get on the road."

"Think I can check in with my family again?" she asked. "Might be able to fill in the gaps in my memory."

His first response would be *hell no*. But the sorrow mixed with hope in her eyes made him think twice.

"We'll look online first. If anything happened to one of your family members, it would be news," he said. "And then we'll play it by ear."

He wasn't exactly promising her contact but knowing everyone was okay would ease some of her stress. He wanted to give her that much.

She twined their fingers and he didn't stop her even though alarm bells sounded off at her touch.

The campsite wasn't more than twenty yards away. As they neared the clearing, Holden heard noises. He stopped and listened, squeezing Ella's hand to catch her attention. He motioned for her to crouch down and then bit back a curse.

Moving stealthily along the tree line, Holden kept diligent watch ahead. Had the teens been a cover, or had they alerted someone to his and Ella's presence? His friend who owned the place wasn't coming back. As they neared, he heard banging on the door.

"David?" an unfamiliar male voice said. "Are you home?"

Holden navigated him and Ella around the woods so that they could get a look at the front door. Branches snapped as Ella moved and that would give them away to a trained ear. No way was he separating the two of them no matter how much noise she made. As it was his heart pounded his rib cage and all his muscles chorded, thinking someone might've found them.

Moving through the underbrush, Holden positioned them so that they could see the front door. A male figure, thin, wearing dress slacks and a collared shirt with short sleeves stood there. He was holding something in his hands and had to reposition it, balancing the bundle against his arm and side in order to free his hand and knock.

The situation looked innocent enough but Holden

wasn't taking any chances when it came to Ella. He held her hand and watched for suspicious activity from the intruder.

After a few more rounds of knocking without an answer, the older man set down the bundle and reclaimed the driver's seat of his vintage Ford pickup. A minute later, there was only dust settling along the drive.

Holden waited just in case the old man returned.

When enough time had passed, he stood. "Stay right here until I give a signal."

"Who was that?" she whispered, her eyes wide.

"Probably a neighbor thinking that David had come home, but I need to check the contents of that package before you get anywhere near it." His tone was emphatic.

"What if something happens to you, Holden? Where does that leave me?" She made a good point. Without him, she had little chance of survival.

"Okay. Together." He linked their fingers and realized immediately that she was trembling. He never would've known she was scared based on her calm exterior. Ella Butler knew how to put on a brave face.

Holden picked up a branch and moved slowly toward the package, measuring his steps carefully. "We treat this like a ticking bomb, okay?"

"Got it," Ella replied. Her palm was sweaty, so he gave her hand a squeeze for reassurance.

"We'll be fine." He moved with precision toward the object. As he neared, he saw the small box filled with what looked like produce. Brightly colored apples, bananas and zucchinis peeked over the rim.

Holden maintained as safe a distance as he could. He didn't specialize in bombs but it didn't take a specialist to know being this close to one wasn't the smartest idea. He tossed a stick at the box.

Thankfully, nothing happened.

"We're good," he said. But they weren't. Just because they'd dodged a bullet this time didn't mean they would the next.

Holden needed to keep that thought close to his heart as they moved into a more densely populated area.

Nowhere was safe.

Chapter Thirteen

The motel not too far from State Highway 151 was sparse but had all the basics—two beds and a decent shower. The best part was that they could pay with cash and Holden seemed to have more than enough to cover the bill.

"I hope you'll let me repay you for all of this," Ella said, grateful for clean clothes, hard walls and a shower. With Holden, she never knew what to expect, and she could admit there was an excitement about that.

He shot her a look that said he wouldn't.

She started to argue but he brought his hand up.

"I haven't done much of anything for anyone for the past twenty-five months, so no arguments," he said with a tone that said it wouldn't do any good to protest.

And on some level, she understood. She would figure out a way to thank him because he'd gone above and beyond anything she could ever expect. It was a foreign feeling being on the other end of someone's kindness. Ella had always been the one taking charge and thinking of everyone else. Maybe she could take what she was learning back to the ranch with her and allow oth-

ers to do more to pitch in. It had felt like the weight of
the world rested on her shoulders her entire life.

"The guy at the front desk said there's an internet
café a couple of miles from here open until 2:00 a.m.,"
he said.

"What kind of place is open that late?" she asked almost to herself as she pulled her hair off her face and
into a ponytail. It was barely dark, so without looking
at the clock Ella knew that it must be after eight o'clock.

"We'll see."

THE PLACE WAS actually a hookah lounge. The atmosphere was perfect for going unnoticed. It was dark inside and surprisingly not as smoky as she'd expected.
There were small round tables with pillows on the
floor. And the place was filled with what looked like
college-aged kids who were chatting in between taking puffs off the hookahs positioned in the center of
their tables. Ella had never been to one before but she
knew others who frequented them in college. Come to
think of it, Ella hadn't done much socializing in the
four years she'd attended university, and she'd gone to
a state school legendary for its parties. She'd never once
thought about letting loose and having a good time. Her
life had been filled with purpose and she'd always been
an overachiever. A thought struck. Had she been trying to find her worth in being the perfect student? The
perfect daughter? The perfect sister?

The revelation caught her off guard. She loved the
ranch but had she thrown herself into her job so that

she could win approval from her dad? The realization knocked her back a step mentally.

"How many?" the hostess said with a smile, interrupting Ella's thoughts. The young woman, maybe twenty, had beautiful dark hair and wore a jeweled dot on her forehead. She batted long dark lashes at Holden and Ella bristled.

"Just the two of us," he said, then added, "and we'll need access to a computer."

She smiled up at him, a mix of courtesy and flirting. Couldn't she see Ella standing right there? Technically, she and Holden weren't a couple, but this woman didn't know it by the looks of them. They *could* be a couple and this woman was being rude.

"Follow me," she said with a silky voice.

Ella rolled her eyes.

Holden laced their fingers and she noticed he was scanning the room as they walked, a sobering reminder of the danger they were in being out in public. Suddenly, she felt silly for being jealous of the hostess. Was that what she was? Jealous?

Ella sighed sharply.

It had been a long week. She was fatigued and sad and had had a personal revelation that still had her mind spinning. Honestly, she was scared no matter how much she didn't want to own up to it. The nightmare that had started with her father's murder and extended to her present situation wouldn't end and it felt like the stakes were growing with every passing day.

"How's this?" the hostess asked, beaming up at Holden.

"Fine." He barely seemed to notice that she was

standing right next to him inside his personal space. Most would consider that rude but Ella decided that it was a cultural thing and not meant to rile her.

"Can I get you anything to drink?" Her gaze dropped to their linked hands and her smile faded just a touch.

A satisfied smile crept across Ella's lips.

"Water for now," he said. "We'll order off the menu after she's had a chance to look over the options."

"Fine," the hostess said before giving Ella a quick acknowledgment and then disappearing.

Ella took a seat at the bar stool facing the wall. Holden glanced around and mumbled something. Best as she could tell, he didn't like the idea that their backs were to the door. He repositioned the chairs so that they could both easily see the screen. His was more to the side, positioned so that he could keep watch on the door.

Holden handed Ella a menu.

"An Americano sounds fantastic," she said, referring to a shot of espresso topped off with hot water.

"We should probably order something for that," he motioned toward the hookah.

Ella scanned the menu. "Sour apple sounds good."

The hostess returned with two glasses of water. Holden relayed their hookah and drink orders—his was strong black coffee—and then he waited for Ella to make a decision on food.

Everything on the menu looked amazing, or maybe Ella was just starving.

"Gyro sandwich," she finally decided.

Holden ordered the same.

The hostess nodded, gave a curt smile and scribbled down their orders on a small pad of paper.

"Do you remember having any arguments with anyone, specifically during any of your meetings?" he asked as soon as the hostess disappeared.

"I honestly can't say anything sticks out. I mean, people fight back all the time over personal gain. It feels like there's something right there—" she motioned toward her forehead "—but every time I think too hard, I get a headache."

"Effects from the blow you took. If I'd been there five minutes sooner I could've saved you all this," he said with a look of frustration. He might've been able to interrupt whoever did this to her but he would've exposed his presence and put himself in more danger, so she was glad that he hadn't in some respects.

"I've been thinking about the shotgun," he said. "Most people have one beside the bed."

"Which means it could've been anyone," she said.

"Exactly."

"Why is that a good thing?" she asked.

"Because it means we're not dealing with a professional. The guys after me would use a Glock or a weapon that is more precise. I would never see them coming because they wouldn't have to get close enough to hit the mark. They're skilled shooters whereas the person who shot at you couldn't hit you at close range," he surmised.

"Okay, but what about one of my father's exes?" she asked.

"I've been thinking about that," he admitted. "The

person who killed your father wanted to make a statement. That could indicate someone angry, vengeful. So, the person kills him and wants everyone to know how mad he or she is. Hurting you doesn't have the same impact because your father wouldn't be around to see it."

"Meaning if this was a revenge killing against my father, they'd save him for last?" she asked.

"Yes," he said. "The first attempt on your life was meant to look like an accident, like you fell and died."

"He goes back to find a body and doesn't. So he sets up and waits," she said. "But the second time around he doesn't care because he figures I'm going to turn him in."

"At that point, he just wants to get rid of you," he said. "He figures that he's got nothing to lose because if you make it to the sheriff, you turn him in. Think you can remember anything about the man in the mask? Height? Weight?" Holden's fingers went to work on the keyboard.

"If my brain will cooperate, I'll do my best." Ella stilled when the hostess returned.

"Do you have a sheet of paper and a pen?" Holden asked, pulling out his wad of money and peeling off a twenty.

"I'll find something in the manager's office," she said, taking the offering with a grateful smile. Ella was pretty certain the woman winked. Wasn't there a waiter in the place? Why did the hostess have to keep coming back? And she did return not two minutes later with a pad of paper and a pen. When she handed the offering to Holden, she brushed her fingers against his arm.

Ella was starting to see red.

"Excuse me," she said curtly. "Those are for me."

Holden gave her a bewildered look. Surely he hadn't been off the grid so long that he didn't recognize when a woman was practically throwing herself at him.

The hostess walked away with a frown.

"I can't believe how rude that woman is being," Ella said.

A quick glance at Holden burned in her belly because he must've caught on and now he was smirking.

"All I'm saying is that it's bad manners to be so obvious," she defended. "And we don't need the distraction with everything else we have going on."

"Are you jealous?" he asked. "Because I'm fairly certain the woman was trying to be nice."

Ella's gaze caught on the ten-digit number scribbled across the top of the page along with the woman's name. She held up the notepad. "And what do you think this is doing on here?"

A bemused Holden broke out into a smile. "Guess you were right."

"I'm not blind," she said. "And she was being so obvious."

The door opened behind her and Holden's smile disappeared. Ella followed his gaze and saw a lively group of college-aged kids walk inside. Holden's relief was almost palpable and this was a good reminder of the tension.

"I don't like putting all these kids in danger with our presence," he said, demonstrating once again that he put others first. Holden might see himself as selfish but she wished that he could see the real him, the man she saw.

"I don't either," she agreed.

"Let's speed things along so we can get out of here." Holden motioned toward the screen in front of them. His left thigh was positioned on the outside of her right, effectively providing a barrier between her and everyone else. The denim material of his jeans against her leg sent volts of electricity at the point of contact.

He did it without thinking, with such ease, yet the dark circles cradling his eyes told another story. He must be exhausted even if he'd never admit it.

Ella tried to ignore the sexual magnetism pulsing between them with contact. When the hostess returned with food she seemed to pick up on it, too. She shot an embarrassed look Ella's way.

At this point, she was too hungry and worried to stress over a little flirting. Holden was a gorgeous man, tall, built like a brick wall, but his body didn't feel like one. When her skin was pressed against his it was the feeling of silk over steel. He was sex appeal and masculinity and resourcefulness wrapped together in one seriously hot package.

A dangerous package.

HOLDEN DRUMMED HIS fingers on the keyboard and then hit Enter.

Maverick Mike's murder still pervaded the headlines.

"My brothers and sister seem to be safe." Ella sighed. "Nothing is going on at the ranch."

Holden entered a new search, using only her last name.

"What's this?" she asked, scanning the stories. "Two men have shown up in town claiming to be heirs."

"Looks like your long-lost brethren are giving interviews," Holden said, pulling up the site running the stories.

"He looks nothing like us," Ella said of the first person who popped onto the screen.

"The amount of money your father owns will bring out a lot of crazy," Holden said, watching as the man claimed Maverick Mike had had an affair with his mother that had produced a son, him. The journalist conceded that the accuser had declined a DNA test to confirm.

The second accuser agreed to a test, but only on his terms. He said he'd bring in his own, whatever that meant.

"I'm pretty sure these guys aren't being taken seriously," Holden said.

"Could either one of them have tried to kill me?" she asked.

"Anything's possible. Your father has enough money that even if it was divided between either or both of these yahoos there'd be more than enough to go around," he added. "I doubt they'd target each of you individually if they wanted to take it all. They'd most likely set a bomb and take all of you out at once. But then that would be too easy, as well."

Ella shuddered.

"Sorry. It must be strange for a civilian to hear someone talk about life and death so casually," he said. "We got used to it in the military. Doesn't lessen the effect of your actions. But I learned to compartmentalize the missions by becoming numb to the words."

"It's okay," she said but her voice was a little shaky. "I'm just still trying to wrap my thoughts around the fact that any of this is happening. Before my father died, my biggest concern was making sure that I secured funding for the new animal shelter being proposed and now death just rolls off my tongue."

"Do either of them match the size of the man who tried to shoot you?" Holden asked.

"This one is too big. I would've remembered someone who looked like he should be a defensive end on a football field."

Holden's dark brows drew together.

"What is it?" she asked.

"You didn't mention the animal shelter before," he said, turning toward the screen.

"I must've forgotten. I don't know if it's from the hit I took or just stress in general," she said.

Holden pulled up a map of Cattle Barge. "Can you tell me where the proposed site is?"

"Yeah, sure." Her look said she had no idea what he was getting at. She took over, zooming the map into a location east of downtown. "There. Right there."

"What's around it?" he asked. "Anything interesting?"

"Pilsner Lake isn't far." She pointed it out on the map. "We have a cleanup project going on there. People love to use the lake and the adjacent park but don't feel the need to clean up after themselves. We get a lot of debris on the beaches and animals are getting sick off the rusting cans tossed around."

"Whose property surrounds the proposed shelter site?" he asked.

"Mr. Suffolk," she said. "Why?"

"Is he against the building being so close to his property?" he asked.

"Not him so much but his son has been cranky about it. Says it'll be too noisy and bother his father," she supplied. "It won't. He's just being difficult. Old Man Suffolk's house is all the way over here."

Ella pointed to a spot on the west end of the property.

Holden leaned back in his chair and brought his index finger to his lips. "Wish we could talk to the old man."

"I guess that's out of the question given our current situation," she said. "Seems like he and my father butted heads from time to time. I might not be his favorite person but I doubt he'd want me dead."

He nodded.

"Are you the only one pushing this project?" he asked.

"Mainly, I guess. Without my support it wouldn't make it far but none of these initiatives would," she admitted. "There was talk of him selling his property a little while ago but I think that's off the table."

Holden needed to figure out a way to talk to the Suffolk family.

Ella tensed as someone approached from behind.

"Hour's almost up," the male voice said.

"Thanks for the heads-up," Holden said to the waiter.

Holden typed his name and a moment of hesitation struck as he wondered what would fill the screen when he hit Enter.

His mind hadn't strayed from the numbers Rose had given to him, 1-9-6-4. Talking about Pop had reminded Holden how much he loved fishing and camping. It was probably just a random thought but it was sticking in his mind for some reason. Maybe there'd be something to point him in the right direction out of the dozens of articles that had popped up in the search engine along with several pictures of him, most of which were in his battle fatigues. Where'd they come up with those pictures? He scanned the stories, noting the strong emphasis on him being ex-military and considered armed and dangerous. Stories like these would bring out all types of bounty hunters hungry for a reward. In his case, it was substantial. Two hundred and fifty thousand dollars were being offered for his safe return to Hampshire Police. That kind of cash would bring people with guns out of the woodwork to hunt him down. No wonder it had always felt like eyes were on him, like he was constantly being watched.

"That seems high," Ella said almost under her breath.

"It is," Holden agreed. He read other headlines. Ex-Marine/Killer Suffers Signs of PTSD.

If the news affected Ella, she hid it well.

"This is untrue," she said hotly. "I don't know that much about PTSD except that you've been around gunfire and I'm pretty sure you would've had some kind of reaction. You have no nightmares, which I've read are part of it. Plus, all the stress we've been under would've triggered something. You're the most calm and collected man I've ever known."

Her indignant tone brought a wave of relief. Holden didn't want her to believe the lies that had been spread about him. For some odd reason that mattered a great deal.

"I thought journalists had a responsibility to print the truth," she huffed.

He covered her hand with his and she looked at him. Those penetrating blue eyes, the ones capable of seeing past the facade to the real him, searched his face.

"Thank you." His throat dried and he had to resist the urge to lean toward her as her tongue darted across her lips. "Your confidence means a lot."

Her eyes darkened as she held his gaze.

"I've been around you long enough to know this is fiction," she said. "You're kind and giving and nothing like the picture painted with these articles."

Well, hell, those words did it. Holden dipped his head and kissed her moist mouth anyway. She'd just taken a drink of her Americano and tasted like coffee.

He caught someone walking toward them out of the corner of his eye. He put his arm around Ella and turned to acknowledge the figure moving their way. Relief washed over him when he saw that it was the hostess.

"Everything taste okay here?" she asked with a glance toward the hookah pipe.

Holden didn't acknowledge the irony there.

"Perfect." And he meant that about Ella. She was the most giving person he'd met. She'd grown up with every privilege but it didn't show. She was down-to-earth and put others' needs first.

The hostess smiled and told them to call for her if they needed anything else.

Holden picked up the mouthpiece as he thanked her. They didn't have to smoke but they did need to put on a better show. He touched it to his lips and then handed it to her. She did the same.

"We should eat," he said as soon as the hostess was out of earshot.

Ella's plate was cleaned and her mug was drained ten minutes later.

"Maybe I can call the sheriff and see if he found any evidence at the scene," she said.

"There should be shell casings," he agreed.

"Is it risky to call from here?" she asked.

"We'll pick up a throwaway phone at a convenience store tonight on our way out of San Antonio. That way you can call in the morning when we're on the road. We'll set out north, make the call and then double back south once you find out what else the sheriff knows," he said.

"He might've solved the case by now and we wouldn't know." Ella motioned toward the screen.

"Are you kidding? You and your family are news." His fingers pounded the keyboard and she saw that he was typing her name.

Socialite Believed to Be Dead read the headline. She stared at the screen. The article went on to say that a substantial amount of her blood had been found at the scene of a shooting and a blood trail ended in neighboring bushes. The suspect was still on the loose. The last line in the article read that her body had not been located and the sheriff's office wouldn't close the investigation until he found answers.

"I spoke to Sheriff Sawmill. There's no way a story like this should run. Why would he say something like this?"

Holden studied the screen. "The way this article reads, the journalist suggested you were dead and the sheriff didn't correct him or her. I'm sure he has reasons for allowing the public to buy into that nonsense."

"May must be worried sick. She reads the paper every day," Ella said. "I can't even imagine what the others in my family must be thinking, my friends."

"We'll get word to May. Let's hope the others aren't watching the news," he said.

"They probably aren't. They've been avoiding the media and I'm sure they won't want to read all the stories that will come out about our father." Ella's gaze narrowed. "I'll never believe another thing I read online again. I had no idea there were so many lies and untruths."

"Agreed. And I don't like seeing this any more than you do, but this is good news for us," Holden said. "The person responsible for the attempts on your life will most likely let his guard down now."

"What if he's smarter than that?" she asked. "What if he realizes that I'm alive and is waiting for me, biding his time?"

"This guy makes a lot of assumptions and mistakes," he stated.

"True." She seemed to catch on to what he was really saying, that if this guy was any smarter, she'd already be dead. "Think we can go back to Cattle Barge if I put on something to cover up my face?"

He remembered why fishing with Pop had stuck in his mind a few minutes ago. Rose had mentioned his father bringing up fishing. It might mean nothing but Holden wanted to explore it anyway. There was a place the two of them always returned to. Maybe something was there?

"There's something I need to do in Colorado first," he said. "We need to go there before we do anything else. I need to look through my father's personal items. My father gave Rose the message 1-9-6-4 for a reason, and we might find answers in his belongings. Are you good with that?"

"I'm all in, Holden."

Chapter Fourteen

"I think my arms are actually going to fall off." Ella gladly climbed off the back of the yellow-and-chrome motorcycle. She shook her hands and wiggled her arms, trying to get blood flowing again. They'd stopped off every few hours on the ride to Colorado for coffee and snacks but hadn't slept.

Holden took off his helmet and cracked a smile that didn't reach his eyes. "You didn't enjoy the open road?"

"I've been on the back of that bike more than I ever want to be on the back of anything ever again. I don't even think I could get on another ATV now." Ella bit back the urge to complain about the fact that they were in a remote area. Granted, it was beautiful. The landscape was filled with dogwood, birch and towering oak trees. She recognized the scent of Douglas firs and it made her think of Christmases back home with her dad. Her heart ached at the thought she would never get to spend another holiday with him. Sadness overwhelmed her and she had to move. Walking helped her refocus on what needed to be done instead of on the hole in her chest when she thought about her father.

The last road sign she'd read said they were in a town called Newburg. Holden had parked near a shed that looked like it could house a minivan. It was old and looked abandoned from outside appearances. She figured this was the perfect location for hiding valuables. The sun would dip below the mountains soon and darkness was imminent. The small shed didn't look to have any power running to it and there was no sign of a light bulb.

"How long do we have before we run out of daylight?" she asked.

"Not long. I'm hoping that the flashlight app on the throwaway I bought will suffice." He'd bought one of those pay-as-you-go cell phones at a gas station convenience store that couldn't be traced back to him.

"I'm guessing there are boxes or containers in there," she said.

"This is where we used to keep camping supplies." The hollow note to his voice reminded her that he hadn't allowed himself a chance to grieve. Work and staying busy were good for sorrow, but bottling up emotions was dangerous.

Ella couldn't imagine that going through his father's personal items was going to be easy for Holden. She couldn't even begin to fathom going through her father's. She and her siblings would have to face that task at some point and she dreaded it with everything inside her. "What are we looking for?"

"Good question." Holden pulled out a small satchel from underneath the seat of his motorcycle and retrieved a key from it. He unlocked the storage shed and opened the doors. The entire building could house a minivan and that was about it.

Boxes were stacked floor to ceiling with a little room for walking to the left. The two of them wouldn't fit inside, not with Holden's sizable build. The idea of climbing in there with spiders and possibly field mice made Ella shiver, so she would let Holden do the honors.

"You don't have to go in there." Holden stood there, looking like he wasn't quite ready to cross that threshold either.

"I'll be fine. In case you hadn't noticed, I grew up on a ranch." She wanted to spare him but knew there wasn't much she could do.

"Right. I did know that," he said. All humor was gone from his eyes and he looked like he was staring at a ghost.

"We don't have to do this today," she offered. "We could grab a room. I saw a town an hour ago. We could eat and you could have a cold drink."

"We're already here." There was a somber quality to his tone. "We might as well get started."

"Is it safe to be here?" she asked.

"If anyone knew about this place, the boxes would already be gone," he informed.

"I can get a box. Step aside," she cautioned as she moved past him. She was pretty sure something moved in the grass next to her and she almost chickened out until she took another look at his face; his eyes were so intent. Her legs felt like she was walking on rubber bands and her stomach clenched, but she forged ahead like nothing was wrong.

He hesitated for a second and then pulled out the first box. "It's light." He opened the top. "Clothes." He picked up a couple other boxes. "Same in here. I doubt we'll find what we're looking for in any of these."

"We can keep going until we find something. I'm sure 1-9-6-4 will make sense when we see it," she said, not sure what *it* was.

"Pop always talked about buying land and building a house in Colorado. He wanted to be closer to Rose so the two of them could keep each other company as they grew old." Holden opened another box. "Maybe he moved some of his valuables here to prepare. He never really talked about retiring but he'd never really talked much about his moving business."

"I'm guessing no one knows about this property," she said.

"Rose would've said something before if she had any idea." He lined up a few boxes on the ground.

Ella began with the one on the end and he moved to the other side.

Carefully, she examined the box for any creepy-crawly bugs that might be lurking inside and especially for anything that might be venomous now that her radar was up.

"We have no idea what we're looking for." Frustration edged his tone.

"We'll know it when we see it," she reassured.

Light had faded and it was hard to see inside the boxes. Ella didn't feel great about sticking her hand inside them in the dark.

"Hold this." Holden held out the throwaway phone.

Ella took it.

"Position it this way," he said, moving her hand.

He moved back to the box he'd been working on. He pulled out two heavy-duty bags by their handles. He set them down in between two tall fir trees.

"What are those?" Ella followed him, positioning the light so he could see what he was doing.

"You'll see." He didn't look up as he unzipped the first and pulled out a bundle.

"That a tent?" Ella had no plans to sleep in there. She hadn't done that since she was a little girl out with her brothers.

"Better. I have a pair of sleeping hammocks." He seemed pretty pleased with himself but they were losing light and her sense of humor was fading along with her energy.

Ella bit back a yawn. Exhaustion made her wish she had toothpicks to prop her eyes open with.

"How tired are you?" he asked.

"There's no end." Her arms had felt like dead weight hours ago on the bike and it would take days to recover.

"You can get some sleep as soon as I get these up." There was no sign of him making a joke.

"You're kidding, right?" She hoped.

"Why? They're still in good shape," he said.

"Because I'll be mosquito food," she stated. "Are there no motels in Colorado? I could've sworn we passed a couple on the highway before our exit."

"Don't worry. These have nets and we'll be safer if we stay away from major roads. No one knows about this place and I have power bars and water in my backpack to keep us from going hungry. They'll get us through the night and morning, when we can finish going through the boxes. We're about to lose light and we should probably save phone battery." He hooked a rope around one of the firs and then secured it with some Boy Scout maneuver she'd seen one of her brothers do when they were kids.

She couldn't argue with his logic. It would most likely be safe for them out here in what felt like the wilderness even if the place did give her the creeps. Living on a ranch was a different beast. Ella was used to wide-open skies after growing up at Hereford. Colorado was beautiful, but it also felt a little claustrophobic with the thick layers of tall trees.

"It'll be good. You'll see," he reassured when she didn't respond.

"I'm sure it will," she said without much conviction. "Want some help?"

He nodded.

Her vision was blurring and sleep, even out here, sounded better than a steak dinner about now.

"Hold here," he said and his fingers brushed hers. He moved next to her and she could feel his masculine presence.

Being out here with no one and nothing besides each other made her miss the ranch. She couldn't remember the last time she'd wanted to leave Hereford, but it had to have been college. She'd gone to state school to be close to home. *Home.* Ella wished she and Holden were there now.

But what was home to him?

She couldn't even imagine this being his life for the past two years. She thought about how alone he must've been feeling, must still feel, being away from everything and everyone he cared about for so long. Two years could seem like an eternity. So much could change.

Holden moved away from her and she immediately felt his absence.

"Thanks for everything you've done for me," she said. "I realize you have a lot going on with your father's case, and yet you're still helping me."

He waved her off like it was nothing. But it wasn't. And when this was all over she would figure out a way to show her appreciation.

After tying off the ropes and ensuring their hammocks were secure, Holden went to work building a fire. His movements were swift and there was a certain athletic grace to them, his muscles tensed and stretched against the cotton fabric of his sweatshirt.

Ella redirected her thoughts. No use going down that road again, the one that had her attracted to a man whose past would always haunt him.

Although the landscape looked completely different, being outdoors reminded her of home. She sat down in front of the campfire. Everything about Hereford reminded her of her father and, once again, she couldn't believe he was gone. Holding on to her knees, she rocked back and forth.

"EVERYTHING ALL RIGHT?" Holden dropped down beside Ella and handed her a power bar and bottle of water.

"I miss him," she said, and he could see tears streaming down her cheeks in the glow of the campfire. She hugged her legs even tighter. "Everything's been happening so fast that my brain hasn't had time to process the fact that when I go home he won't be there. He's never coming back."

"I'm sorry." Those were the only two words he could think to say and they fell short of what he wanted to communicate.

"He was larger than life. He was just this huge presence. You know? And now there'll be a gaping hole in his place at the ranch," she managed while fighting off sobs threatening to suck her under. "I can't imagine life on Hereford without him, and that's exactly what I'm going back to. A life where he doesn't exist. Going through your father's belongings made me realize that I'll be doing the same thing very soon."

"He sounds like he was a good man underneath it all. I have a lot of respect for him," Holden said. He knew firsthand what it was like to lose a father, and that meant he also knew there was nothing that he could say to take away the pain. Instead of issuing empty words, he put his arm around her and drew her close. She responded by leaning into him.

"He was," she said quietly.

To say the day had been difficult was a lot like saying bears had fur. Being around his father's things brought back all kinds of memories, most of them good. Hell, Pop's clothes still smelled like him.

Being here made Holden feel close to Pop, in a way. Holden remembered the first time his father had taken him fishing. He'd caught a large-mouth bass twice the size of his fist and they'd gone most every weekend until Holden reached the age hanging out with his old man on the weekends wasn't cool. Then they'd gone on holidays like Father's Day and Fourth of July. Forget barbecuing hamburgers—they'd clean the fish they caught and toss them around in batter. They'd fill up on fried catfish until neither could walk. There'd been hard times, too.

Growing up without a constant feminine presence, save for occasionally spending time with Rose, had brought its own set of challenges. Holden couldn't help but notice the similarities between his father and Ella's in that regard. The men were completely different but each did his best to bring up his family.

Despite any hardships, Ella had turned out all right. It couldn't have been easy for a girl to grow up without a mother. Nurses and caretakers only went so far. But she'd grown into a caring, intelligent, giving woman. *Beautiful woman*, a little voice felt the need to remind him. He wouldn't argue. She deserved better than this.

For tonight he was pleased that she had a soft hammock, warm covers and food in her stomach.

THE SOUND OF twigs breaking underneath shoes woke Holden with a start. He glanced around quickly, gaining his bearings. He didn't mention to Ella that black bears can be up to nine feet tall and weigh in at close to seven hundred pounds.

He closed his eyes and listened.

The twig snaps grew louder, indicating that the snapper was heading toward their campsite.

Holden moved into action, swiftly and quietly. He was at Ella's side in a heartbeat, gently shaking her.

Her eyes opened and he said, "Someone's coming. It's okay."

He deliberately said someone and not some*thing*. Startle her and she might panic, drawing unwanted attention toward them. "We need to move away from camp as fast as possible."

She nodded and bolted into action, throwing off the blanket he'd placed on her last night. He handed her her shoes and she put them on and laced them up in a snap.

The sounds were getting closer and this time he heard voices. It was a relief on some note because that meant they weren't about to encounter a bear. However, people often turned out to be far more dangerous than wildlife. Wildlife made sense. They simply followed the natural order and acted according to laws of nature and their DNA's programming. Humans were unpredictable.

"What is it?" Ella whispered, and the sound of her voice first thing in the morning stirred dormant places inside him that he couldn't afford to let wake. Not when everything in his life was uncertain.

"Hikers," he said. "I need to get a closer look to evaluate the threat. I'm not leaving you here alone."

"Okay." She yawned. "Let's go."

"Stay low and close," he said.

He led her into the woods, far beyond the hikers. He wanted to come up on them from a different angle, from behind. And especially so that he could draw them away from camp.

There were two males and a female. They were chatting easily and looked to be in their early twenties. They were dressed like L.L. Bean models and the female had a black bandana tied around her head. Their hiking boots were clean, which meant they'd just been bought or didn't get taken out much.

Holden looked at Ella and whispered, "Follow my lead."

She smiled her response.

He took her hand, stood up straight and said, "It's chillier this morning than I expected even at this altitude."

"I know, right?" She beamed at him as he made an effort to stomp through the underbrush toward a path. "Brrr."

"Oh, hey. Morning," Holden said to the trio as he and Ella approached.

"Morning," the female said as the guys nodded and smiled. She had dark hair in twin braids running halfway down her torso. Up close, the guys looked to be nineteen or twenty at the most. His estimate of the group being college coeds seemed to be spot-on.

"Been up here long?" he asked.

"Aiden had the bright idea to wake up at four this morning," one of the guys said. "I'm Patrick, by the way. And this is Keisha."

Holden shook hands with each of the guys and then Keisha offered her hand. The group exchanged perfunctory greetings before Holden laced his fingers with Ella's.

"We ran into a park ranger a mile or so back. He said to watch out for black bears. A big one was spotted heading south," Holden lied. He pointed almost directly toward camp.

Ella's hand tensed. She must not have considered the possibility of bears last night, and that was probably for the best. Holden had learned that being stressed about danger didn't make it go away. Stress was an unnecessary distraction on a mission. All a man needed was enough fear to keep him sharp and give him a clear mind and the confidence that he could handle whatever he faced.

Damn, it dawned on him that he'd strayed far from the one philosophy that had kept him alive through countless missions as a marine. As soon as he figured out what the men after him wanted and who was ultimately behind the murders, he had every intention of reclaiming his life.

"How big?" Keisha asked.

"Maybe eight feet tall and close to six hundred pounds," Holden stated.

"Thanks for the heads-up, man," Aiden said with wide eyes as he repositioned his body east. "We'll keep watch."

"The ranger said we should make a lot of noise," Holden added.

"Cool. Good idea." Patrick paused, his gaze landing on Ella. "Do I know you?"

"I doubt it," Ella said a little too quickly, giving away her nervous tension.

Patrick's eyebrow shot up as he studied her face. "I know I've seen you before."

Chapter Fifteen

Holden squeezed Ella's fingers for reassurance. All she had to do was breathe and she'd be fine.

"I'm not from around here," she clarified, and that seemed to satisfy the coeds for the time being.

They turned to face the same direction as Patrick.

"Wouldn't hurt to find a big stick and carry it with you just in case you run into that bear," Holden said, turning in the opposite direction, west.

"Thanks for the tips," Patrick said. His gaze was fixed on Ella. "I could swear that I've seen you before. Have you been on TV?"

"Me? TV?" She shook her head and laughed. "Nah."

Patrick seemed to accept the answer but the puzzled look stayed on his face. He was scanning his memory for where he'd seen her before and that wasn't good.

"Keep watch out for that bear," Holden reminded, trying to distract Patrick.

"You got it. You, too," Patrick said before shaking his head and refocusing on his group.

When the trio disappeared, Ella exhaled.

"That was close," she said. "I almost panicked."

"You were fine," Holden reassured her, wanting to give her confidence.

"I thought I almost blew our cover," she continued as he redirected their movement toward base camp.

"We deflected them for now but there could be more hikers, and since your face has been splashed all over the media we can't be too careful," he said.

"Right," she agreed.

"So, we find what we came for and get out of here before we run into anyone else." Holden located a walking path.

"I thought your dad owned this land," she said. "Why not just kick people off?"

"First of all, I didn't want to attract any more attention to us than we already had. And this land is very near a hiking trail, so it'd be easy to end up on Pop's property," he clarified.

Back at camp, he produced a couple of power bars and bottled water. Ella already had her own travel toothbrush that she used after breakfast. Holden made quick work of doing the same and then built a small fire. Ella was already through the first box when he produced two tin cups of coffee.

The idea of going through more of his father's personal effects sat hard on Holden's chest.

"I'll never figure out how you do this so well, but I will forever be grateful that you can," she said with a little mewl that made him think of the similar sound she'd made when the two of them were in bed at Rose's house.

"You learn to make do with what you have in the military."

"Thank you for your service, by the way. I meant to say that earlier," she said, and the reverence in her voice made his chest fill with pride.

"You're welcome." Holden drained his cup and joined her at the boxes.

The ones with clothes had already been stacked next to the storage shed, so he pulled out a few more. One by one they were working their way through them. Nothing stood out in the memorabilia, except the depressing note that the most important items in his father's entire life could fit into a ten-by-twelve-foot shed.

"I thought for sure we'd find something here," he said, doing his best to hide his frustration as he stared at the last couple of boxes. This was turning out to be another dead end and they needed to get on the move again before anyone else stumbled upon the place.

"We've checked everything in these." Ella motioned toward the line of opened containers. There were a couple dozen. "Unless you think there might be something in one of those clothing boxes."

Going through his father's personal effects caused a lump to form in Holden's throat. He could only imagine what it would be like to go through the old man's clothes. His trophies and metals were personal items, but garments were even more so.

"I guess it's worth a try," he agreed.

"We don't know what we're looking for, so how can it hurt?" she asked.

"True."

"This must bring back a lot of memories," she said and there was a sad note to her voice.

"It does," he admitted. "A lot of good memories."

She smiled.

"I just saw something move and I'm pretty sure it's a copperhead." The haughtiness in his voice should've warned her that he was goading her, but she hopped to her feet faster than he'd ever seen lightning strike.

"Where?" She froze, holding perfectly still as she searched the grass.

Hearing Holden's laugh rumble from his chest had her swatting his arm. She drew her hand back pretty fast, and that got him laughing more. It was probably the stress of the last few days that had him needing a break.

"If you want my help, you're going to have to quit giving me a hard time." The pout to her lips made him want to kiss her again.

"Fine. We'll call a truce." He offered a handshake. She took it.

"No more teasing," he said. "It's just nice to have a normal conversation for a change."

Ella nodded. She shot him a look that said she got it. They both could use a sense of normalcy after everything they'd been through and what they faced ahead.

She dropped onto her knees and opened another box. "Do these make you think about what happened?"

"Yes. At first, I was filled with so much rage. I wanted to track down the men responsible for his and Karen's deaths." Holden paused, fighting back the images of Karen on his bed with blood everywhere and where his imagination always went thinking about what they'd done to his father. Guilt tore into him at the memories.

"What changed your mind?" Ella asked.

"I realized that if anything happened to me, the men responsible would never be brought to justice. I wanted to wait so I could get revenge on my own terms," he said.

"Being angry must come with the territory," she said. "I feel that way now sometimes and I get frustrated. It doesn't change anything. Won't bring back my father."

"Don't be too hard on yourself. From where I sit, you have amazing strength," he stated.

"Maybe from the outside." She pointed to the center of her chest. "In here, I feel like a fragile mess."

"Believe me, you're not." Holden moved to her side and tucked a stray strand of wheat-colored hair behind her ear.

"I wish I was more like you," she stated and it caught him off guard. "You're strong." She glanced at his chest. "And resourceful."

"You think that you're not?" he asked, trying not to let his emotions get the best of him because they had him wanting to pull her close. There was always an undeniable draw toward Ella. Were his emotions getting the best of him being around his father's things?

"I'm nothing like you," she pointed out.

Holden broke into a smile. "That's probably a good thing. I'm stubborn and difficult."

"I was going to say focused and intelligent." It was a good thing she didn't look up at that moment. Holden fisted his hands to keep them from reaching for her.

"You said your dad was into baseball." She held up a card. Holden took a couple of strides toward her. The card was encased in plastic, a collector's edition Hank Aaron. "He was my father's all-time favorite player."

"He's a legend," she agreed.

"You know Hank Aaron?" Holden asked.

"Everybody knows him," she said matter-of-factly. And then she rewarded him with a smile. "Plus, I have brothers who were obsessed with baseball."

That made more sense.

"This is the only card in here. The only thing to do with sports at all." She held it up.

A flood of warm memories bombarded Holden as he took the offering. "I haven't even seen a game in years."

"Do you miss it?" Ella asked, and the question caught him off guard.

"I guess I haven't allowed myself to think about it. You get focused and shove everything else out of your mind in order to survive. All you think about is making it through each day."

"There's something perfectly simplistic sounding about that," she said. "No complications."

"Not much of anything. You can't let yourself focus on what isn't in your life." Holden looked at the card. "To do otherwise would ensure a slip."

"You didn't miss home?" she asked.

"Only one place remotely felt like home to me. Your ranch." He didn't look at her. Before he could get too caught up in nostalgia, he reminded himself the longer they hung around the more danger they were possibly in. They needed to stay on the move and they needed to get going.

"I'm glad you found me, Holden," Ella said.

"Yeah?" he asked.

She nodded. "Not just for the obvious reason that you saved my life. I mean that I'm glad it was you who found me."

He offered a smile. He was, too. He pocketed the card, hoping that keeping it with him would make him feel somehow closer to his father. The past two years had been about trying to forget. It was time to remember. Everything.

"I'd forgotten about how much Pop loved his favorite player," he said appreciatively.

"It was in there all by itself, so I thought it might be important to him." Ella went to work on another box.

Holden dug into the clothing box in front of him and his hand hit something hard. He felt around and realized it was metal. It was the size of a small cash box but sturdier. He pulled it out.

"What is that?" Ella stopped what she was doing and moved beside him.

Holden played with the heavy metal in his hands. "Some kind of lockbox."

He looked around for something he could use to break it open.

"I'm guessing you don't have the combination." She examined the strongbox along with him.

"All I need is a crowbar." He didn't have anything close on hand.

Ella disappeared inside the shed. "There's nothing in here."

Holden picked up a rock and Ella shivered when she got a good look at it.

He set the box down and dropped the rock. Nothing happened. Not even a dent. Holden dropped down to his knees and slammed the hard edge again and again against the box. Nothing.

"My dad has a few things like that at the ranch. He uses our birthdays as combinations." She pointed to the numbers on the side.

"Here goes." Holden entered his birthday.

More nothing.

Except voices. Holden listened. It was the trio from earlier and their voices were drifting up.

"Let's clear out," he said. "We'll take this with us and play around with it once we settle into a motel."

Side by side they took down the hammocks and replaced the moving boxes.

"Where are we going next?" She looked up at him with bright, trusting eyes after he closed and locked the doors.

"I plan to find a hot shower and a soft bed for our next stop," he said.

"That sounds like heaven." She clucked her tongue. "Actually, better than heaven. But I'm grateful that I got to brush my teeth this morning."

"Little things like that make a huge difference when you've lost everything," he agreed, securing the strongbox on the back of his motorcycle.

"They really do," she agreed. And then she took one look at the bike before shaking her head. "I don't think my body will allow me to get on the back of that thing again."

"It would take a lot longer to hike down the mountain, but we can if you want," he offered.

She eyed the motorbike and then the woods. "Were you kidding about black bears earlier?"

"Afraid not," he admitted. "We can do like I told the others and make a lot of noise on our way down. Believe it or not, those bears don't want to be around us any more than we want to run into them."

"As much as that may be true, we can't walk all the way back to Texas," she said on a sigh.

"I have a surprise waiting," he said. "If you can make it down the mountain."

"Then I'll get on the back of that thing again," she said, and he almost laughed at the sound of dread in her voice.

He handed over her helmet. At least it shielded her face. Especially when she put the visor down.

"If I end up with bugs in my teeth, I know who to blame," she said as she climbed on behind him.

"I'll take the hit for that one. Just don't smile," he quipped. Despite himself, Holden laughed and it was good to get a break from his somber mood. Going through Pop's things proved more difficult than Holden had expected, but having Ella there made it tolerable. He'd forgotten what it was like to have real companionship with someone he cared about, partly because he'd never connected with someone like he did with Ella. Yeah, he cared about her. He'd fallen down that rabbit hole. Couldn't say he was especially sorry either.

Talking to Ella was easy and he was starting to enjoy the way they bantered back and forth. This was real conversation and the closest he'd come to talking about something normal in two years. Before her, he didn't realize how much he missed it. Or course, he couldn't deny that he liked talking to her more than he'd ever liked talking in general. In fact, he didn't remember being all that into conversation before spending time with her. Few people made him laugh. Fewer got his sense of humor and laughed with him.

There was something special about Ella Butler.

ELLA LET OUT a yelp of excitement as she followed Holden into the standalone garage and stood in front of the sport-utility vehicle.

"This is our ride?" she asked. "Are you serious?"

"Belongs to a friend of mine who said I could take it anytime I needed to," Holden said. "I figured this was as good a time as any to take him up on it."

"Won't he miss it?" she asked.

"He would if he was in the country." Holden moved to the workbench in the detached garage. "As for now, he's a contractor for the US military and living in Jerusalem."

"You're sure he won't be upset?" She clapped. She couldn't contain her excitement any more than a kid could refuse an ice-cream cone on a hot summer day. This was just as good. It would have AC and doors and a real seat. The banana-like wedge on Holden's motorcycle had her bottom completely numb after an hour.

"Are you kidding? He'd insist." Holden felt along a wooden workbench before his hand stopped and he came up with a set of keys.

"We won't be putting him in danger, will we?" The last thing she wanted to do was involve anyone else in their problems.

"None that he wouldn't welcome if he were stateside," Holden said. He jangled the keys. "Ready?"

"Am I?" she said. "Are you kidding? I could kiss you."

Those last words hung in the air and had come out completely on impulse.

"I didn't mean," she started to say, but words were pretty useless. Her cheeks felt like they were on fire.

"Don't be embarrassed," he said. "I want you to feel like you can relax around me."

"I got a little too comfortable," she said along with an apology. "Because I wasn't joking."

"Don't be sorry," he countered.

"The problem is that I do want to kiss you, Holden. And that's not where we need to be right now," she said and walked to the passenger's side. She didn't exhale until the SUV blocked her view of him. It was true. She liked kissing him. And where would that get either one of them? They were on the run and their heightened emotions were running away with them. Realistically, Holden would move on as soon as she was out of danger. Sure, they had chemistry. That was obvious. But real feelings?

Ella couldn't even go there. Not with him. Not with anyone. Not until she sorted out her life and got a handle on the property. Once she was clear of this danger, she'd go back to her life on the ranch, her charity projects. That life made sense to her. This, being on the run with a magnetic roamer wouldn't last. He'd get bored and move on.

Besides, Holden was in love with a ghost and Ella couldn't compete with that. Not to mention the fact that neither had a future at the moment. She expected him to unlock the door but he didn't. Instead, he came up from around the back of the SUV.

"Where should we be?" he asked, and there was so much torment in his voice. Even so, his deep timbre washed over her, warming her.

"Probably inside this vehicle and on the road to Texas," she said, turning until her back was against the door. She couldn't look at him. Not right then. Because all her defenses would come crashing down around her feet and she couldn't be that vulnerable to him right now.

"Why not right here?" he asked, and his voice was husky as he trailed his finger along the line of her jaw. He dipped down and kissed her collarbone. A thousand volts shot through her as need welled up, low in her belly.

"Holden," she started but stopped.

"What about here?" He caught her stare for a few seconds and then dipped his head down again. This time, he kissed the spot where her pulse pounded at the base of her neck.

"We shouldn't…"

"Tell me to stop and I will," he said, holding her gaze. There was so much power and promise in that one look from him. This time, she knew better than to seek comfort in his arms. How many times had he pulled away from her every time they got close already?

She tried to form the words but couldn't. She wanted him to keep going until they were lost in each other, in complete bliss and a tangle of arms and legs.

So she looked him dead in the eyes.

"What if I can't?" she asked. "What if I want this?"

Holden swallowed, slicked his tongue across his lips and captured her mouth. He was warm and tasted like the coffee they'd had earlier. Awareness trilled through her at his nearness, at how fast his heart pounded. She brought her hand up to his chest and ran her fingers along the layers of muscle. She smoothed her hand over his masculine pecs.

He captured both of her hands in his, braiding their fingers, and lifted them over her head. Movement thrust her breasts forward and he groaned when the tips of her nipples brushed against him. They beaded and her breasts swelled, needing to be touched. He let go of her right hand and palmed her breast as she arched her back.

Ella opened her eyes and the world tilted when Holden did the same. A bolt of electricity shot through her and she immediately realized that she was in deep trouble.

"Can I keep going?" he asked.

"Yes," she responded without thinking—thinking would have her realize this wouldn't go anywhere. One night sounded amazing and great sex would dim some of the tension pinging between them...

All rational thinking stalled when he brushed his thumb across her nipple and her stomach quivered. Tension corded her muscles, needing relief that only Holden could give.

Ella leaned against the solid vehicle behind her and brought her hands up to Holden's shoulders. Her fingers dug into his shirt as he made her body hum with need by trailing his tongue across her collarbone. Not having sex had never felt so sexy.

His hands cupped her bottom and she wrapped her legs around his toned midsection after he lifted her off her feet. She tunneled her fingers in his hair and his tongue slid in her mouth as his erection pressed into her sex. A familiar force started building inside her body as her tongue roamed freely. She bit his bottom lip as ecstasy pulsed through her. All her senses heightened, her breath started coming out in quick bursts and she could feel that his was, too.

The fact that they were in a garage fully clothed took nothing away from the intimacy and heat of the moment.

"Holden," she managed to say against his mouth, breathless.

"I know." He nipped the conversation in the bud. "This can't go any further."

"Not right now," she said, trying to steady her rapid breathing.

He didn't immediately move and she was grateful.

"This, whatever's happening between us, is moving too fast," she said.

"I know." He surprised her with his response. "We need to take it slow."

"That would be smart," she said, even though her body begged for more.

"We have time to do this the right way," he continued.

A trill of awareness goose bumped her arms and her stomach free-fell. He feathered a kiss on her neck. And then another slow one against her lips. She loved the way he tasted.

"That's the only way I know how to do things," she said. There was so much craziness going on all around them, and yet this was the only thing that made sense to her. She'd never felt this strong of a pull toward another man and that excited and scared her at the same time.

"I could really like you," he said so quietly she almost didn't hear him.

Ella didn't respond. She just stood there with Holden for countless minutes, letting the world stop for just one moment. She wasn't grieving or running or scared. And the world had a strange sense of rightness that she'd never felt before.

Without analyzing it, she breathed in the calm feeling that came over her. Then she wrapped her arms around Holden's neck and looked him in the eye. He had that same hunger she felt deep in her stomach and she needed to let go with him. Life was crazy. Tomorrow wasn't guaranteed. They had *this* moment. Right now. Letting it slip through their fingers would be a costly mistake.

Ella pressed up onto her tiptoes and his mouth came crashing down on hers. No words were needed to move things forward. She could feel his body humming with the same awareness and desire rippling through her.

He brought his hand up and cradled her neck, tilting her head back a little as his tongue brushed against the tips of her teeth. She pushed him back long enough to help him out of his shirt and a few seconds later hers joined his on the floor.

Holden pressed his lips to hers as he cupped her breasts and groaned. "You're beautiful."

"So are you," she said against his mouth.

His hands wrapped around her back, unsnapped her bra and then it joined the shirts on the floor.

Her chest rose and fell quickly as tension heightened her nerves with anticipation. She brought her hands to the waistband of his jeans and tugged at the zipper. He helped her take his off and then her jogging shorts and panties flew to the floor.

She pulled his masculine body against her, her back against the SUV. His erection pulsed against her stomach and she wrapped her legs around his midsection as he lifted her. He eased her down on his full shaft, dipping the head inside and groaned with pleasure when he discovered that she was ready for him. She wiggled her hips until she could take in his full length.

"Holden," she whispered, tangling her fingers in his thick, wavy hair. The feeling of her naked skin against his brought on a wave of ecstasy and anticipation.

He drove himself inside her, his hands on either side of her hips as his mouth found hers.

She said his name again and he thrust deeper in response. Her entire body hummed with need as all her emotions heightened. She matched his thrust this time and then the next. Faster. Harder. Deeper. Until her entire body begged for release. His hands caressed her bottom as he drove inside her until she tipped over the edge of the precipice and free-fell as explosions filled her.

"Holden." She breathed his name as she felt him reach the peak. His muscles corded with tension as she ground her sex on his erection until he rocketed toward the same release.

She had no idea how long he stood holding her in the garage before he finally opened his eyes.

"Ella." Hearing her name spoken softly into her ear was the sweetest sound coming from him.

As her breathing returned to normal, Holden pressed his forehead to hers. He didn't immediately move away and she liked that he didn't. His hands cupped her neck and hers had dropped to his waist. It felt so right to stand there with him in the quiet.

Neither spoke as he eased her to her feet. Neither had to. The silence was comforting. He picked up her clothes first and she admired his glorious body for another few seconds before he dressed.

He gazed at her with a look of appreciation as she dressed and it felt like the most natural thing to be naked with Holden, another foreign feeling.

Once they were dressed, he palmed the keys. He clicked the button to unlock the door and then opened her side first.

Life was short and all her careful planning felt stifling now. Being with him made her feel alive. At first, she'd chalked it up to adrenaline rushes and danger. But it was Holden. What was so wrong with taking it a step further? Of completely letting go and being with this man in every sense of the words?

One word came to mind. *Love.*

Ella had fallen down that slope and risked her heart being shattered. Sure, she'd been with other men, but she'd never felt this deep of a connection during sex than she did with Holden. Mind-altering, heart-all-in sex.

And when he walked away, her heart would be shattered into a million tiny pieces and scattered across the ranch. She'd already lost her father. While this was no comparison, she couldn't risk losing anyone else. There wouldn't be enough pieces of her to pick up.

Their temporary shelter against the world was about to disappear. She knew full well that they couldn't stay there forever. And yet a piece of her heart wanted exactly that, to hide out with Holden until the rest of the world forgot about both of them, to stay in each other's arms, found instead of lost in the world.

"Ready?" he asked, turning the key in the ignition.

"As much as I'll ever be," she responded.

"Let's see what kind of trouble we can get ourselves into," he said with a wink and a smile that unleashed a thousand butterflies in her stomach.

Ella, who never let anyone break inside her walls, was in serious trouble.

Chapter Sixteen

The highway stretched on for miles. Ella had finally fallen asleep in the passenger seat. And Holden tried to ignore the ache in his chest. He'd stepped in where he had no business going earlier. Caring about her more wasn't going to help their...*situation*, for lack of a better word, one bit.

The physical attraction pinging between them was one thing. This was another. It was so much deeper than that. The air had changed between them after sex and he needed to protect her more than he needed to breathe. The problem was that nothing had changed. Being seen with him was still a death sentence. He had to figure out a way to give her back her life. He'd bring justice to the men who'd killed his loved ones. Holden was alive again for the first time in two years and his anger bubbled to the surface—anger that had been at a steady simmer since he'd walked inside his house and seen that lifeless body.

And he had a problem because his feelings for Ella were out of control. He needed to bring them back down to earth because they were dangerous for her. It didn't matter the pain it would cause him; he had to push her away for her own sake.

Could he, though?

Holden watched as cars zipped around him. Morning light was close and there was a motel off the highway where they could get a couple of hours of shut-eye. He grabbed a room key and walked her inside.

The place had two full-size beds and a decent shower, so they could clean up and get a nice meal not far from there. Holden had made this drive on his motorcycle more than once over the years. A piece of him felt contentment with Ella that he'd never experienced before. Leaving her was going to hurt like hell.

"You shower first," he said.

"Okay." She blinked her eyes up at him and he'd be damned but he kissed her.

Holden palmed his father's favorite baseball card as he waited for Ella to finish her shower. When this was all over, he would circle back to Rose. One way or another, this would end. Ella made him see that he'd stopped living, stopped caring. The only thing that had been keeping him alive was his promise to his father and the fact that Rose needed him.

He flipped the card around his fingers, frustrated that he was missing something. His father had been obsessed with Hank Aaron and then Rose had passed along the message 1-9-6-4, which could be a combination or address.

Holden studied the card.

"What are you thinking about so intensely?" Ella

asked, and he hadn't even realized she'd turned off the water.

"I'm missing something." He sighed sharply. "What does 1-9-6-4 mean?"

"A home address?" she asked.

"I thought about that, too. Seems like I would remember something and that could be anywhere." He held up the card and flipped it around his fingers. Staring at the back, he said, "1-9-6-4 could be 1964, as in the year."

Hank Aaron's batting average in 1964 was 340.

"What does 340 mean?" she asked.

He pulled the strongbox from his duffel and set it on the bed in between them. She looked up at him and it seemed to dawn on her.

"The combination." Holden punched in the numbers and the box cracked open. He thumbed through ledgers, pages and pages of documented illegal activity. His father was involved in illegal activity?

"Pop got himself into trouble," he said. From what Holden could tell, his father was being forced to use his interstate moving company to move other things. "And the Hampshire Police Chief is involved."

Ella touched his shoulder.

"They were after Pop all along," he said, and it was like a balloon in his chest had deflated when he exhaled.

"Why? Seems like he was cooperating." Ella studied the documents over his shoulder.

An envelope fell out of the papers with Holden's name on it.

He ripped it open. The note from his father read "If

you're reading this, things must've gotten bad. Chief Mallory approached me a year ago with an offer he said I couldn't refuse. He wasn't kidding and made it clear. I cooperated. At first, it was small stuff, a little bit of narcotics and weapons. It grew fast. Then one of my drivers disappeared with a shipment. Forgive me? Love, Pop."

"They must've tried to get to him through you," Ella said.

"All this time I thought it was my fault. I thought I did something to cause the deaths that followed me. I thought I was responsible for Pop being killed." Holden fisted the paper. A mix of sadness and anger and a little bit of hope that this could end filled him.

"I bet the people who showed up at your place that morning thought they would find you, wanting to use you against your father." Ella sat back on her knees. "Karen was in the wrong place at the wrong time."

"That cost her her life, which is something I take seriously."

Ella nodded. "The cop tried to kill you. The police chief must've believed you knew or were in on it somehow."

"And then I went into hiding and they couldn't track me. They tortured and killed Pop because they believed he was involved in that shipment disappearing," he said, anger filled him. "I wish I'd known what Pop had gotten involved in."

"Your dad must've realized how deadly this information could be," she said. "He was trying to protect you."

Holden no longer cared what happened to him. He

had to bring the chief to justice for his father and Karen's sakes. Otherwise, their deaths meant nothing. "There was a young attorney general who'd been trying to make a case against the chief for something. I can't remember what exactly. I don't even know if he's still after the chief, but I need to turn this information over to him."

"First, we'll call. Make sure he knows this is coming from you and that you are in no way involved," she said. "And then we'll FedEx the documents. This is all the proof he'll need to bring the chief to justice."

"I don't want to wait. We can stop off on the way to Cattle Barge to send these," he said.

"We'll make a copy. Just in case," she said.

"Let's get out of here." Holden dared to imagine a normal life again. Friday night date nights and a cold beer while watching a game. It had been out of reach for so long that it seemed foreign now. Like all that was a lifetime ago, similar to when he'd returned from overseas after three tours.

And it was still at arm's length. Because he was still wanted for murder.

THE MOTEL ROOM was wiped down and empty inside of twenty minutes. Tension radiated from Holden as he took the wheel of the SUV.

"It's going to work out," Ella reassured, noticing the white-knuckle grip Holden had on the steering wheel.

"What if they've gotten to the attorney general?" He started the engine and navigated out of the pay-by-the-night motel parking lot. "He may want to strike a deal instead of clearing my name."

"He won't," she reassured. "We have definitive proof that you weren't involved and if the attorney general doesn't want to do the right thing, we'll go to the media."

Holden nodded and she was satisfied that he believed her.

"I wish Pop would've told me before. I could've prevented his death." He pulled onto the highway.

"And involve you even more?" she asked. "He loved you too much for that. You would've taken this up for him and he knew it. You would've ended up dead and he wouldn't have been able to live with himself."

"I had a chance. I could've gotten to him sooner," he said, and she could see the torment he was putting himself through.

"You have to accept the fact that even though you're a grown man capable of defending yourself and everyone else around you, your father is still your father. If he's anything like you, and I'm guessing the apple didn't fall far from the tree, then he would rather trade his life if it meant saving yours. Besides, he probably blamed himself for not figuring a way out of this sooner."

Holden paused thoughtfully. He focused on the patch of road ahead with a nod.

"I just wish he hadn't been so stubborn," he said. "I could've kept him alive."

"I'm sorry, Holden. I really am. Fathers are hardwired to protect their children no matter how old we are. Yours sounds like a good man, an honest man until his back was against the wall. He didn't deserve what happened to him. And neither did you." She twirled a pen in between her fingers.

Holden gave her a look of appreciation.

"There was no way I could've hurt Karen. I hope the attorney general will be able to see it. I wasn't even there when it happened," he said.

"The attorney general won't overlook that fact," she reassured.

"I hope you're right because you know what the implication is if you're wrong," he said.

She did know. It meant that they were about to turn over the only true evidence in the case, the only evidence that could clear Holden. "We'll make a copy and keep the original. We'll threaten to use the media if he doesn't cooperate. It'll work out."

"I wish I had your optimism."

Morning traffic was thickening as the sun rose.

Ella sipped the coffee that he'd bought from the minimart. It tasted burned in comparison to the stuff Holden made over nothing but a few fire logs, but the caffeine would do the trick. "This attorney general person, is he legitimate?"

"I believe so," he said.

"First impressions are usually right." Even when he had a beard covering his face and hadn't spoken to a person in almost two years, Ella had known that there was something still good about Holden. She was intuitive enough to realize that he was holding something in, too.

His demeanor had changed like it did every time their defenses started tumbling down. It never lasted long and she could see that he was still holding on to the past. He'd never be able to move into the future—a future that she was beginning to hope that the two of them could spend getting to know each other better— if he couldn't let go of the past.

"I guess." He shrugged, keeping his focus on the stretch of highway in front of them. "We'll stop off along Interstate 40 to give the impression we're heading west. It'll add time to our trip but it'll be worth it. In case."

Holden didn't finish. The rest of that sentence involved what would happen if the attorney general didn't believe him. And they both knew what that meant. She could eventually go home but he would have to disappear. Again.

THE CALL WITH the attorney general, Calvin Edwards, had gone better than expected. Holden had tilted the phone so that Ella could hear. He'd said he wanted her perspective. She'd had a good feeling when they ended the conversation.

An hour later, they stopped off at a mailing center.

"This will give Edwards everything he needs to go after them," Holden said to Ella under his breath at the copy company's business center. He placed the package inside the small mailing box and sealed it at the self-check counter. "If it makes it."

"It will," she urged. "Make sure to get a signature."

"And receive confirmation where?" he asked.

She thought about it for a moment. "My email should be fine."

"No way," he said.

"Why not?" she asked. "It's perfect. You don't have one and no one involved would connect me to your father's case."

Holden conceded. He punched in the mix of letters and numbers as she spoke. He printed the mailing label and placed it on the small box before taking to the cashier.

"Two years is a long time." Holden leaned down and brushed a kiss on her lips after taking a deep breath.

"The timing of this is perfect," she said. "Everyone involved has moved on. No one is expecting evidence to show up now. It'll come out of the blue. You stay under the radar a few more weeks, like Edwards said, and the key players will already be in jail."

As they walked out, Holden fished his cell out of his pocket and held it flat on his palm. "Your turn."

"Sheriff Sawmill, this is Ella Butler," Ella said into the phone after dialing a number.

"I have good news for you, Miss Ella," Sheriff Sawmill said. "We have Suffolk's son in custody."

"Why? What happened?" She tilted the phone so that Holden could hear.

"The shell casings on his father's shotgun matched those at the crime scene. When we hauled his father in, he did the right thing and stepped forward," he said. "Suffolk's gun wasn't stolen and his son took it right from inside the back door."

Ella looked at Holden, searching for something that she wasn't sure could exist so early in their relationship.

"It's over, Miss Ella. We got him. Handcuffed him this morning," he said. "It's safe for you to come home."

"He's responsible for both attacks? For the rock at Devil's Lid?" she asked. Tears brimmed at that last word because without her father she wondered if Hereford would still feel like home. What would it be now? An odd feeling settled in her chest. Nothing felt the same anymore, nor had it since her father's death, and she doubted it ever would again. And she had to wonder how much the man standing next to her influenced that.

"We believe so," Sawmill supplied.

"Thank you, Sheriff," Ella said.

"I didn't want to release a statement to the media until I delivered the message to you personally," he said. "They're outside now."

It would be all over the news soon.

"I appreciate it," she said. "Can you give me five minutes to tell my family that I'm okay?"

"You bet," Sheriff Sawmill said.

The two exchanged goodbyes and she made a quick call to May, who promised to let the others know immediately.

"Everyone's fine, other than my sister having the flu. It's over. And I should feel more relieved," Ella said to Holden.

"Do you think they have the wrong guy?" he asked.

"I wouldn't say that exactly. I'm not sure what's wrong." She couldn't pinpoint what was going on in her mind. "It's probably just me. I'm off. This whole experience has been surreal and it's just hard to believe that it's all over. Everything feels different about the ranch now. The second I start to feel relief about going home

I realize that my dad's not going to be there. Suddenly, Hereford doesn't feel as much like home as it used to."

Holden took her in his arms and she buried her face in his strong chest. Those strong arms of his wrapped around her and she couldn't deny that this felt like home.

"Will you come back with me?" She blinked away tears and looked up at him.

"I should check on Rose," he said before pressing a kiss to her forehead.

"We could send for her. She hasn't been away in a while and she might enjoy being on the ranch for a few days." Ella wasn't sure if she'd convinced him but Rose was always welcome at Hereford.

Holden stood there for a long moment. Ella pressed up to her tiptoes and placed her hands on his shoulders. She looked into his eyes before kissing him. There was no hesitation in his reaction, his lips pressed to her and his tongue tasting her.

Ella pulled back first and looked into his intense blue eyes. "Can you give me a few more days?"

His face broke into a smile as he trailed his finger along her cheek. "You can be convincing when you set your mind to something, can't you?"

"Only when it's the right thing to do," she countered, matching his smile. "Does that mean you'll stay?"

"Yes."

She wrapped her arms around his neck and rewarded him with another kiss. Happiness lifted the weight from her shoulders. They were going home. Even if Hereford was a temporary stop for Holden.

Chapter Seventeen

Being back in Cattle Barge reminded Ella of what a media circus the town had become. A hot shower, May's cooking and Holden nearby would go a long way toward making her feel like she could deal with it all again.

Of course, she would feel better if she could access the memory buzzing around in the back of her thoughts. Trying to force it threatened to split her head open. "Remind me to take a couple of ibuprofen the minute we get to Hereford."

Even with the pain, her excitement was building.

"We have some." Holden kept one hand firmly on the wheel and the other reached around and retrieved the duffel.

"I forgot all about these," she said. They'd been on the road twelve hours steady aside from a pair of bathroom breaks since leaving the motel. Ten was pretty much her limit. Even in the comfortable SUV, the ride dragged on and it was probably because she missed being home so much.

"Are you hungry?" Holden asked.

"I can make it. Another forty minutes and we're

there." She was already thinking about May's cooking, the kitchen. The place was an old-world farmhouse with the oversize single sink, and had white cabinets and granite countertops. There was a hand-carved wooden table in the kitchen that stretched almost end to end. One side was used for food prep and the rest of the table was used for eating. She couldn't wait to show Holden around the main house.

To avoid traffic, she'd directed Holden to a back road. There was no way she wanted to face the media. Not now. All she wanted to do was get home and call her brothers. She wanted to check on her younger sister, Cadence, to see if she was recovering from the flu she'd caught as everything was going down about their father. Cadence rarely ever got sick and stress had most likely weakened her immune system.

"Feeling better?" Holden asked a few minutes later.

"They're starting to kick in." Thank the stars for pain relievers.

"Are you worried about being home again?"

"Not as much as I thought I would be," she admitted, and it had everything to do with the man sitting next to her. The feeling of missing her dad wasn't going away anytime soon, but she felt ready to face the fact that he was gone, and that was a huge step for her.

Ella leaned her head back. A comfortable silence sat between them as Holden navigated the country road and she waited for the last of her headache to ease. She checked the time. They were ten minutes from home now and Ella's excitement only increased now that she was so close to Hereford.

Out of nowhere, the sound of a bullet split the air and the SUV spun a hard right. Ella gasped as the vehicle rammed into a tree. Airbags deployed. The next thing she knew she heard a door open and saw Holden being dragged out of the driver's seat.

It took a second to register that he wasn't fighting back. Was he conscious?

Ella tried to work her seat belt but it wouldn't budge and her fingers were so shaky. Panic seized her lungs as she tried to climb out anyway. How had the man gotten Holden out so quickly? She craned her neck to the left and then to the right but couldn't find him. "Holden."

The fact that there was no response chilled her to the bone.

"Holden," she shouted, louder this time.

A hand wrapped around her mouth. She tried to bite the fingers. Failed.

"You just won't die," the masculine voice said. And she absolutely knew that this man was there for her. Because that memory she'd been trying to reach came crashing down around her at the sound of his voice. He'd shouted for her to stop when she'd taken off running. He was the man who was trying to kill her, Troy Alderant. He was the developer who'd tried to buy Suffolk's land.

Old Man Suffolk's son was in jail. He'd confessed. Why would an innocent man confess to a crime he didn't commit? All the details of the conversation she'd had with the sheriff jammed in her brain. Nothing made sense. Except from somewhere deep down she knew this was the man Sheriff Sawmill should be looking for.

She was jerked out of the passenger seat and then

thrown onto the unforgiving dirt. Her hands were rammed behind her back and tied. She struggled, kicking and screaming.

But Alderant was strong. Too strong.

"Holden," she shouted out of panic and desperation.

She rolled over in time to see a leering face coming toward her. "Why are you doing this?"

"You and your little pet projects. You couldn't leave well enough alone, could you?" he mumbled. "You don't have my vision for Cattle Barge and that's your problem. Donating more land for animals instead of taking advantage of the lake as a destination is beyond me."

What was he talking about? He'd been around the past year or so, trying to get involved in local politics. Was he trying to develop the land for something? He must've had his eye on Suffolk's land and the surrounding area.

And she'd accidently gotten in his way.

"We were coming to terms until you ruined it," Alderant said, dragging her by her feet behind the SUV.

If he'd put his plans out in the public too early, residents would've denied it. People had been trying to develop the lake for as long as Ella could remember. Proposals were always being shot down in town hall meetings. This guy must've figured if he bought up enough of the land, he'd have more voting rights. Once he hit the tipping point he could make his plans known and no one would be able to block him.

Ella gasped. Could he be responsible for her father's murder? "Why'd you kill my father? Did he find out about your plans?"

A strangled noise tore from his throat. "I didn't. Your father's death was the best thing that ever happened to me. He was always in Suffolk's ear and the old man wouldn't have sold his land without Butler's approval. I wish I'd thought of killing him. I seized the moment, figuring if I got rid of you I'd be set. Your siblings don't share your passion for animals. No one would've been left to block me. I'd followed you for days when you took that walk on Devil's Lid. I saw my chance to make this go away, to make *you* go away and to keep my name out of it. Everyone would assume your father's killer had set his sights on you."

Ella kicked harder as she realized the other end of the line that tied her hands together was being secured around the back of the SUV.

"But there was a confession," she said.

"To keep his old man out of jail, I presume." The icy voice sent chills down her spine. "You can fight all you want. This time, you die."

A figure launched toward Alderant. Holden?

The two went down in a tangle of fists.

"Grab the phone, call 9-1-1 and get out of here," Holden shouted to Ella.

She used the SUV as balance to get to her feet. Her hands were still tied together behind her back and she needed something to cut the tie. Her pulse raced as she moved toward the open door of the SUV and raked the corner between her hands. Her wrists hurt like hell but adrenaline dulled the pain.

It felt like it took forever to break free from her bindings. She immediately located the cell and called 9-1-

1, as instructed, keeping one eye on the fight going on a few yards away from her. The two were on their feet now as she relayed details of their location to the dispatcher.

Holden slammed his fist into Alderant's face. His head snapped backward. The two struggled for something. *A weapon?* And she watched in horror as a metal blade was driven into Holden.

Ella screamed and Alderant glanced toward her, giving Holden the second he needed to regain the upper hand. Holden took the knife, tossed it far away and landed a punch so hard Alderant fell backward.

In a beat, Holden was straddled over Alderant, pounding him until he went still. And then Holden dropped, too.

"Holden." Panicked, Ella ran to him as he lay splayed out on his back. He looked like a doll someone had tossed onto the floor in a hurry and then left behind. His legs were bent and twisted at odd angles. There was blood everywhere, soaking his shirt and jeans. She couldn't even allow herself to think that anything had happened to him as she dropped down beside him. Her lungs felt like they would collapse and her throat closed up. Her chest seized as she saw him there, helpless. He'd taken that knife for her.

Ella folded forward next to his ear. His eyes were closed and he didn't move. Was he breathing? Panic squeezed her chest, making it almost impossible to take in air as she heard the faint sounds of sirens in the night air.

"Breathe," she said in his ear, fighting against the

wall of emotions threatening to break down and come crashing around her. She searched for a pulse on his wrist, any sign to tell her that he was still alive.

And then his eyes blinked open. Those gorgeous blue eyes of his. Tears streaked her cheeks.

"I love you," she whispered into his ear. "Stay with me. Please."

His eyes closed as the cavalry arrived.

"Help us, please," she said to the first officer on the scene. "That man caused us to wreck and stabbed my boyfriend."

Alderant was still knocked out cold as he was cuffed. He was going to jail for the rest of his life.

At least for Ella, justice would be served. As for her father, she was resolved to help the sheriff find the person responsible.

THE RIDE TO the hospital in the sheriff's SUV seemed to take forever. Once there, the coffee tasted watered-down but she was grateful for the caffeine boost after she'd downed several cups. There never was much else to do in a hospital while waiting on a loved one than drink cup after cup. She'd paced the halls the entire night even though the doctor had visited with her hours ago and said that Holden would be okay. She'd asked to see him but the doctor asked her to wait until Holden woke. That was four hours ago.

"Ma'am?" a female voice said, startling Ella out of her thoughts.

"Yes."

"You can go in now," the nurse wearing the name tag Roberta said.

"Thank you." Ella didn't waste time turning down the hall and rushing past the nurses' station. She already knew Holden was in room 132. She pushed open the door, scared of what condition she might find him in.

"Finally, the view is worth looking at in here," he said with a smile that reminded her of the fact he was on pretty good pain medication.

"Holden." She rushed to his side and took his hand. "How do you feel?"

"Better now."

She eased onto the side of the bed, afraid she'd hurt him if she moved too fast.

"You can't hurt me," he said with the smile that was so good at breaking down her walls.

"Doctor says you're going to be fine." She looked into those blue eyes of his. Those gorgeous blue eyes.

"He'll let me out later today if everything goes well," he said.

"Is that a good idea?" Panic gripped her.

"Yeah. I want to be with you."

"I'll stay here," she offered.

"It's not a bad injury. I'll be fine by dinner. And there's something I need to say that can't wait."

Ella tensed, afraid he was about to drop the bomb that it was time the two of them parted ways. Her heart would shred but she forced a game face.

"Life without you isn't living, Ella. I'm all in. I'm in love with you and I'd be the happiest man on earth if you would do me the honor of marrying me. I know it's early and we haven't had a long time to get to know each other. But I feel like I've known you all my life. I've made a lot of mistakes but this is a choice I feel good about. The choice I'm making is *you*."

Ella dared to hope this could be real because she felt it just as strongly. "Are you sure this isn't the medication talking?"

"Not a chance. I want to spend the rest of my life with you, but I'll wait until you're sure."

"I don't need time. I need you. Yes, I'll be your wife." Ella wiped away joyful tears streaming down her cheeks. "I fell in love with you the second I looked into your eyes and saw what kind of man you really are, the one I want to spend the rest of my life getting to know even better."

"I love you, Ella," Holden said as he looked up at her. There was so much love in those blue eyes. "I'm done drifting. You're my home."

A WAVE OF gratitude washed over Ella as she woke from a good night's sleep in her own bed for the second time since Alderant's arrest. The other side was empty, so Holden must already be up. The doctor wouldn't be thrilled but she had a feeling that Holden had a good handle on what was best for him while he recovered.

Besides, knowing him, he was probably making a cup of coffee for May. Lucky her. Ella was more than pleased that two of the most important people in her life got along so well. Her brothers would most likely be more critical, protective instinct being what it was, but Holden was exactly the kind of guy they'd hang out with. And soon the two of them would be married. Her brothers would never argue against a man who made her this happy.

Ella stretched and pushed off the covers. She could use caffeine and a pair of pain relievers.

The news had broken last night about the scandal involving the chief of police. Apparently, the attorney general had wanted to act fast before word leaked of the kind of evidence in his possession. The internet couldn't get enough of replaying a police chief in handcuffs. Holden would finally see justice served for his father and Karen. And when he'd gone to bed last night, it was as if a weight had been lifted.

Ella moved to the dresser to find a pair of jogging pants to throw on so she could find her fiancé. Rose would be flying in later today and Ella couldn't wait for her to see Hereford.

A folded piece of paper caused Ella to freeze. She'd forgotten about the note her father had left there before his death. She picked it up, thinking that his hands had touched the same places not so long ago. Ella pressed the paper to her chest and forced back the tears threatening.

She opened the paper and read the words.

You haven't hiked Devil's Lid since you were little. A trip there might just help you find where you belong.
—D

Ella's heart fisted and tears streamed down her cheeks as she realized that her father had been trying to lead her to Holden. That, even now, she felt like her father was looking out for her.

And even though he was gone, she knew in her heart that he would always watch over her.

* * * * *

SCENE OF THE CRIME: MEANS AND MOTIVE

CARLA CASSIDY

To Bob and Jenny Offutt, thanks for the
wonderful hospitality we received when we
stayed with you at your beautiful resort,
Crystal Cove Bed and Breakfast in Branson.

Chapter One

FBI Special Agent Jordon James hated two things—winter and murder—and she was about to be immersed in the middle of both. She frowned and stared out the small window of the helicopter that had carried her from Kansas City to the rousing tourist town of Branson, Missouri.

When they'd left Kansas City the ground had been winter brown and the temperature had been a balmy forty-five. Unfortunately, as they approached the Branson airport, the temperature had dropped into the teens and four inches of snow had fallen in the small vacation destination overnight.

As the helicopter circled for the landing, visions of a beach with a bright sun, a chaise lounge and a fruity alcoholic drink flirted in Jordon's head. She'd booked a long-awaited vacation in Florida for the end of next week. Hopefully, this mess in Branson could be cleaned up soon enough that she wouldn't have to postpone the long-awaited vacation.

She was here only in an advisory position as a favor between her FBI director and the Branson mayor. All she knew was that there had been three murders in as many months committed in a popular bed-and-breakfast. The latest murder victim had been stabbed to death and discovered by a maid in her room the day before.

Jordon played nice with others when it was absolutely necessary, but she preferred to work alone. She had a feeling that Director Tom Langford had tapped her for this job, knowing that she would have to try to work with a police chief who probably didn't want her here.

"It builds character to step out of your comfort zone." She wished she had a dime for every time Tom had said that to her in the last couple of years. "Don't be a cowboy, Jordon. That's what nearly got you killed a year ago," he'd reminded her right before she'd left.

The heart-shaped pattern of cigarette-burn scars on her left hip itched as memories of an old cellar and a serial killer named Ralph Hicks flashed in her head.

It had been nearly a year since she'd almost become the sixth victim of the man who had tortured and killed five other women over a six-month period in the Kansas City area. Thankfully, she had been the one who had walked out of that dank, terrifying cellar and Ralph Hicks had come out in a body bag.

The bump of the helicopter touching down snapped her back to the here and now. Jordon thanked the pilot, grabbed her two bags and climbed down to the tarmac, where a uniformed police officer greeted her.

"Agent James, I'm Lieutenant Mark Johnson." He shouted above the whoop whoop of the helicopter blades as the aircraft took off once again.

He grabbed her bags from her. "Good to have you here. My car is parked over here." He turned and headed for the parking lot in the distance. An icy gust of wind half stole her breath away as she quickly followed behind him.

Within minutes they were in his patrol car with a steady flow of heated air blowing in her face. "Have you been to Branson before?" he asked when they pulled away from the airport.

"Never, although I've certainly heard a lot about it from coworkers who have been here," she replied. She held her hands up to the air vents and squinted against the late-afternoon sunshine that glared off the snow cover.

At least the highway they traveled had been cleared, but as he turned onto a narrow snowpacked street that headed straight downhill, her breath caught in the back of her throat.

They had gone from city highway to thick woods and a precarious country road with a simple right-hand turn. "Diamond Cove is down this way," Mark said. "Chief of Police Gabriel Walters is waiting for you there." He eased up on the gas as the back end of the car slid ominously to the left.

Every muscle in Jordon's body tensed and didn't relax again until they had turned into a driveway in front of a cozy-looking log cabin. He parked next to a police car that was already there and shut off the engine.

"Welcome to Diamond Cove Bed-and-Breakfast," Mark said. "This is the main office and dining area." He pointed to the right. "As you can see through the trees up on the ridge there are four cabins that hold two suites each. The latest victim, Sandy Peters, was found in her bed in unit three yesterday morning by one of the housekeeping staff."

Jordon gazed at the four small log cabins with front porches. With the lack of leaves on the trees they were easily visible. Outside each doorway were two rocking chairs for the guests' pleasure.

In the spring and summer the thick woods that surrounded the cabins would hide them from view. The air would be filled with birdsong and squirrels would provide comic relief with their antics. Those rocking chairs would make perfect perches to nature-watch.

On the surface, the Diamond Cove resort appeared to be nestled on a secluded mountainside and promised peace and seclusion for the city-weary. But the peace had been shattered by three horrendous murders.

Mark opened his car door and Jordon did the same.

A gust of frigid air greeted her and snow crunched underfoot as she got out of the car. Once again she thought of the beach and released a frosty, deep sigh.

"Follow me," he said after grabbing her bags from the backseat.

He bypassed the front door and instead led her around the building on a wraparound porch. They passed a beautiful waterfall that was obviously heated as the water trickled merrily over rocks and into a small pond despite the below-freezing temperature.

They entered the building and stepped into the main dining room. The air smelled of a hint of cinnamon, wood smoke and rich, freshly brewed coffee.

It was a small, cozy area with two long tables draped in elegant white cloths. Fat white candles and crystal salt and pepper shakers marked the center of each table. A bookcase holding preserves, jellies and cookbooks for sale was against one wall, and a fireplace with two chairs added to the homey atmosphere.

Jordon took all of this in with a single glance, for it was the man seated in one of the chairs by the fireplace that captured her full attention.

Chief of Police Gabriel Walters held a cup of coffee in his hand and stared into the flames of the crackling fire. He was apparently so deep in thought he hadn't even heard them come in.

His black hair was neatly cut and broad shoulders

filled out the dark blue uniform shirt. His profile indicated a strong jawline and a perfectly straight nose.

"Chief?" Mark said hesitantly.

He shot up out of the chair and a touch of annoyance flashed across his handsome features. It was there only a moment and then covered by a smile that warmed Jordon right down to her frozen toes.

He might not mean the smile, but it didn't matter. He wore the gesture well even though it didn't quite light up the depths of his intense blue eyes.

"Special Agent James… I'm Chief Walters," he said and took her hand for a firm, no-nonsense shake.

"Please, make it Jordon," she replied.

He nodded and released her hand. "Jordon it is. Please, have a seat. Can I get you a cup of coffee?"

"That would be great," she replied. She unzipped her coat, shrugged it off and sat in the chair next to his in front of the fireplace.

He walked over to Mark and spoke so softly to the man that Jordon couldn't hear. Mark nodded a goodbye to Jordon and left the way they had come.

She watched as Gabriel moved over to a small table that held a coffeemaker and all the accoutrements for all tastes. "Cream? Sugar?" he asked.

"Black is fine," she replied. The man was definitely hot. He boasted not only wonderfully broad shoulders, but also slim hips and a stomach that didn't appear to hold an ounce of body fat.

He hadn't offered her the choice of calling him

by his given name and that alone told her he might not be happy to see her. She'd seen him for only a minute and already she had him pegged as intense and probably uptight and rigid.

His physical attractiveness definitely stirred a little fire of heat in the pit of her stomach, but if her suspicions about his personality were right, then she had a feeling it wouldn't be long before she might want to pinch his head off. Time would tell.

He held the coffee cup out to her and she took it with a murmured thanks. Then he returned to the chair next to her. "I don't know how much you know about what's going on here."

"No real specifics. I was only told that there have been three murders here, the most recent victim discovered yesterday morning."

He nodded. "Sandy Peters. She was thirty-four years old and a mystery writer. According to the owners of the resort, she came here every year in January to spend a couple of weeks holed up and writing."

"Married? Divorced?"

"Single, and according to everyone I spoke to yesterday who was close to her, she wasn't dating anyone," he replied. "Besides, she was killed in the same manner as the other two victims."

"Stabbed to death," Jordon said.

"That's right. My investigation hasn't turned up anything the three victims have in common other than they were all guests here at Diamond Cove at the time of their deaths. In fact, they were the only guests here at the time when they were killed."

Jordon took a sip of the coffee and leaned back in the chair. The warmth and scent of the fire combined with the deep smooth tone of his voice would make it easy to be lulled into a semicoma if they weren't talking about murder.

She leaned forward and caught a whiff of his pleasant, woodsy-scented cologne. "So, this doesn't sound like it's about any specific victimology, but tell me about the other victims anyway."

"The first one was twenty-five-year-old Samantha Kent. She and her husband had rented a suite just before Thanksgiving to celebrate their first wedding anniversary. She was stabbed to death on a trail near their cabin on a Tuesday morning."

He grimaced and then continued. "The second victim, Rick Sanders, booked a room a week before Christmas. He was found stabbed in the guest shed. Samantha was a schoolteacher from Kansas City. Rick was a restaurant owner from Dallas who had come here to check out some of the local food. Sandy was from St. Louis."

Jordon was impressed by how easily he rattled off the pertinent information of each victim without any notes. It meant he'd embraced the victims. They weren't just dead bodies to him... They were people. She liked that.

She took another sip of her coffee as he continued. "When Samantha was found on the trail, the first person we looked at hard was her husband, Eric. But he had a solid alibi. He'd been here having breakfast with the owners when she was killed and I could find no motive for him wanting her dead."

"What was she doing outside all alone?" Jordon asked, mentally taking notes of all the information he was giving to her.

"She was an amateur photographer...a nature buff, and according to her husband, she'd decided to skip breakfast on that particular morning to take some photographs. She had a quick cup of coffee here with the owners and her husband to start the day and then she left by herself."

"Who found her body?"

"Billy Bond, the groundskeeper. When he found her she was still breathing but unconscious and bleeding out. She died on the way to the hospital. According to the doctor, she had been attacked only minutes before she was discovered."

"So, the killer is probably local and you have no clue as to the motive," Jordon said.

Gabriel's lips thinned slightly. "No clue as to who or why. I guess that's why Mayor Stoddard thought it was important to bring in the big guns."

A small laugh escaped her despite the obvious displeasure on his face. "Don't worry, Chief Walters.

This gun doesn't intend to get in your way. You're the big Uzi and I'm just a little backup handgun."

She held back a sigh. She'd been here only half an hour and already the very hot chief of police appeared to be attempting to engage her in a spitting match.

SHE DIDN'T INTEND to get in his way.

But something about FBI Special Agent Jordon James was already under his skin.

As Gabriel led her out of the main cabin and toward the smaller cabins so that she could see each of the crime scenes, his gut twisted tight in frustration.

He hadn't been happy when the mayor had insisted they get help from the FBI, even in just an advisory position. He'd taken it as a vote of no confidence from the man who was his boss.

Jordon James had said nothing out of line. She'd been a complete professional so far, but while they'd talked he'd had some very unprofessional thoughts roll through his head.

She was strikingly pretty with her short curly dark hair and green eyes that sparked not only a keen intelligence, but with what he sensed was also a glimmer of humor.

When she'd shrugged out of her coat it had been impossible not to notice the length of her legs encased in the tight black slacks and the thrust of her full breasts against the white cotton of her blouse.

Even the holster around her waist didn't detract from her innate femininity.

He'd been living and breathing murder since the first body had been found here almost three months ago. His instant, sharp physical attraction to Jordon had momentarily shaken him.

He now followed her up the wooden stairs that led to the ridge where the cabins were located. At least out here in the cold air he couldn't smell the enticing flowery perfume that had permeated the air the moment she'd sat next to him in the dining room.

She reached the top of the ridge and turned back to wait for him. When he joined her he pointed to a small structure just to the right.

"That's the guest shed where Rick Sanders was found." She fell into step next to him as they approached the building where a cheerful hand-painted Welcome sign hung over the door.

They stepped inside to the tinkle of a little bell, and even though he'd been in the shed at least twenty times since the night that Rick's body had been found, his gaze took everything in as if it was the very first time he'd been inside the small building.

A bifold door to the left hid a stackable washer and dryer. A round table and chairs to the right invited the guests to sit and relax. Beyond that was another closed door that led to a small storage room.

A counter held a fancy coffeemaker with a carousel of little flavored coffees, and beneath the counter, a glass-doored refrigerator displayed a variety of sodas and bottled water for the guests to enjoy at no cost.

"What a nice idea for the people staying here," Jordon said.

Gabriel nodded, although his head filled with the vision of Rick Sanders dead on the floor, his back riddled with stab wounds. "He never saw what was coming. It appeared that he was standing in front of the coffeemaker waiting for a hot chocolate when he was attacked from behind."

She looked up at the bell hanging over the doorway. "He didn't hear it coming?"

"The bell wasn't hung there until after his murder," Gabriel explained. He watched Jordon closely as her narrowed gaze once again swept the room. He couldn't help but notice the long length of her dark eyelashes and the slightly pouty fullness of her lips.

She opened the door to the storage room, where Gabriel knew the space held only cases of soda, boxes of the little coffee pods, paper napkins and other supplies.

"Okay," she said and gazed at him with eyes that gave away nothing.

"See anything me and my men might have missed?"

"Yes. In fact, I think I've solved the case. It was Colonel Mustard in the library with a wrench," she replied flippantly. He stared at her in stunned surprise. "Where to next?" she asked before he could even begin to formulate a response.

They exited the guest shed and he led her down a path that would eventually take them to the place where Samantha Kent's body had been found.

"There's about seven acres of trails here," he said.

"Good grief. I hope we aren't walking them all now." She pulled her coat collar closer around her slender neck. "I hate this weather. I've got a date with a beach in Florida at the end of next week and I can't wait to get in a bathing suit and enjoy a fruity, fun alcoholic beverage."

"Then I guess you'll need to hurry to solve this case in time to get to the beach," he replied. He took another couple of steps then halted when he realized she wasn't with him.

He turned around. She stood stock-still, her green eyes narrowed as if he was a puzzling crime scene she was analyzing. "Are you normally a jerk or are you just acting like one especially for me?"

Despite the cold air, a wave of warmth filled his cheeks. "No, I'm not normally a jerk," he replied. He drew in a deep breath and released it slowly. "But I guess I have been acting like one since you arrived and I apologize." He had to admit to himself that he'd been a bit antagonistic with her. It wasn't her fault she was here. She was just doing her job like he was trying to do his.

"Apology accepted," she said easily and grinned. "Can I expect more jerk from you or are you over it now?"

"I'm not sure," he admitted. He shoved his hands into his coat pockets. "It's not you personally."

Her grin widened. "Trust me, I didn't think it was about me personally. You haven't known me long enough to have attitude with me, although I'm sure if I'm here for a few more days that will eventually come."

He gazed at her curiously. "Why? Are you difficult to work with?"

"I'll let you draw your own conclusions." Her smile fell and she wrapped her arms around her chest. "Look, I get it that you probably aren't happy about FBI presence here. But I am here, and we might as well try to work together to solve these murders. Now, can we get on with this? I'm freezing my tush off."

And a fine tush it was, Gabriel thought as they continued walking on the narrow trail. Within minutes they were at the spot where Samantha Kent's body had been found.

"The trees were still fairly full of leaves when she was killed," he said. "Although you can see the cabins from here now, they weren't visible at the time of the murder."

Once again Jordon silently surveyed the scene.

"She didn't scream or cry out for help? Nobody heard anything?"

"Nobody admitted to hearing anything. She was attacked from behind like Rick. She didn't have a single defensive wound and Billy didn't see or hear anyone else in the woods when he found her." The frustration of the cases burned in his stomach as once again his mind provided a memory of this particular crime scene.

Samantha had already been carried away to the hospital by the time Gabriel had arrived on scene, but her blood had stained the autumn leaves where she had fallen, transforming this piece of beautiful woods to a place of haunting, violent death.

"I've seen enough," Jordon said softly.

They were both silent as he led her to unit number three, where Sandy Peters had been found stabbed in her bed.

"Wow. Nice room," Jordon said after they'd stomped the snow off their boots and stepped inside. They both had donned gloves and bootees, as the room was still officially a crime scene.

"All the rooms are this nice," he replied. He stood by the door as Jordon wandered the area.

A king-size log bed was the center focal point, along with a stone fireplace and a sunken Jacuzzi tub for two. The bed had been stripped down to the mattress, but Sandy's suitcase was still open on one of the chairs in front of the fireplace, and a thick pink robe still hung on a coat tree next to the dresser.

He'd kept things intact in the room as much as possible for Jordon's perusal, although his men had already taken Sandy's cell phone and computer and the bedclothes into evidence. The room had been gone over with a fine-tooth comb and fingerprinted, so this evening he'd have some of his men clear the rest of Sandy's things from the room.

Jordon disappeared into the adjoining bathroom and then reappeared and stared at the tub, where a little basket held packets of bubble bath and two wineglasses with a bottle of white wine perched on the tile.

"There was obviously not a struggle." It was a statement of fact rather than a question.

"And the door wasn't forced," he replied. "It appears that she opened the door and was immediately stabbed. She fell backward to the bed and the attack continued there. She was stabbed a total of twelve times."

A frown danced across Jordon's features. "Overkill… That indicates a rage."

He nodded. "The same kind of rage was evident with the other two victims, as well."

"And the time of death?"

"The coroner placed it between around midnight and five in the morning," he replied. "Hannah, the owners' fifteen-year-old daughter, saw Sandy leaving the guest shed at around nine in the evening. She had a soda in her hand and told Hannah she planned on being up late working."

"What was Hannah doing out and about at that time of night in this weather?"

"One of her jobs here is to make sure the refrigerator is restocked each evening. She was later than usual that night." He looked toward the window where dusk had moved in. "I've arranged interviews with all the staff here to start in the morning at eight. In the meantime, we should get you settled in for the night. I've made arrangements for you to stay at a motel not far from here."

She looked at him in surprise. "Why would I stay at another motel? I'm assuming there are vacant rooms here?"

"Yes, but there is also a killer using this bed-and-breakfast as his personal playground."

"All the more reason for me to stay here," she replied.

Gabriel frowned. "I really don't like the idea. I think it would be much better if you stayed somewhere else."

"I'll be fine here. I'm armed and I'm trained. Just get me a key and point me to a room."

The burn in his gut intensified. Even though he barely knew Jordon, he recognized the stubborn upward thrust of a chin, the resolute shine in her eyes.

The killer was savvy enough not to leave any evidence behind. In savagely murdering three people he hadn't made any mistakes that Gabriel had been able to find.

The last thing Gabriel wanted was for FBI Special Agent Jordon James to become the fourth victim.

Chapter Two

When they returned to the main dining room, two adults and two teenagers awaited them. Gabriel introduced them as owners Ted and Joan Overton and their two children, fifteen-year-old Hannah and seventeen-year-old Jason.

"I made fresh coffee and some sandwiches," Joan said as she and her husband jumped up from the table where they'd been seated. She hurried over to stand next to the table with the coffeemaker and twisted her hands together as if unsure what to do next.

"Thank you—I'd love a cup," Jordon said. "And the sandwiches look wonderful." Joan's pretty features lit up as if she was pleased to be able to serve somebody.

"We've canceled all of our reservations for the next two weeks," Ted said. Jordon took a seat across from him and Gabriel sat next to Jason.

"There weren't that many to cancel," Joan said as she set a cup of coffee in front of Jordon and then sat next to her husband. "This is our slowest time of year, but reservations had already fallen off because of the bad publicity we've received. Social media is destroying us."

"Your place is lovely," Jordon said. "How long have you all owned it?"

"We bought it a little over a year ago," Ted said. "We'd talked about leaving the rat race behind and doing something like this for years, and then this place came on the market as a foreclosure and so we bit the bullet and made the move."

"Made the move from where?" Jordon asked. She took half of one of the thick ham-and-cheese sandwiches that were on a platter and placed it on the small plate in front of her.

"Oklahoma City," Ted replied. He was a tall, thin man with dark hair and brown eyes, and his children took after him rather than their shorter, blond-haired, blue-eyed mother.

"Do we need to be here?" Jason asked. His cheeks colored slightly as Jordon turned her gaze on him. "I don't know anything about what's happened around here and I've got homework to finish."

Jordon shifted her gaze to Gabriel, who shrugged. She turned back to Jason. "I don't see any reason for you to hang around here while we talk to your mother and father." The young man was nearly out of his chair before Jordon had finished speaking.

"What about me?" Hannah asked. "I've already told Chief Walters everything I know."

"As long as it's okay with your parents, you both can be excused for tonight," Jordon replied. Hannah also flew out of her chair and pulled a cell phone from her pocket.

"Go directly to the house and no place else," Ted said.

"Where's the house?" Jordon asked as the two teenagers left the building.

"Across the street. It came with this property," Ted replied. "It's a nice three-bedroom with a lake view."

"And it has a huge detached garage that's far enough away from the house that I can't hear the banging and curses or noises that Ted makes when he's working on one of the cars or in the middle of a woodworking project," Joan added.

For the next hour Jordon questioned the couple about the murders, the victims and the daily operation of the bed-and-breakfast.

Gabriel was mostly silent during the conversation. She was grateful he allowed her to go over information she was certain he already knew.

The body language between the couple indicated a close, loving relationship, and Jordon sensed no underlying tension other than what would be deemed normal under the conditions.

By the time they'd finished up, night had fallen outside. "Agent James would like to stay here," Gabriel said when the interview had wound down. A deep frown cut across his forehead. "That wouldn't be a problem, would it?"

"Of course not," Joan replied with a touch of surprise.

"Are you sure you want to do that?" Ted asked.

"Positive," Jordon replied without hesitation. Gabriel's silent disapproval of the plan wafted in the air, but Jordon's mind was made up.

"We'll put you in unit seven," Ted said. They all got up from the table. "I'll just go get the key for you." He left the dining room through a door that Jordon assumed led into the main office.

"Breakfast is served from seven to nine. If that doesn't work for you just let me know," Joan said. "We'll be glad to do whatever we can to accommodate you while you're here."

"I'd like you to keep things the way you would for any other guest," Jordon replied.

"And I'll be here around seven in the morning so that we can begin interviewing the staff at eight," Gabriel said. "I hope you don't mind me joining Agent James here for breakfast."

"You know you're always welcome here, Chief Walters," Joan said warmly.

Ted returned to the dining room and handed Jordon a room key. "I'll just grab my coat and show you to the room."

"Don't worry about it, Ted. I'll see her to the room,"

Gabriel replied. He pulled on his coat and Jordon did the same.

"Thank you for the sandwiches. It was very thoughtful of you," Jordon said to Joan.

"It was my pleasure," Joan replied.

"And I won't be needing daily maid service while I'm here. Once a week or so would be fine just for clean towels and sheets, and I can change my own bed."

Joan nodded. "If that's what you want. Hopefully the case will be solved soon and you won't even be here long enough for that."

"We'll see you in the morning." Gabriel picked up Jordon's suitcases.

Jordon took the smaller of the bags from him. "They seem like a nice couple," she said when they were out of the building and heading up the stairs to the cabins.

"They are. They have good kids, too. Both Jason and Hannah are excellent students and they work here for their parents after school." He shifted the suitcase he carried from one hand to the other. "But these murders are quickly destroying their livelihood."

"So, who would want to do that?" The cold air nearly stole her breath away as they trudged up the stairs to the row of cabins. She sighed in relief as they reached the unit she would call home for the duration of her stay.

"A few people come to mind."

She set the suitcase she carried down and retrieved the room key from her pocket. Although she was intrigued by any suspects he might have in mind, at the moment all she wanted to do was get out of the frigid night air.

She sighed in relief as she stepped into the warm room. Gabriel followed her just inside the door and set her suitcase on the floor. She shrugged out of her coat, flipped the switch that made the flames in the fireplace jump to life and then turned back to look at him. "So who are these people who come to mind?"

"Actually, I'd rather not get into all that tonight. It's getting late and I'll just let you get settled in. Why don't I meet you in the dining room at seven tomorrow morning and we can discuss it more then."

It was only eight o'clock, hardly a late night, but it was obvious by the rigid set of his shoulders and how close he stood to the door that he wasn't comfortable having a long conversation in the intimacy of the room.

Maybe he had a wife to get home to, she thought, although there was no wedding ring on his finger. She pegged him in his midthirties, certainly not only old enough to be married, but also to have some children running around.

"Okay, then I guess I'll see you in the morning," she said. "Oh, and one more thing. If it's possible, I'd like to have a car at my disposal while I'm here."

He gave a curt nod. "I'll see to it that you have one first thing in the morning. And we should exchange cell phone numbers." He pulled his phone from his pocket.

With her number in his phone and his in hers, Gabriel stared at her for a long moment. "You know I don't approve of you staying here. You need to call me immediately if you feel uncomfortable here or believe you're in any kind of danger."

The only danger at the moment was the possibility of getting lost in the simmering depths of his eyes. She'd watched those blue eyes through the course of the evening. She wondered if he had any idea how expressive they were.

As she'd spoken to the Overtons, his eyes had alternately radiated with a soft sympathy and a deep frustration. It was only when he gazed at her that they became utterly shuttered and unfathomable.

"Jordon?" he said, pulling her from her momentary contemplation.

"Don't worry about me. I'll be just fine." Her hand fell to the butt of her gun to emphasize her point. "Good night, Chief Walters. I'll see you in the morning."

He gave her a curt nod and then left the room. Jordon locked the door behind him. There was no dead bolt, only the simple lock in the doorknob. Apparently security had never been a real issue before the murders. She was vaguely surprised dead bolts hadn't been installed since then.

She sank down on the chair next to the fireplace, her thoughts consumed by the man who had just taken his bedroom eyes and his heady woodsy scent with him.

She had no idea how well they were going to work together. She wasn't sure yet how open he was to hearing anything she might have to say about the cases. But the bottom line was she had a job to do and she would do her best with or without his cooperation.

She pulled herself up off the chair and opened one of the suitcases on the bed. It took her only minutes to unpack and then place her toiletries in the bathroom.

She set up her laptop computer on the small coffee table in front of the fireplace and for the next half hour typed in notes and impressions while things were still fresh in her mind.

By the time she finished, she was still too wound up even to think about going to sleep. She should just pull her nightgown on and go to bed, but she had a feeling she would just stare at the dark ceiling while sleep remained elusive.

Although the idea of going outside in the cold night air was abhorrent, she pulled on her coat and snow boots with the intention of retrieving one of the flavored coffees that tasted like dessert from the guest shed.

The path to the shed was lit by small solar lights in the ground, and despite the frosty air, she kept her coat open and her hand on the butt of her gun. The night was soundless, the eerie quiet that thick snow cover always brought.

All of her senses went on high alert. There was no way she intended to be careless on her first night or any other night she stayed here.

A faint scent of pine lingered in the air and she noticed through the bare trees that the main building was dark. She was all alone on the Diamond Cove grounds.

When she reached the guest shed and stepped inside, a light blinked on and the bell tinkled overhead. She made sure the door was closed firmly behind her and then checked behind the door that hid the washer and dryer to make sure nobody was hiding there. She then moved to the storage room. With her gun in her hand, she threw open the door and breathed a small sigh of relief.

Assured that she was alone, she picked out a chocolate-flavored coffee, placed it in the coffee machine and then faced the door as she waited for the foam cup to fill.

This was what poor Rick Sanders had done. He'd come in here seeking a nice cup of hot chocolate and instead had ended up stabbed viciously in the back.

When the coffeemaker whooshed the last of the liquid into the foam cup, she turned and grabbed it and went back out into the quiet of the night.

She was halfway to her cabin when the center of

her back began to burn and she had the wild sense that somebody was watching her.

She whirled around, her sudden movement sloshing hot coffee onto her hand as she gripped the butt of her gun with the other. Nobody. There was nobody on the path behind her.

There was no sound, no sign of anyone sharing the night with her. She hurried the rest of the way to her room, unlocked her door and went back inside. She set her coffee on the low table in front of the fireplace and then moved the curtain at the window aside to peer out.

Despite the fact that she saw nothing to cause her concern, she couldn't shake the feeling that somebody had been out there, somebody who had been watching her...waiting for the perfect opportunity to strike.

GABRIEL WAS UP before dawn, his thoughts shooting a hundred different directions and making any further sleep impossible. He got out of bed, pulled a thick black robe around him and then padded into the kitchen to make coffee.

As it began to brew he took a quick shower, dressed for the day and then sank down at the kitchen table with a cup of hot coffee before him.

He should be thinking about murder. He should be thinking about the interviews he'd set up for the day, but instead his head was filled with questions about the long-legged, green-eyed woman who had blown into his case…into his town on a gust of cold air.

Could she accomplish what he hadn't been able to do? Could she somehow identify the killer, who had remained elusive so far to him, and get him behind bars? If she could, then it would be worth whatever he had to put up with to work with her.

All he wanted was to get this murderer off his streets. He'd never dreamed when he'd left the Chicago Police Department behind three years ago to take this job that he'd be dealing with a serial killer in the town known as America's family destination.

He'd also never imagined he'd be working for a mayor who was contentious and petulant, a man who was also a pompous ass and passive-aggressive. It was no wonder the last chief of police had quit after only less than a year on the job. More than once throughout the past three years Gabriel had considered walking away from here and starting over someplace else.

Once again his thoughts went to Jordon. There was no question that he found her extremely attractive. He even admired the fact that she'd called him out on the jabs he'd shot at her. But that didn't mean he was going to like her and it certainly didn't mean he was going to work well with her.

She already had one strike against her. He hadn't approved of her decision to stay at Diamond Cove. She'd known he didn't like it and yet she'd done it anyway. She was placing herself in the eye of a storm, and as far as he was concerned, it was an unnecessary, foolish risk.

By the time he finished two cups of coffee and his scattered musings, the morning sun had peeked up over the horizon and it was almost six thirty.

He made a call to arrange for a patrol car to be taken to the bed-and-breakfast for Jordon to use and then pulled on his coat to head out.

It was going to be a long day. Diamond Cove employed four people full-time and he'd arranged for all of them to be interviewed today along with a few others away from the bed-and-breakfast, as well.

As he got into his car he swallowed a sigh of frustration. Everyone they would be interviewing about the latest murder were people he'd interviewed at least twice before with the first two homicides.

He was desperate for some new information that might lead to an arrest, but he really wasn't expecting to get any that day.

Thankfully, the road crews had handled the snowfall well and the streets had been cleared for both the locals and the tourists who braved the winter weather for a vacation.

There was another snowstorm forecast for early next week. Jordon better enjoy the next few days of sunshine because, according to the weather report, the approaching snowstorm was going to be a bad one.

Maybe they'd get lucky and solve the case before

the storm hit. She could keep her date with the Florida beach and he could get back to dealing with the usual crimes that always occurred in a tourist town.

He arrived at the bed-and-breakfast at ten till seven and parked next to the patrol car that Jordon would use. He retrieved the keys from under the floor mat and then headed to the dining room.

Jordon was already seated at a table and he didn't like the way his adrenaline jumped up a bit at the sight of her. Once again she was dressed in the black slacks that hugged every curve and a white, tailored blouse—the unofficial uniform of FBI agents everywhere.

"Good morning," she said. Her eyes were bright and she exuded the energy of somebody who had slept well and was eager to face a new day.

"Morning," he replied. He took off his coat and slung it over the back of a chair and then got himself a cup of coffee and sat across from her. The scent of fresh spring flowers wafted from her.

"Are you a morning person, Chief Walters?" she asked.

He looked at her in surprise. "I've never thought about it before. Why?"

"My ex-husband wasn't a morning person and he found my cheerful morning chatter particularly irritating. If you need me to keep quiet until you've had a couple of cups of coffee, that's information I need to know."

"How long have you been divorced?" he asked curiously.

"Three years. What about you? Married? Divorced? In a relationship?"

"Single," he replied, although he'd always thought that by the time he reached thirty-five years old he'd be happily married with a couple of children. That birthday had passed two months ago and there was no special woman in his life, let alone any children.

"Here are the keys to a patrol car you can use while you're here." He slid the keys across the table.

"Thanks. I appreciate it," she replied.

"Good morning, Chief," Joan said as she came into the room carrying two plates. "We heard you come in and I figured you were both ready for some breakfast."

"Oh my gosh, this is too pretty to eat," Jordon said as she gazed at the huge waffle topped with plump strawberries and a generous dollop of whipped cream.

"Speak for yourself," Gabriel replied as he grabbed one of the pitchers of warm syrup from the center of the table. "As far as I'm concerned, Joan makes the best waffles in town."

"Appreciate it, Chief," Joan replied with a smile of pleasure. She poured herself a cup of coffee and then joined them at the table. Within minutes Ted also appeared to drink coffee while Gabriel and Jordon ate their meal.

For the next half hour the conversation remained

light and pleasant. Ted and Joan told Jordon about the various shows and attractions offered at the many theaters and establishments along the main drag.

"If you have time to do anything, you should go to the Butterfly Palace," Joan said. "It's one of my favorite places here in Branson. It's like walking in an enchanted forest with different species of butterflies everywhere."

"That sounds nice, but I don't plan on having any downtime to enjoy the local flavor while I'm here," Jordon replied. "I've got a vacation planned in Florida next week so I can get away from the cold and the snow."

"So you think you'll be able to have this all solved by the end of next week?" Ted's voice was filled with hope as he looked first at Jordon and then at Gabriel.

The frustration that had been absent while Gabriel had eaten his waffle returned to burn in the pit of his belly. "Unfortunately, I can't promise to solve this case in a timeline that would accommodate Agent James's vacation plans."

"And certainly that isn't what I meant to imply," Jordon replied with a slight upward thrust to her chin. "Vacation plans can be postponed. I'm committed to being here as long as I need to be in order to be of assistance to Chief Walters." She gave him a decidedly chilly smile.

"And I appreciate any help that I can get," he replied, hoping to diffuse some of the tension that suddenly snapped in the air.

"Speaking of help..." Joan looked out the door where housekeeper Hilary Hollis and her daughter, Ann, stomped their boots before entering the building.

Joan cleared the table and then she and Ted disappeared into the office so Gabriel and Jordon could get down to work.

The interview with the two women didn't take long and Gabriel let Jordon take the lead. It had been twenty-one-year-old Ann who had found Sandy Peters's body when she'd entered the room to clean it.

The young woman's eyes still held the horror of the gruesome discovery as she recounted to Jordon the morning she would never forget.

Jordon took notes on a small pad and handled the interview like the pro she obviously was, not only gaining the information she needed from the two women, but also earning their trust, as well.

"Do you intend for me to conduct all the interviews?" she asked when the women had left and she and Gabriel were alone in the room.

"If you're comfortable with that. I've already spoken to these people several times before with the previous two homicides. Maybe you can get something out of one of them that I couldn't get."

She narrowed her eyes. "Are you being sarcastic?"

He smiled at her ruefully. "No, although I guess

I shouldn't be surprised that you think I am." His smile fell into a frown as he continued to gaze at her. "I'm frustrated by these murders. I'm ticked off at the mayor, who has made me feel inadequate since the moment I took this job, and I guess I've been taking all that out on you."

The smile that curved her lips warmed some of the cold places that had resided inside him for months. "Apology accepted," she replied.

"That's twice you've easily accepted an apology from me. Are you always so forgiving?" he asked curiously.

"I try not to sweat the small stuff, although I have been known to have a temper. Now, who are we seeing next?"

Before he could reply, the outer door swung open and groundskeeper Billy Bond walked in. "I don't know why I've got to be here," Billy said after the introductions had been made and he'd thrown himself into a chair.

He looked at Gabriel, his dark eyes filled with his displeasure. "You've already talked to me a dozen times before when those other two people got killed. I don't know any more now about murder than I did then."

"But I don't know anything about you or anything you've told Chief Walters in the past, so you'll have to humor us and answer some questions for me." Jordon gave the surly man a charming smile. "Why don't we start with you telling me what your duties are around here?"

"I take care of the grounds."

"Can you be a little more specific?"

For the next forty-five minutes Jordon questioned the thirty-two-year-old man who had worked for the bed-and-breakfast since Joan and Ted had opened the doors for business.

Once again admiration for Jordon's interrogation skills filled him as he sipped coffee and listened. And as before as he watched Billy closely, as he heard what the man had to say, he couldn't help but believe the man was hiding something...but what?

"He's a charming guy," Jordon said wryly when Billy left.

"He definitely lacks some social skills," he replied.

She looked down at her notes. "He answered all of my questions fairly easily, but his posture and facial expressions indicated to me that he wasn't being completely truthful." She looked at Gabriel. "For most of the interview he refused to meet my gaze and I could smell his body sweat. He just seemed a bit shady to me."

"Billy is at the top of my potential suspect list because I have the same concerns about him, but I haven't been able to find anything to tie him to the murders and I can't figure out what he could be lying about."

"He would be on my suspect list simply because he's the one who found Samantha Kent in the woods," she replied. "He could have stabbed her and then waited until he knew she couldn't say anything to identify him and then played the hero in calling for help, knowing that she was going to die before she could say anything to anyone."

He nodded. The same thought had definitely been in his head. "But what's his motive? There's certainly no financial gain in him killing the guests and he doesn't seem to have an ax to grind with the Overtons."

"Crazy doesn't need a rational motive," Jordon replied. Her eyes simmered with what appeared to be a whisper of dark ghosts and Gabriel fought against a sudden dark foreboding of his own.

Chapter Three

It was just before noon when thirty-eight-year-old handyman Ed Rollings sat at the table for his interview. Ed had the face of a cherub, slightly plump and with the open friendliness of a man who'd never met a stranger in his life.

However, the pleasant man was another at the top of Gabriel's list of suspects. Before Ed had arrived, Gabriel had given Jordon just enough information to aid her in her questioning of Ed.

"I understand your brother Kevin owned this place before the Overtons bought it," Jordon now said.

Ed nodded and a strand of his blond hair fell across his broad forehead. "That's right. Kev had big dreams for Diamond Cove but he was short in the financial-planning area." Ed laughed and shook his head. "That's the story of Kevin's life... Big dreams and no smarts for the follow-through."

"And you weren't upset when the Overtons took over here?"

"Why would I be upset? I was just glad they hired me on. I'd been working here when my brother owned it and jobs aren't that easy to find around here. I don't have any hard feelings against Ted and Joan. They didn't screw things up for Kevin. He did that to himself."

"What about your brother? Does he have a grudge against the Overtons?" Jordon asked.

"Kevin has a grudge against the whole world. Most of the time he doesn't even like me or our brother Glen," Ed replied with another laugh.

Gabriel listened to the back and forth and thought about that moment when Jordon's eyes had darkened so much. Although he shouldn't be curious, he was.

He was intrigued about those dark shadows that had momentarily danced in the depths of her eyes. He wondered what had caused her divorce, if her curls were as soft as they looked and what her slightly plump lips might taste like.

He also wondered if the stress of these cases was making him lose his mind. Certainly his thoughts about Jordon were completely inappropriate.

As Jordon continued questioning Ed, Gabriel got up from the table and walked over to stare out the window. From this vantage point he could see not only the cabins up on the ridge, but also the guest shed.

The scene of each murder flashed in his head, along with all of the people he'd interviewed after each one had occurred. Had he interviewed the murderer twice before already? Had he sat across from the person who had viciously stabbed Samantha Kent, Rick Sanders and Sandy Peters and exchanged conversation? Had he somehow missed something vital? That was one of his biggest fears.

"So, where were you on Sunday night when Sandy Peters was killed?" Jordon asked Ed.

Gabriel turned from the window to gaze at the man. "Where I usually am on most nights…at home with my wife."

"And she can corroborate that you didn't leave the house all night?"

Ed laughed yet again. "That woman knows if I turn over in my sleep. She'd definitely know if I left the house, which I didn't." His blue eyes shone with what appeared to be open honesty. "Look, I've got no reason to kill anyone and no reason to hurt Joan and Ted. Ted pays me a good wage for a day's work. Besides, I don't have it in me to murder somebody."

"I think that's it for now," Jordon said and looked at Gabriel to see if he had anything to add.

"I'm sure Ed will be available if we have any further questions for him," Gabriel said.

"You know where to find me. I'm either here or at home with Millie most of the time," Ed assured them as he got up from the table.

"How do burgers sound for lunch?" Gabriel asked when Ed had left the building.

"Sounds good to me. I'm starving." She got up

from the table and reached for her coat slung across the back of her chair.

"I thought we'd grab some lunch and then head into the station. I figured you'd want to look at all the files of the other two murders."

"Definitely," she replied.

It took them only minutes to get into Gabriel's car and he headed for Benny's Burgers, a no-nonsense joint just off the main drag that didn't cater to the tourist trade.

"I seriously doubt that the two housekeepers had anything to do with whatever is going on," she said once they were on their way.

"I agree." The warmth of the heater seemed to intensify the fresh floral scent of her that he found so appealing. He tightened his hands around the steering wheel.

"Tell me more about Ed Rollings and his brothers."

"They were all born and raised here. Ed and his wife have no children but he has two brothers who also live in the area. Glen is two years younger than Ed. He's single and works as a clerk in one of the souvenir shops. And as you now know, his older brother, Kevin, owned Diamond Cove but lost it in bankruptcy."

He pulled into Benny's Burgers' parking lot, pleased to see that the lunch crowd was already gone and only three cars were in the lot.

Within five minutes they had their burgers and were seated across from each other in a booth near the back of the place. At least in here the odors of fried onions and beef were heavy enough to overwhelm Jordon's evocative scent.

"I'm assuming you've interviewed Kevin Rollings," she said and then popped a French fry into her mouth.

"Several times, but not in relationship to Sandy's murder. He's on my list to speak with later this afternoon. He's another one who has been on my short list of suspects."

"You mentioned that Billy Bond was on your list, as well. Anyone else I need to know about?"

He shook his head. "My list is depressingly short and everyone on it has had some sort of an alibi for the first two murders. You can get a better idea of what we've done to investigate those murders when you read the files."

"I'm looking forward to that," she replied.

For the next few minutes they were silent and focused on their meals. The cheeseburger and onion rings were tasteless to Gabriel as thoughts of the three murdered people weighed heavily in his head.

Jordon's appetite didn't appear to suffer at all. She ate her burger and fries, and then, with an assenting nod from him, she pulled his plate closer to her and picked at the onion rings he'd left on his plate.

"This has got to be somebody who wants to hurt Ted and Joan personally," she said.

"I was hesitant to make that call until now." He

leaned back against the red leather of the booth. "I've investigated their background thoroughly and so far haven't found anything or anybody that would send up a real red flag."

"What did they do back in Oklahoma City?"

"Ted sold home and vehicle insurance and Joan was a third-grade teacher. According to all their friends and relatives, they're solid people who didn't have enemies. Their coworkers also spoke highly of them. Kevin Rollings might want to destroy the business just for spite and I can't figure out if Billy Bond is hiding something or not."

"He definitely has a bit of a creep factor going on." She shoved his now-empty plate away.

"Unfortunately, I can't arrest Billy for being a creep and I can't arrest Kevin Rollings on just my suspicion alone. Why did you get a divorce?" The question was out of his mouth before he realized he intended to ask it.

Her eyes widened slightly in surprise and then she smiled. "I was madly in love and got married in an effort to play grown-up and be a traditional kind of woman. It took me two years to realize I wasn't a marriage kind of woman after all." She took a quick sip of her soda, her gaze curious. "What about you? Are you a marriage kind of man?"

"Definitely," he replied firmly.

"Then why aren't you already married? You're a

hot-looking guy with a respectable job. Why hasn't some honey already snapped you up?"

"I'm cautious," he admitted. "I want to make sure that when I finally marry it's a one-shot, forever kind of deal. My parents just celebrated their fortieth anniversary together and I want that kind of a lasting relationship for myself."

"Footloose and fancy-free—that's the life for me," she replied.

The threat of his intense physical attraction to her eased in his mind. She was somebody he would never be interested in pursuing no matter how alluring he found her.

This brief conversation was enough to let him know that he and FBI Special Agent Jordon James wanted very different things in life. He wasn't sure why, but this fact gave him a bit of peace of mind.

For the first time since she'd arrived he relaxed. "I'm glad you're here, Jordon."

"Thanks, Chief Walters. Does that mean lunch is on you?"

He smiled at her. "Yes, lunch is on me, and please call me Gabriel."

The sexy smile she flashed him in return instantly surged an unwanted tension back in his belly.

JORDON STRETCHED WITH her arms overhead and got up from the table. She'd been seated in the small conference room alone for the last couple of hours reading all the information that had been gathered on the murders at the bed-and-breakfast.

She definitely admired how Gabriel and his team had conducted such thorough investigations following each of the crimes. She'd also been aware of the respect shown to Gabriel among everyone in the station.

Nobody had joked or been overly familiar with him, indicating to her that he ran a tight ship and kept himself somewhat distant from his staff. Despite that fact, she'd sensed that he was not only respected, but also well liked.

She paced the length of the table, and her brain whirled with all the information she'd gained in the past three hours of intense study. Still, as thorough as the investigations had been, it was all information that yielded no answer as to who was responsible for the three homicides.

Several times throughout the past couple of hours of being cooped up in the conference room, a female officer named Jane Albright had occasionally popped her head in to see if Jordon needed anything. Only once had Jordon requested a cup of coffee.

The murder crime photos had been utterly gruesome and had built up not only a surge of frustration, but also a rich anger inside her. She wanted this perp caught before another person was killed and before Joan and Ted Overton were forced to close their doors and lose their livelihood.

She opened the conference room door, stepped out into the short hallway and headed to Gabriel's office. She gave two quick raps on his door, and when she heard his deep voice respond, she walked in.

He looked ridiculously handsome seated behind a large wooden desk, a computer on one side and a stack of files at his right. He started to rise but she waved him back down and sat in a chair opposite the desk.

"Looks like a lot of work," she said and pointed to the files.

"The usual...break-ins, purse-snatchings, robberies and the occasional car theft." He leaned back in the leather chair, his blue eyes gazing at her expectantly.

"If you're waiting for me to give you the name of the killer, don't hold your breath. After reading the files I'm as aggravated as I'm sure you are. This guy is obviously smart and organized. He's not only managed to commit three hideous murders but he's also escaped each scene with nobody seeing him and leaving nothing behind."

He stood. "We can talk about it more on the drive to Mouse's Maze of Mirrors."

A knot spun tight in her chest. "Mouse's Maze of Mirrors?"

He nodded. "It's a fairly new attraction on the strip, and on most afternoons and evenings Kevin Rollings works the door."

She got up from her chair and fought against the unsteady shake of her legs. "I definitely think a chat with Kevin is in order."

Minutes later they were in Gabriel's car and headed to the popular 76 Country Boulevard, where, he explained, most of the theaters, eateries and attractions were located.

As he pointed out places of interest, she tried to still the faint simmer of panic inside her. *See how I got mirrors all set up so you can see yourself? You can watch yourself scream.* Ralph Hicks's gravelly voice filled her head.

The creep had placed three large mirrors in front of all of his victims so they could watch while he tortured them. It had been a horrid form of torture in and of itself.

Buck up, buttercup, she told herself firmly. She'd survived the mirrors and Ralph Hicks. She refused to let those long hours in the cellar affect her now or define who she was. She could deal with a silly maze of mirrors without freaking out.

"I definitely think Kevin Rollings looks good as a potential suspect. His alibis for the other murders weren't exactly stellar," she said, shoving away the haunting memories of her past to focus on the here and now.

"It's tough to break an alibi substantiated by another family member. His brother Glen swore Kevin was at his house drinking and then passed out on his sofa at the time of both the previous murders."

"And of course Glen would have a motive to lie to save his brother's hide," she replied.

"I turned up the heat when I questioned Glen, but he stuck with the story." Gabriel turned into a parking lot in front of a large brown building with a huge picture of a demented-looking mouse painted on the siding. "We'll see what kind of alibi Kevin comes up with for the time of Sandy's murder."

As they got out of the car and approached the building, the sun broke out of the layer of clouds and gleamed on the rich darkness of Gabriel's hair.

He walked with confidence, as if he owned the space around him. Salt of the earth…a traditional man with traditional values and three murders that he was desperate to solve.

He seemed to have taken these crimes personally, otherwise she'd be working with somebody else rather than the chief himself. She hoped together they could get this killer behind bars, where he belonged.

There were no other cars in the lot. There had been few cars on the road. Obviously mid-January after a snowfall was a slow time for the entire town.

They entered into a small lobby with a turnstile and a counter behind which Kevin Rollings sat. Although considerably older than Ed, Kevin had the same blond hair, the same round face as his brother, but that was where the similarities ended.

"I figured you'd be coming to talk to me," he said with a deep scowl that transformed his pleasant features into something mean and ugly.

"You figured right," Gabriel said and then introduced Jordon.

"Got the feds involved in local business." Kevin shook his head and sniffed as if he smelled something dirty.

"Nice to meet you, Kevin. We had a nice chat with your brother Ed early this morning and he had so many wonderful things to say about you." Jordon beamed a smile at the man.

"Ed's a damn fool," Kevin replied. "He's nothing more than a glorified lawn boy."

"What I'd really like to know is where you were on Sunday night," Jordon replied, cutting to the chase.

Kevin smiled, a tight slash of lips that didn't begin to reach his eyes. "That's easy. I met up with a couple of buddies for beers at Hillbilly Harry's. We were there until about midnight and then I went home and crashed out. I've got to admit I was pretty trashed. I could barely stumble from my car to the front door."

"Good thing I didn't meet you on the road. You'd have been looking at a little jail time and a DUI," Gabriel said.

"Kevin, do you live by yourself?" Jordon asked, not wanting the conversation to get off track.

"Yeah. My wife left me two months after the Diamond Cove went into bankruptcy. And yeah, I hold a grudge about the whole thing. If the damned bank would have just given me a little more time, things would have been fine."

His nostrils flared as he continued. "Now I'm working a minimum-wage crap job and barely making ends meet. I don't have anything to do with the Overtons. It's bad enough their kids hang out here with their snot-nosed friends all the time. Do I wish Diamond Cove would fall off the face of the earth? Damn straight. Did I kill those people? Hell, no." He drew in a deep breath and stood from the stool.

"We'll need the names of the men you were with on Sunday night," Jordon said. She was shocked by the venom Kevin hadn't even attempted to hide. He certainly had said enough to keep him high on the suspect list.

"Names?" Gabriel said and pulled a small notebook and pen from his coat pocket.

Kevin heaved a deep, audible sigh. "Glen was there and so was Wesley Mayfield, Tom Richmond, Dave Hampton and Neil Davies. You can check with all of them. They'll tell you I was with them on Sunday night and I wasn't anywhere near Diamond Cove."

"Don't worry. We will check it out." Gabriel tucked the pen and notepad back into his pocket.

"Maybe while you're here do the two of you want to go through the maze? I get a percentage of the till each night and today has definitely been a slow day." The anger that had gripped Kevin's features transformed to a mask of mock pleasantry. "Go see the mouse inside."

"It might be the only fun you'll have while you're here," Gabriel said to Jordon as he pulled his wallet from his pocket.

He paid for their admission and Jordon swallowed against the faint simmer of alarm that attempted to grip her. *It's just a silly tourist attraction*, she told herself. She went through the turnstile with Gabriel just behind her. *Don't freak out. Mirrors can't hurt you.*

A dark corridor led into the maze, where she stepped into a space with five reflections of herself staring back at her. Gabriel was right behind her, a calming presence as the back of her throat threatened to close up.

"This way," he said and led her into a corridor of mirrors to the right.

"Have you been in here before?" she asked.

"No, it's my first time, too." They both jumped as one of the mirrors lit up and displayed an image of the demented mouse and a loud, wicked cackle sounded from overhead.

"If I find you, Mouse, I'll tie your tail into knots," Jordon said as the mirror returned to normal.

"Come on. Let's find our way out of here."

She followed Gabriel's lead through the disorienting corridors as she fought against dark flashbacks. The scars on her hip burned and the phantom scent of cigarette smoke and sizzling flesh filled her nose.

Mouse suddenly appeared behind another mirror.

"Beware. If you aren't fast enough I'll pull you into my mouse hole and nobody will ever find you again," a deep voice whispered over the speaker.

Jordon stared at the fat mouse with the oversize teeth and she was back in the cellar clad only in her bra and panties, her arms above her head with her wrists in shackles connected to chains that hung from the low ceiling.

Nobody will ever find you here. You're mine to play with until I get tired of you. Ralph Hicks's voice exploded in her head. *I'm going to take my time and have lots of fun with you, and you get to watch.*

She closed her eyes to dispel the memory and when she opened them again Gabriel was nowhere to be seen. She was alone…with the mirrors, and a deep, gripping panic froze her in place.

Help! Somebody please help me. The pleas filled her head. *Don't let him burn me again. Don't let him do all the things to me that he did to the other women. I don't want to die this way. Please help me!*

"Gabriel?" His name croaked out of the back of her throat, which had become far too narrow. "Gabriel!" This time the cry was a half scream.

"I'm right here." He appeared next to her.

She grabbed on to his hand and forced a bright smile. "Whew, I thought you were lost." She hoped her voice betrayed none of the sheer panic that had momentarily suffused her.

"I think I found the exit—follow me."

She dropped his hand and practically walked in the backs of his shoes and cracked several bad jokes in an effort to relieve her own tension. After several twists and turns and more warnings from the mouse, they found the door that led outside.

"That was sort of lame," she said as they walked toward his car.

"From what I've heard, this is a really popular attraction among the teenagers in town. And as Kevin said, Jason and Hannah and their friends enjoy it."

"Probably because the girls scream and clutch on to the nearest testosterone-filled boy," she replied drily.

He smiled. "You want to get some dinner before I take you back to your room?"

Knots of tension twisted in her stomach and the taste of panic still filled the back of her throat. "I'm really not that hungry right now. Maybe you could just stop someplace and I'll grab a sandwich to take back to the room for later. I can put it in the mini-fridge until I'm ready to eat."

"There's a sub place not far from here—we can stop there."

They got into the car and Jordon was more than grateful to leave Mouse's Maze of Mirrors behind. She hated her own weakness. She hated that she still felt a bit shaky and dark memories clutched at her heart and invaded her brain.

The last thing she wanted was for Gabriel to sense

any weakness in her. "So, what's on the agenda for tomorrow? A roller-coaster ride through a cave? A tour through Ripley's Believe It or Not?" She forced a flippant tone in her voice, determined not to let the memories pull her down.

"Nothing quite so grand. We need to chase down all the men Kevin said he was with Sunday night and confirm his alibi."

"Even if his alibi is confirmed until around midnight, that doesn't clear him for the murder, which took place much later than that," she replied.

"True, but in order to make a solid record, we need to corroborate everything." He pulled into the parking lot of a small place called Subs and Such.

"I'll just run in and grab something," she said. "You want anything?"

"Nah, I'm good. I've got some leftover meat loaf waiting for me at home."

It took her only minutes to get a submarine sandwich, several bags of chips and peanuts and then return to the car. All she wanted now was a long soak in the tub and time to put the mirrors and her memories behind her.

She might not have been woman enough to make her marriage work and she might not have been the daughter her parents wanted her to be, but she was one hell of an FBI agent. That was all she needed to be.

"Do you want me to drive into the station tomorrow morning or are you planning on picking me up?" she asked once they were back in the Diamond Cove parking lot.

"Why don't I come here around seven in the morning to get you? That way I can start the day with one of Joan's breakfasts."

"Sounds good to me." She gathered her purse and the white bag holding her sandwich and snacks. "Then I'll see you in the dining room at seven in the morning."

She gladly escaped the car and stepped into the cold night. She just needed a little time to get herself centered again. The little foray through the maze of mirrors had definitely shaken her up more than she'd expected.

She carried both her purse and her bag of food in her left hand, leaving her right hand to rest on the butt of her gun as she made her way down the path toward her cabin.

The night was once again silent around her and smelled of the clean evergreen that reminded her of Gabriel's attractive woodsy cologne.

She breathed a sigh of relief as she reached her door. She stepped into the warmth of the room and noticed a folded white piece of paper that had apparently been slid beneath the door at some point while she'd been gone.

It was probably something from Joan and Ted, perhaps concerning breakfast the next morning.

She dropped her purse and the sandwich bag on the coffee table and then picked up the paper. She unfolded it and a sizzle of adrenaline whipped through her as she read the message written in red block letters.

U R Next.

Chapter Four

For the first time in months Gabriel's thoughts weren't filled with mayhem and murder. Instead they were filled with a woman who smelled like spring and had almost had a panic attack in a tourist attraction meant to be fun.

She'd played it off well, but he'd picked up on the signs of her distress while they'd gone through the maze. Although she'd made a few jokes, her voice had been slightly higher in pitch and with a hint of breathlessness. When she'd grabbed his hand hers had been icy cold and had trembled. What had caused her such distress?

She was a curious contradiction—tough enough to insist that she stay in a room that might put her at risk as a target for a vicious serial killer, yet shaken up by a silly maze of mirrors. Definitely intriguing.

He turned onto the road that would eventually lead to his house, thoughts of Jordon still taking up all the space in his mind. She was not only beautiful, but also intelligent and with a sense of humor that reminded Gabriel he had a tendency at times to take life and himself a little too seriously.

He'd been sorry that she hadn't been up for dinner with him. Her company was far more appealing than leftover meat loaf and complete solitude.

His cell phone rang. He punched the button on his steering wheel to answer. "Chief Walters," he said.

"Gabriel, can you come back here?" Jordon's voice held a touch of simmering excitement.

"Of course. Is there a problem?"

"Unless I'm the victim of some sort of a sick prank, I think our killer just made contact with me."

Every nerve in his body electrified. "Are you safe?"

"Yes, I'm safe. We'll talk when you get here." She disconnected before he could ask any other questions.

He turned around in the closest driveway and headed back the way he'd come. Adrenaline rushed through him, along with a mix of uneasiness and cautious excitement.

The killer had made contact. What did that mean? His investigation into the other murders hadn't indicated any kind of contact between victim and killer.

He drove as fast as possible and within five minutes was back at the Diamond Cove and out of his car. He hurried toward unit seven, his heartbeat racing.

A rivulet of relief flooded through him when Jordon opened the door to his knock. She'd taken off her coat and boots and appeared to be just fine.

"Thanks for coming back," she said as she closed the door behind him. She pointed to a white piece of paper on the bed. "That was slid beneath my door at some point or another while I was gone today."

He walked over to the bed and stared down at the note. Jordon moved to stand next to him, her fresh scent filling his head as the blatant threat of the words on the paper tightened his gut.

"Do you think it's really from the killer?" she asked. "I didn't see anything in the case files about notes to the victims."

"This is something new and we have to treat it as a serious threat."

"Not that many people know I'm here," she replied.

"This is a small town with a healthy gossip mill. By now probably dozens of people know you're in town and staying here." He turned to look at her. "You need to get out of here. Pack your things and I'll check you into a nearby motel."

She took a step back from him and put her hands on her hips. "I'm not going anywhere." Her eyes flashed and her chin thrust upward. "If that note is from the killer, then it's the first real piece of evidence we have. Hopefully, you can lift a fingerprint off it."

"And it shows that you now have a bull's-eye on

your head. I can't allow you in good conscience to remain here." The idea of anything happening to her absolutely horrified him.

She laughed, a low husky sound. "Guess what, Chief Walters—you don't get to allow or not allow me to do anything. You aren't my boss."

He stared back at the note and then looked back at her. "Jordon, be reasonable. You're setting yourself up as bait for somebody who has already killed three people." A new frustration burned in his chest. She was right. He couldn't force her to do anything, but he definitely wanted to change her mind.

"I am being reasonable." She stepped closer to him and placed a hand on his chest. "Gabriel, please don't fight me on this. This is what I'm trained for. This is what I do."

The warmth of her hand seemed to burn right through his coat, through his shirt and into his bare skin. He fought a sudden impulse to grab her in his arms and pull her tight against him.

Crazy. These cases were definitely making him crazy. She dropped her hand back to her side and grinned up at him. "This little gun just might be your best opportunity to catch a killer."

"I would prefer for the little gun to stay safely in a holster," he replied.

"Hey, you made a joke," she said.

He frowned, not comforted by her light tone. This

was serious business. "I can't change your mind?" he finally asked.

"No way. I'm a chatty, cheerful morning person and I'm stubborn as hell. Just ask my ex-husband."

He released a deep sigh. "I've got an evidence bag and gloves in my car trunk. I'll just go get them and I'll be right back."

A wealth of worry rode his shoulders as he headed back outside to his car. There was no question he wanted the killer caught, but not at the expense of Jordon's safety.

She's trained, he told himself. *She's an FBI agent. She knows the risk and obviously embraces it.* But that thought certainly didn't comfort him in any real way.

He grabbed an evidence bag and a pair of gloves from his trunk and then hurried back to the room with a heavy concern still burning inside him.

As he placed the paper in the bag, she sat on the edge of the bed, her eyes glittering brightly. "This is the break you've needed," she said. "I feel it in my bones and my bones rarely lie."

He sealed the bag and then sank down in the chair next to the fireplace, reluctant to leave her alone. "You know I'd feel better if you'd leave here and stay someplace else."

She shook her head. "This is where I need to be. First thing in the morning I'll talk to Ted and Joan and ask them if they saw anyone unusual on the premises today."

He frowned thoughtfully. "Kevin Rollings didn't have time to get here and leave a note after we left the maze."

"That note could have been slipped under my door at any time during the day after we left here. He's not coming off my suspect list so easily and neither are his brothers."

"As far as I'm concerned, all of the Rollings brothers are up there on the list. Before I head home I'll stop at the Overtons' and see if they saw anyone on the property today who shouldn't have been here." He released a deep sigh. "I should put a couple of men on duty here so that you aren't so vulnerable."

"Don't you dare," she replied fervently. "This place is relatively isolated and any men you put here would be visible. Their presence would drive the killer underground. If he doesn't come after me, then he might be patient enough to come after another guest when Joan and Ted open the doors again."

She leaned forward. "You have to trust me, Gabriel. You have to believe that I know the risk and I accept it. He's not going to get the jump on me."

A helpless inevitability swept through him. She was right. The last thing he wanted was for the killer to fall off the radar only to target another guest, and sooner or later, the Overtons would need to open their doors and have paying guests staying here again.

The only thing he could hope was that the note might yield a clue, a fingerprint, an unusual watermark…anything that might lead to the guilty.

"Now, unless you want to watch me slosh around naked in a tub of bubbles and hot water, you'd better get out of here," she said.

His mind was suddenly seized with erotic visions that heated his blood. He consciously willed them away and stood. "I hope whatever you do you'll keep your gun right next to you." He picked up the bagged note from the coffee table.

"Don't look so grim," she said as she got up from the bed. "You need to remember that the other three victims weren't armed and were unaware of the danger that was present here."

There was some comfort. Still, even as she walked him to the door, he realized he'd never been so reluctant to leave a woman. "Stay alert," he said.

"Always. I'll see you in the morning." She opened the door and he walked out into the cold, a cold that couldn't begin to rival the chill in his heart as he thought of Jordon being the next potential victim.

JORDON BOLTED UPRIGHT and grabbed for her gun. She gasped for air as she struggled to leave her nightmares behind. The room was cast in shadows, partially lit by the bathroom light she'd left on all night.

As her breathing returned to normal, she placed

her gun back on the nightstand. There was no danger here except for in the dreams she'd left behind.

A glance at the clock on the nightstand let her know it was just after five. It would be another hour before her alarm would ring, but she knew there was no way she'd go back to sleep.

She flopped back on the mattress and stared up at the dark ceiling. It had been months since she'd had any nightmares, but last night her sleep had been filled with them.

Ralph Hicks and his mirrors had invaded her dreams, yanking her back to that cellar and the terror of those long hours. She'd also dreamed of a faceless figure she knew was the killer who had now marked her for death if she was to believe the note left for her.

And there was no reason for her not to believe. Like the other victims, she was the only guest here, and from past actions, that was what the killer liked.

She'd be stupid not to feel a healthy dose of fear, but she knew that specific fear would help her stay alive. She hadn't been afraid on that day a year ago when she'd knocked on Ralph Hicks's door to ask him some questions about the murders going on in the neighborhood.

The forty-six-year-old man hadn't been on anyone's radar as a suspect, but he had lived next door to the latest victim and so was on the list to be interrogated. She hadn't known she was in danger until he smashed her over the head and rendered her unconscious.

The experience had taught her a valuable lesson, that everyone was a potential suspect and danger could leap out of nowhere. With a sigh she slid out of the bed, grabbed her gun once again and padded into the bathroom to get ready for the day.

As she dressed she thought of the people they'd interviewed the day before. Certainly Kevin Rollings hadn't hidden his resentment of this place, but did that make him their killer? Or was he simply a bitter man who verbally railed against all the perceived injustices of his world? Billy Bond had been sketchy, but that didn't make him a killer, either.

They just didn't have enough information yet. Today they would be pounding the pavement and asking more questions, and hopefully something they stumbled on would help break the case wide open.

She was huddled by the dining room door, freezing her butt off, when Joan unlocked and opened the door at quarter till seven.

"I positively hate winter," she exclaimed as she shrugged off her coat and then headed for the coffee.

"I really don't mind it too much." A frown dug into Joan's forehead and her eyes were dark. "Gabriel told us about the note you got. We didn't see anyone around your door yesterday and we didn't notice any strangers on the property. I wish we would have seen somebody. I can't tell you how much I wish we would have seen the person responsible and you and Chief Walters could make an arrest and end all this."

Jordon poured herself a cup of coffee and then sat at the table and gestured for Joan to join her. "Is running a bed-and-breakfast something you always dreamed about doing?" she asked in an attempt to change the subject and erase Joan's worry at least for a few minutes.

"Always, although it took me some time to get Ted completely on board with the idea. I think he worried that it would be too much work for me, but I absolutely love it. I love that the entire family is involved, and I was ready to get the kids out of the city and into a more family-oriented environment."

"Were you having problems with the children?" Jordon asked curiously.

"No real problems, although Jason had started hanging out with some kids I didn't really approve of and his grades were dropping and Hannah had started getting attitude."

Jordon smiled. "What fifteen-year-old girl doesn't have a little attitude with her mother?"

Joan laughed, but the laughter was short-lived and once again her eyes darkened. "We took such a gamble by making the move here. We put our entire life savings into buying this place. If it doesn't work out for us I don't know what we'll do."

"We're going to get this person, Joan. We're going

to get him, and all of your rooms will fill up once again and you all will be just fine."

Joan gave her a grateful smile. "Chief Walters has been wonderful through all of this. He's been working so hard and I know these murders are eating him alive. I'm glad you're here to help him."

"We're definitely doing everything we can," Jordon replied.

Joan leaned back in her chair. "I'm just sorry you aren't going to get a chance to see some of the sights and have some fun while you're here."

"Actually, I did manage to go through Mouse's Maze of Mirrors."

"Hannah and Jason love that place," Joan replied.

"I wasn't a big fan," Jordon admitted.

"Really? Why not?"

"I don't like mirrors, but that's another story altogether."

Both women turned toward the door as Gabriel came inside. "Good morning," he said.

"Back at you," Jordon replied.

Joan got up from the table. "I'll just go see to breakfast." As Joan left the room, Gabriel took off his coat and sat across from Jordon.

His gaze was dark and intense. "You doing okay?"

"I'm fine as a fiddle."

"No problems overnight?" he asked.

"None at all. Do you know it takes more muscles to frown than it does to smile?"

He sat back in the chair and a smile curved his lips. "Is that better?"

It wasn't just better—it was freaking amazing. He had a smile that could light up the darkest corner of the earth. There was no question that she was intensely attracted to him and she thought he might be more than a little bit drawn to her.

But she also had a feeling Gabriel wasn't interested in a hot sexual fling, and that was all it would be. That was all she would ever be to any man. That was her choice.

For the next fifteen minutes they drank coffee and talked about the plans for the day. Joan brought in plates of biscuits and gravy with sausage patties on the side and a fresh fruit salad. Ted came in and joined them for small talk while they ate.

It was just after eight thirty before they were in Gabriel's car and headed to their first stop for the day to check Kevin's alibi for the night Sandy Peters had been murdered.

"Dave Hampton and I have a bit of a history," Gabriel said. "I've had to arrest him several times for drunk and disorderly. The man loves his booze, and when he drinks too much, he gets stupid and nasty."

"Are you expecting trouble with him? Because if you are, I've got your back, partner."

He cast her a quick glance. "Are you always so sure of yourself?" he asked wryly.

"Only when I'm on the job," she replied. "I know what I'm good at."

"And what are you good at besides being a kick-ass FBI agent?"

Not much. She shoved the two hurtful words away. "I'm great at zapping food in a microwave. I can do five cartwheels in a row without getting dizzy, and when I sing I can make every dog in a five-mile area howl."

He cast her a charming grin. "I'm impressed."

"What about you? Besides being a kick-ass chief of police, what else are you good at?"

He frowned thoughtfully and then the frown lifted, and when he shot her a quick glance, his eyes were a lighter, more inviting blue that she hadn't seen before.

"I can twist an aluminum can into a work of art. I can get almost any dog to eat out of my hand if I'm holding a good piece of steak, and I know all the lyrics to Manfred Mann's 'Blinded by the Light.'"

"Whew, now I'm the one impressed." What impressed her more than anything was that he had responded with the same silly lightness as her. She didn't think he had it in him. There was nothing sexier than a man who didn't always take himself and the world too seriously.

However, the light mood disappeared as he pulled into Charlie's Brake and Muffler Repair. "Dave works here as a mechanic," he said.

"Let's go talk to Dave the drunk and see if he can corroborate Kevin's alibi."

Gray clouds hung low in the sky as they walked toward the large building with four bays. Men's voices rang out along with the sound of noisy tools being used.

They entered into a small office where a man stood behind a counter. "Charlie," Gabriel greeted the man. "How's business?"

"A little slow, but not too bad." His gaze swept the length of Jordon. "I'm hoping you're here because you or the little lady needs a brake job."

"This *little lady* doesn't need brakes," Jordon said drily.

"Actually, we're here to speak to Dave," Gabriel said.

Charlie frowned. "Good grief. What has he done now?"

"Nothing. We just need to ask him a couple of questions," Gabriel replied.

Charlie pointed to a nearby door. "You can use the break room. I'll go get Dave and send him in."

The break room held a card table that cast slightly to one side and was littered with what appeared to be petrified crumbs from meals past, a couple of chairs and a soda machine. The air smelled of grease and oil. Neither of them sat.

Dave Hampton was a big man with a shock of thick dark hair and a scowl that appeared to have been etched permanently into his face. "I haven't done anything wrong. What's this all about?" He glared first at Gabriel and then at Jordon as he wiped his hands on a filthy rag.

"We just need to ask you a couple of questions and then we'll let you get back to work," Gabriel said.

"Questions about what?" He stuffed the rag into his coverall's pocket.

"About last Sunday night," Gabriel said.

Dave narrowed his eyes. "What about it? I didn't do anything stupid. If somebody said I did then they're a damned liar."

"It's nothing like that," Gabriel assured him. "We just need to know where you were and who you were with."

"A bunch of us went to Hillbilly Harry's to shoot some pool and have a few beers." Dave visibly relaxed.

"Who was with you?"

"Wesley Mayfield, Neil Davies, Tom Richmond and Kevin and Glen Rollings. Is this about that woman's murder?"

"What time did you all leave the bar?" Gabriel asked, ignoring Dave's question.

"I guess it was around midnight or so."

"And none of you left early?"

Dave rocked back on his heels and smiled slyly. "It's Kevin, isn't it? You're wondering if he killed that woman." Dave shook his head and released a small laugh. "Those Rollings boys are thick as thieves, and Kevin hates anything and anyone that has to do with Diamond Cove."

"I got the impression that Kevin didn't get along well with his brothers." Jordon spoke up for the first time.

"That's definitely not true. Kevin raised Glen and Ed after their mother died," Dave said. "According to what Kevin told me, their father was a no-account drunk and Kevin had to step up to be both mother and father to his younger brothers. Like I said before, those three are thick as thieves."

"Was Kevin drunk when you all left the bar?" Jordon asked.

Dave frowned. "We were all a little toasted, but he was no drunker than the rest of us. Is that all? I really need to get back to the shop."

"That's it for now," Gabriel replied.

She and Gabriel didn't speak again until they were back in his car. "There's definitely no honor among thieves," he said as he started the car. "Dave threw Kevin under the bus pretty quickly."

"Kevin told us he got completely trashed, but Dave didn't indicate that Kevin was all that drunk," Jordon replied.

"He was sober enough to drive himself home," Gabriel said. "And Ed has always given me the impression that Kevin isn't close to him or Glen."

Jordon pulled her collar up more tightly around

her neck as a cold wind of uneasiness blew through her. "What worries me now is the possibility that we aren't looking for just one killer, but maybe we have a brotherhood of murderers, and that's definitely only going to complicate things."

Chapter Five

"Where to now, boss?" Jordon asked as they pulled back on the main road.

"How do you feel about a little shopping?"

"Like any reasonable woman, I'm always up for some retail therapy," she replied.

"In the store we're going to you can buy a Branson T-shirt or a corncob pipe, a refrigerator magnet or any one of a thousand other items."

"And I'm guessing that Glen Rollings might be my personal shopper?"

He flashed her a quick smile. "Glen is definitely the charmer of the Rollings boys, but I doubt that you need a personal shopper. You strike me as the kind of woman who usually knows exactly what she wants and you don't stop until you get it."

"You've got that right." She turned her head to look out of the passenger window. At the moment she'd like Gabriel Walters's very kissable mouth to be on hers.

The errant thought could only be because she was cold and she knew being in his arms and kissing him would warm her. She'd been cold since she'd arrived in Branson, if not because of the wintry weather, then from the chill of hunting down a cold-blooded serial killer.

Were they up against a single murderer or was it a tag-team effort? Were Glen and Ed helping the brother who raised them get his revenge on Diamond Cove? It was crazy to think somebody would go to such lengths to destroy a business, but revenge killings had happened for far less.

She turned back to look at Gabriel once again. "What I don't understand is if Kevin really wants to destroy Diamond Cove then why not just set fire to the place? Why not build a bomb and blow it all up?"

He turned into the parking lot of the Ozark Shed of Souvenirs and released a deep sigh. "I don't know. I haven't been able to get a handle on this from the very beginning. This is far more evil than a fire or a bomb. It takes a special kind of killer to stab somebody. This person apparently likes to kill up close and personal."

With his words ringing in her ears, they exited the car and headed for the huge shop.

Evil. The word echoed in her brain. Yes, whatever was going on here was definitely evil.

She knew all about evil. She'd been locked in a

cellar with evil personified for hours, just praying for death to take her quickly.

She shoved the thought away when they entered the store. She gazed around in amazement. Never had she seen so much stuff in one place. Tote bags and camping lanterns, wooden signs and toilet-paper holders in the shape of outhouses fought shelf space with traveler-size toothpaste and T-shirts and blinged-out wallets and purses.

She followed Gabriel to a sales counter where a gray-haired woman greeted them. "Gabriel," she said with a big smile that lifted all of her wrinkles upward. "I hope that's a girlfriend with you and you've come in to buy one of our real, stunning Ozark gold rings."

Gabriel laughed, a low, deep and appealing sound. "Special Agent James, meet Wanda Tompkins, the orneriest woman in the entire town."

"Nice to meet you, ma'am," Jordon said.

"You, too," Wanda replied and looked back at Gabriel. "So, if this pretty woman isn't your girlfriend and you aren't here to buy anything, then what can I help you with?"

"We need to speak with Glen," Gabriel said.

"He's upstairs in the back room." Wanda gave Jordon a sly smile. "A shame you aren't his girlfriend. He's a good man who needs a good woman."

"Be careful or I'll arrest you for attempted matchmaking," he replied in a mock-stern voice. "And do I need to remind you that this isn't your first offense."

Wanda laughed and waved a hand at him. "Go on with your bad self." She turned her attention to a group of tourists who had entered the store.

"So Wanda has tried to hook you up?" Jordon asked as they climbed a narrow set of wooden stairs to the second floor.

"When I first arrived in town this store was robbed and that's when I first met Wanda. There was about six months after that when she made finding me a wife her life's mission. She still calls me occasionally to tell me about some nice woman I should meet."

"And did you ever meet any of them?" she asked.

"A few."

"They weren't wife material?"

"They were for somebody, but just not for me."

They reached the top of the stairs and she followed behind him as they wound through several aisles of merchandise. The man was drop-dead gorgeous, wore a respected uniform and seemed to be a genuinely nice guy.

There must be plenty of women in this town who would love to get hitched to a man like him. Cautious, that was what he'd told her he was, but she wondered if maybe he wasn't just super picky.

Jordon had believed she'd married a man like Gabriel, a man who was well respected, principled and moral. She'd been head over heels in love with Jack and after that debacle she never wanted to give any man her heart. Although something about Gabriel made her think some time in a bed with him would be totally awesome.

As they reached the doorway to a storage room, she mentally kicked herself for her errant thoughts. She wasn't here to have a quick, hot hookup. They had a killer to catch.

Like his brothers, Glen Rollings had pleasant features, blond hair and light blue eyes. He was tall and thin, and when Gabriel made the introductions, Glen's gaze swept the length of her.

"You're an FBI agent? Wow. That's hot." He gave her a wink that she assumed he thought was sexy. It was totally lame.

"We want to ask you a few questions," Gabriel said.

Glen gazed at Jordon once again. "Maybe the superhot FBI agent wants to tie me up to interrogate me." He winked at her again.

"Knock it off, Romeo. We're here on serious business," she said with narrowed eyes.

The smile on his face slowly faded. "I know why you're here. Everyone knows a woman was murdered at Diamond Cove." He shook his head. "I wish my brother had never bought that damned place and I also wish he'd keep his mouth shut about how much he hates it."

"So where were you last Sunday night?" Gabriel asked.

As Glen told the same story that Dave had told them earlier, Jordon listened carefully for any inconsistencies.

"And what did you do after you left the bar?" she asked when he was finished.

"Went home…unfortunately alone," he replied.

"Did any neighbors see you? Anyone call you?" she pressed.

"My closest neighbors are a retired couple who go to bed at the crack of dusk, and no, I didn't get any calls." Glen frowned and gazed at Gabriel. "I told you the last time you talked to me that you're barking up the wrong tree. I'm a lover, not a killer."

"Do you text?" Jordon asked.

Glen's frown deepened. "Occasionally. Why?"

"Just curious. Can I see your phone?" Jordon asked.

Glen cast her a sly look. "I may be a dumb country hick, but I've watched enough cop shows to know you need a warrant for that."

Jordon wasn't surprised that he didn't hand it over. Cell phones were as intimate as underwear. You could tell a lot about a person just by looking at their text messages.

Their questioning ended and they headed back downstairs. "I can't leave here without buying a Branson T-shirt," she said. "I love sleeping in oversize T-shirts."

It took her only minutes to find a hot-pink shirt with *Branson* written in bold black letters across the chest. She paid Wanda and then they returned to the car.

They managed to hunt down two more of the men who had been at Hillbilly Harry's with Kevin and Glen on the night of the murder, and then at six thirty they stopped in a pizza place for dinner.

"So, we know Kevin and Glen have a solid alibi until midnight on the night Sandy was murdered," Jordon said as she pulled a piece of the pie onto the smaller plate in front of her.

"But none of the Rollingses can prove that they were home all night after midnight except Ed, who was supposedly home with his wife." He frowned. "We need to touch base with her."

"Could you prove where you were on a specific night between midnight and five or six in the morning?" She didn't wait for his reply. "Unless you have somebody in bed with you, it's hard to have an alibi for that time."

"It's a good thing I don't need to provide an alibi for the middle of the night." He took a bite of the pizza and stared off into the distance.

A lonely man. He wore his loneliness in quiet moments. She recognized it. She understood it because she had a same core of emptiness inside her. She'd had it before her marriage and even more so since the day she'd walked out on her husband. It was a part of her that she tried not to acknowledge.

"I love pepperoni," she said to break the silence that had stretched too long between them. She picked a piece of it off her pizza slice and popped it into her mouth. "Thick crust and pepperoni—there's nothing better."

For the next ten minutes they talked about the merits of different kinds of pizza. It was a welcome respite after the murder talk that had been the subject of most of their conversations during the day.

It was almost eight when he pulled up in the Diamond Cove parking area. The sun had gone down and dusk had given way to night.

"See you for breakfast?" She grabbed her purse and her shopping bag with the T-shirt.

"I'll be here. Stay safe through the night."

"Stop worrying about me. I'll be just fine," she replied. She got out of the car and opened her coat so she had easy access to her gun.

As she walked to her room, the loneliness she'd sensed in Gabriel resonated deep inside her. There were moments when she wished she had somebody meaningful in her life, somebody to share the ups and downs of the days and hold her in big strong arms through the night.

At one time she'd wanted that, she'd believed she deserved that, but she no longer believed.

"Been there, done that," she muttered as she unlocked her door and went inside. And it had been a heartbreaking experience that she never wanted to repeat.

She tossed her purse on the bed and pulled the T-shirt out of the shopping bag and carried it and her gun with her into the bathroom.

After a quick shower she pulled on the soft cotton shirt and then climbed into the comfortable big bed with her laptop. As she had before, she typed notes into a growing file she'd named Means and Motive.

It was often those two elements that ultimately solved a case. Who had the means to execute the crime and who had the motive?

She'd been typing in notes for about half an hour when a bump sounded against the building near her door. Every nerve inside her electrified. Her heartbeat raced as she grabbed her gun from the nightstand.

U R Next.

The words screamed inside her head as she slid out of bed and approached the door. If she opened it, would she be met by somebody wielding a deadly sharp knife, ready to follow through on the threat? Was this potentially an attack like the one that had taken Sandy Peters's life?

She gripped her gun more firmly. She wasn't Sandy Peters and nobody was going to take her by surprise. Drawing a deep breath to steady herself, she reached out, turned the lock and then jerked open the door.

She was greeted only by a cold gust of wind that

momentarily stole her breath away. No knife-wielding maniac, no quick attack.

Nobody.

She took a step outside onto the porch and looked around. Nothing. She wouldn't see anyone in the area. The darkness of night would cover anyone's presence.

It was only when she turned to go back into the room that she noticed one of the rocking chairs in front of her window had been moved.

It looked as if somebody had been trying to peer into her window and had accidentally bumped into the chair. Whoever it was, there was definitely no sign of the person now.

She stepped back into the room and closed and locked her door. Her heart still raced as she climbed back into the bed and pointed her gun toward the door.

"Come and get me, you creep," she whispered.

THE NEXT FOUR days passed far too quickly. Jordon had told Gabriel about the Peeping Tom incident and again he'd tried to get her to move to another motel, but she was adamant that she was right where she wanted…where she needed to be.

She'd been right. She was definitely stubborn and he'd tried a dozen ways to change her mind, but she wasn't budging. The fact that she'd been warned that she was the next victim and she continued staying at Diamond Cove had given him several nightmares over the last couple of nights.

They had interviewed all the men who had been at Hillbilly Harry's on the night of Sandy's murder, they'd pored over the files in an effort to find something they might have missed, and by late Sunday afternoon, Gabriel had all kinds of anxiety burning in the pit of his stomach. He figured by the time these cases were solved he'd have ulcers as big as the Ozark foothills.

The Rollings brothers remained high on the suspect list, along with Billy Bond, who as groundskeeper had easy access to all the victims and might have known their routines, but no new evidence had been revealed to make an arrest.

Unfortunately, the note that had been left for Jordon had yielded nothing...no fingerprints and no distinctive features. The paper was ordinary copy paper that could be bought almost anywhere in town and beyond.

Because it had been written like somebody would write a text, they had questioned everyone again about texting, including Jason and Hannah Overton, who might have thought leaving such a note would be funny.

The two teenagers had proclaimed their innocence passionately and Gabriel had been surprised to learn that almost everyone these days texted in abbreviated language. It had made him feel like an ancient old man.

He now closed the file that held the crime-scene photos and looked across the conference table where Jordon had been reading through the interviews they'd conducted over the last several days.

"Why don't we knock off early, and instead of grabbing a burger out somewhere, I'll take you to my place and fix us a home-cooked meal," he said.

"That sounds absolutely marvelous," she replied. Her eyes were a warm green as she rose from the table and reached for her coat. "A little break will be nice. I've been thinking about murder for the past week."

"Then let's make a pact that for the next couple of hours we won't talk about work at all."

"That's a deal," she instantly agreed.

Within fifteen minutes they were in Gabriel's car and headed to his house. Although he'd certainly had his head immersed in these cases for the last seven days, he'd also had far too many inappropriate thoughts about his "partner."

Her scent invaded his senses when he was sleeping; the visions of her clad only in bubbles in the oversize tub haunted his dreams. He could easily imagine her in bed and clad only in the hot-pink oversize T-shirt she'd bought.

He had no idea if taking her to his house for a meal was a good idea or not, but he did know they both needed a break from the mind-numbing routine of the investigation and the endless fast food they'd eaten over the past week.

"It doesn't look like you're going to make that beach in Florida unless we get a break pretty fast," he said.

"I already canceled my reservations. I also heard on the weather last night that we're supposed to get a big snowstorm here starting tomorrow night." She leaned forward and adjusted the heater vents as if just thinking about the upcoming snow made her cold.

"I'm sorry about your vacation plans."

She leaned back in the seat again. "The beach will still be there after we catch this creep. What's for dinner?"

"How does spaghetti with meat sauce sound?"

"Fantastic. Do you like to cook?"

"I do. I find it a good stress reliever." He shot her a quick glance. "What do you do to relieve stress?"

"I've always thought primal screaming sounded like a great idea but it's hard to find an empty forest when you need one," she said jokingly. "Actually, stress rolls off my back pretty easily."

"I've noticed that about you." He'd definitely noticed that she used humor to ease tension and alleviate any stress that might be in the air. He wondered what might lurk beneath her humor. What depths of emotions, if any, did she mask with laughter?

And then he wondered why he cared. She was here only temporarily. Despite his visceral attraction to her, there was no way he intended to pursue anything remotely romantic with her.

"Nice place," she said as he pulled up in front of the three-bedroom house he called home. It was a neat place painted a dark brown and flanked by two tall, beautiful evergreen trees.

Still, the Christmas tree lights remained hung and an inflatable Santa had lost his wave as the air had seeped out. He'd had more important things on his mind than taking down Christmas decorations.

"Santa looks pretty sad," she said as they walked up to the front door.

"Yeah, it was a pretty grim Christmas," he replied.

"Have you been here long?" she asked.

"It's a rental but I've been here for the last three years, ever since I moved here from Chicago." He unlocked the front door and ushered her inside.

They entered into the large living room with the open kitchen to the right. "Make yourself at home," he said as he hung his coat in the closet and then did the same with hers.

She walked around the room, her eyes narrowed as they had been when she'd looked at the crime scenes. He looked around the space in an effort to see it through her eyes.

The overstuffed gray sofa was comfortable for sitting and watching the flat-screen television on the opposite wall. The black coffee table held only a small fake flower arrangement that a woman he'd briefly dated had given him. Lamps were on each of the end tables.

She looked at him and smiled. "Your living space is exactly what I expected it to be."

He raised an eyebrow. "What does that mean?"

"It's neat and uncomplicated. A place for everything and everything in its place." She released a short laugh. "You'd go stark raving mad if we lived together."

"You're messy?"

"I like to call it controlled chaos," she replied.

"Interesting," he said. "How about you bring your controlled chaos into the kitchen so I can start working on the meal."

"Sounds like a plan."

Fifteen minutes later he had a pot of seasoned tomato sauce simmering on one burner and stirred a skillet of frying hamburger, garlic and onions on another.

Jordon sat at the table with a beer and filled what was normally the silent hours he'd grown accustomed to with cheerful chatter that he welcomed.

She was so bright and witty and he was vaguely surprised to realize how much he enjoyed her company. Within thirty minutes he learned that she loved old rock and roll, Chinese food and her neighbor's Yorkie named Taz. She loved to dance in her underwear in her living room and preferred white cheddar to yellow.

As they ate the salad, garlic bread and spaghetti, they argued politics and discovered they watched the same television shows and had read many of the same books.

She asked him about his time working in Chicago and he related many of the cases he'd worked on there. She helped clean up the dishes and they settled side by side on the sofa for coffee.

"I needed this," she said as she eased back against the gray cushion.

"The coffee?"

"No, silly man. I needed this break away from thinking about serial killers and the potential demise of Diamond Cove."

He smiled at her. "Nobody has ever had the nerve to call me a silly man before."

She gave him a brash grin. "I call 'em like I see them, cupcake."

He laughed. "I needed this, too. Maybe after this little break we'll approach everything with fresh eyes tomorrow."

"What we need is fresh evidence, and until this creep makes another move, we're in a holding pattern." A frown danced across her forehead as she lifted her coffee cup to her lips.

"And we're doing exactly what we said we wouldn't do by talking about the case."

She took another sip of the coffee and nodded her

head. "You're right. So, tell me, Gabriel Walters, what is your deepest fear?"

She constantly surprised him. A long look at her features let him know the question was serious. He feared being alone for the rest of his life. He feared that he would never have the family he desperately wanted, but those were things he didn't share with anyone.

"I'd say my biggest fear right now is that we won't catch this guy and somebody else will wind up dead." He couldn't tell her that he worried that particular somebody would be her. "What about you? What's your deepest fear?"

"Big hairy spiders, especially the jumping kind," she replied flippantly.

He gazed at her for a long moment. "Are you ever serious?"

"I'm serious about getting bad guys off the streets," she replied with a slight upward thrust of her chin.

God, she looked so beautiful with that spark of defiance in her eyes. She intrigued him like no other woman had ever done before.

Despite their long hours of working together over the last week, in spite of all the conversations they'd shared, he felt like he'd just scratched the surface of her. He shouldn't want to go any deeper. A superficial relationship was all he needed for them to work well together.

However, right at this moment with her scent wafting in the air and her eyes the soft green of a beautiful spring day, he wanted more. "Tell me why you're afraid of mirrors," he said.

Her eyes instantly darkened and her chin shot up once again. "What makes you think I'm afraid of mirrors?"

He held her gaze intently. A faint color danced into her cheeks. She set her coffee cup on the table in front of them and wrapped her arms around herself. She shifted her gaze to someplace in the distance just behind him and released a shuddery sigh.

"His name was Ralph Hicks." Her voice was soft and her eyes remained shadowed. "He had already tortured and killed five women before I knocked on his door to interview him. I was officially off duty for the day, but I decided to go ahead and get the interview done on my way home from work." She shook her head and her face paled. "I should have gone straight home and danced in my underwear."

He fought the impulse to move closer to her. She looked small and achingly vulnerable as she pressed herself farther into the corner of the sofa.

She drew in a deep breath and continued. "He was so pleasant and unassuming-looking. He invited me inside and nothing rang a bell of alarm in my head. I stepped in and he bashed me over the head with a small bat. I never saw it coming."

She unwound her arms and leaned forward to grab her coffee cup, but before she did, he reached out and took her hand in his. Icy cold and so achingly small. She wound her fingers with his and he slid closer to her. Her face had paled to an unnatural white and her lower lip trembled for just a moment.

"I'm sorry I asked," he said regretfully.

"It's okay." She gave him a small smile that did nothing to light up her eyes. "Thankfully, after he hit me, the last thing I did before I passed out was slide my cell phone under his sofa. When I regained consciousness I was in my underwear and strung up with chains and there were three floor-length mirrors in front of me. Ralph liked his victims to watch themselves as he tortured them."

Gabriel tightened his hand around hers, his stomach churning with sickness as he could only imagine the horrors she had endured. He wanted to rescue her from her past, from that horror, something that he knew wasn't possible.

"I was lucky. By the time he had me trussed up, he decided it was his bedtime. I didn't see him again until midmorning the next day. By the time he came down the stairs to have his fun with me, my fellow agents already knew I was in trouble because I hadn't shown up for work and I never, ever missed work."

"They traced your phone," he said.

She nodded. "They came in hard and fast, but not before Ralph had played on my hip with a lit cigarette." She released his hand and leaned back once again. "The good news is Ralph got a bullet in his chest and I walked out of there with just a heart-shaped scar."

"And an aversion to mirrors," he added.

"Only if there's more than one," she replied as her face regained most of its color. "And now I think it's time you get me back to Diamond Cove."

He wanted to protest. He wanted more time with her, but her eyes remained hollow and he realized that sharing her story had taken an emotional toll on her.

Twenty minutes later they were back at the bed-and-breakfast and Gabriel got out of the car as she did. "What are you doing?" she asked.

"I just thought I'd walk you to your door," he replied. She'd been quiet on the way back and he'd cursed himself for digging deep enough to dredge up what must have been horrendous memories for her. If he had any questions about whether there was something behind her humor and laughter, he now had the answer.

"That isn't necessary," she protested.

"I know, but it's something I feel like doing. Besides, if the weather forecast is right, by Tuesday morning I might not be able to make it here at all." He walked behind her on the small path.

"Ugh, don't remind me. More snow, more winter—it makes me want to throw up," she replied.

They reached her door and she turned to face him.

Her features were softly lit by the nearby solar lamps. "Thank you for the meal and the conversation."

"I'm sorry some of the conversation was difficult for you."

She smiled up at him. "It's something that happened to me, but it's in the past and I survived." Her gaze softened. "When I first arrived here I was sure you were going to be an inflexible, boneheaded pain in my butt, but I was wrong about you. Thank you for putting up with me, Gabriel."

He watched her lips moving, and before he realized his intent, he covered her mouth with his. The evening air was cold, but her lips were wonderfully hot and inviting.

She opened her mouth to him, welcoming him as his tongue deepened the kiss. White-hot desire seared through him. All rational thought momentarily left him, and it wasn't until she raised a hand to gently touch his cheek that rational thought slammed back into his head.

He broke the kiss and stepped back from her, appalled by what he'd just done. It had been a total lack of control. "I'm sorry. That was completely unprofessional and wrong."

"It sure didn't feel wrong," she replied, her cheeks flushed with a becoming pink.

He took another step backward. "Still, it won't happen again."

"Don't bet on it." She dug her key out of her purse

and then smiled at him. "Good night, Gabriel. I'll see you in the morning." She opened her door and disappeared inside.

He stared at her closed door for a long moment as he waited for the desire inside him to ebb. Finally, with the frigid night air seeping into his bones, he turned and hurried to his car.

Jordon James was like no other woman he had ever dated. *She's a partner, not a date*, he reminded himself firmly as he started his engine and pulled out of the Diamond Cove parking lot.

They needed to get this case solved sooner rather than later. They needed to find the murderer so Jordon could get back to Kansas City before he really did something boneheaded.

Chapter Six

The snow began to fall at six o'clock the next evening. Jordon sat at the conference room table and stared out the window at the fat, fluffy flakes drifting down from the heavy gray skies.

She was alone in the room. Gabriel had left almost twenty minutes ago to deal with an armed robbery that had taken place at one of the convenience stores.

She'd been distracted all day...distracted by a single kiss. It surprised her how much she'd liked that darned kiss, how much she wanted to repeat it... and more.

Neither of them had mentioned it throughout the day and she had a feeling Gabriel definitely wished it had never happened. But it had and she'd thought about it far too often as the long hours had gone by.

Releasing a deep sigh, she focused back on the files in front of her. Although neither of them had said it out loud, they were at a dead end.

They had checked and rechecked the Rollings

brothers and Billy Bond, and while they remained on the suspect list, she and Gabriel had no real evidence to point a finger at anyone. They had also dug a little deeper into the Overtons' background, but nothing in their past had raised a red flag or indicated any reason why somebody would want to hurt either one of them.

Now there was a blizzard forecast for overnight and it would probably stymie any further investigation at least through the next day or so. Jeez, she hated winter and she hated this killer.

She stared out the window once again, her thoughts flittering back to the evening before. She hadn't meant to tell Gabriel about Ralph Hicks and what had happened in that cellar. She'd thought she'd covered her anxiety well, but Gabriel had obviously picked up on her panic attack in the mirror maze.

He'd offered her just the right amount of support... a warm and strong hand holding hers and not so much sympathy that she felt guilty about sharing the events of that dark moment in her past.

He'd seen her more vulnerable, more fragile than she liked anyone to see her, but for some reason Gabriel felt safe. She knew instinctively that he was a man who would keep all of her secrets. Funny. She was a woman who didn't trust easily and yet within seven days she trusted Gabriel implicitly.

Not that any of that mattered. Once they caught the killer she'd go back to Kansas City, and within a month or two Gabriel probably wouldn't even remember her name. She wasn't sure why that thought depressed her a bit.

"Sorry about that," he said as he breezed back into the room.

"Not a problem. I know as head of this department you have lots of other things to attend to besides this case."

"Thank God I've got good men and women working with me and for the most part the department practically runs itself." He sank down in the chair across from hers and raked a hand through his thick, shiny hair. "I assigned a couple of men to investigate the armed robbery, but before I could get out of my office, I got a butt-chewing phone call from the mayor."

She raised an eyebrow. "Does he think we're not doing whatever we can to solve this?"

"He was all puffed up like a peacock and talking about his responsibility to the town. He reminded me that a serial killer running amok hurts the tourist trade Branson depends on, as if I'm too dense to know that."

"You might be a silly man, but I would never call you dense," Jordon said in an effort to lighten the dark frustration in his eyes.

It worked. His eyes lightened a bit and he leaned back in his chair. "What I'd like to be right now is a magician. I'd like to wave a magic wand and have all the answers to solve this case in my hand once and for all."

"Unfortunately, we're both short on magic wands at the moment," she replied. "Face it, partner. We've conducted a solid, thorough investigation but we're kind of at a dead end at the moment. We've hit a brick wall."

He leaned forward and released a deep sigh. "I know and it's frustrating as hell."

"Look on the bright side. The perp could attack me at any moment and then I'll nab him," she said lightly.

His gaze darkened once again. "Jordon, don't even joke about that." He scooted his chair out and stood, walked to the window and peered outside. "We probably need to head out of here. The snow is coming down pretty hard. We should also stop someplace on the way and pick you up some supplies in case I can't get to you first thing in the morning."

"Don't worry about supplies—I'll be fine. Before you arrived for breakfast this morning, Joan told me no matter how bad the weather gets, breakfast will be served as usual and she'd make sure additional meals would be available if we all get snowed in."

"Should we pick you up a sub sandwich or something else for later tonight?" His gaze once again went out the window.

"Not necessary. I'm still full from the burgers we ate earlier. I've also got some chips and peanuts left in the room if I get the munchies. I'll be fine for the rest of the night." She got up and pulled on her coat.

As they left the building to get into Gabriel's car,

she was surprised to see how quickly the snow was piling up on the road. Already a couple of inches of new snow had fallen on everything.

"Just drop me off and get yourself home safe and sound. The roads look like they're already getting treacherous," she said.

Minutes later her words proved true as Gabriel slowly maneuvered the snow-covered streets with blowing snow that made visibility difficult.

She grasped the edges of her seat as the back wheels slid out and he quickly corrected. A muscle throbbed in his jawline as he frowned in concentration. They didn't speak until he reached the Diamond Cove parking lot.

"Don't wait another minute. Get someplace safe for the night," she said as she unbuckled her seat belt.

"I'll call you in the morning," he replied.

She nodded and got out of the car. The wind stole her breath and the snow stung her face and any bare skin as she hurried up the path that would take her to her room. When she reached her door she looked behind her, grateful to see the faint red glow of Gabriel's taillights as he drove away.

She hated winter more than she hated fried liver, more than she despised her ex-husband. She hoped Gabriel got home safe and sound. This was definitely not a good night to be out on the roads.

Her fingers trembled from the frigid air as she put her key into the doorknob and opened the door.

A person exploded out of the room toward her. She had only a second to register a black ski mask, a black or navy coat and the glint of the long, sharp knife as it slashed at her.

She stumbled backward, dropped her purse and fumbled for her gun as she raised her other arm defensively in front of her. She gasped as the blade sliced through the arm of her coat.

Before she could clear her gun from her holster, the figure shoved past her and ran toward the woods. Jordon nearly fell backward, but quickly regained her balance and followed. There was no way she was going to let the perp get away.

"Halt, or I'll shoot," she cried just before the person darted behind a tree.

Jordon raced ahead, the wind howling in her ears and her face and fingers freezing. She had no time to process the attack that had just occurred, a surprise attack that might have killed her. All of her training kicked in and she had only one goal in mind.

This was the perfect opportunity to bring him down. She refused to let the cold and the near-blinding conditions stop her. She absolutely refused to give in to any fear that tried to take hold of her. She didn't have time for fear.

There was no question in her mind that this was the serial killer they sought. He'd obviously hoped to stab her in the chest, to incapacitate her and then finish her off, just like he'd done to Sandy Peters.

If he'd been successful just moments before in his attack, then Gabriel or somebody else would have found her body on the porch sometime the next morning.

The only sound in the woods was the sharp pants of her own breaths as she raced forward and tried to see the dark, deadly figure who shared the area with her.

She paused and swiped at the snow on her face. Where had he gone? Was he hiding behind a tree just waiting to strike out at her again?

Was he behind her? She whirled around, every nerve tense and her heartbeat racing frantically. Her head filled with images of Samantha Kent, who had entered these woods to take pictures but instead had wound up stabbed in the back.

Swirling wind-driven snow made it impossible for her to see more than five feet in front of her. Her lungs ached with the freezing air.

Each tree she passed was a potential hiding place. Every tree in front of her could hide the knife-wielding killer. She walked slowly now, pausing often to listen to see if she could hear anything, but there was nothing but the thundering boom of her heartbeat in her head.

Bitter disappointment filled her as she realized she had no idea where he'd gone. It was possible he wasn't even in the woods anymore.

The wind cut through her, and her face and fingers had gone numb. The snow was coming down so hard now she could barely see her hand in front of her face. It was a whiteout condition.

She had to give it up. It was foolish to hunt a person in these circumstances, especially not knowing the area or if her prey was even still nearby.

She turned to head back to her room and froze in her tracks. She was in a snow globe and completely disoriented. She hadn't paid attention to the direction she'd run.

Was her cabin in front of her or to the left? Was it behind her or to the right? How far away was she from her room? How long had she been running?

Squinting, she tried to see something that would orient her, but there was nothing but snow and wind. She was in trouble. She hadn't been truly scared before, but now she was terrified. She was lost in a blizzard and had no idea where to go.

IT WAS GOING to be a long night. Jordon had assumed Gabriel was going to go home to ride out the storm in the comfort of his own home, but that wasn't happening.

As chief of police, he needed to be out on the road, seeing to stranded motorists or any accidents that were certain to occur with this kind of weather.

He'd left her and driven straight back to the station, where the garage mechanic had put snow chains on his tires. He should have had them put on earlier in the day before the storm was upon them, but he'd been busy.

Thankfully, it took only a few minutes and then he headed for the main drag, grateful to see that it appeared everyone had taken the storm warnings seriously.

Branson appeared like a ghost town. All the stores and restaurants had closed up. Shows had been canceled and there was virtually nobody on the streets.

With the near-whiteout conditions, he intended to park in one of the lots in the middle of the strip and ride out the worst of the storm. Hopefully, from here he could respond quickly to anyone who needed help. His police radio crackled as his men on duty gave updates from where they were located.

He'd just parked when his cell phone rang. A jangle of nerves coursed through him as he recognized the number as Jordon's.

"Jordon?"

"I'm sorry… I'm lost, Gabriel. I'm lost and so cold."

He sat up straighter, his heart racing. "Jordon, where are you?"

"In the woods. I'm someplace in the woods. He came after me and I chased him, but now I don't know where I am. There's so much snow. Everything is white, so white." Panic screamed from her voice and a sickness surged inside him.

"Jordon, stay where you are. I'm coming to find you."

"Okay, and, Gabriel, please hurry."

He was already racing down the street as fast as the conditions would allow him, which wasn't half-fast enough for his panicked alarm. Damn the snow that now fell in sheets.

He kept her on the phone as he radioed for more men to meet him at Diamond Cove. Once he'd called for help, she told him in a halting voice about the person waiting for her in her room and attacking her with a knife.

His heartbeat thundered inside his chest. She'd nearly been stabbed but he couldn't fully process that now. The biggest threat to her at the moment was the weather, and if she'd run from her room as soon as Gabriel had left the bed-and-breakfast, then she'd been out in the elements far too long.

By the time he reached Diamond Cove, her chattering teeth were audible over the phone as she kept up a stream of conversation.

He was grateful to see two of his men already there and waiting for him. "Agent James is someplace in the woods. We'll stick together and cover the area," he said to them. "It's also possible that our killer is someplace out here, so stay alert.

"Jordon, we're here and we have flashlights," he said into his cell phone. "Let me know when you see or hear us."

"I'm officially now a snow cone. A cherry snow cone because that's my favorite flavor. If I was from Italy I'd be an Italian ice," she said and released a small burst of laughter that bordered on hysteria.

He wasn't surprised that she'd defaulted to humor. He'd known her long enough to realize it was her way to deal with stress or fear. "We're on our way, Jordon."

"Maybe it's better to be a snow angel than a snow cone," she said and rambled on about making snow angels when she'd been younger and had lived in Denver with her parents.

Gabriel led the men to her suite, where the door was still open, her key remained in the doorknob and her purse was on the ground. He threw her purse inside the room, pulled the key out, shoved it into his pocket and then closed the door.

It was impossible to follow any footprints. The wind and the falling snow had already covered whatever prints there might have been. As they stepped off the porch and entered the woods, all three of them began to yell her name as their flashlights scanned the snowy landscape.

Gabriel could only pray they were going in the right direction. After only a few steps, the cold ached inside him and his face stung. He couldn't imagine how frozen she must be.

It was slow going as visibility was nearly down

to nothing, and the men walked side by side so that none of them would get lost, as well.

As Jim and Bill yelled her name, Gabriel kept the phone pressed tightly against his ear. "Maybe I'm a snow woman," Jordon said. "If somebody is making me into a snow woman then I definitely want bigger boobs."

Gabriel was grateful he didn't have her on speaker. He knew without a doubt she wouldn't want anyone else hearing this conversation but him.

How much longer could she stay out here in the cold? She already sounded half-delirious. He was also aware that she could be vulnerable to another attack by whoever had gone after her in the first place.

His brain flashed with visions of what Samantha Kent must have looked like when Billy Bond had found her. According to the groundskeeper, she'd been facedown on the ground and bleeding out from the vicious stab wounds she'd suffered.

They had to find Jordon. They had to find her right now. The wind seemed to swallow the men's cries and Gabriel realized Jordon had stopped babbling.

"Jordon?" he asked urgently.

"I'm here... I think I heard somebody shouting my name."

"Scream...scream as loud as you can," he replied. He took the phone away from his ear.

A raw, ear-piercing scream shattered the silence.

It not only sounded from the cell phone in his hand, but also from someplace to the left of them.

"This way," Jim said urgently and headed in that direction.

Suddenly she was in front of them. Snow covered her dark hair and her shoulders, and her eyes glowed wild in the light. "Jordon!" Gabriel shut off the cell phone and stuffed it into his pocket as he ran toward her.

"Gabriel!" She met him and slammed her body into his, her arms wrapping tightly around his waist. "Thank God you found me," she said with a half sob.

He held her tight for only a couple of seconds. "Let's get you out of here." With his arm around her shoulders, the four of them headed back to the cabin.

First he wanted her safe and warm, and then he wanted to know every single detail that had led up to her being out in the woods in a blizzard.

Once they reached her suite, he thanked Bill and Jim and they left to get back on the road to help anyone else who might be in trouble.

Gabriel's first order of business was Jordon. As she stood shivering, he shrugged out of his coat and then pulled hers off. "Sit," he said and pointed to the chair next to the fireplace. He turned on the flames and then hurried to the bathroom for a towel.

His blood ran cold as he saw that the window in the small room was open and the screen was nowhere to be seen. He grabbed a hand towel and used it to slam it shut. He tried to lock it, but the lock didn't work. This answered how the perp had gotten inside.

He took a couple of bath towels from the stack on the back of the commode and hurried back to her. She'd taken off her boots and socks and rubbed her bare feet together. At least she didn't appear to be drowsy or suffering from hypothermia.

"I'm sorry. I didn't mean to be any trouble." Her voice broke with a hiccuping sob.

"Here, dry off your hair," he replied softly. She did as he instructed, and he went to the small closet and pulled down a blanket that was folded on the top shelf.

He wrapped the blanket around her. "Let me see your fingers."

He took one of her hands in his, grateful to see her fingertips were red but didn't show any indication of frostbite. "Now your feet."

She hesitated a moment but then raised her legs so he could grab her ankles. Her toenails were painted a pearly pink and he was grateful again that her toes were cold, but didn't appear to suffer frostbite.

"Okay," he said and she lowered her feet back to the floor. For the first time since he'd answered her call on his phone, his stomach slowly began to unclench. He leaned over her, pulled the blanket more tightly around her and then sat opposite her chair on the edge of the bed.

The beige blanket emphasized the bright green of

her eyes and her dark, damp tousled hair. She looked so fragile and he wanted nothing more than to pull her into his arms and comfort her…warm her. But he had business to attend to.

"Feeling better?"

"A little," she replied.

"Now, tell me exactly what happened after I dropped you off here," he said.

She grimaced and sat up straighter in the chair. "He was waiting for me in here. I opened the door and was met by a knife. He tried to stab me but thankfully only sliced through the arm of my coat. Before I could grab my gun, he pushed past me and ran into the woods. I didn't want him to get away."

Her eyes blazed bright. "I didn't think about the weather. I didn't think of anything except catching him. But it didn't take long for the storm to make it impossible for me to find him."

"Did you get a good look at him?" He asked the question even knowing that if she'd been able to identify him she would have already done so.

"Black ski mask, black or navy coat." She frowned. "It all happened so fast."

"Height…weight?" he asked.

"I…I'm not sure. Maybe taller than me? And with his coat it was difficult to tell body weight." She shrugged the blanket off her shoulders and expelled a deep breath of obvious frustration. "I'm an FBI agent and I can't even tell you exactly what my attacker looked like. I can't even tell you what material his coat was made of."

"Jordon, cut yourself some slack. You were caught by surprise in the middle of a snowstorm. Whoever it was, entry was made through the bathroom window. It looks like the lock doesn't connect right."

She frowned and pulled the blanket back around her shoulders. "I wonder who around here knew the lock wasn't working properly?"

"Our handyman, Ed Rollings, might know," he said grimly.

She stared at him for a long moment. "Don't tell me again you want me to move to another motel. You're right—I was caught by surprise tonight, but that won't happen again and I'm not going anywhere."

Gabriel grimaced. It was as if she'd read his mind and he wanted to shake her for her stubbornness. He walked over to the window and moved the curtain aside to peer outside.

There appeared to be about five inches of snow already on the ground and it was still coming down fast and furiously. Even if there hadn't been any weather conditions to contend with, his decision would be the same.

He turned back to look at her. "I'm not leaving you alone here until that window is fixed, and that won't happen before tomorrow."

"So, I get a snuggle buddy for the night. I like it."

Her lips curved into a smile and her eyes held an inviting light that twisted Gabriel's gut with a new kind of tension.

Chapter Seven

She couldn't get warm.

She felt as if she'd never be truly warm again. Even with the blanket clutched tightly around her shoulders and the knowledge that Gabriel was going to be with her through the night, Jordon still possessed a stubborn inner chill that wouldn't go away.

It wasn't the fear of the close call with the killer that kept her frozen, but rather the moments when she'd been surrounded by the harshness of winter. At least that was what she told herself.

Gabriel wandered the room, obviously looking for something…anything the killer might have left behind before his attack. His shoulders were rigid with tension and his frown was as deep, as dark as she'd ever seen it.

How she wished things had played out differently tonight. If not for the damned winter weather she was certain she would have managed to capture the killer and the case would have been solved.

It would be nice if they found the killer's body in the woods sometime tomorrow, frozen to death and no longer a threat to anyone. But she knew fate wouldn't be so kind.

They wouldn't find anything in the woods. The snowstorm would have effectively erased or covered any evidence the killer might have left behind.

Gabriel disappeared into the bathroom, and she closed her eyes and tried to access any minute detail about the attacker that she might not have thought of before. Hidden face, dark bulky coat and big, wicked knife—that was all she'd seen and it wasn't enough.

She'd been anticipating a potential attack, had been so careful, so cautious whenever she'd come and gone from her room. In her wildest nightmares she'd never dreamed the danger would explode out at her from inside her suite.

The whole room felt slightly tainted now. Her privacy, her safe place had been violated by the mere presence of the killer. Still, she was more determined than ever to remain here.

"I should go get a print kit from my car and see if I can lift anything," Gabriel said as he came back out of the bathroom.

"It wouldn't do any good. He had on gloves." She'd seen the knife and she now realized she'd also seen the hand that held it. "Big, black gloves. You won't find anything in here. You didn't find anything in Sandy Peters's room or at the other two crime scenes.

This creep is careful and he still hasn't made a mistake."

Once again he sat on the edge of the bed facing her. She pulled the blanket closer around her throat. "I don't think it was Ed."

He sat up straighter. "Why do you say that?"

She frowned and once again went over every detail of the surprise assault. "Ed is a bit heavyset and I think our killer is leaner."

"Even if it wasn't Ed that still leaves Glen, Kevin and Billy Bond as potential suspects. None of them are particularly big men."

"Billy Bond would know the woods intimately. As groundskeeper, he probably knows the trails better than anyone else," she replied. "The person I was chasing didn't seem to be running willy-nilly. He seemed to know exactly where he was going."

"You shouldn't have gone out there all alone. You could have been killed, Jordon." His gaze remained dark and troubled as he looked at her.

"Then I would have died doing what I love. Besides, it worked out okay. The only way things would have been better is if I'd managed to get him and you hadn't had to ride to my rescue. Did you search all of the woods after Samantha Kent was killed?"

"Every inch of them," he replied.

"Is there anything on the property besides trees and brush?"

"A couple of old outbuildings," he said. "One of

them is nothing more than a lean-to shed where lawn equipment is stored. The other one is just a little bit more substantial."

"Substantial enough to harbor somebody overnight in a snowstorm?"

He ran a hand down his jaw where a five o'clock shadow had begun to appear. "Doubtful. There are no windows or doors in it and it lists badly to one side."

She couldn't control a shiver that overtook her as she remembered the horror of the frigid temperature and the snow that had been everywhere.

"You're still cold. I saw a little coffeepot on the vanity in the bathroom. Do you want me to make some?"

"Not unless you want a cup." She knew what would warm her up. He could. If he'd just wrap her in his arms and kiss her, the inner chill would finally ease. If he took her to bed and made love to her, she'd be wonderfully warm.

With the deep frown cutting across his forehead and the set of his shoulders, the last thing he appeared to have on his mind was any kind of intimacy with her. He probably thought he was going to spend the night on one of the chairs rather than sharing the bed with her.

But he had kissed her and his lips had held the heat of desire and the taste of deep yearning. In the past week she'd felt his attraction toward her. Furtive heated glances, a casual touch that lingered a little too long.

Whether he knew it or not, he'd definitely been sending signals she'd received.

"There's only one way for me to get warm," she said. She shrugged off the blanket and stood. "I need a nice hot bubble bath."

His eyes widened. "Now?"

"Right this very minute." She walked over to the oversize tub and started the water. He turned on the bed to continue to stare at her.

She ignored him and adjusted the water temperature and then added some of the lilac-scented bubble bath to the tub. When she looked at him again, his eyes were still widened with an expression she couldn't quite read.

He cleared his throat. "If you're going to take a bath then I'll just go sit in the bathroom until you're finished," he said.

"Don't be silly. If it makes you that uncomfortable then you can just sit there and stare at the fire." She began to unbutton her blouse.

He whipped his head around to face the opposite direction but not before she saw the searing desire, the raw, stark hunger that lit his eyes momentarily.

"You like baths," he said, his voice sounding slightly strained.

"I love a nice soak. Now that I think about it, I guess it's one of my major stress relievers," she replied.

By the time she'd stripped off the rest of her clothes, the tub was full of steamy, scented water. She eased down into the warm depths and pushed the button to get the jets working.

Leaning back in the tub built for two, she knew it wouldn't be enough. She wanted a bath, but at the moment what she needed, what she wished for more than anything was the man who sat on the bed.

She wouldn't be happy, she wouldn't find the warmth she craved until Gabriel held her in his arms.

TORTURE.

The sounds of sloshing water, the whir of the jets, and the faint sensual moans she emitted were sheer torture to Gabriel.

He stared intently into the fireplace, but instead of seeing the dancing flames there, his head filled with visions of a very bare Jordon in the tub.

Her skin would be warm and soft and sweetly scented by the fragrance of lilacs. He was jealous of the jetted water that swirled around her naked body. He was on fire with the desire for her that had simmered inside him for the last week.

The memory of the kiss they had shared burned in his head. Her lips had been so soft, so hot, and just thinking about it heated his blood.

"I think this is a perfect night to open this bottle of complimentary wine," she said. "Would you like a glass?" There was a sweet invitation in her voice.

She was seducing him.

It was evident in her tone of voice, in the fact that

she'd gotten into the tub with him sitting right here. She was seducing him and he was helplessly faltering in his desire to not respond.

Don't turn around, a little voice whispered in his head. He somehow knew that if he turned around, if he saw her in that tub, he'd be lost.

Still, even knowing that he was making a mistake, in spite of all the internal alarms that rang in his head, he stood and turned around.

Her beauty squeezed the air out of his lungs and shot a burst of fiery adrenaline through his veins. Her hair looked even more charmingly curly than it had before, and her creamy shoulders and a hint of her breasts were visible above the bubbles.

He had no conscious memory of crossing the room, but suddenly he stood by the edge of the tub. She smiled up at him and held out a glass of wine. "Why don't you join me. The water's just fine."

She was a wicked temptation, and any good sense he had fled beneath the sensual assault she presented to him. He was cold, and the only way he could get warm was to join her in the tub.

Her eyes beckoned him like a silent siren song. As if in a trance, he took off his belt and dropped it to the floor and then unbuttoned his shirt and shrugged it off. He was making a mistake and someplace in the back of his mind he knew it, but nothing short of the apocalypse could keep him out of that tub.

He took out his gun and set it on the tiled area next

to the bathtub and then kicked off his shoes, bent down and peeled off his socks. As he unfastened his slacks and stepped out of them, that inner voice whispered that this was his last chance to stop the madness, but he didn't listen.

He'd never been a shy man. He knew he was physically fit, but as he took off his boxers and then eased down into the tub, the smile Jordon gave him made him feel like Adonis himself.

She was curled up on one side of the tub and he was on the other. His legs stretched out to the left. She did the same so they didn't touch each other. She leaned forward and handed him the glass of wine and then grabbed hers.

"Here's to warm baths and snuggle buddies," she toasted and then clinked her glass with his.

He didn't draw a full, deep breath until she leaned back again. If he didn't touch her then there would be no harm, no foul.

If this was the only intimacy they shared, then they could face each other in the morning without any regrets. He took a big swallow of the wine.

"I'll admit, this does have its merits," he said as the warm water swirled around him.

She smiled. "And you're going to smell like a beautiful spring flower when you get out." She downed her wine and then poured herself some more. She held the bottle out to splash more in his glass but he shook his head.

"I'm good." The last thing he needed was to add too much alcohol to the fire. Besides, he was already half intoxicated by her.

She took another sip from her glass and then set it on the side of the tub, closed her eyes and released a sigh of obvious pleasure.

How could she look so relaxed? Only hours before, she had been attacked by a killer and faced freezing to death in the middle of a snowstorm.

He'd wanted to be angry with her for chasing the perp without calling for backup, without giving any thought to the consequences. However, it was difficult to be angry with her when he knew he would have reacted the same way.

It was equally difficult to sit across from her and gaze at her without wanting her. The bubbles were slowly dissipating and in desperation he looked up at the ceiling. The last thing he needed was to do something stupid that might complicate their partnership.

The water sloshed and he knew she was changing positions, but he kept his gaze upward. "Gabriel? Would you mind washing my back?"

Every muscle in his body tensed as he looked at her once again. She held out a wet washcloth and a small beige soap bar, and there was not only a warm invitation in her eyes but also that damned soft seduction. "Please?"

He was helpless to deny her. Hell, he was helpless to deny himself. He took the washcloth and soap from her and moved his legs so that he was sitting cross-legged, and she sat the same way directly in front of him with her back turned toward him.

He wasn't touching her—the washcloth was, he told himself as he caressed the soapy cloth over her slender back. But he knew he was only fooling himself. He wanted her and it was obvious she wanted him, too.

Good sense be damned, he knew with a sweet inevitability there was no way they would exit this room in the morning without having made love if that was what she wanted.

As soon as the thought filled his head, she turned to face him. The washcloth and soap slid from his hand the second she leaned into him.

Her bare breasts pressed against his chest at the same time their lips met. As the kiss deepened, he stretched out his legs and pulled her fully on top of him.

Warm soft skin, hot lips and the heady scent of lilacs cast all other thoughts out of his head. There was just him and Jordon and this single night.

"I want you, Gabriel," she said softly as their kiss ended. Her eyes shone with a brilliance he could drown in.

"I want you, too, Jordon." The words issued forth from the very depths of him.

She placed a finger over his lips. "I love the way my name sounds on your lips. I love the way your body feels against mine. Now I think it's time we move this to the bed." She moved away from him and hit the knob that would empty the water.

He stepped out of the tub and onto the bath mat and then grabbed one of the fluffy oversize towels and quickly dried himself off. He took a second towel and beckoned her out of the tub.

He'd officially lost his mind and he knew it, but they were both in too deep to stop now. She stood with her back to him and he began drying her shoulders. As he did so he leaned forward to kiss just behind one of her earlobes.

She leaned her head back and released a small moan that shot fire through his blood. He moved the towel down the length of her slender back, over her perfectly rounded butt and then down her shapely legs.

The tight control he'd maintained since the moment she'd started the water in the tub snapped. He dropped the towel, scooped her up in his arms and carried her to the bed.

There was no time to fold down blankets or turn out the lights. They were on each other like two hungry animals. He took her mouth in another kiss and reveled in the full-body contact with her.

This time when he broke the kiss, he moved his mouth slowly down the length of her neck, across her delicate collarbone and then to the raised nipple of one of her breasts. He teased it with his tongue, loving the taste of her and the way her fingers splayed in his hair as if she couldn't get enough of him.

He definitely couldn't get enough of her. He raised his head and gazed at her. "You are so beautiful, so perfect."

"I almost believe it when you say it," she replied in a husky voice.

With his desire a barely controlled beast inside him, he continued to explore her body. It was only when his fingers touched the raised scars on her left hip that desire was tempered by empathy and an anger that she had ever been in a cellar where a madman had played on her body with a lit cigarette.

He ran his fingers over the raised area and then followed the caress with his lips. He'd like to be able to kiss away not only the physical scar, but also the memory of that time, of that horrible pain she had to have endured. He wished he could kiss away the fear that she must have experienced knowing she was in the hands of a brutal serial killer.

He moved his hand to her inner thigh and then to the soft folds of her center. She moaned and whispered his name as he moved his fingers faster against her.

She arched her hips upward to meet him, and within minutes she gasped and stiffened as she climaxed. She shuddered and reached up to grab his shoulders.

Her eyes glowed a deep green. "Take me now, Gabriel. I want you inside of me."

He didn't hesitate. He moved between her thighs and slowly entered her. Her warm, moist heat surrounded him as her fingernails dug into his back.

He fought to maintain control, to last for as long as he possibly could. But as he began to stroke inside her, intense pleasure washed over him and he feared he'd lose it far too quickly.

His lips took hers once again in a fiery kiss that stole all thought from his mind. She met him thrust for thrust as fevered pants escaped them both.

She cried out his name as she stiffened against him and then moaned as she found her release once again. Gabriel's climax came hard and fast. He groaned and half collapsed on top of her.

He remained there only a moment and then rolled to the side of her and waited for his heartbeat to resume a more normal pace.

She rose up on one elbow and gazed at him with a soft smile. "I don't know about you, but I think that was pretty amazing."

He reached up and caressed her cheek. "'Amazing' doesn't even begin to describe it."

She leaned over and kissed him, a soft sweet kiss that stirred him on a completely different level altogether. "And now I'm wonderfully exhausted. All I need to do is get you out of this bed so that we can get under the covers."

She got off the bed and he did the same. As she stood, he saw the heart-shaped scar on her hip and once again his heart squeezed tight for the fear, the pain she must have gone through.

"Get your gun," he said. "I'll be right back." He took his gun from the edge of the bathtub and then went into the bathroom and closed the door behind him.

This night had been all kinds of wrong. He checked the window to make sure it was properly locked and then stepped up to the mirror and stared at his reflection.

From the moment the attacker had leaped out at Jordon, mistakes had been made, first by her and then by him. Making love to her had definitely been a huge mistake. Hell, they hadn't even used protection.

She touched him like no other woman had ever done before in his life. She made him laugh and she made him think. He wanted to know all of her thoughts, every one of her innermost emotions and dreams.

She was exactly the kind of woman he wanted in his life and she couldn't be more wrong for him. She'd told him she wasn't interested in marriage. Footloose and fancy-free—that was the way she wanted to live her life. They just wanted different things in their lives.

Starting tomorrow, he had to distance himself from her. They had to get back on the course of being strictly partners trying to hunt down a killer and nothing more.

But first, he was going to return to the bedroom and

climb into bed with her. She would snuggle against him and he would want her all over again.

He leaned closer to his reflection. "Bonehead," he whispered to the man in the mirror.

Chapter Eight

Jordon awoke before dawn. Gabriel was spooned around her back with his arm thrown across her waist and his deep, even breathing warmed the back of her neck.

She closed her eyes again and embraced the moment of feeling loved even though she knew it was a false sentiment. Gabriel Walters could never love a woman like her. Nobody could really love her. Still, it was nice to pretend for a little while.

Certainly making love with him had rocked her world. He'd been so passionate and so wonderfully intense. He'd made her feel incredibly beautiful and desired.

They'd come together again sometime in the middle of the night, and then their lovemaking had been sleepy and slow and all kinds of wonderful.

However, she knew when dawn broke and a new day began, it would be business as usual between them. She didn't expect the soft glow in her heart to remain. She wasn't here for romance. She didn't *do* romance. She was here to catch a killer.

She remained in bed, wrapped in Gabriel's warmth and listening to her heartbeat mirror the slow steady beat of his until the sound of a snowblower shattered the silence. Gabriel stirred and slowly unwound himself from her.

"Good morning," he said as he sat up and raked a hand through his hair.

"Back at you," she replied.

He leaned over and grabbed his cell phone from the nightstand. "Jeez, it's just after seven. I haven't slept this late since before the first murder."

She slid out of bed. "I get the bathroom first." She grabbed a fresh pair of slacks, a blouse and her underwear and then went into the bathroom.

She hoped he didn't want to talk about last night. She didn't want to hear the regrets he was probably feeling in the light of day.

While she suffered not a single regret about what they had shared, she also wasn't eager to delve too deeply into exactly what her own feelings were.

Dressing as quickly as possible, she tried to get her head back into the game of murder and away from the night of passion. The killer was escalating in his quest. He'd almost gotten to her last night. She'd been lucky that the first knife strike hadn't hit her chest and incapacitated her.

When she left the bathroom Gabriel had already

dressed and made the bed. He stood at the window with the curtain pulled back allowing a faint stream of sunshine to seep into the room.

"If you don't like the weather in Missouri just wait a minute and it changes," she said.

He turned away from the window with a nod. "It's hard to believe we were in blizzard conditions last night. It looks like the sun is going to shine today."

She walked over to stand next to him and peered outside. The morning sun sparkled on the five or six inches of additional snow that had fallen overnight. In the distance she saw Billy Bond working a snow-blower around the dining room porch and Ted Overton was shoveling off the paths in front of the cabins.

"It looks like everyone is working hard except us," she said.

"Why don't we head in for coffee and breakfast and then we'll get to work."

Within minutes they were both in their coats and snow boots and heading toward the dining room. Billy and his snowblower had disappeared, but Ted greeted them on the path with a quick, cheerful "good morning" as he continued to shovel.

WHEN THEY ENTERED the dining room, not only was Joan there, but also Jason and Hannah were seated at the table eating breakfast. Billy had apparently come in to get warm and stood by the fireplace sipping a cup of coffee.

"Good morning, everyone," Gabriel said.

They all returned his greeting except Billy, who gave a curt nod and then turned to face the fire. All of Jordon's muscles tensed. Was it guilt that had him facing away from them or just the desire to warm up?

They each got a cup of coffee and then sat at the table with the two teenagers while Joan scurried into the kitchen to see to their breakfast.

"Billy, why don't you join us?" Gabriel said. His tone of voice indicated it was a command, not a simple request. Billy got the message, for he moved away from the fire and sat in the chair opposite Jordon.

She stared at him but he refused to meet her gaze. He looked at a place just over her shoulder and then into his cup as if the contents were of great interest.

Was he the person who had been in her room last night? Was he the cold-blooded killer they sought? He'd probably know about the window lock and could have even set it so that it appeared to be secure when it wasn't.

"Heck of a night," Gabriel said. He took a sip of his coffee then turned to look at the groundskeeper. "How are the roads out there?"

"Side streets are a mess, but it looked like the road crews had already hit the main streets when I came in," he replied.

"Where did you ride out the storm, Billy?"

The man shot Gabriel a quick glance. "At home,

where any sane person would be in that kind of weather," he replied.

"Anyone with you?" Jordon asked.

For the first time since they'd entered the room, his gaze met hers. Cold and flat, his eyes stared into hers and she fought against an inner chill. "It wasn't exactly a good night for socializing."

"What about for a walk in the woods?" Gabriel asked. Jason and Hannah had stopped any pretense at eating as they listened intently to the conversation.

"I don't know what you're talking about." Billy took a sip from his cup and then leaned back in the chair. "Why would I go for a walk in the woods in the middle of a snowstorm?"

"That's what we're trying to figure out. Jordon thought she saw somebody in the woods last night," Gabriel said. It was apparent by the way he framed his words that he intended to play the attack close to his chest.

"Well, it wasn't me," Billy said. "Getting out in weather like that for a walk would be just plain stupid. I might be many things, but I'm not that dumb."

At that moment Ted came in from outside. "Billy, you warmed up enough to get back to work?"

"I am." Billy got up from the table, put on his coat and then headed out the door.

"Do you think Billy is the killer?" Hannah asked half-breathlessly.

"We're still investigating," Jordon replied as the snowblower outside once again started up.

"He's always been kind of weird," Jason said and then popped a piece of bacon into his mouth.

Ted wore a deep frown. "Is Billy a suspect?"

"Like Agent James said, we're still investigating," Gabriel replied.

Joan entered the room carrying their plates and then sat at the table next to her husband. "I see you two got through last night okay. According to the weatherman, we're supposed to get above-freezing temperatures tomorrow and it's supposed to be in the midforties for the rest of the week."

"Ah, sweet music to my ears," Jordon said. She took a sip of her coffee and then looked at Ted. "I was wondering about the outbuildings in the woods. Gabriel said there is a lean-to shed out there and also a building that's a little more substantial."

"That's right," Ted replied. "They're really nothing but eyesores. One of my goals for this spring is to tear them both down and put up a nice, new shed."

"Is there electricity out there?" Jordon asked.

"Not in the lean-to shed but in the other building there is, although we don't use that building at all," Ted replied.

"Mom, can we be excused?" Jason asked Joan.

"Go ahead, but get your morning chores done. Just because you have a snow day at school doesn't mean you don't keep your usual routine."

"We know, we know," Hannah replied, earning her a stern look from Joan. The two kids quickly got up, grabbed their coats and left.

"What's with all the questions about the outbuildings?" Ted asked.

"Jordon was attacked last night and whoever did it ran into the woods," Gabriel replied.

"Attacked?" Joan raised a hand to her lips in horror. "What happened?"

"He was waiting for me in the room. He got in through the bathroom window. He tried to stab me and then ran off into the woods," Jordon explained.

"Oh, sweet Lord," Joan exclaimed. "I'm so glad you're okay."

"I'm fine," Jordon assured her. "The arm of my coat was the only casualty."

"Thank goodness," Joan replied, her voice still filled with a touch of shock.

"That lock on the window in Jordon's room needs to be replaced or fixed," Gabriel said. "And hopefully it can be done today."

"Ed should be in within the next couple of hours. I'll get him right on it," Ted replied and then looked at Jordon. "Did you see who it was?" He grimaced. "I guess you didn't since you're sitting here instead of making an arrest."

Jordon shook her head. "He had on a ski mask and it was impossible for me to make an identification."

"We're hoping maybe there might be something in

the woods or in one of those outbuildings that might yield a clue," Gabriel said.

"I certainly hope so. I want this nightmare to be over," Joan replied fervently.

Jordon ate quickly as did Gabriel. If they were going to head into the woods to see what they could find, then she wanted to do it sooner rather than later.

The very idea of traipsing through the snow made her want to shiver, but if they found something that would help them catch the murderer then it would be worth every agonizingly cold moment.

It was almost eight thirty by the time they left the dining room. There was no sign of Billy and the sound of the snowblower had stopped.

"You might want to put your gun in your coat pocket so you can zip up your coat," Gabriel said and his breaths hung on frosty puffs.

"I definitely want my coat zipped," she replied. "That hot beach in Florida would be nice right about now."

"A beach anywhere sounds good to me," Gabriel agreed.

They took off walking toward the woods. Both of them had their guns in hand.

"I've got to confess, I'm not feeling optimistic about us finding anything out here," she said.

Gabriel smiled at her, that beautiful smile that sparked warmth through her entire body. "I thought you were the optimist in this partnership." His smile faded and he stopped in his tracks, his eyes slightly darker in hue. "Do we need to talk about last night?"

"As far as I'm concerned, there's nothing to talk about. We were just two cold souls who warmed each other up on a cold wintry night." She forced a lightness into her voice. As crazy as it sounded, it had been more than just a hot hookup for her.

He held her gaze for a long moment, his features radiating with an emotion she couldn't discern. "Okay, then let's get this done." He trudged ahead and she quickly followed.

As they got deeper into the woods, Jordon tried not to remember the panic that had nearly crippled her the night before when she'd been lost in a snow globe.

She also had to swallow down the fear that had gripped her, knowing that at any moment a knife could stab her and she would become the fourth victim to die at Diamond Cove.

There were places where the snow had drifted and others that appeared barely touched by the new snowfall. The tree branches sparkled in the sunlight. It would have been a beautiful winter wonderland if they weren't hunting for clues that would lead them to a savage killer.

They walked slowly, scanning the area silently and with focused concentration. If only they could find a scrap of material from a torn coat, something dropped out of a pocket, anything that would identify who had been in her room and had tried to stab her.

When they approached the lean-to shack that Gabriel had described, he motioned for her to go to the left and he went to the right.

She tightened her grip on her gun, even though she didn't really expect trouble. Whoever had been in the woods last night would have beat feet to get out of the area long before now.

The shed held a riding lawn mower, rakes and shovels, and other yard equipment, but nothing that didn't belong there. They checked the entire structure but didn't find anything that would indicate that anyone had been there the night before.

The sun grew warmer on her shoulders as they left the shed and continued on. Once again she scanned the pristine landscape for anything that was out of place, something that didn't belong.

In the distance was the other outbuilding Gabriel had mentioned. It was bigger than the other shed and had a doorway without a door and two windows with no glass.

It appeared completely abandoned and like a stiff wind would bring it down. She couldn't imagine anyone huddling inside for the duration of the snowstorm. A sigh escaped her. This whole search had been nothing but more dead ends.

How she wished she would have been able to catch the person the night before. She'd been so taken by surprise. Somehow, she should have managed to take down the perp before he ever shoved past her and jumped off her porch.

The crack of gunfire split the air and a bullet dug into the snow at Jordon's feet. She scarcely had time to register it when Gabriel slammed his body into hers and took her down to the ground.

GABRIEL'S HEART THUNDERED as he returned fire into the building. Jordon wiggled out from beneath him. "See if you can get around to the back," she said. "I'll cover you and get behind a tree trunk."

Although his first instinct was to protect her, he reminded himself she was a trained professional and as it was they were both sitting ducks with their dark coats against the white snow. They needed cover.

He gave a curt nod. She fired into the building and he raced to the right, praying that she would manage to get behind something before a bullet found her.

As he darted to the back of a tree, he looked back and sighed in relief when he saw that she had rolled sideways and now crouched behind the trunk of a large oak.

Several more shots came from the shed, one of the bullets pinging off the tree behind which he hid. Who was in the shed? There had been nothing to indicate in the past that the killer they sought had a gun.

Jordon returned fire and Gabriel darted to another tree, moving him closer to the back of the shed. There was no way he intended to allow whoever was inside to escape.

If it was the killer, Gabriel had no idea why he would be here now. But certainly with the attack and the flight last night, he had to believe that the person they had sought was the same person shooting at them.

Adrenaline pumped through him as he moved again. Jordon was no longer in his sight, and as gunfire sounded from the shed once again, he could only hope that no bullet found her.

At least he didn't hear a scream of agony or any cry for help. But would she shout for aid if she'd been shot, or would she lie in the snow and die silently? She was so tough and obviously a lone wolf.

He made it to the rear of the shed just in time to see a figure dart out of the back door opening. He recognized the cut of the dark coat and the baggy jeans beneath. He'd seen them earlier in the dining room.

Billy Bond.

"Jordon, in the back," he yelled and took off running after Billy.

Billy ran fast, but Gabriel ran faster, fueled by anger and determination. "Billy, halt! Don't make me shoot you in the back."

Instead of shooting at him, Gabriel got close enough to lunge at his back. Billy hit the ground hard with Gabriel on top of him.

Jordon appeared and leaned down to place the

barrel of her gun against the side of Billy's head. "If you twitch, I'll shoot," she said firmly.

"Please, don't shoot me!" Billy exclaimed.

"Billy, what in the hell are you doing?" Gabriel said as he got to his feet and yanked the man up by the back of his coat. As Gabriel handcuffed Billy, Jordon searched his pockets and pulled out his gun, then did a more thorough pat-down.

"It's a meth lab," Jordon said. "I ran through the shed and there's enough material in there to keep the whole state high for a very long time."

"I don't know what you're talking about," Billy replied, a surly snarl curving his lips.

"Then why were you shooting at us?" Gabriel asked as he led the man back the way they had come.

"I wasn't shooting at you. It must have been somebody else. I was just out here trimming some tree branches."

"And I'm the freaking queen of Scotland," Jordon retorted with a laugh.

Gabriel led Billy into the shed, where he looked around in stunned surprise. A hot plate was plugged into an electrical socket that hung from the lightbulb in the ceiling. Mason jars gleamed red and purple, and jugs of drain cleaner, paint thinner and a variety of other items used to make the deadly drug littered what was left of the workbench.

Anger once again ripped through Gabriel. Fighting the making and use of meth was a full-time job.

It was a scourge that not only ripped apart families, but killed. And this had been going on right under his nose.

Was Billy just a dope manufacturer and dealer or was he a killer, as well?

"Let's go," he said and roughly yanked Billy out of the door.

Within minutes they were in his car and headed to the police station. They rode in silence. Gabriel drove slowly although he was eager to get Billy into an interrogation room and have a long talk. He needed to find out if they now had the killer under arrest.

Thankfully, the main roads had been cleared, but the side streets remained a grim testimony to the storm that had roared through overnight.

He felt the tension that wafted from Jordon and knew that she had the same questions that he had about Billy Bond and his potential relationship to the murders that had taken place.

Had he been the person who had attacked Jordon? Had he climbed through the window with the intention of killing her? Gabriel gripped the steering wheel tightly and tried to quell his anger.

Once at the station, he put Billy into the small interview room and then instructed his right-hand man, Lieutenant Mark Johnson, to gather up the team trained for cleaning up drug labs in the area and get out to Diamond Cove.

Jordon stood just outside the interrogation room

door, peering in through the small window to where Billy sat at the table with his head in his hands.

"We now know why we thought he was a creep," she said. "He definitely had something to hide."

"A damn meth lab." Gabriel shook his head.

"And potentially our killer?" Jordon looked at him with darkened eyes.

"Let's get in there and see just how much he has to hide," Gabriel replied, hoping that this would be the end of the search for their murderer.

Billy looked up as the two of them entered the room. His smirk was gone, replaced by eyes that held nothing but despair and hopelessness.

Gabriel sat across from him and Jordon remained standing just behind Gabriel's chair. He read Billy his rights and thankfully the groundskeeper waived his right for a lawyer.

"I'm in big trouble, aren't I?" he asked.

"You're looking at fifteen years just for the drug charges. If I add in attempted murder then you're probably looking at life," Gabriel replied.

Billy's eyes widened slightly. "I wasn't trying to kill you. I just wanted to scare you off. Dumb, huh."

"Duh, we're the law. We run toward bullets, not away from them," Jordon said drily.

"Methamphetamines? What on earth were you thinking, Billy? Just how long has this been going on?"

Billy grimaced and shook his head. "My sister

was diagnosed with breast cancer three months ago. She needs money for treatment and I was desperate."

"Desperate enough to murder three innocent people?" Jordon asked.

Billy's gaze shot to her and then back to Gabriel, his eyes widened once again. "Don't try to pin that on me. I don't know anything about those murders—you've got to believe me." He leaned forward, his eyes filled with fire as he held Gabriel's gaze. "I'll admit I'm guilty of the meth lab, but I did not kill those people."

A weight dropped inside Gabriel's chest and lay heavy in the pit of his stomach. He believed Billy. And if Billy wasn't their killer, then who was?

Chapter Nine

They interviewed Billy for almost two hours, and it was only when Gabriel wanted the names of anyone else involved in the meth operation that Billy finally demanded a lawyer.

He was taken to a jail cell to await a meeting with legal counsel, and Jordon and Gabriel got in his car to head back to Diamond Cove.

"I hate to admit it, but I believe him," Jordon said as she adjusted the car heater vents for maximum warmth on her face. "I believe that he wasn't in the woods last night and I believe him when he said he wasn't the person who attacked me. I just don't think Billy is our man."

"I agree and that's good news and bad news," Gabriel replied. "The good news is we can take him off our suspect list. The bad news is that means our murderer is still out here somewhere."

Jordon stared out the passenger window, her mind working over the few suspects they had left. The

Rollings brothers, they were it. Was one of them the killer or was the person they sought completely off the grid, flying under their radar? That was definitely a depressing thought.

She gazed back at Gabriel. "I'm assuming we'll be checking some alibis for last night at some point today?"

"Definitely, although the first order of business is seeing to it that the window in your room is fixed."

He pulled into the Diamond Cove entrance, where two police cars and an evidence van were already parked. Several officers stood around, and it appeared that the van had been packed with all the items that had been in the shed.

"Chief," Mark greeted them as they got out of the car. "We're loaded up and ready to leave. Thank God it looked like he hadn't cooked for a couple of days and the fumes weren't too bad at all. It definitely helped that there were no closed windows or doors and the storm blew through the building."

"Good," Gabriel replied.

"Did you find any actual meth?" Jordon asked.

Mark grinned. "Enough to keep Billy cooking up slop in prison for a very long time."

"One more bad apple off the streets," Jordon replied.

"We'll just let you finish up." Gabriel touched her arm. "Let's go check in with Ted and Joan."

She followed behind Gabriel as they headed inside. She couldn't help but think about how nice it had been to have his arms around her through the night, how comfortable she felt with him. Their conversations were so easy, as if they'd known each other for months instead of days. She didn't feel the need to censor herself with him. She trusted that she could just be herself and that was okay with him.

She'd misjudged him at first impression. He wasn't inflexible; he was determined. He wasn't uptight—he was focused, and he was so much more than those things. He was intelligent and could be funny. More important, he seemed to *get* her.

Maybe she was just feeling particularly soft about him because he'd thrown her to the ground and covered her body with his own when the bullets had flown. His first instinct hadn't been to get to cover himself, but rather to protect her.

Not that any of that mattered. She tamped down a strange wistfulness that tried to take hold of her as they entered the main dining room.

Ted sat on one of the chairs by the fireplace and Joan sat at one of the tables. There was an underlying thrum of tension in the air. Joan stood as they entered and worried her hands together.

"We didn't know," she said. Her blue eyes were darker than Jordon had ever seen them. "You have to believe me—we had no idea what Billy was doing out there in the shed."

"A meth lab...murder," Ted said in disgust and

gazed at his wife. "All of it happening right here where we live with our children. This would have never happened if we'd stayed in Oklahoma City, where we belonged."

It was obvious the crimes were fracturing what Jordon had presumed was a good and loving relationship.

"Sit down, Joan," Gabriel said calmly. "Nobody believes that you and Ted had anything to do with Billy's meth business."

Jordon walked over to the coffeepot to get a cup of the hot brew while Gabriel took a seat next to Joan.

"How long has this been going on? How long has Billy been cooking drugs on this property?" Ted asked, his voice almost a growl.

Jordon sat at the table next to Gabriel and faced the fireplace and Ted. A rich anger radiated from the man, an anger that appeared to be pointed not only at the circumstances, but also specifically at his wife.

"I checked that shed when Samantha Kent was killed in the woods and there was nothing there. According to what Billy told us, he started just after Christmas when he found out his sister had cancer and needed money," Gabriel said.

"Did he kill those people?" Ted asked. "Is he the killer who is trying to destroy us?"

"We don't believe so," Jordon said.

Ted frowned. "So, we still have a killer running loose around here." He shook his head and gazed at

Joan once again. "Happy wife, happy life—yeah, right." He got up from his chair and slammed his coffee cup down on the table. "I've got work to do in the office."

"I'm sorry," Joan said as soon as he'd left the room. "He's upset. We're both upset. This has all been so difficult." She looked utterly miserable as the glint of tears shone in her eyes.

"Don't worry—we understand," Jordon said softly.

"Has Ed come in yet?" Gabriel asked.

"He arrived just a few minutes before you did." She glanced at Jordon. "I sent him right to your room to take care of the window issue."

Gabriel stood. "We'll go check out the progress."

Jordon took a big gulp of her coffee and then got up, as well. "Joan, stay strong. We're going to get this all taken care of."

"I hope so. I was the one who insisted we make this move. Ted really only did it to make me happy." Her hand trembled as she reached up and tucked a strand of hair behind her ear. "I just want this to all go away so we can live the dreams we had."

"We'll do everything we can to make that happen, Joan," Gabriel replied.

"Tensions are definitely rising," Jordon said once they were on the path to her room. "I hate to see what's happening between Joan and Ted."

"Collateral damage," Gabriel replied. "There are

always more victims than the dead ones when something like this happens."

"The ripple effect," she replied. Her stomach clenched. "I want to get this guy so badly I can taste it."

"Speaking of tasting it, we'll stop and get lunch after we leave here and before we start interviewing anyone."

Jordon glanced at her cell phone, shocked to see that it was almost three. It was amazing how a chase in the woods and an interview with a drug dealer could eat up the hours of the day.

The door to her room was unlocked and they walked in to find Ed in the bathroom installing a new window lock. "I put up a new screen and this should take just a minute," he said after their initial greetings. "I told Ted a month ago that this lock had an issue, but with everything else going on around here, I guess we both forgot about it."

He finished using his screwdriver and then opened the window and tried the new latch several times. "That should do it," he said.

"Just a minute, Ed," Gabriel said before the handyman could leave the suite. "We have a few questions to ask you."

"Questions about what?"

"Where were you last night?"

Ed looked at them in surprise. "I was at home. In fact, Kevin and Glen came over and wound up spending the night. We played cards and drank some beer, and this morning Millie made us all sausage and French toast with my favorite strawberry syrup."

Jordon stared at the man with a rising frustration. She still couldn't be certain if he was off the hook for being the man who had attacked her, but how convenient that he'd just provided an alibi not only for himself but also for his brothers.

"Is there anything else?" Ed asked with his usual pleasantness. "I've got some other work to attend to around here."

"That should do it," Gabriel replied. Once Ed was out the door, Gabriel turned and looked at Jordon. "We'll grab some lunch and then I think it's time we talked to Millie."

"Do you really think she'll say anything different than what Ed told us?"

"Doubtful, but maybe we'll see something in the house that will tell us something different."

"If you don't mind, I'd rather talk to her first and grab lunch afterward," Jordon said. She wanted to tie up any loose ends that they could from the attack the night before as soon as possible.

He shrugged. "Fine by me."

"Will she even let us in the front door?" Jordon asked as they left her room.

He flashed her a quick smile. "It would be downright rude to keep people standing on the front porch on a cold winter's day."

"And Branson is known for its down-home friendliness," she replied.

Why couldn't she get Gabriel's *friendliness* out of her brain? Throughout the interview with Billy, she'd flashed back to the night before and the intimate moments with Gabriel. When they'd entered the room to find Ed, her gaze had shot to the bed where they'd made love the night before.

He'd somehow managed to get under her skin in a way no man had done since Jack. She'd hoped never again to feel the wild electricity, the slight flutter in her heart, for any man. As crazy as it sounded, when she left here the chief of police would have more than just a little bit of her guarded heart.

She mentally shook herself and realized there was an unsettled piece of her brain, as if she'd forgotten something important. But, try as she might, she couldn't figure out what it was, like having a snatch of a lyric to a song going around and around in her head and she couldn't quite remember the title.

Gabriel pulled down a narrow road that thankfully had been plowed earlier in the day. The houses were small and set far apart.

"Unfortunately, Ed's house is fairly isolated and the last place before a dead end. It's doubtful that anyone in the neighborhood would know whether Kevin's and Glen's cars were parked there overnight or not."

Jordon released a deep sigh. "A dead end is where we're at. Nothing is coming easy with this case. I can't go back to Kansas City without this being solved. It would totally ruin my reputation."

"And what reputation is that?" he asked.

"My kick-ass-and-get-it-done reputation," she replied.

He cast her another one of his charming grins. "I certainly wouldn't want to mess with that reputation, so that means we need to kick ass and really get it done."

"Amen," she replied.

He parked in front of a little house painted a dreary brown with a bright red front door. Unfortunately, the driveway was completely shoveled, making it impossible to see whether one car or three cars had been parked there overnight.

She definitely hoped an answer was inside. She not only wanted to catch this guy sooner rather than later, but she also needed to get back to Kansas City before Gabriel dug any deeper into her heart.

MILLIE ROLLINGS WAS a painfully thin woman with mousy brown hair and faded blue eyes that gazed at them warily as she ushered them into a small neat living room that smelled of lemon furniture wax and old coffee.

Gabriel had never had much to do with Ed's wife, whom he saw only occasionally at the grocery store. He'd always gotten the impression of a nervous little bird, and as he introduced her to Jordon, his impression of Millie didn't change.

"Ed told me there was a pretty FBI lady staying at Diamond Cove," she said and self-consciously reached up to touch a strand of her limp hair.

"Do you mind if we have a seat and ask you a few questions?" he asked.

"Of course, please, although I can't imagine what you would want to ask me." She gestured toward the sofa and sat in a chair opposite them.

"We spoke with Ed earlier and he mentioned you had houseguests last night," Jordon said. "Is that correct?"

"Yes. Ed's brothers came by to play cards and got snowed in until this morning. I made them a big breakfast of sausage and French toast and the strawberry syrup that's Ed's favorite." She reached a hand up once again to pat her hair and her gaze shifted slightly above Jordon's head.

Interesting that she'd used almost the precise same words that Ed had used when he'd described the morning meal. Gabriel would love to get a look at her phone to see how quickly Ed might have called his wife after they'd spoken to him.

"You do realize we're searching for the person who has killed three people in cold blood. If you know anything about these crimes or if you're lying about Kevin and Glen being here last night, you could go to prison for a long time," Gabriel said.

Millie shot back in her chair as if he'd physically struck her. Her lower lip trembled slightly, and this time when she reached up to her hair, she grabbed a strand of it and twirled furiously.

"I'm not a liar. I'm not," she replied. "I'd never risk going to prison for anyone, especially the likes of those two. Me and Ed, we're good people."

"Sometimes good people make mistakes when it comes to protecting their family," Jordon said softly.

"I wouldn't do that and now I think it's time you both leave." She stood and looked at them expectantly... and defiantly.

The mouse had roared, Gabriel thought. He didn't know whether to be amused or ticked off. He and Jordon rose from the sofa.

"Mrs. Rollings, if you know anything about these murders, anything at all, now is the time to speak up," Jordon said.

"I can't help you and if you have any more questions you talk to Ed." She opened the front door. "Now, please go."

"What do you think?" Jordon asked when they were back in the car.

"I honestly don't know what to think." He started the engine and then pulled away from the house. "She might be telling the truth and she might be lying."

"Have you heard any rumors about her being an abused wife? Is it possible that she's scared of her husband and so would say anything to us that he told her to say?"

"I haven't heard any whispers of abuse," he replied. "But you never know what goes on behind closed doors."

"True. Maybe we should check with the neighbors. Maybe somebody saw or didn't see the cars here that would either prove Millie truthful or a liar."

It took them almost an hour to check with the other people who lived on the same street as Ed Rollings. Unfortunately, it had been a night where most people had hunkered down and weren't paying attention to what their neighbors were doing.

"Now I need to eat," Jordon said as they drove back toward the main strip. "Breakfast seems like it was served a lifetime ago."

"What sounds good?" he asked. Another night in her bed sounded good. Another night of holding her sweet, soft body against his sounded great. "How about a juicy steak?" He hoped his voice didn't betray his physical frustration.

"Hmm, perfect," she replied.

It was almost six when they pulled into a popular steak house where Gabriel often ate. There were only two cars parked in front of the building despite the dinner hour.

As they got out of the car, Gabriel was struck by a bone-weariness. Between the trauma of the night before, the shoot-out with Billy and all the other events that had occurred within the past twenty-four hours, it was no wonder he was tired.

This case was eating him alive, and when he wasn't thinking about murder, he was thinking far too much about Jordon. Before he'd gone to sleep the night before, he'd been determined to put a little distance between himself and his partner. However, they'd shared another bout of lovemaking in the middle of the night, and so far the distance he'd thought he'd be able to maintain wasn't happening. Hell, he wanted her again right this minute.

The owner of the restaurant, Bob Carson, greeted them at the door. "Slow night with the weather, Chief. You've pretty much got your pick of tables or booths." He held out two menus.

"Thanks, Bob." Gabriel took the menus and then led Jordon to a booth toward the back of the restaurant. There was only one other couple seated at a table in the same general area.

They had just gotten situated and peered at the menus when Bob appeared at the booth with an order pad. "My waitresses didn't show up tonight due to the snow."

"Does this mean you'll also be cooking our meals?" Gabriel asked with a touch of humor.

Bob laughed. "No. You're in luck—the chef actually made it in along with one busboy. Now, what can I get for you two this evening?"

Jordon ordered a strip steak and a loaded baked potato and Gabriel got the rib eye with creamy mashed potatoes. They both ordered soft drinks and then Jordon leaned against the high, red leather booth back.

She looked achingly beautiful but her eyes appeared tired and slightly hollow.

"You look exhausted," he said softly.

"I am," she admitted.

"I think we've done enough today. After we eat I'll take you back to your room, unless you're finally ready to agree to get a room at another motel," he said, desperately wishing she would agree to go someplace safe.

She laughed, the slightly husky sound that stirred him on all levels, and shook her head. "You're nothing if not consistent, Chief Walters."

"Jordon, I care about your safety," he replied.

"I care about my safety, too, but that doesn't mean I'm going to run and hide. Ed fixed the window lock, and if it makes you feel better then you can walk me to my door each night and check the room before I settle in."

"Do you have some sort of a death wish?"

"Of course not," she replied quickly. "I'll admit I take some risks, but they're always calculated ones."

Their conversation was interrupted by the arrival of their meals. Unlike most of the meals they had shared, Jordon was unusually silent and appeared distracted.

Gabriel didn't know if it was because she was

tired or if he might have made her angry with his death-wish question. Although he would have liked to prod her into telling him more about herself, about her current mood, instead he gave her space and remained quiet.

They were halfway through the meal when she placed her fork down and stared at him thoughtfully. "Something has been bothering me all afternoon and I finally figured out what it was."

"What's that?" he asked curiously.

"Ted."

Gabriel looked at her in surprise. "What about him?"

"I'm just wondering how hard Joan really had to twist his arm to move here." Her eyes darkened slightly. "I'm wondering what lengths he might go to in order to get back to life in Oklahoma City."

Gabriel sucked in a deep breath. Was it even possible? Would Ted sabotage the family business by killing three people in cold blood to ruin his wife's dream and get her and their children back where he thought they belonged?

"That's sick and it's crazy," he finally said.

"I know, right?" she replied. "But we knew we might be chasing crazy. Ted lives right across the street. He'd have access and intimate knowledge of the area."

"But he had a solid alibi for Samantha Kent's murder. He was having breakfast in the dining room with other people when she was killed," Gabriel protested.

"The medical examiner only has to be wrong about the time of the attack by twenty minutes or so. That would have given Ted time to stab her, clean himself up and appear for breakfast."

She leaned forward, her eyes blazing with the spark of life that had been missing before. "Ed mentioned that he'd told Ted about the window lock not working a month ago and yet he put me in that very room. Why not one of the other empty rooms? I know we checked into their backgrounds, but we were looking at it from the viewpoint that they were victims. I'm just saying maybe we need to approach an investigation into Ted from a new angle."

She picked up her fork once again and Gabriel set his down, his appetite gone as he realized they had managed to take one suspect off their list but had just added another one.

Chapter Ten

Another week passed far too slowly. The cases had all gone cold, and although the investigation continued, they were grasping at straws. One of the only good things that had happened was the weather had warmed up and the snow had finally melted away.

Jordon now sat in the conference room alone. Gabriel was attending to other duties in his office and she'd been reading through the interviews and the background material they'd gathered throughout the past week.

They'd spoken to Glen's, Ed's and Kevin's neighbors and friends in an effort to get a handle on the three brothers who topped their list of suspects.

They'd also spent hours on the phone speaking to anyone they could find who had been in Ted's and Joan's lives in Oklahoma City before they'd bought the Diamond Cove. This time the investigation wasn't seeking to find somebody who was an enemy of the couple.

Much of their efforts had been focused on digging

into Ted's past to see if there was any indication that he harbored a dark and twisted soul. He had no criminal record other than a speeding ticket he'd received four years ago.

They'd spoken with former coworkers, and Jordon had spent hours digging into social media where he was fairly active. She'd studied his posts and stared at his photos for so long he invaded her dreams, but she'd found nothing out of the ordinary.

She'd not only delved into Ted's social media, but had also looked at Joan's. She'd even been desperate enough to study Jason's and Hannah's online presences, figuring sometimes children might share something about family tension.

Joan had posted fairly regularly when she'd been a teacher but had apparently put her blogging efforts into the official Diamond Cove website when they'd moved here. Her cheerful, inviting blogs had fallen off after the first murder.

Jason posted irregularly, mostly sharing things that teenage guys would find interesting. He had been unhappy about the move and talked about leaving his friends, but later posts indicated that he'd adjusted okay and had made new friends. Hannah had little social media, which was rather surprising for a fifteen-year-old girl.

Jordon sighed and cast her gaze out the nearby window where dusk was just beginning to paint the world in deep purple shadows. Another night nearly gone and they weren't any closer to solving the case.

However, she had definitely grown closer to her partner. He invaded her dreams, as well. They were not just sizzling erotic dreams, but also sweet and filled with all kinds of wonderful that she knew she'd never have in her real life.

She'd grown to care about him deeply and she had a feeling he was feeling the same way about her. That only made her need to solve this case more pressing than ever.

Even though they'd known each other for only a little over two weeks, they had probably spent more time together than most couples who had been married for six months or so.

They'd learned each other's little quirks. She knew he liked his burgers without ketchup and with extra mayo and that he refused to drink cold coffee. His energy level fell somewhat in the late afternoons, but he got a second wind after eating dinner.

Those were just the superficial things she'd discovered about him. She'd also learned he had a kind heart, that he had a secret passion for supporting animal rights and that his eyes softened and lightened in hue whenever he gazed at her.

The very last thing she wanted to do was break his heart. He was such a good man and he deserved a good woman. As much as she'd like to think otherwise, that woman would never, ever be her.

A wave of loneliness, of quiet sorrow struck her, piercing through her heart and bringing an unexpected sting of tears to her eyes.

She'd once had such dreams of sharing her life with a special man. She'd once believed she'd have a husband who would be her soft place to fall, a man who would be by her side until death. But those dreams had been stolen and she refused to believe in anything like that ever again.

This case was definitely not only getting to her on a professional level, but also on a personal one. Angrily she swiped at her eyes and sat up straighter in the chair. She was good alone. That was the way it was supposed to be and there was no sense getting all teary-eyed about it.

The conference room door opened and Gabriel swept in, filling the room with his solid presence, with his male vitality. "Now, where were we?" he asked.

She shoved the files away. "At the same dead end we were at a week ago," she replied with an uncharacteristic pessimism darkening her tone. "It would be nice if we could just identify somebody with the means and a clear motive, but I'm beginning to wonder if any of our suspects are really good for these murders." She released a heavy sigh.

He frowned. "That doesn't sound like the kick-butt partner I've come to know and love."

"I guess I'm just not feeling it right now," she replied.

"Has all work and no play made Agent James a grumpy woman?"

"Possibly," she admitted.

"My recommendation is we grab our coats, get out of here and go someplace where we can kick back and have a couple of drinks," he replied.

She immediately stood and pulled her coat from the back of her chair. "Just lead me to the nearest bar."

He grinned at her. "Now, that's the go-get-'em spirit."

Fifteen minutes later he pulled up in front of a small tavern off the main drag. A wooden sign across the doorway proclaimed the place to be Joe's.

"I know, it's a bit of a dive, but it's my favorite place to come to and unwind," he said as he turned off the car. "The music is low, the drinks are good and strong, and here nobody expects anything from me except that I pay the tab before I leave."

"Sounds like the perfect place to end a fairly depressing day," she replied.

They got out of the car and he ushered her inside with his hand in the middle of her back. It was just one of many of the casual touches they'd shared since the night they'd made love, but tonight she felt particularly vulnerable and it affected her more deeply than ever before.

Joe's held a long polished bar with a dozen stools. Two men sat on opposite sides of the bar and an older man with a graying beard stood behind it and nodded in greeting to them as they entered.

Gabriel led her to one of the handful of booths where a small bowl of peanuts was the centerpiece. A country song about lost love and a broken heart played on speakers overhead. Jordon took off her coat and then slid into the black leather booth.

"What can I get for you?" Gabriel asked her.

She frowned thoughtfully. "A gin and tonic with a twist of lime," she finally replied. She didn't want a civilized glass of wine. She wanted...needed something stronger to take the edge off her uncharacteristic blue mood.

She watched Gabriel as he walked to the bar. It wasn't her growing feelings for him that had her so discouraged. It wasn't, she told herself firmly.

The real problem was that she was afraid she'd be called back to Kansas City before they caught the bad guy. The job was the only successful part of her life, and she was afraid she'd leave here as a failure, and she'd already been a failure in so many other areas of her life.

He returned to the booth with their drinks and sat across from her. "What is your poison tonight?" she asked.

"Scotch and soda. My father introduced me to the pleasure of fine scotch when I got old enough to have an occasional drink with him."

"You're close to your parents?"

"Very," he replied. "They moved from Chicago to Florida several years ago, but they come up to visit me at least once a year and we stay in touch by phone."

"They must be very proud of you," she replied.

He smiled. "They are, but I think they'd be proud of me no matter what I chose to do for a living."

The front door opened and she glanced over to see Glen Rollings come in. The relaxation that had been about to take over her came to a screeching halt as every muscle in her body tensed.

Gabriel followed her gaze and muttered a small curse under his breath. "What in the hell is he doing here?"

Glen ambled over to their booth with a wide smile. "What a small world. Chief Walters, I didn't know we shared the same drinking hole. I was just driving by here and saw your car and thought I'd stop in to say hello." He winked at Jordon. "Figured I'd take the chance at seeing the hottest woman in town one more time."

"Hello and goodbye," Jordon replied, not attempting to mask her irritation.

"Move it along, Glen. We're busy here," Gabriel said, his eyes narrowed as he glared at the blond-haired man.

"Jeez, you guys don't have to be so unfriendly," Glen replied.

"We're both not feeling too friendly right now," Jordon said.

"Wow. Okay, then. I guess I'll just see you later." Glen turned around and headed for the bar, where he sat on one of the stools.

"In all the times I've been here, I've never seen any of the Rollings brothers," Gabriel said. "I don't like this sudden appearance."

Jordon cast Glen another glance. He had a beer in front of him and was half-turned on the stool so that he could see them. She looked back at Gabriel. "Do you think he followed us here?"

"I don't know. Maybe he is a regular here and I've just never seen him." He took a drink and then grabbed a handful of peanuts. "Just ignore him."

For a few minutes they sat silently. Jordon felt Glen's steady gaze on her, making it impossible for her to just ignore him as Gabriel had advised.

Was he their man? Was it possible he had seen the car outside and wondered if maybe she was inside here by herself? Alone and vulnerable?

All the other murders had taken place on Diamond Cove property, but that didn't mean the next one would. The killer could always change up his game. Maybe for him it was enough that she was a "guest" at the resort.

Thankfully, Glen finished his beer fairly quickly

and then left. It was only then that her muscles began to slowly unknot. "That was weird," she said.

"Maybe it wasn't as weird as it felt. It's possible he really did see the car and maybe thought he could charm you. I think he has a crush on you."

Jordon was somehow grateful that Gabriel's thoughts about the situation hadn't gone as dark as hers had. She sat up straighter in the seat and picked up some peanuts.

"Tell me about your parents," he said. "You've heard all about mine, but you never mention yours."

"That's because we aren't real close. My mother and father own a successful law firm back in Denver. They're both defense lawyers who specialize in high-profile cases. They wanted me to follow in their foot-steps and work at the firm, but that wasn't the side of the law I wanted to work."

"They were unhappy with your decision to be-come an FBI agent?"

An old pain attempted to grab hold of her, but she shoved it away. She'd long ago made peace with the fact that she hadn't been the daughter her par-ents had wanted.

"They weren't happy about my career choice and they weren't happy that I never had an interest to rub shoulders with their society friends." She smiled at him wryly. "I think they were probably disappointed that I had curly dark hair instead of beautiful gleam-ing blond tresses, too."

"I love your hair," he replied. "And I love that you're

an FBI agent and here with me right now." His eyes gleamed in the low lighting.

"Thanks." She grabbed some of the peanuts, aware that his gaze was a little too soft and filled with a lot of inviting heat.

"So, what are some other places where you hang out in your downtime?" she asked, determined to steer the conversation onto a lighter topic.

"I occasionally go to the local animal shelter and play with the dogs."

"Why don't you have one?" she asked curiously. "You know, man's best friend and all that."

"My lifestyle wouldn't be good for a dog. I work long hours and it wouldn't be fair."

"Working long hours makes any kind of a relationship difficult," she replied.

He nodded. "People who aren't in the life don't understand the drive, the passion we feel for this work." He cocked his head to the side and gazed at her curiously. "Was that an issue in your marriage?"

"Not really. Jack loved the fact that I sometimes worked long hours. It gave him an opportunity to cheat with women who were better than me." She looked down into her empty glass, shocked that she'd spilled this particular piece of her past.

"Better than you? What in the hell does that mean?"

She looked up to see his intense gaze boring into her. "Can I get another drink?"

He held her gaze for another long moment and

then got up from the booth and headed for the bar. Jeez, what had made her dredge up the failures of her marriage? With the arrival of Glen and now the conversation, this downtime definitely wasn't as refreshing as she'd expected when they'd left the station.

As she stared at Gabriel's back, she knew the answer as to why she'd brought up her marriage. She had to remind herself that she wasn't fit to be a wife, that she wasn't good for any real relationship. Something about the way Gabriel watched her made her want to believe differently about herself, but she knew the truth and she had to cling to it.

He returned to the booth with her drink. "Now, tell me all about this creep that you married."

She took a big swallow of her gin. "He wasn't a creep," she said as she set her glass down. "I met Jack at a charity function. He owned an insurance company and was a well-respected figure in the community. He was handsome and smart and charming, and I fell hard for him. We dated for eight months and then got married."

She'd been so happy, so certain that she'd found her soul mate. Even her parents, who had never been particularly pleased with anything she did, had approved of Jack.

"We had a blissful couple of months before the cracks started to appear," she said. "He thought I was messy, so I tried really hard to keep things neat and tidy. He didn't like my jokes and so I tried to be more serious. The first year was definitely an adjustment for us. And then I heard from a mutual friend that he was seeing another woman."

It was an old hurt that had scabbed over long ago, but as she remembered that time, she was surprised to realize it still hurt just a little bit.

"Did you confront him?" Gabriel asked softly.

She nodded. "I did, and he confessed that he'd met her a few times for drinks and that was all there was to it. He swore he wouldn't see her again, that he wanted our marriage to work, and I believed him."

"And so the marriage continued."

"I didn't want another failure. Marrying Jack was the one thing I'd done that my parents approved of, so I was desperate to make it work. Then I found some sexy text messages on his phone that made it clear he was having an affair, and yes, I was snooping."

She took another big gulp of her drink and realized she was more than a little bit buzzed. She'd always been a lightweight when it came to hard liquor.

She offered Gabriel a rueful smile. "The problem wasn't Jack—it was me. I didn't know how to make him happy. I didn't know how to be a partner. I'm just not good wife material."

"That's not true." His eyes filled with a warmth that washed over her. "You just weren't Jack's wife material and I still think he's a creep."

She laughed. "Partners are supposed to be loyal to each other. I promise I'll hate anyone who breaks your heart, and now I think it's time for me to get back to my room for the night."

They got up and pulled their coats on, and Jordon stood by the door while Gabriel paid the tab. When he ushered her outside, a deep scowl possessed his features.

"What's wrong?" she asked him once they were in the car.

He buckled his seat belt and then turned to look at her, his eyes so dark she fought against an inner shiver. "Joe just told me that he'd never seen Glen in the bar before tonight."

All the black thoughts she'd momentarily entertained when Glen had sat on the bar stool staring at her rushed back into her head.

"He implied to us that he was a regular customer," she said.

Gabriel pulled out on the road to take her back to the bed-and-breakfast. "I don't know if he's a real threat or if he just really drove by and saw the patrol car like he said. We know for sure now that he's a liar."

Jordon leaned her head back and closed her eyes. The travel back to her broken marriage, coupled with the new concern of a stalking Glen, swept away any pleasant buzz the alcohol might have given her.

She turned in her seat and glanced behind them, but no cars shared the secondary road with them.

"Don't worry. I'm watching, too," Gabriel said.

"I just don't understand these men. It's like Kevin and Glen are intentionally doing things to make them look like suspects. Are they just stupid or are they that calculating and they're trying to muddy things up for us?"

"Neither of them are rocket-scientist material, but they are cunning. I'll call Mark and have him assign somebody to keep an eye on Glen. I want to know what he's doing and when he's doing it."

"Sounds like a plan," she replied.

"I'm sorry the night ended up like this. I was hoping we'd both relax and kick back a bit."

"It's not your fault Glen showed up and ruined the mood."

It took only minutes to arrive back at Diamond Cove. They both got out of the car and walked up the path to her room, guided through the dark night by the solar lights.

Gabriel pulled his gun as she unlocked her door. This had become their routine since the night she'd been attacked.

She opened the door and they both went inside fast. Immediately he went to the bathroom, where she knew he'd check to make sure nobody was hiding and that the window remained securely locked.

She checked in the closet and under the bed, and when the room was cleared, he sat in the chair next to the fireplace and she sat on the edge of the bed facing him.

"Looks like I'm good for another night," she said.

He nodded, his eyes holding a gleam of hunger. "Jordon, about your marriage… The only mistake you made was not marrying a man who loved your sense of humor, a man who didn't care about housekeeping or cooking and such nonsense. You just need to be with a man who understands you and loves you just the way you are."

She jumped up from the bed, afraid that he was going to say something stupid, afraid that she would fall for his sweet words and ultimately he'd only wind up being another person she disappointed.

"I'm tired, Gabriel. I don't want to talk anymore about my past or Glen Rollings or murder or anything else." She stood by the door. "I just need to get some sleep."

He got up from the chair and joined her at the door. "Then I guess I'll just say good-night." There was a wistfulness in his tone that held the promise of the warmth of his arms, the heat of his body against hers.

She could have him if she wanted him for the night. All she had to do was ask him to stay and she knew he would. The idea was definitely tempting, but she steeled her heart.

"Good night, Gabriel," she said and opened the door.

He stepped outside and then turned to look at her. "You know I'm more than just a little bit crazy over you."

Her heart squeezed tight. "Get over it," she replied forcefully. "I've never lived up to anyone's expectations, Gabriel, and I certainly wouldn't live up to yours."

She closed the door before he could respond and leaned her head against the wood. She wished he'd never told her what he felt about her. She wished he was the antagonistic bonehead she'd initially thought he was going to be.

Instead he was a man she could love, a man who could fill the empty spaces of her life. But she refused to love him. She cared about him too much to fall into a rosy glow with him that would only end in flames of regret.

Chapter Eleven

He'd wanted her tonight. He'd wanted to hold her in his arms and make love to her. He'd needed to somehow erase whatever insecurities her ex-husband had scarred into her soul. Although she hadn't gone into great detail, she'd said enough to let Gabriel know that the marriage had wounded her in a way to make her believe she was unworthy.

Instead of going home, Gabriel returned to the station, thoughts of the conversation they'd shared in the bar still haunting him. She had so much to offer a man who captured her heart, but she didn't believe she had anything to give.

There was no question that she'd rebuffed him tonight. She'd shoved him out of the door as if he was the devil himself. He didn't know what to do with the feelings he had for her, but it was obvious she had no interest in them.

He parked in front of the station and went inside, unsurprised to find Mark working at his desk. "You know we don't pay overtime," he said and sank in the chair across from Mark.

Mark smiled. "Sheila flew out this morning to spend a couple of weeks with her parents. The house was so quiet without her I decided to come in and catch up on some paperwork. What are you doing here so late? I thought you and Agent James had knocked off for the day."

"We had," Gabriel replied and then told Mark about Glen showing up at the bar. "I want a tail put on him. I don't know what his game is, but I don't like it. Him showing up at Joe's just didn't feel right."

"I'll take care of it," Mark replied. "I'll talk to Ben before I leave here. You know how good he and his team are at undercover surveillance."

Gabriel nodded and released a deep sigh. Ben Hammond ran a private investigation agency in town and was often tapped to help out the small police department.

"This is a tough one," Mark said.

Gabriel didn't have to ask him what he was talking about. Mark had been part of the team of officers working alongside Gabriel and Jordon on the cases.

"I thought when I left Chicago behind I was also leaving behind these kind of tough cases," Gabriel said.

"You probably also thought you'd be working for a mayor who was a normal, rational human being,"

Mark said wryly. "He's thrown us all under the bus in his last couple of news conferences."

Gabriel leaned back. "We're all busting our butts to solve this case and he's whining about our lack of progress." He shook his head ruefully.

"How's Agent James holding up?"

"Like all the rest of us she's frustrated and weary." And she'd never lived up to anyone's expectations. Gabriel frowned as her parting words played in his head. Something about the funny, brash Agent Jordon James broke his heart just a little bit.

"She's a tough one," Mark said.

"She is," Gabriel agreed.

"I heard from the grapevine that Ted Overton has been spending a lot of time alone in some local watering holes lately," Mark said.

Gabriel frowned thoughtfully. "Wish I knew if he's trying to drown his guilt or just drinking his misery away."

"I don't know, but from all my sources he's definitely trying to drown something."

Gabriel stood abruptly and released a weary sigh. "Go home, Mark. Get a good night's sleep."

"And you do the same," Mark replied, although he made no move to get out of his chair.

A few minutes later Gabriel was back in his car, but he wasn't heading home. He wouldn't rest easy unless he knew exactly where Glen Rollings was right now. He needed to make sure the man wasn't parked down the street from Diamond Cove and potentially planning some sort of an attack on Jordon.

Glen lived not too far from Ed, but unlike Ed's small neat house, Glen's place was a tiny cabin that appeared not to have enjoyed any outside maintenance for the last twenty years or so.

The window shutters had either fallen off or hung by a single nail, and it was impossible to tell what color the cabin might have once been painted, for it had weathered to a dull gray.

Gabriel breathed a sigh of relief as he saw Glen's car parked outside and lights beaming out from the windows. He pulled to a stop just past the house and called Mark.

"I just wanted to let you know that Glen Rollings's current location is his home. I thought you might want to tell Ben that when you speak to him."

"I already talked to him. I gave him Glen's address and he's going to have somebody in place within the next half hour."

"Thanks, Mark. I appreciate it."

The two men hung up and Gabriel left, this time heading for home. If he couldn't put a man on Jordon, then this was the next best thing. He would have liked to put a tail on all their suspects, but it simply wasn't financially feasible. Glen's appearance in the bar had been odd and unsettling enough that he could justify the expense of a tail. Although he was certain that Mayor Donald Stoddard would bitch and moan about the use of the private agency.

I've never lived up to anyone's expectations.

Jordon's words haunted him as he entered his house and as he undressed and got into bed. She'd far exceeded his expectations of her professionally, and she'd also exceeded his expectations of her as a desirable, exciting woman.

He fell into a troubled sleep filled with images of a shadowy person with a wicked-looking knife chasing Jordon through the woods. He ran after them, desperate to help her, but the trees all came to life, their limbs grabbing at him to hold him back.

It was just after seven the next morning when he walked into the Diamond Cove dining room, where Jordon and Joan were already seated at a table.

Joan looked haggard and as if she hadn't slept in days. The pleasant sparkle that normally lit her eyes was gone, replaced by the dark pall this case had cast over everyone involved.

Joan and Jordon greeted him before Joan jumped up from the table and hurried into the kitchen. "Everything all right?" he asked after he'd poured a cup of coffee and sunk down in the chair opposite Jordon.

After the conversation they'd had the night before, he wasn't sure what kind of mood to expect from her this morning. "According to Joan, Ted is drinking too much, the kids are starting to act out and she feels like her entire world is falling apart." Her eyes sparked with anger. "This case is really ticking me off."

"We can only chase what leads we get, and right now there aren't any to chase," Gabriel replied. "We've now got a tail on Glen, so if he's our man and he makes a move, we'll be on him before anyone else gets hurt."

"And if he isn't our man?" She raised one of her eyebrows.

Gabriel frowned. "Then we'll find the person who is our man. I don't know what else to say." He still couldn't quite gauge her mood.

"I know you don't. I'm just frustrated." She released a deep sigh. "Maybe I just need to make myself a bigger target. I need to appear as more vulnerable bait. I could spend the nights sitting in a rocking chair outside of my room…or maybe…"

"Stop." Gabriel interrupted her in horror and leaned forward in his chair. "You aren't going to do anything like that."

"You're right—I'm not. I just wish this creep would make another move." She took a sip of her coffee and then set the cup back down on the table. "You know I can't stay here forever." Her gaze held his intently and then she stared down into her coffee cup.

"Do you know how much longer we've got with you here?" His heart suddenly felt too big for his chest and he had to talk around a lump that rose up in his throat.

He'd known she was here only temporarily, but in

the past week or so he'd somehow buried that fact deep in his mind. It had been easier to not think about the time she'd have to go.

"I spoke to my director last night and he's giving me another two weeks and then it's time for me to go back home," she replied.

"Here we are," Joan said as she entered the dining room carrying two plates of scrambled eggs, toasted English muffins and strips of crispy bacon.

Two weeks. It wasn't a lot of time. Gabriel picked up his fork even though his appetite had fled. They had fourteen days to catch the killer.

And he had two weeks to try to stop falling deeper in love with her.

JORDON SAT IN the center of her bed and stared at her laptop monitor. It was just after nine and the frustration of another fruitless day burned hot in her belly.

That wasn't all that burned inside her. She was in love with Gabriel and she wished he was beside her right now, in her bed...in her life forever.

The night that they'd slept together she'd thought he would just be a fling, a warm memory for her to embrace on lonely nights. Gabriel in her bed had been exciting and wonderful, but Gabriel out of her bed was everything she had ever wanted, everything she had ever dreamed of in a man.

But she knew he wouldn't settle for anything less than marriage and she wasn't willing to go through that again. He was terrific husband material and she was nothing more than mistress material. And to believe anything otherwise would be a disservice to them both.

With a deep frown, she got up from the bed, refusing to think about all the things she wouldn't allow in her life. She knew who and what she was, and whether Gabriel knew it or not, he deserved much better.

She'd almost been grateful when Director Langford had told her he was pulling her off the case after another two weeks. All she had to do was hang on to her heart and remember she was a lone wolf for the next fourteen days.

What she needed now was a cup of coffee from the guest shed and then a good night's sleep. She wrapped on her gun belt, pulled on her coat and stepped out of her room.

The temperature had dropped again but not before the last couple of warm days had melted the snow left by the night of the blizzard.

As always when she left her room at night, she kept her hand on the butt of her gun and her senses on high alert. The night was silent around her, but she scanned the area with narrowed eyes.

There was no way she was going to let somebody get a jump on her. She was ready for anything that might come out of the darkness. She would never be taken by surprise again.

She reached the guest shed and opened the door.

Instantly every nerve in her body electrified and her muscles tensed. There had been no welcoming tinkle of the bell. In fact, the small silver bell that had hung over the door was gone.

Her breaths became shallow as she yanked her gun from her holster and fell into a crouch. Was he inside here with her, or was he just outside and had hoped she wouldn't notice that the bell was missing.

Was he just waiting for her to turn toward the coffee machine and watch a drink fill a cup and then he'd come at her and stab her in the back like he had Rick Sanders?

She twirled toward the door and then pivoted to face both the laundry room door and then the storage room door. Her heart ticked like a time bomb in her chest. Despite the cold of the night, her fingers grew slick with sweat on the gun handle.

Where was he? She turned sideways so both the laundry room door and the entry into the shed were in her vision. She pulled the laundry room door open and released a frantic gasp of air.

Nobody there.

She refused to give in to the shudders of fear that attempted to possess her. She still had to clear the small storage room and watch her back for anyone coming in from outside.

Heart still racing, she grabbed the storage room door handle, turned it and then kicked the door open.

Despite the relative darkness of the room, it was easy to see that nobody was inside.

She whirled to face the door that led back outside. Any desire she might have had for a flavored coffee was gone, vanished by the sick knot of nerves that twisted inside her.

The bell over the door had been there two nights ago when she'd come inside to get coffee. It hadn't just dropped off to the floor and there was absolutely no reason Ted and Joan would have had it removed.

She stepped back outside, her gaze frantically shooting in all directions. She got back safely to her room and sank down on the edge of her bed, and only then did her heartbeat begin to slow.

It was him. The killer had taken down the bell. He was toying with her. Had he been someplace nearby? Watching her search the room? Laughing at her fear?

Her stomach clenched, this time not in fear, but rather in anger. He was so close…so damn close. He had to have known about the bell over the door. He had to know that about every other evening she made the trek to the shed for a late-night cup of coffee.

Had he hoped she wouldn't notice the missing bell? Had he hoped that she'd be unaware enough to go into the shed, stand in front of the coffeemaker and be attacked from behind?

If that was the case then he must think she was stupid. She frowned. And why wouldn't he believe that? They hadn't caught him yet even though apparently he was moving around right under their noses.

She carried her simmering anger with her the next morning into the dining room, where Gabriel was already seated at a table, chatting with Joan.

"Good morning," she said curtly. "The bell over the door in the guest shed is gone," she added before either of them could reply.

"What do you mean gone?" Joan asked in surprise.

"The bracket is still there but it looks like the bell was torn off." Jordon stalked over to the coffeemaker.

"Who would have done such a thing?" Joan asked.

Jordon turned to look at her.

Joan raised a hand to her mouth. "The killer. He didn't want anyone warned of him coming in behind them."

"Give the little lady a stuffed bear," Jordon replied as she poured herself a cup of coffee. Once she was finished, she walked back to the table and sat across from Gabriel.

He gazed at her with a deep frown. "When exactly did you discover this?"

"Last night it was just after nine when I decided to get myself a cup of coffee from the shed. The minute I stepped through the door I realized the bell hadn't tinkled."

"How often at night are you leaving your room to get coffee?" he asked, his voice holding a wealth of disapproval as his gaze bored into hers.

"I'll just go see to breakfast," Joan said and quickly left the room.

"Every other night or so," Jordon said in response to Gabriel's question.

"Tell me, Agent James—on those nights do you really want a cup of coffee or are you taunting the killer to make a move on you?"

He was definitely angry. As if calling her Agent James wasn't enough to let her know, the deepening frown across his forehead and the taut slash of his lips was a sure sign of his ire.

She smiled at him. "I told you when we first met that if you hung around me long enough you'd get irritated with me."

"This isn't funny, Jordon," he replied. "I have nightmares about something happening to you."

She looked at him in surprise. "You dream about me?"

He shook his head. "Don't change the subject. Answer my question."

"I forgot what the question was."

He leaned back in his chair and released a deep sigh of obvious frustration. "Have you been intentionally taunting the killer to come after you?"

She thoughtfully stared down into her coffee cup and then looked back at him once again. "I don't know," she finally answered truthfully. "I mean, I'm definitely a coffee freak and I like to drink a cup in the evenings, but maybe subconsciously I was hoping the killer would come after me."

"You aren't alone in this. We're a team, Jordon. It's bad enough that you're staying here. The last thing I want is for you to take any additional chances that put you in greater danger." His gaze softened and his mouth relaxed a bit.

"I won't get coffee at night anymore," she said quickly, afraid by the look on his face that he was going to say something stupid...something that might twist her heart.

"That only makes me feel a little better," he replied.

Joan came in with their breakfast plates, thankfully ending that particular conversation. "I'll have Ed hang another bell in the shed as soon as he comes in this morning."

Jordon exchanged a pointed gaze with Gabriel and she knew he was thinking the same thing. It was very possible that the man who would be replacing the bell was the same one who had yanked it off.

Was she mistaken in her belief that her attacker on the night of the snowstorm hadn't been Ed? In retrospect she really couldn't be sure. It had all happened so very fast.

Or had he taken down the bell to clear the way for one of his brothers to make a move on her? The idea of three of them working in concert was so disturbing.

The day had barely begun and already a dull throb pressed tight across the back of her skull. She had a deadly man to find and a wonderful man to forget.

Chapter Twelve

Ten days.

And tomorrow it would be nine more days and
Jordon would be gone. Gabriel turned around at his
desk and stared out the nearby window where another day had ended and night had fallen.

When the bell had gone missing in the guest shed,
he'd added a tail to both Kevin Rollings and Ted Overton, but over the past couple of days neither one of the
men had gone anywhere or done anything suspicious.

Gabriel knew he couldn't justify the tails remaining in place for too long, especially not having any
concrete evidence to tie them to the crimes other than
Kevin's vocal hatred of Diamond Cove.

A knock on his door turned him around in the
chair. Mark entered the office and sank down in the
chair in front of his desk. "Another frustrating day,
huh," he said. "Maybe the killer is done. Maybe he
figures the three murders have already ruined business for Diamond Cove and he's finished."

Gabriel smiled. "Thanks for trying to inject a little optimism into my heart, but we both know he isn't finished." His smile fell. "And right now it appears that we're stuck just waiting for his next move."

"He's marked Agent James as his next victim, but so far he's been unsuccessful in getting to her. Let's just hope he doesn't change his mind and decide to go after somebody else, like a member of the Overton family."

"There's been no indication that the family is at risk, which makes Ted even better as a potential suspect," Gabriel replied. "However, I have warned them all to not be on the property alone, especially at night."

"I know Agent James is leaving town soon. What happens when his target goes away?"

Gabriel's gut tightened, and he didn't know if it was because Jordon would be gone or knowing that the killer would probably find another target.

"I don't know," he finally replied. "I can't stop Ted and Joan from reopening their business and that means any of their guests could be potential victims."

"If they have any guests."

"Oh, they'll have guests. If nothing else they'd get stupid people who want to stay in a place where murder has taken place." Gabriel swallowed against a bit of disgust.

"So, I guess the only thing we can hope for is that our man comes after Agent James within the next week or so," Mark said.

That was the last thing Gabriel hoped would happen. He wanted the killer caught but he didn't want Jordon involved. He was torn between being a chief of police who trusted that an FBI agent could take care of herself, and being a man who wanted nothing more than to protect the woman who held a big chunk of his heart.

"I guess I'm out of here," Mark said and got up from the chair. "I'll see you in the morning."

"Good night, Mark." Gabriel shut down his computer and then stood. It was time to get Jordon back to her suite. He put on his coat, left his office and then walked down to the conference room where she had been working alone for the last hour while Gabriel caught up on all the other crimes in the area.

He opened the conference room door and her fresh, floral scent instantly assaulted his nose. She looked up from whatever she'd been reading and her smile warmed him to his very soul.

"Another day is done," she said. She slid the paper into one of the manila folders on the table and then stood.

"Another day of more dead ends," he replied.

She pulled on her coat. "Don't beat yourself up, Gabriel. We both know we're at a point in the investigation where the ball is in the killer's court."

"Don't remind me," he said drily. "Are you hungry? Want to grab something before I take you back to Diamond Cove?" They had eaten a late lunch, but he'd much prefer the final meal of the day spent with her than alone in his kitchen.

"I'm really not very hungry. I'm good just going to my room," she replied.

He nodded despite his disappointment. She'd been rather distant with him all day. During lunch she'd been quiet, far more introspective than he'd ever seen her. It was as if mentally she was already moving on and putting him and these crimes behind her.

She was quiet as they left the building, got into his car and left the station. "The weather report says more snow coming in sometime tonight," he said to break the silence.

"Hopefully it isn't going to be another blizzard," she replied.

"Nah, right now they're just calling for an inch or two."

"That's good." She stared out the passenger window and the silence resumed.

He tried to think of something inane, any light topic that would draw her out, but the things he really wanted to talk about with her weren't light or inane.

Tonight the depth of his feelings for her begged to be spoken out loud. They filled his heart with a fullness that was difficult to hold in. As crazy as it was, he knew in his very soul that she was the woman he wanted not just for the next ten days, but rather for the rest of his life. And until this moment he'd believed that she was falling in love with him.

They reached Diamond Cove and they both got out of the car. As always, he drew his gun as she unlocked her suite door. Once the room was cleared, they took off their coats and he sat on the chair next to the fireplace.

"How about a cup of coffee before I take off?" he asked.

"Okay, I'll make a pot, although this isn't as good as the flavored ones in the guest shed." She walked over to the vanity where the little coffeepot sat next to a small basket that held coffee packages, creamers and sugar packets.

He watched her covetously as she poured the water into the back of the machine, set the coffee packet inside and then turned it on to brew.

She was so beautiful and seemingly so unaware of her own attractiveness. It wasn't just her physical charm that drew him to her, but also the spirit and beauty that shone from within.

As she turned around to face him, he got up and flipped the switch that made flames jump to life in the fireplace. He sat back down in the chair and knew this night wouldn't end without him speaking exactly what was in his heart.

"Long day," she finally said when the coffee was finished and she'd poured them each a cup. She set hers on the nightstand and moved aside what appeared to be a red nightgown that was on her bed, along with a can of hair product and a tube of mascara, and then sat down.

"They're all long lately," he replied. When he'd worked as a cop in Chicago, he'd once faced down a man high on PCP and armed with a machete. He and his partner had gotten into a firestorm of flying bullets with a handful of dangerous gangbangers.

However, nothing he'd ever experienced before in his life had made him as nervous as he now was as he faced a woman with soft curls and green eyes and a spirit that made him smile.

"You've been terribly quiet all day," he observed.

She nodded. "I guess I've just been trying to figure out where we go from here."

"I know where I'd like us to go from here." He set his coffee cup on the table and ignored the sudden dryness of his throat as he held her gaze intently.

"Where is that?" she asked. She picked up her coffee cup and took a sip.

"Jordon, I'm not talking about these cases. I'm talking about us...you and me."

Her eyes became guarded as she set her cup back on the nightstand. "Gabriel, there is no you and me."

"Jordon, I'm in love with you and I think you feel the same way about me." His heart thundered in his chest as he spoke the words that had been burning inside him.

She averted her gaze from his. "You just feel that way because we slept together."

"Jordon, I loved making love with you, but my feelings for you certainly aren't just based on a physical level. I love the way your eyes light up just before you say something funny. I adore how they narrow when you're deep in thought."

He leaned forward, the words now falling out of his mouth as if released from a pressure cooker. "Jordon, at the end of this, no matter how the investigation goes, I don't want to tell you goodbye. I want you in my life forever. I want…" He paused as she held up her hand.

"Stop, Gabriel. Please stop." She got up from the edge of the bed and walked several steps back from where he sat.

He drew in a deep breath and then continued. "I know the distance thing might be a bit of an issue at first, but it's less than a four-hour drive from here to Kansas City. There's no reason why we couldn't continue to see each other on days off and eventually I'd be willing to relocate."

There was no joy on her beautiful features. Instead she gazed at him in what looked like stunned horror. She closed her eyes for a brief moment, and when she opened them again, a reckless smile curved her lips. "Sorry, sailor. You've obviously got me mixed up with somebody else."

"Stop it, Jordon." He stood, all of his muscles tense. "Don't make jokes when I'm pouring out my heart to you."

A slight flush filled her cheeks and she averted her gaze from him. "Then stop pouring out your heart," she replied in a soft voice.

"Okay, I'll shut up after you tell me you don't love me." He took several steps closer to her. "Tell me that I mean nothing to you and I'll leave here and won't speak of this again."

He saw it in her eyes, a soft yearning, a sweet wistfulness, but it was there only a moment and then her chin shot up and her gaze was once again shuttered.

"I told you I wasn't marriage material, that I'd never lived up to anyone's expectations," she replied.

"Oh, Jordon, you've not only lived up to mine, but you've far exceeded them," he said softly.

Her lower lip began to tremble and she turned away from him. "Please go, Gabriel. Before you say anything more that you'll regret."

He stared at her stiff back and he didn't see an impenetrable wall. Rather, he saw a woman who was afraid to believe she was worthy of being loved by anyone.

He didn't know how to make her not be afraid. He didn't know what else to say and so he simply stood still and loved her.

JORDON WAITED FOR the sound of the door opening and then closing, indicating to her that Gabriel had left. But several long minutes passed and it didn't happen.

Her heart hurt as it had never ached before in her life.

Falling in love with Gabriel had been so incredibly easy, but this...this rejection of him was so achingly difficult. She desperately wanted what he was offering her, yet of all the men in the entire world she knew, she couldn't be more wrong for a man like him.

She stiffened as his hands fell on her shoulders. "Jordon," he whispered, his breath a warm delight on her ear. She closed her eyes and fought against the sting of tears. "Jordon, don't throw away what we have."

She drew in a deep breath and whirled back around to face him, dislodging his hands from her. "You obviously took things too seriously. We don't have anything, Gabriel. We slept together. It was no big deal. We've had a few laughs and some good times, but that certainly doesn't equate love."

He stared at her and the intensity of his gaze made her feel as if he was peering into her mind, into the very depths of her soul. "What are you so afraid of?"

"I'm not afraid of anything," she replied with a rise of anger filling her. Why was he making this so difficult? Why couldn't he just accept the words she said and go away?

"You know what I think? I believe your parents and your ex-husband did a real number on your head. They have made you feel like you're unworthy of loving... of being loved, and nothing could be further from the truth."

"Thank you, Dr. Gabriel, for the quick psycho-analysis," she retorted.

He had the audacity to smile at her. "You have no idea how adorable, how utterly wonderful I find you. I've been waiting years to find you. You're the woman I want to build a life with. I want you to have my children and I want to grow old with you."

His words painted a picture of a beautiful future, one that she'd once dreamed of and one that still resonated with desire in a small piece of her heart.

There was a part of her that wanted to reach out and grasp on to what he offered, but there was a bigger voice inside her head that told her she'd be all kinds of fool to believe that kind of future with him could be hers.

"You're just trying to grasp on to something good because your investigation has stalled out and you're frustrated," she replied.

A flash of anger lit the depths of his eyes. "You really believe my feelings for you are simply born out of my frustration with the investigation?" He released a dry laugh and shook his head. "Don't try to tell me how I feel and why. I'm not afraid to take a leap of faith with you."

"Then you're a fool," she exclaimed. "And stop implying that I'm afraid. I'm a realist, Gabriel, not a coward."

"I think you're a coward," he replied. "I think you love me, Jordon, and you're just too scared to give us a chance. You'll invite a serial killer into your life, but you won't allow in a man who loves you. You're more afraid of giving your heart than you are in giving your life."

"Get out." A deep rich anger filled her. "Get out now." She stalked to the door. She didn't want to hear anything else he felt the need to say to her.

He stood perfectly still, the only movement his gaze as it searched her features. He finally walked over to the chair, grabbed his coat and put it on.

She opened the door, allowing in the cold of the night, a cold that couldn't begin to compete with the chill that encased her heart.

He walked over to her and reached up as if to stroke her cheek, but she jerked away from him, not allowing him the touch. A muscle ticked in his jaw and his eyes darkened.

"You aren't just a coward, Jordon. You're also a beautiful fool," he said and then walked out.

She slammed the door after him. She locked it and then leaned with her back against it as tears blurred her vision. A beautiful fool...a coward. How dare he say such things to her.

Who did he think he was? He didn't really know her and he certainly couldn't be in love with her. He was just kidding himself and she refused to be pulled into his fantasy.

Still, her heart squeezed tight, so tight in her chest she could scarcely draw a breath. He was the fool to think that she could be the woman he wanted in his life.

She moved away from the door and sank down on the bed, tears still stinging her eyes and an imminent threat of sobs only making her even angrier with him.

He was just a silly man who had confused a wonderful bout of lovemaking and a few laughs with love. She'd told him right up front how she felt about marriage and relationships. He should have just kept his feelings to himself.

But what if he does really love you, a little voice whispered in her head. *What if fate brought you together to finally know happiness? To finally have what you've always dreamed of in the deepest recesses of your heart?*

"No," she said aloud, effectively silencing the voice in her head. She wasn't a coward, but she just wasn't willing to put her heart on the line again.

She'd be gone from here before long and eventually Gabriel would find the woman who was really right for him. She'd be a woman who had a place for everything and everything in its place. She'd be able to cook hearty meals for him and whatever children they might have. She'd be everything Jordon wasn't and couldn't be.

Damn him for his bedroom eyes and gentle ways. Damn him for making her love him when she didn't want to love anyone. Tears began to chase themselves down her cheeks, and instead of attempting to stanch them, she gave in to them.

She curled up on the bed and wept. She grieved

for the woman she had once been, a young woman who had believed in dreams of marriage and happily-ever-after.

She mourned the fact that she no longer believed in those dreams, that they had been shattered by a man who had taken her love and then betrayed it over and over again.

It felt as if she cried for hours, and finally, her tears wound down to little gasping sobs. She rolled over on her back and stared up at the ceiling. How was she going to continue working with Gabriel when she was so angry with him?

And why are you so angry?

The reason wasn't clear, but she embraced the emotion and held tight to it. She was a lone wolf and he should respect that. The idea that he thought she could be anything else just ticked her off.

She got up from the bed and went into the bathroom, where she sluiced water over her face and then stared at her reflection in the mirror.

Finish this assignment and then get the heck out of Dodge, she mentally said to her reflection. *Do your time and then get back to the safe, alone life you've built for yourself.*

Eventually she'd forget that she'd ever loved a good man like Gabriel. She had to forget him because there was no place in her life for him.

She left the bathroom and started to unbuckle her holster, but stopped as she spied a piece of paper peeking out from under her door. Her heartbeat clanged a discordant beat as she pulled her gun. She raced to the door, unlocked it and yanked it open. The porch was empty and she narrowed her eyes to attempt to see through the darkness.

She remained standing on alert for several long moments, the night feeling ominous and fraught with new danger. Slowly she bent down, picked up the paper and then closed and locked her door.

The white paper burned in her hand as she carried it with her and perched on the edge of the bed. When had it been shoved under her door?

It had to have been left after Gabriel had gone, otherwise he would have seen it. While she'd been crying about broken dreams and Gabriel's love, the killer had left her a new calling card.

Her hands trembled as she opened the paper and read the bold letters.

Play a game of cat and mouse
In Mouse's Maze of Mirrors
Come alone or I won't play
At midnight face your fears.

She read the note a second time and then looked at the clock on the nightstand. It was twenty till midnight.

She jumped up off the bed and pulled her cell

phone from her pocket. *Come alone or I won't play.* The words reverberated in her head.

This was a final showdown. She knew it in her gut. With her hand still trembling and a healthy fear squeezing her lungs, she repocketed her cell phone.

She threw on her coat and then grabbed the keys to the patrol car that she hadn't used since she'd been here. She left the room and headed for the parking lot.

She was a lone wolf, and she was going to meet the killer in a place where her nightmares began.

Chapter Thirteen

Who was she going to face in the mirrors? Jordon clenched the steering wheel tight as she drove through the dark night toward the tourist attraction.

Would it be Kevin Rollings, who worked the admission gate and probably knew every inch of the maze? Was he the one they sought?

Or would it be one of his brothers? Was Ed not the pleasant handyman he pretended to be? Had Glen managed to lose his tail? Had he parked his car at his home and then sneaked out of a door or window to come here for a final confrontation with her?

A simmering panic rose up the back of her throat and she swallowed hard against it. Would she get into the maze and get lost in her past? Captured and helpless by visions of Ralph Hicks and that cellar where she'd thought she would die?

She couldn't let that happen, otherwise whoever was in the maze would manage to accomplish what Ralph hadn't managed. If she gave in to her panic, then she knew without a doubt she would wind up dead.

It was three minutes until midnight when she pulled into the Mouse's Maze of Mirrors parking lot. There were no other cars in the lot and the place was dark and formidable.

She got out of the car with her gun in her hand, every muscle tensed and her heart racing a familiar rhythm of fear. Would he be here? Or was this just another little game of taunting like the missing bell in the guest shed?

She wouldn't know until she went inside. She licked her dry lips and drew on every ounce of training she'd had. She had to remain cool and calm and completely in control.

The front door was unlocked, an invitation to enter and face the killer. She eased the door open and went inside in a crouched position. Security lights gave the small lobby a ghostly illumination.

She checked behind the counter where Kevin had sat when she and Gabriel had been there before. Her lungs expelled a deep breath as she saw that nobody was there.

She stared at the turnstile, knowing that once she went through it she would be in the maze of mirrors. *You can do this*, she told herself. *You're a kick-butt FBI agent and it's time to put an end to the killer's madness.*

Her stomach twisted in knots so tight she was

half-nauseous. Her lungs constricted, making deep breaths impossible. *Just do it*, a voice screamed in her head.

She pushed through the turnstile and stepped into the maze. Lights turned on and five reflections of herself stared back at her. She appeared wild-eyed and terrified...just like she'd appeared in Ralph's mirrors.

She drew in several deep breaths to center herself. She refused to be that frightened woman in the reflection. She didn't move until she'd calmed herself and was prepared for whatever might happen.

"Hello?" she called out.

Silence.

Was she here all alone or did she share the space with the person who had brutally killed three people? Somebody had to have turned on the lights. She couldn't be alone. After taking several steps to her right, she found herself facing another set of mirrors.

Which way had Gabriel led her out of here? She couldn't remember how to find the exit, and in any case, she expected to meet somebody before she ever reached the end of the maze. "Is anybody here?"

"Beware. If you aren't fast enough, I'll pull you into my mouse hole and nobody will ever find you again."

The words boomed overhead and ended on the mouse's cackle. Jordon whirled around and five Jordons moved in the reflections. Her taut nerves ached as she waited for somebody to show themselves.

Was she supposed to wait for someone to appear or walk the maze to meet her tormentor at another junction? The uncertainty of the situation had her silently screaming inside her head.

She took several steps forward only to realize it was a mirror and not a passageway. She walked to the left and found another corridor.

A flash of movement behind her spun her around, but then she realized it had been a reflection and she had no idea where the person was and how close he was to her.

The vision had been so brief there was no way she could make an identification. She didn't even know if it had been a man or a woman. It only confirmed to her that the killer was here and toying with her.

She walked slowly, the panic still attempting to close off her airway as she faced her own reflection again and again. The odor of cigarette smoke seemed to linger in the air, along with the acrid scent of burning flesh.

The scars on her hip burned and itched, a reminder of her nightmares, of Ralph and his torture. *Be in the moment*, she commanded herself. She couldn't be pulled back to that cellar where she'd thought she was going to die a slow and painful death.

"Bring it on, you little creep," she yelled.

A girlish giggle filled the air. "You're gonna die in here tonight, Agent James."

Jordon froze, her mind working to make sense of the familiar voice. It couldn't be... Hannah? Was this some sort of a teenager's sick joke? Was she here with some of her friends? Spooking the FBI agent? Was this their idea of a little fun?

"Hannah? Stop playing. This isn't funny. Stop this nonsense and come out and talk to me right now," she said.

"I don't want to talk. You're the next victim, Jordon. You're staying at Diamond Cove and that means you have to die."

Jordon's skin crawled. Was it possible? Surely the murders couldn't have been committed by a fifteen-year-old girl. But even as she tried to deny the possibility, she knew the facts, and the fact was even teenagers could be deadly killers.

Something flashed in her peripheral vision on her left and pain sliced into her upper arm. She whirled around, but Hannah was gone, once again hidden within the maze. Her breath caught in her throat as the warmth of blood leaking down her arm attested to the depth of the wound.

This was definitely no joke. This wasn't a silly game, not when blood had been drawn. Her brain whirled. None of the murdered guests would have felt threatened by Hannah. Hannah knew the woods and she would have known the guests' routines. She had the means to commit the murders, but more than anything Jordon needed to understand the motive.

"Why, Hannah? Why are you doing this? Why did you kill those people?"

"Because I want to go home!" Hannah's voice was filled with a bitter rage. "I didn't want to move to this stupid place in the first place. I don't belong here. Now nobody will want to stay at Diamond Cove and my mom and dad will take us back to Oklahoma City, where I have my own friends."

Jordon was stunned, first by the vitriol in Hannah's voice and second by the unbelievable cunning that had hatched this whole deadly plot.

She tightened her grip on her gun and a vision of Joan's face flashed in her mind. Joan, with her sweet blue eyes and her love for her family—there wasn't going to be a happy ending for her.

But could Jordon shoot Joan's daughter? Could she really take the life of a fifteen-year-old girl? Hopefully, it wouldn't come to that, but if it came to which one of them was going to walk out of here alive, Jordon would pull her trigger without regret.

She screamed as a knife sliced out at her from the left, catching her in the middle of her thigh. She pivoted and ran to the left and caught a glimpse of Hannah ahead of her.

"Stop! Hannah, don't make me shoot you!"

Hannah laughed and instantly disappeared from Jordon's view. Jordon stopped her forward run and instead crept forward slowly...cautiously, unsure from where the next attack might come.

Her biggest fear was that the attack would come from behind. That she wouldn't see Hannah coming, she wouldn't hear her approach until a knife plunged into the center of her back.

There was no question the surroundings were disorienting for Jordon, and it was equally obvious Hannah was perfectly at home in the maze. Like the mouse that ruled this environment, Hannah was the rodent that knew all the secrets of the mirrors.

The sticky wetness on her arm and the blood that now had soaked through her slacks concerned her, but she couldn't focus on that now. She had to figure out a way to somehow disarm and contain Hannah without either of them getting killed.

GABRIEL DROVE AIMLESSLY in his car, the argument with Jordon playing and replaying in his head and sickening his heart. He'd been a damned fool to tell her how he felt about her.

He should have at least waited until the day before she was leaving. Maybe with another week of spending more time together she would have been more open to the possibility of a continuing relationship.

She obviously hadn't been ready to hear what he had to say. Maybe his timing sucked, but he didn't believe she didn't care about him. He'd seen love or something very much like it shining in her eyes when she gazed at him in quiet moments of their days. He'd felt it wafting from her when they touched and when they laughed.

What he hated was that they'd parted with harsh words. While he believed what he'd said to her about being afraid to reach out for love, he'd probably been too harsh with her. He'd let his emotions get ahead of him.

He hated that her cold, demanding parents and a cheating ex-husband had made her believe that she was unlovable. He hated that she didn't believe she deserved to be loved.

He found himself parked back in the Diamond Cove parking lot and realized he was here to apologize to her. He'd pushed her too hard and he didn't want to go to bed until he told her he was sorry.

A glance at the clock told him it was a few minutes before midnight. It was possible she was already sleeping. He could always apologize to her in the morning. Still, he didn't turn around and leave.

Just as he'd needed to tell her how he felt about her earlier, he knew he needed to apologize to her this very moment. The cold air gripped him as he got out of his car. The same cold had encased his heart since he'd left her room earlier.

He certainly didn't intend to apologize for loving her, but he wanted her to know he hadn't meant to get upset with her and that he just wanted her to be happy. At least that way hopefully there would be no unresolved tension between them in the morning.

The last week with her shouldn't be uncomfortable for them both. That wasn't the impression he wanted her to take away from here.

As he approached her door, he was relieved to see light casting out from her window. Good—apparently she was still awake.

He rapped lightly on the door and waited for a reply. When none came he knocked a little harder. "Jordon, it's me. I'd like to talk to you. Please open the door."

Several seconds passed and a rivulet of uneasiness swept through him. There was no way he believed her to be the kind of woman to just ignore him. He knew her well enough to know that if she was still angry with him she'd open her door and meet him with both barrels loaded.

He froze. Had the patrol car he'd left for her to use while here been in the parking lot? He'd been so buried in his own head, so deep in his own thoughts, he hadn't paid any attention.

He turned and raced back to the parking lot. The uneasiness turned to panic as he saw the car was missing. Where could she have gone? Why would she leave her room at this time of night?

Would she have been angry enough to get in the car and go for a drive? That just didn't feel right. For several long seconds his brain refused to fire.

Had something happened after he'd left her earlier? What could have possibly led her to leave her room at this time of night?

Had the killer made contact with her again?

He stared across the street where the Overton house was dark. He needed to get into Jordon's room. He had to see if there was any clue inside as to her whereabouts. Maybe she just needed to get out and clear her head, he thought again as he raced across the street. Maybe she got hungry and decided to grab something to eat.

However, in winter in Branson on a weeknight, most places shut down early. Besides, he just didn't believe one of those rational explanations was right.

Although he hated to bother the Overton family, an alarm bell was ringing loudly in his head, an alarm that told him Jordon might just be in trouble.

He pushed the doorbell and heard the ding-dong echo someplace inside the house. He waited only a minute and then rang it again. Lights went on inside and Ted came to the door clad in a T-shirt and plaid sleep pants and holding a gun.

"Chief Walters," he said in surprise.

"I need you to open Jordon's door for me," Gabriel said without preamble.

"Give me a minute." He opened the door to allow Gabriel to step into a small entry and then Ted disappeared down a hallway. He returned a few moments later wearing his coat and jeans and they both left the house.

"Is there a problem?" Ted asked.

"I'm not sure." Gabriel's gut twisted into knots of tension. He'd half hoped that by the time they got back to her suite she'd have pulled in, sheepish that she'd worried anyone and carrying a bag of goodies from the nearest all-night convenience store.

"I hope I didn't wake everyone in your house," he said.

"Just me and Joan. It would take a bomb going off to wake up Jason or Hannah at this time of the night," Ted replied.

When they reached her room, Ted pulled from his pocket a ring full of keys. He fumbled with them for a moment and then got to the one that would unlock her door.

Gabriel stepped into the room and gazed around, his heart beating wildly. Almost immediately he saw the white folded piece of paper on her bed.

His chest tightened. It looked just like the previous note she'd received from the killer. He picked it up and opened it. His blood chilled as he read the sick poem.

"I've got to go," he said to Ted. "Don't touch anything in here. Just lock up after me."

He didn't wait for Ted to reply. He ran out of the room and down the path to his car, his heartbeat thundering loudly in his head. He had to find her. Dear God, he had to get to her as soon as possible.

When he got into his car, he looked at the time.

Twenty after midnight. She'd met the killer twenty minutes ago in a place where she'd frozen in a panic attack when they'd been there before.

She would not only be vulnerable to a bloodthirsty, knife-wielding killer, but also to the horrible demons of her past. Why hadn't she called him the minute she'd received the note?

Even as the question formed in his mind, he knew the answer. She'd been so angry with him and the note had said for her to come alone. Dammit!

He tore out of the parking lot and tried to call her, but the call went directly to her voice mail. What was happening? He glanced at the clock. What had already happened? It had been almost half an hour since the rendezvous was supposed to occur. So many horrible things could transpire in that amount of time.

He tried to call her again and got the same result. He then called Ben Hammond. The private investigator answered on the second ring.

"You have men on Glen and Kevin Rollings?"

"Yeah. When my guys last checked in they were both at their homes."

"Have them knock on the doors and get a visual confirmation that those two are where they're supposed to be and then get back to me as soon as possible," Gabriel said urgently.

Ben called back just as Gabriel turned into the

Mouse's Maze of Mirrors parking lot, where Jordon's car was the only other vehicle in the lot.

"Both men are confirmed at their homes," Ben said. "My men spoke to each of them."

"Thanks, Ben."

Gabriel pulled his car to a stop, his brain whirling with not just fear, but complete confusion. If Ted was at home, and Kevin and Glen Rollings were also in their houses, then who the hell was inside with Jordon?

"HANNAH, COME OUT and talk to me," Jordon shouted. For the last few minutes the girl had been ominously silent. Jordon had no idea where she was in the maze now or how to find her to end the madness.

She'd wandered down corridors, wound up in dead ends, and all the while her nerves had screamed with tension as she anticipated another attack.

She thought the bleeding of her wounds had finally stopped, but the anxiety of the situation was definitely wearing on her. She had no idea how much time had passed since she'd first entered the maze but it felt like an eternity.

The recorded cackle of the mouse split the air and Jordon dropped into a crouch, prepared for an attack that might come from any direction.

Her own reflections haunted her. Her mind attempted to drag her back into the torment of her past. There were times she saw only herself and other times she saw the ghost of Ralph Hicks just behind her. She wanted to scream with the anxiety that bubbled inside her.

"Hannah, this needs to stop now."

"You're right."

The girl's voice came from all around her and a sharp pain in the back stole Jordon's breath away. She jerked around to see Hannah's reflection in four mirrors. The girl smiled and held up her bloody knife.

Jordon's knees tried to buckle as she took a step forward and the warmth of blood worked down her spine. Her gun hand shook as she stared at the four Hannahs.

Which one was real?

Time seemed to stand still and then everything happened in the space of a single heartbeat. Jordon fired at one Hannah. Glass shattered to the floor. Damn, she'd shot a mirror.

She gasped in agonizing pain and tears blurred her vision. If she had to shoot out every mirror in the place, she'd do it. She scarcely took time to breathe before she fired again, and this time her bullet found its mark.

Hannah screamed and dropped her knife as she bent over to grab just above her left knee. She took a step forward and then fell out of the reflections and to the floor.

It was over.

Case solved.

Jordon tucked her gun into her holster, the simple action taking up nearly all of her energy as her chest squeezed tight and her back screamed in pain.

She walked over close enough to kick the knife out of Hannah's reach and then took several steps backward. She was so tired...so very tired as the adrenaline that had pumped through her for so long seeped away.

She'd just sit for a minute to catch her breath and then she'd call Gabriel. She sank down and leaned back. She was light-headed and cold chills raced through her.

Hannah continued to yell and curse and cry, but the sound seemed to come from very far away. Jordon saw herself in three reflections and she was vaguely surprised that no visions from her past haunted her, no images of Ralph Hicks and that cellar tried to intrude. She saw only herself, alone as she had always been.

The pain in her back intensified, making it difficult to breathe. She wondered if she might be dying. The thought made her so sad.

She should have called Gabriel. Her heart squeezed tight at thoughts of him. He'd have to clean up this mess she'd made. At least Hannah would no longer be able to hurt anyone again.

White dots like snowflakes danced in her vision.

Cold. She was so very cold. She was back in a snow globe, immersed in a brutal, bitter winter.

She closed her eyes.

She should have gone home and danced in her underwear.

Chapter Fourteen

Gabriel approached the front door of the maze with his heart beating out of his chest. He had no idea what to expect or who besides Jordon he might encounter inside.

Billy Bond was in jail and all their other suspects were accounted for, so whoever had written that note hadn't even been on their radar. Who could it be?

He went into the front door fast and with his gun ready. The small lobby was empty. He shoved through the turnstile and entered the maze. Instantly he heard female cries for help coming from someplace within the mirrors.

His nerves electrified. Was it Jordon? No...he didn't think so. Whoever it was, she was not only cursing but she was also crying for her mother.

Definitely not Jordon.

His mouth dried. So, where was Jordon? The unknowns of the situation balled a huge knot of anxiety in his stomach. He should call for backup, but until he knew what he faced, he was afraid that the extra manpower might only complicate things.

He stood in a corridor where he saw nothing but visions of himself. He walked forward and took the first turn to the right. Another empty passageway.

The cries for help had stopped and a frightening silence ensued. A horrible dread seeped into his bones as he continued walking slowly, aware that somebody could jump out and attack him with every step he took.

Had the cries for help been a ploy? A ruse to get him to rush to the rescue only to be stabbed by the killer? Was that what had happened to Jordon?

Oh, God—please, no. She might not want to have a meaningful relationship with him, but he certainly wanted her alive and well and with a future that would hopefully bring her to the point where she could love some special man. He didn't want her hurt. He prayed she wasn't hurt.

Walking the maze was agonizingly slow as he constantly turned first one way and then the other to clear any corridors he came to.

He finally stopped with his back to a dead end. "Jordon!" Her name released from the very depths of him with more than a hint of despair. "Jordon, where are you?"

"I'm here. Please help me. I'm hurt." The female voice came from his left and he suddenly recognized it.

"Hannah?" he called out incredulously. What on earth was she doing in here?

"She shot me. I just came here to help her and she accidentally shot me," Hannah cried.

"Where's Jordon?" Gabriel tried to move in the direction of the voice.

"She's here. She's…she's dead. He stabbed her and then he ran away."

Gabriel stumbled into one of the mirrors as all the breath in his body whooshed out of him. *No!* The single word screamed in his brain. It couldn't be. An all-encompassing grief pierced through him as he shoved off the mirror and continued walking.

He couldn't think about Jordon right now. He had to shove the grief away. He needed to focus. He pulled his radio from his belt and called in the troops.

From what little he knew, this was definitely a crime scene and the killer was still on the loose. With the call made, he reattached the radio to his belt.

"Hannah, keep talking so I can find you." He pulled on every ounce of professionalism he had. Jordon was gone. Jordon was dead. Despite the utter tearing of his heart, he had a job to do.

Hannah continued to yell to him, and with two more turns, he was there. His brain worked to take in the scene before him. Hannah lay on the floor, bleeding from what appeared to be a gunshot wound in her leg. A bloody knife was also on the floor not too far away.

It was the sight of Jordon that once again stole his breath away and squeezed his lungs so hard he could scarcely breathe. She was seated and leaning against one of the mirrors, eyes closed and utterly lifeless.

He rushed to her side and crouched down, his fingers going to her neck to check for a pulse. *Please be there*, he prayed. *Please don't be dead.*

Yes! Yes, there was a pulse.

He grabbed his radio once again. "I need an ambulance at Mouse's Maze of Mirrors. Officer down. I repeat, officer down!" He touched her face. Her skin was cold and pale.

"Jordon? Jordon, can you open your eyes? Can you talk to me?" There was no response.

Her slacks were ripped and bloody across her thigh, but it appeared that the wound had stopped bleeding. He had no idea what other injuries she might have sustained.

He was afraid to move her to even check. Hannah had said she'd been stabbed by the killer. More injuries had to be in her back or someplace where he couldn't see them beneath her coat.

"What about me? I'm hurt. She shot me," Hannah cried plaintively.

Reluctantly, he left Jordon's side and moved to Hannah. The bullet had caught her just above her knee, and while she was bleeding, it was apparent that nothing vital had been hit because there wasn't too much blood.

"Just hang on," he said to the girl. "Help is on its way."

"Is Agent James going to be all right?" Hannah asked and there was a glint of fear in her dark eyes.

Gabriel took a step back and surveyed the scene once again. Hannah shot and Jordon apparently stabbed and the knife was on scene.

There was no way the killer would have left his weapon behind. It didn't make sense and the murderer they'd been chasing didn't make those kinds of mistakes. There was no way he could believe things had happened as Hannah had said.

A new quiet horror swept through him as he looked back at her. Was it possible that the tall, slender girl was responsible for all the deaths and destruction?

"It's over, Hannah," he said in calculation. "Agent James is going to be just fine and she'll be able to tell me everything that happened here tonight." He wanted to believe it. He needed to believe that Jordon would be okay.

Hannah's features twisted with rage. "I just wanted to go home! If nobody stayed at Diamond Cove because of the murders then Mom and Dad would move back to Oklahoma City and I'd be where I belong."

"Chief Walters," a deep voice cried out. "We're here."

Gabriel recognized the voice as belonging to Ty Kincaid, an EMT. "We need two boards," Gabriel replied.

It seemed to take forever for the medical team to find them in the maze and then get both Hannah and Jordon loaded into the ambulance.

Jordon didn't regain consciousness as they took off her coat to reveal the bloody wound on her back. Gabriel officially placed Hannah under arrest before the ambulance pulled away.

He followed the ambulance to the hospital, where both patients were whisked back into the emergency room and he was left alone in the lobby.

Gabriel paced the room, his thoughts a riotous mess in his head. Hannah was their killer. How deep were Jordon's wounds? A fifteen-year-old kid had kept them all hopping around like maniacs all because she didn't want to live here. Had he gotten there in time or had Jordon been stabbed deep enough in her back to cause her death?

Only now did he fully process the sheer anguish that ripped through him, bringing the sting of tears to his eyes and squeezing his heart with an agony he'd never known before.

He was ragged with emotions by the time Mark walked in to join him in his vigil. "How is she?" he asked.

"Nobody has told me anything yet." He sank down on a chair and Mark sat next to him.

"She's a fighter," Mark replied.

"She is that," Gabriel agreed, but that didn't stop the frantic claw of despair inside him.

"The men were all working at the crime scene when I left them. I contacted Kent Myers to let him know he'd have to keep the attraction closed until we're finished with it."

"At least it's over now except the evidence gathering and the cleanup," Gabriel replied as he stared at the emergency room door and willed a doctor to come out with good news.

"Who would have thought our perp would turn out to be a teenage girl? You think the prosecutor will push to try her as an adult?"

Gabriel turned to look at Mark. "I'm certainly going to encourage him to. These murders weren't the result of a school yard fight or something else spontaneous. She carefully plotted this out. She showed enormous cunning in both the planning and the execution. She needs to be locked up for a very long time."

He turned to stare at the door once again. What was taking so long? Why didn't somebody come out to talk to him?

"Want some coffee?" Mark asked.

"No, thanks. I'm good." As sick as his stomach was at the moment, there was no way he wanted to attempt drinking anything.

Dr. Gordon Oakley came through the emergency room door. Gabriel and Mark both sprang to their feet. "Chief... Mark," he greeted them.

Gabriel searched the ER doctor's features. "How is she?"

"Agent James is resting easy now. She needed seven stitches in her leg and twenty-one in her back. Thankfully, both were slashing wounds and not stabbing injuries. She was also cut on her arm, but that didn't require any stitches."

Gabriel released a deep sigh of relief and then frowned. "So, why was she unconscious?"

"I'd say she might have suffered a touch of shock and utter exhaustion. She's hooked up to an IV. We've cleaned her up and administered pain meds. We'll keep her under observation until sometime tomorrow."

"Can I see her?"

"I'd prefer that she not be disturbed for the rest of the night. From what I understand, she's been through quite a trauma and what she needs now is complete rest," Gordon replied. "You can see her in the morning."

Although disappointed, Gabriel nodded. He wanted whatever was best for her. For the next ten minutes the doctor filled them in on Hannah's wound. At the moment she was in surgery. Her parents had been contacted and were in a private waiting room.

"I'll go talk to the Overtons," Mark said when the doctor had left them again.

"And I want a full-time guard on Hannah while she recuperates here," Gabriel replied. "I need to get back to the crime scene."

"I'll take care of everything here," Mark assured him.

The two men parted, as Mark headed to talk to

the Overtons and Gabriel left the building. It wasn't until he was in his car that the emotions of the night nearly overwhelmed him.

As his car warmed up, he leaned his head back and closed his eyes. She was going to be just fine. Tears of relief burned at his eyes.

He'd been so scared for her. He'd been so afraid that this night would end differently. It was already tragic enough that a girl's life, for all intents and purposes, had come to an end.

It was utterly inconceivable that three innocent people had been brutally murdered because a kid didn't like where she was living. But if Jordon had lost her life tonight, the depth of the tragedy would have been beyond anything he could even imagine.

She was fine. The case was solved, and within the next twenty-four to forty-eight hours, she would be gone from here, gone forever from his life.

He tightened his hands on the steering wheel, opened his eyes and realized it had begun to snow.

JORDON AWOKE SLOWLY. Before she opened her eyes the scent of fresh coffee and bacon drifted to her nose along with a faint antiseptic smell. Shoes squeaked on the floor from someplace in the distance and a blood-pressure cuff began to pump up on her arm.

She opened her eyes to find herself alone in a hospital room. The cuff around her arm released and the blood-pressure monitor displayed numbers that assured her she'd made it through the long night despite the aches and pains that attempted to tell her otherwise.

She glanced out the nearby window and frowned. It was snowing again. She couldn't wait to get to that beach in Florida, where it would be wonderfully warm and sunny.

"Ah, good—you're awake." A blonde woman in purple scrubs entered her room. "My name is Marjorie and I'll be your nurse for the day." She walked over to Jordon and held out a thermometer. "Open."

Jordon did as she was told.

"You're normal," Marjorie replied as she removed the thermometer.

"I know some people who would argue with you about that," Jordon replied and then frowned as Marjorie didn't react. Great—a nurse without a sense of humor.

"On a scale from one to ten, how do you rate your pain level?"

Jordon changed positions and winced. "About a seven, but I don't need any more pain meds." She almost welcomed the pain that was a reminder that she'd survived. "What I would like is a big cup of coffee."

"I'll contact the kitchen and let them know you're ready for a breakfast tray."

"Perfect," Jordon replied.

She stared back out the window as Marjorie left the room. Gabriel. A vision of him jumped into her head. So handsome and with those piercing blue eyes that warmed her from the inside out.

She channeled her thoughts into another direction. She didn't want to think of him with his gentle touches and strength of character.

Instead she closed her eyes and thought about Hannah and the confrontation from the night before. She'd been a fool to go in there alone, especially not knowing whom she might face.

It had been a reckless move not to call for backup. She wasn't a cat with nine lives. She'd already had two near-death experiences because of her lone-wolf attitude. It was past time to be a team player.

Thankfully, these troubling thoughts were interrupted by the arrival of breakfast. As she ate she was haunted by every breakfast she had shared with the Overtons, by each conversation she'd had with Joan.

Hannah's crimes would haunt them. Their lives would never be the same again. How did a parent ever find any kind of peace knowing that one of their children had committed three horrible murders? That she would be in lockup for years to come?

She cleaned off her plate and then fell back asleep. She had no nightmares haunted by Ralph Hicks or Hannah. Rather it was Gabriel who filled her dreams. They were sweet dreams of laughter and love, and she awakened with both deep longing and agonizing regret.

By that time lunch was served and then the doctor arrived. "When can I get out of here?" she asked him.

"How are you feeling? We did a lot of stitching on you last night."

"I'm sore," she admitted. "But I'm hoping to get a ride out of here as soon as possible and get back home to Kansas City. I can see my doctor there for any follow-up."

"Why don't you enjoy dinner on us this evening and then we'll see about releasing you," he replied.

She nodded her agreement, but there was no way she was spending another night here. She needed to get home. She had to get her feet back on the ground in her own space and put this place and a certain man far behind her.

After the doctor left the room, she called Director Tom Langford to fill him in on everything that had happened. He arranged for a helicopter to pick her up the next afternoon.

She'd just hung up when Gabriel came in. She stared at him in stunned surprise. In one arm he carried a huge, inflatable palm tree and in the other he had a pink fruity drink with a little umbrella stirrer.

"If Jordon can't get to Florida, then a piece of Florida will come to her," he said. He set the palm tree next to her bed. "Unfortunately, there's no alcohol in here." He held out the drink.

She took it from him and fought against the huge lump in her throat that made speech impossible for a moment. He looked so wonderfully handsome in his uniform and without the stress of the cases weighing him down.

He sat in the chair next to her bed and smiled at her. "Go on—take a sip. I wasn't sure exactly what you liked, so it's a strawberry smoothie with chunks of pineapple, berries and mango."

She took a drink and she didn't know if it tasted so good because she loved smoothies or if it was the fact that he'd gone to all this trouble just for her. The silly man was breaking her heart.

"Delicious," she said and then pointed to the palm tree. "Where did you manage to get that?"

"A couple of years ago the police department threw themselves a luau. There are five more of those in storage." His smile faded. "How are you doing?"

"I'm okay. I guess I'll be sporting a new scar across my back."

"She could have killed you." His voice was husky and his beautiful eyes were dark and filled with an emotion she didn't want to acknowledge.

"Is this the part where you yell at me for being a reckless fool?"

He leaned back in the chair. "It's enough for me that you recognize that you were reckless."

"I should have called you the minute I got that note. I'm done being a cowboy. I got lucky when Ralph Hicks had me in that cellar. I got lucky again last night, but I can't depend on luck anymore."

"If you've realized that then I guess your time here wasn't for nothing." His gaze on her was so intense she had to look away.

"How is Hannah?"

She needed a conversation about something… anything that would ease some of the tension in the room.

She stared out the window and listened absently as he caught her up on everything that was going on with the teenage killer. Hannah had come through surgery fine and was recuperating with a guard at her door.

"We found Joan's car parked a block away from the maze. She sneaked out of the house and took the car. Ted and Joan heard nothing. Hannah intended to kill you and then get home and back into bed before morning," he said.

"How are Ted and Joan?"

"Broken and in complete shock."

"They'll eventually get through this," Jordon replied. "They're strong people." She cast her gaze out the window. "And now, on another note, I should be released sometime this evening and I've made arrangements to leave tomorrow. I was wondering if you could pick me up later and take me to a motel for the night," she said.

She looked at him once again and saw in his eyes words he wanted to speak, emotions he wanted to share. But she didn't want to hear him. They had said everything necessary the night before.

"You know I'll be here whenever you need me," he finally replied.

Once again the lump was back in her throat and the pain that had been in her back moved around to pierce her in the heart.

"I'll call you later," she said and set the drink on her tray. "I think what I need right now is a nap."

He got up from the chair. "Then I'll just wait for your call." With those words he was gone.

She squeezed her eyes closed against a sudden burn of unexpected tears. The whole visit had been stilted and uncomfortable, nothing like the relationship they'd shared in the time she'd been here.

He'd brought her a palm tree and a fruity drink. His eyes had spoken of a love that invited her into something she'd never believed she could have.

She was doing what was best for both of them.

She had to tell him goodbye.

GABRIEL PARKED IN front of the motel room door and dreaded the goodbye that was to come. The sun was bright and the snow that had fallen the day before had been negligible. It was a beautiful day for a helicopter ride.

He'd brought Jordon to the motel room the night before and their ride from the hospital had been quiet, their only conversation dealing with the aftermath of the cases.

He now opened his car door and started to get out, but Jordon flew out of the door with her two bags in hand. "Don't get out," she said. "I've got this."

She opened the back door and threw her bags into the seat and then got into the car. She cast him a cheerful smile that only managed to break his heart just a little bit more.

"Thanks for taking me to the airport," she said.

"No problem," he replied and pulled out of the motel parking lot. "How are you feeling today?"

"Not too bad. I'm going to be sore for a while, but it's nothing I can't handle."

Her scent filled the car, evoking desire and love even as he drove her to the place where she'd leave him forever. Throughout the long night a weary resignation had set in. He loved...and he'd lost.

He couldn't make her love him if she didn't. He couldn't force her to understand that they belonged together if she didn't believe that in her very soul.

He could only let her go to find her own kind of happiness. She was the bravest woman he knew and yet he still believed it was fear that held her back.

"Nice day to fly," he said. "And now you can take that vacation you've been waiting for. You've definitely earned it."

"What about you? When was the last time you had a vacation?" she asked.

"I haven't taken one since I took this job," he admitted. He wasn't going to tell her that the idea of going off somewhere alone simply wasn't appealing to him.

"I'd definitely say you've earned one, too."

Why were they talking about vacations when his heart ached so badly? He didn't want inane conversation and yet he knew that was all that was left between them.

They reached the small airport, and as he parked, he had a perfect view of the helicopter that waited to take her home. "Looks like your ride is here."

"You don't have to get out." She unbuckled her seat belt.

"I'll walk you to the door," he replied. Just like he had every night since she'd been attacked by Hannah and had gotten lost in the snowstorm.

He got out of the car and grabbed the larger bag from her. Silently they entered the airport and then exited to the tarmac, where the helicopter pilot stood waiting.

When he saw them approaching, he climbed into the plane and the blades began their whooping swirl as they prepared for takeoff. Jordon took her bag, and when she looked back up at Gabriel, her green eyes simmered with emotion.

"Gabriel, I can't thank you enough for everything you've done for me while I've been here," she said.

"Jordon, I…"

She held up a hand. "Please don't say anything. This is hard enough already. Goodbye, Gabriel."

She didn't wait for his reply. She hurried to the helicopter door and climbed inside. He backed away, grief ripping another hole in his heart.

The helicopter blades spun faster and the engine began to whine. An empty, hollow wind blew through him as he turned to go back to the parking lot. It had taken him so long to finally find the woman he wanted forever in his life and now she was gone.

"Gabriel!"

His name carried on the breeze and he turned around to see her running toward him. Had she forgotten something? When she reached him, she threw her arms around his neck and smiled up at him.

"I want it," she said. Her eyes sparkled with a light that half stole his breath away. "I want life with you. I thought I could just walk away from you, but I can't. I love you, Gabriel, and I'm willing to take a chance on us."

He couldn't speak. Instead he took her lips with his in a kiss that held all his hope, all his dreams and every ounce of his love for her.

"I'd wrap you up in my arms right now if you didn't have stitches in your back," he said when the kiss ended.

She laughed, that husky sound that delighted him. "I don't know how this is going to work, but I do know my vacation is going to be right here with you."

"What about the beach?"

"To heck with the beach. I want to spend my time wherever you are."

"I want that, Jordon," he replied fervently. "We're going to make this work. We'll figure it all out as long as we love each other."

"You know I'm messy and I don't cook."

"And I love that about you," he assured her.

She cast a quick glance back at the helicopter. "I've got to go."

"I know." He kissed her again and this time he tasted her love for him and the promise of a future together. "I'll call you."

"I'll be waiting." She backed away from him and then turned and ran back and disappeared into the helicopter.

Gabriel remained in place and watched as the bird lifted off to carry her away. He missed her already, but his heart was filled with a wealth of happiness.

The sun glinted on the helicopter as it circled the airport once, and the shine was warm in Gabriel's heart. He loved and she loved him back, and he'd never been more certain of his future.

She might not know it yet, but Jordon was the woman he was going to marry. She was the woman who would have his children.

This wasn't a goodbye; it was only the beginning.

He had no doubt in his mind that life with Jordon would be a wonderful adventure and he was more than up for the challenge.

Epilogue

The sun was hot in Florida in late August. Jordon sat on the chaise lounge and sighed with happiness. "This is positively wonderful," she said as she closed her eyes and raised her face.

"You just think it's wonderful because you have a handsome devil to rub sunscreen on your back," Gabriel said as his hands sensually worked the coconut-scented cream across her skin.

"You're right—the beach is definitely better with you," she replied.

He kissed the back of her neck and shivers of pleasure worked up her spine. "If you keep doing that we won't have much time in the sun. We'll wind up back in the room like we have done every afternoon since we arrived here."

He laughed and moved back to his chair next to hers. "Vacations are definitely better with a snuggle buddy."

She looked at him and grinned. "You're a great

snuggle buddy." She leaned back in her chair and closed her eyes once again.

There were still moments when she needed to pinch herself to make sure this was real and not a dream. The last six months had been magical.

She and Gabriel had taken every opportunity to see each other despite the distance. She'd spent weekends at his house and he'd come to Kansas City every chance he got and had stayed with her.

Each and every day their love had only grown deeper, her confidence in what they had together grew stronger. He had made her believe in herself in a way nobody had ever done before. He made her a better woman and she liked to believe she made him a better man.

She hadn't been surprised when he'd told her Joan and Ted Overton had decided to remain in Branson and continue to run Diamond Cove. The couple had decided that despite their heartbreak over Hannah's crimes, they couldn't allow her plot to succeed.

She'd been happy when Gabriel had told her that the couple appeared to be closer than ever, and while they planned to support their daughter, they also believed she belonged behind bars.

"Whew, it's really hot out here," Gabriel said, pulling her from her thoughts with a seductive lilt to his voice. "I'll bet our room is nice and cool. We could probably crank up a little music and dance in our underwear in the air-conditioning."

Jordon laughed, but didn't open her eyes. "You definitely look hot dancing in your underwear," she replied. She was so in love with this man.

"If we go inside we could probably even request room service to bring us a bottle of champagne to celebrate."

She turned her head to look at him. "And what would we be celebrating?"

He swung his legs over the side of his chair to face her and pulled their beach tote bag closer to him. His ocean-blue eyes gazed at her softly. "Jordon, these last six months have been the happiest I've ever been in my life."

Her heart squeezed. "You know I feel the same way. I thought I knew what love was, but it took you to really show me what it's all about."

"You know I'm all in with you, Jordon."

"Since you put in your resignation and are going to be part of the men in blue in Kansas City and move in with me next month, you'd better be all in," she said with a laugh.

"The real question is, are you sure you're really all in?" He slipped a hand into the tote bag and pulled out a small velvet box.

Her breath caught in her throat and she sat up to face him as he got down on one knee in the sand. His eyes suddenly held a touch of uncertainty. He opened the ring box to display a sparkling princess-cut diamond ring. "Will you make me the happiest man in the world and marry me, Jordon?"

Her heart trembled inside her, not with fear, but rather with a kind of wild joy she'd never known before. "You silly man, take that worried look out of your eyes. Yes, yes, a thousand times yes, I'll marry you."

He slipped the ring on her finger and then pulled her up off the chaise and into his arms. The kiss they shared was filled with unbridled passion and enduring love.

"Hey, get a room," a male voice called from nearby.

She broke the kiss and turned her head to see a skinny old man eyeing them. She grinned at him. "We have a room and we're going there right now." She placed a hand over Gabriel's heart. "This is the man I'm going to have babies with."

The old man's lips turned up in a smile. "Then get off the beach before you start that kind of business."

"Come on, fiancé. You heard what he said," she said to Gabriel.

He grasped her hand and together they ran across the sand toward the hotel, toward their future filled with love and laughter and family.

* * * * *

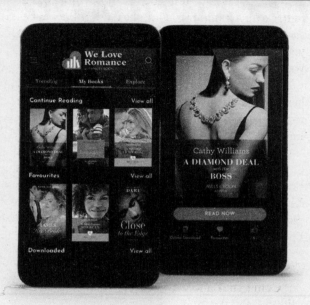

LET'S TALK
Romance

For exclusive extracts, competitions
and special offers, find us online: